THE COLOUR
OF NIGHT

DAVID LINDSEY

WARNER BOOKS

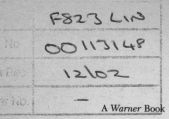
A *Warner* Book

First published in the United States by Warner Books Inc.

First published in Great Britain in 1999
by Little, Brown and Company

This edition published by Warner Books in 2000

A CIP catalogue record for this book
is available from the British Library.

ISBN 0 7515 2889 7

Typeset by Palimpsest Book Production Limited
Polmont, Stirlingshire
Printed and bound in Great Britain by
Clays Ltd, St Ives plc

Warner Books
A Division of
Little, Brown and Company (UK)
Brettenham House
Lancaster Place
London WC2E 7EN

For Joyce,

whose
black and white
illuminates
my
gray

"We are, I know not how, double within ourselves, with the result that we do not believe what we believe, and we cannot rid ourselves of what we condemn."

Michel de Montaigne
Essays (II, 16, 469 C)

CHAPTER 1

VENICE, SESTIERE DI DORSODURO

It was the middle of the afternoon, and the windows of the old palazzo were partially opened to the crisp spring air. The study, filled with books and artwork obsessively arranged and cataloged and situated, overlooked the narrow canal, and the light that the room received was reflected off the buildings opposite, their weathered colors throwing off pale hues of apricot and lilac, wan ocher and coral and vanilla.

The sounds of the canal rose up on the summer heat and drifted into the room as well, carrying the voices of tourists strolling on the small *fondamenta*, the slosh of a passing gondola, the voices of merchants unloading produce from a small barge, water lapping under the bridge just beyond the window, a woman's laughter.

"Just put them here," the German said to the dealer, spreading his arms out over the long refectory table at which he sat and that he used as a working desk. He had moved aside orderly piles of paperwork and books to provide a clean surface.

The dealer nodded deferentially and approached the table with an oversize leather portfolio. His name was Claude

Corsier, and he was a private art dealer from Geneva. He specialized in the drawings of artists of the nineteenth and twentieth centuries, the secondary market. That is, deceased artists. His unusual ceremonious manner was not a demonstration of particular respect for the German client. Corsier was known for his courtesy to everyone, billionaire and housemaid alike. It was said that his manner was a reflection of his lifelong respect for the artwork in which he traded.

Corsier put his portfolio on a small, marble-topped side table a step or two from his client and opened it. He was a large man, with big hands that one normally associated with farmworkers and laborers. But Corsier's hands were pale and soft, his nails manicured; they had never been darkened by the sun or stained by soil or lifted anything heavier than a folio reference book. His burly physique was genetic, not occupational. He had been bookish since childhood.

Each drawing was enclosed in its own acid-free paper folder to protect it. After opening the first folder, Corsier turned it around and placed it on the table before the German.

"First, the Italians you wanted to see. Giovanni Boldini. Becoming very difficult to find these days. Six images here, and a small, quick sketch of a hand on the back of the sheet. These are studies for portraits, it seems, but the finished work, if it was ever completed, has never been identified." Leaning over the refectory table, he gently pointed to an image with the barrel end of a marbled fountain pen. The pen was less intrusive than using one's finger. "The turned head is quite good here," he said.

The German, whose name was Wolfram Schrade, nodded, bending over the sketch to look at it closely. He picked up a horn-handled magnifying glass from the table and examined each image on the sheet of paper. There were six.

"These are very nice," Schrade said. His accent was heavy, but attractive, sophisticated.

"I like them," Corsier agreed modestly.

The German picked up the paper and looked at the drawing on the back. Corsier watched him as he turned and held it up to the diffused light from the windows. He was a handsome man, tall and lean, in his early fifties. His hair was thick and coarse, and Corsier had always marveled that it very nearly was the exact color of old vellum. His features were fine, a straight, narrow nose, a rather wide mouth with a full lower lip. The irises of his eyes were odd, almost lacking in any pigmentation at all.

Without commenting further, Schrade closed the folder, set it aside, and looked at Corsier, who was already turning to get a second one.

"Ettore Tito," Corsier said, placing the next opened folder before his client. "Studies for *La Perla*, now in a private collection. Very fine nudes . . . The treatment here"—again the fountain pen pointed out a delicate line—"is exquisite, the way he handled the shadow at this concavity on the shoulder."

Schrade closed the folder and set it aside with the other one.

"And this artist is most difficult to find . . ." Corsier was unfolding a third folder.

The presentation took up the better part of an hour, and by the time Corsier had shown his client nine works, the most he had ever shown him at one sitting, the light coming into the room from the canal had become richer with the lower angle

3

of the sun. The circular *rulli piombati* panes in the Renaissance windows were now concentric smears of pastel.

The drawings were stacked at Schrade's left elbow, and
Corsier stood in front of the refectory table and folded his soft
hands, looking down at the seated client.

"I will have all of them," Schrade said.

Corsier made a slight "as you wish" gesture with his
hands. He had sold this man a fortune over the past dozen
years, and this lot alone was a small fortune in itself.

"A drink to celebrate?" the German asked.

Corsier tilted his head forward, a bow of assent. Schrade
got up from behind his desk and stepped across the marble
floor to a sixteenth-century cabinet of dark walnut and opened
the doors to reveal bottles of liquor. Two bottles were already
opened, and he poured Corsier a glass of Prosecco, the dealer's
favored drink with which to close a sale, and a glass of Bor-
dolino for himself.

"Please, sit for a while," he said, giving the *aperitivo* to
Corsier and gesturing to a pair of heavy, X-frame wooden
armchairs nearer the windows. When they were seated, the
German raised his glass and said, "To resolution."

Corsier was already drinking the Prosecco when he realized the toast didn't make any sense to him. He was still swallowing, relishing the movement of the drink on his palate,
when Schrade continued.

"I assume you've observed your usual discretion about
bringing these to me," he said.

"Of course."

"There is no record that you've come here?"

"None."

"You've always been reliable on that score," Schrade conceded.

"All of my clients require discretion." Corsier took another large drink of the Prosecco.

The next few minutes were spent in casual conversation about drawings. The German was a voracious collector, and Corsier knew that he had large personal collections in his homes in Paris and Berlin. More than likely the drawings Corsier had just sold him would go to one of these two locations, where his client had elaborate archival spaces for exhibiting his collections.

"As for the matter of payment," Schrade said offhandedly, "I'm sure you won't mind if I settle with you later."

Corsier's last sip of Prosecco stuck in his throat and refused to go down. He struggled with it as his thoughts suddenly swarmed, turning, tacking, veering first in one direction, then in another, as he tried to concentrate on the most important implications of what his client had just said.

First of all, this was now the second time. Wolfram Schrade already owed Corsier for a group of symbolists' drawings that Corsier had brought him four months before, perhaps the best group of symbolists that Corsier had ever had in his possession and which he had collected over a period of nearly a year, specifically with this client in mind. There had been an even dozen drawings of extraordinary quality. It had come to 1.3 million Deutschmarks. Corsier had taken them to the German's Berlin home. Where he had left them. With only a promise of payment.

That was not so extraordinary. It wasn't an entirely comfortable position to be in, but he had known his client for

5

twelve years and had never had any trouble collecting. So he had taken a deep breath. . . .

Now this. Nine drawings by the increasingly popular nineteenth-century Italian realists. Almost a million Deutschmarks. The German's assumption that Corsier would carry him yet again was appalling. Especially since in the corner behind the refectory table sat a computer. Its screen was dark, but a small lime green light burned on the keyboard, proving to Corsier that it still had a heartbeat. On more than a few occasions Schrade had turned around at his desk—in Paris or Berlin or here—and paid Corsier instantly from his accounts in Liechtenstein or Cyprus. So Corsier knew that it could be done. He was just an electrical spark away from two million Deutschmarks.

He managed to swallow the Prosecco.

The more serious implication of Schrade's remark, the one that had caused a sudden empty space in Corsier's chest, a huge cavity without tissue or feeling or breath, was the implication that these two reversals in their relationship—for, to a man of Corsier's sensibilities, they were irrefutably reversals—were premonitory.

Schrade *knew*!

Corsier looked at his client, whose neutral coloring was a perfect foil for the dusty colors that fell on him, the failing light passing through the concentric striations in the small panes of the windows. He heard a gondola, the thick *chuck-chuck-chuck* of the oar in the rowlock as the boat was propelled along the canal. He concentrated, desperate to absorb everything in these last moments. Was that a cat mewing? A barrel, or something like it, being rolled along the *fondamenta*? What could it be if not a barrel? A cart?

All of this aural sensitivity had gone through his brain in an instant, no longer than it had taken him to swallow the imperceptibly hesitant Prosecco. After all, Corsier was a professional. He had been an operator most of his adult life, and he had done nearly all of his work in the brutal, high-stakes world of wealthy men. He had survived, and he had been successful. Corsier had brass balls, as a matter of fact. Though, to be sure, he himself would never, ever, have expressed it in such crass language.

"Oh," he said, lowering his glass. "This is very awkward for me, I'm afraid." He knitted his brow and looked squarely at Schrade. "This seriously affects my liquidity. After accommodating your last request . . . well, this is most difficult."

"Difficult?" Schrade smiled ever so slightly. "Well, I certainly understand the awkwardness of a loss of . . . liquidity."

It was a pointed remark. Corsier knew that his client was never going to baldly state the real subject of this conversation. Corsier pursed his mouth thoughtfully as though he were trying to ferret out a mutually agreeable resolution. In fact, he was concentrating as he had never concentrated before in his life, bringing to bear his entire genetic code on one single thing: not bolting for the door.

He was stunned at how complete, how all-consuming, was his fear.

How would it happen? A gunshot? Poison? Torture to make him tell everything, even things he could no longer remember himself, and then end it with simple asphyxiation? Why this charade first? This cruel pretense of civility? He couldn't imagine, but he struggled with the nausea and continued to play his own part flawlessly.

"This is really quite irregular. Very difficult for me."

"I'm sorry," Schrade said, which he clearly was not.

"How long do you think you will need to delay payment?"

"Payment? Oh, I plan to resolve this as quickly as possible."

The double meanings shimmered before Corsier's sightless eyes. Venice, he thought, what a monumental surprise to die in Venice. He would never have imagined it. Never.

As he rode in his host's private launch back down the Grand Canal on his way to Marco Polo Airport, Claude Corsier was numb with fear. He was also tremulous with hope. There was the launch driver and a companion. After they passed through the mouth of the Grand Canal and skirted San Giorgio Maggiore, more than ten kilometers remained across the lagoon to the airport. He looked at the two men in front of him. Was one of them the executioner? Surely not. They hardly paid him any attention.

My God, Corsier thought, if he ever got away from this situation, he would disappear so thoroughly that he would become as invisible as breath.

The wind picked up and the launch slapped the waves with a hard, rhythmic jolt, throwing a light spray from the hull. A short distance away he could see the public *vaporettos* filled with tourists headed to the same destination. He fought to avoid hyperventilation. His thoughts swung wildly back and forth between black, oppressive fear and an almost giddy exhilaration.

Then he thought of the drawings. Holy Mary. The wretched German was going to get twenty-one of some of the finest drawings Corsier had ever possessed . . . for absolutely nothing.

8

CHAPTER 2

HOUSTON

The first time he saw her was through the clear, moonstone colors of water. Suddenly she entered his peripheral vision, gliding past him in the opposite direction, her long legs close together and scissoring gently, trailing an unstrung necklace of tiny silver bubbles.

She wore a black, membrane-sheer suit, and her dark hair, pulled back from her face and held in place by a single band at the nape of her neck, spread out behind her like a billow of ink let loose in the water. Though she wore a small pair of swimming goggles that partially obscured her eyes, he could see from the shape of her face and mouth that she was Asian.

That morning she got out of the pool only a few minutes before he did. By the time he had completed his last lap and pulled himself from the water, she was nearly finished drying off, bending to towel between her thighs, her wet hair pulled to one side and draped over her shoulder. Without acknowledging him, she turned and walked away beside the pool toward the women's dressing room, nonchalant, as though they had done this together for decades, leaving a code of damp footprints behind her.

❖   ❖   ❖

At seven o'clock in the morning the Olympic-size lap pool at the River Oaks Swimming Club is deserted. The water is glass still. The fresh early light, entering obliquely through the upper windows, refracts off the arched angles of the lofty groined ceiling and plunges into the water, penetrating all the way to the pale floor of the pool. It is quiet.

Every day for nearly four years Harry Strand had come here to swim, well before even the earliest club member appeared at eight o'clock. It was a routine he had interrupted only once, for a period of three weeks, when his wife died. That had been eleven months ago. Her death had shaken him more deeply than anything that had ever happened to him. She had come to him late and had left him too soon, a flash of clarity in a life tangled with obscurities. He was approaching fifty when she died, and she had been eleven years younger. Though they were not in their youth anymore, they had no reason to believe that time was short. Her sudden death had sent him reeling, wobbling to the far edges, where he had teetered precariously, dangerously close to breaking down, before wobbling back toward a holding pattern, to the old, anxious tensions of former times.

For the three rare years of his marriage to Romy, he had actually felt as though he had accrued some real measure of an elusive emotional equanimity. She had redeemed him from a lifetime of dissembling and increasing self-dissatisfaction and had taught him to believe in the simple reality of virtue. Then she was gone.

The morning swim was one of the things he did to keep his brain from flying apart. It was a place and a way to begin the day with a reliable rhythm, an affirmation of purpose on a small scale and of peace at the heart of the universe. The aquatic ritual had been Romy's idea, a regimen deliberately put into play to contravene nearly twenty years of obfuscation. She had said, only half-joking, that the daily immersion would cleanse him, a circadian baptism to remind him that his life had changed.

So, after the funeral, after the horrible, soul-consuming afterbirth of death had passed and he was left with the silence and the solitude, he had returned to the rhythms of the water and the light to try to steady himself all over again. Even in Romy's absence, he found himself turning to her for help, to her idea of a proper ceremony for rebirth and a new beginning.

The woman in the black Lycra tank suit came to swim laps beside him in the long empty pool every day for twelve consecutive days. She swam exactly half an hour. Sometimes she was there when he arrived, though she seemed to have preceded him by only minutes, and left while he was still swimming. Sometimes she came after he was already well into his laps, and she was still there when he left. Either way, for nearly two weeks they shared the same water and the same silence and the same light.

During those days it had happened a few times, by sheer chance, that they would swim for a while in tandem, and as he turned his head to the side with every other stroke of his arm, he would see her long, sleek body slipping through the water as smoothly as it had ever been done, perhaps as smoothly as it could be done. Her form was impeccable. Then, gradually, his longer strokes would separate them again, and he would see her only in passing.

The twelve days they swam together were odd in just about every respect. Inevitably during that time their eyes connected briefly, but neither of them ever acknowledged the other. They never spoke. Yet by the twelfth day Strand had grown comfortable with her company, something he would not have expected. If he had been told in advance that another person would begin swimming with him at the exact same hour, he would have resented the intrusion immensely. It would have ruined everything that he sought in that particular hour of the day.

As it turned out, that hadn't happened. Very quickly, by the fifth day, he had begun to accept that she was going to be there. She possessed a discernible serenity that easily counter-balanced what he would otherwise surely have considered a disruption. She blended remarkably well into the equation he sought in those sequestered mornings.

Then she stopped coming. That had been over a month ago, and he hadn't seen her since.

He had inquired about her. The swimming club was pri-vate and very discreet. The only thing he could learn about her was that her name had been listed as Mara Song, recently ar-rived in Houston from Rome. No address, of course, and no telephone number were available to him. For an instant he thought about leaving a message for her at the club, in the event that she had begun swimming at another time of day, then immediately rejected that as being far too overt. In fact, he didn't know why he wanted to meet her at all. Just about everything argued against it. If he wanted companionship, if he wanted to begin seeing someone, it didn't have to happen like this. He knew a number of women who were respectfully keeping their distance—some keeping less of a distance than others, to be sure—waiting for him to decide to resume his life.

He was also aware of the irony of what he wanted. He could easily have spoken to her a dozen times—literally—during the two weeks she had joined him in the water, but he hadn't. Now that he couldn't, he wanted to.

So, with some effort, he tried to put the prospect of meeting Mara Song out of his mind. It didn't really make any sense. But he never swam now without thinking of her, thinking that at any moment she might suddenly be there, slipping through the light-illumined water, a dizzy trail of bubbles shimmering behind her like a visible scent.

CHAPTER 3

After leaving the club, Strand went slightly out of his way home to a small neighborhood bakery with a dozen tables under a rattan-covered patio surrounded by catalpa trees. Every morning Strand was the first of a loyal clientele to arrive.

He always sat at the same table in the patio, the nearest to a large and unusual outdoor aquarium watched over by a pair of small, brilliantly colored macaws that looked as though they had flown through a freshly painted rainbow. He ate breakfast—the only meal served at the bakery—and read the newspaper while the macaws scolded and cajoled the fish and each other, and anything that moved, sometimes inching to the near end of their perch to read over Strand's shoulder.

Around nine o'clock he pulled into the porte cochere at home and went straight to the kitchen to make a pot of coffee. Harry Strand lived and worked in a two-story home in the museum district, an expensive address just a few streets off Bissonnet. The home was old, with Mediterranean influences and made of stolid, gray limestone. The minute he and Romy had seen it they had loved it and bought it within a week of arriving in Houston. They had lived in Vienna before they were married, and the warm and fertile Mexican Gulf coast was an exotic and welcome change for them.

The house was on a quiet, narrow lane that meandered among other aged and behemoth domiciles, most of them only partially visible behind a well-groomed wilderness of oaks and palms, azaleas and laurel, boxwood, quince, and bougainvillea. Encompassing stone or brick walls shrouded in vines were de rigueur, and privacy was as precious as time itself.

Built on all four sides of a central courtyard, the home sheltered a large carved stone fountain at its heart. Semitropical plants filled the courtyard, and their care and cultivation had been Romy's abiding passion. Often Strand would watch her from the windows by his desk as she dawdled among the tiled paths, pinching a faded blossom here, monitoring a pale new shoot there, checking the progress of the long awaited efflorescence of a favorite species.

She had been content here, in this home and its environs, and Strand had frequently reminded himself that their shared happiness was uncommon good fortune. It wasn't anything he had ever experienced before, and he had told himself that he would be a fool if he ever, even for a moment, took for granted the wonderful balance they had managed to achieve together.

He had also known that balance, by its very definition, was fragile.

Meret Spier, Strand's assistant, had become irreplaceable after Romy's death. She had begun working for them two years earlier, when their workload had increased to the point that they couldn't handle it between them. Fresh out of graduate school at the University of Chicago, Meret had recently returned to Houston after failing to find a position with the museums in the Chicago area. After Romy's death, Meret simply became indispensable. Strand paid her very well and even increased her salary significantly when she had to take over so many of Romy's responsibilities. She was worth every dime of it. Aside from her impeccable scholarship, she was intelligent and low-key, facile at reading between the lines, and perceptive when assessing personalities, all invaluable attributes when dealing with art collectors, who could be as eccentric as the artists they collected.

The rooms that formed Strand's offices also served as the showrooms for the drawings he owned and sold. They occupied the entire left wing of the house as seen from the front entry. Most of these rooms were accessible from the peristyle that surrounded the courtyard. The porch of the peristyle was deep, providing a buffering shade from the summer heat and reducing the glare from the sunny courtyard.

Strand's office was the first in order from the front of the house to the back. It opened onto the broad front entry hall as well as into the courtyard, with a third door communicating with the library that separated Strand's office from Meret's. The walls of both offices were covered with framed drawings and a few paintings. In the library a long antique walnut table used for research sat squarely in the center of the room and was usually cluttered with recently consulted volumes, slips of paper protruding from their pages. All of these rooms were generous spaces with sitting areas and comfortable furnishings, and each of them communicated with the others through a short arched passageway with a wrought-iron gate the height of the passageway placed midway. The gates were covered on one side with plate glass to muffle sound for privacy when the gates were closed. A fourth room was for storage, where rows of thin, vertical shelving for paintings and drawings lined the walls. This was also a work area for packaging artwork to be shipped and for receiving.

Every morning at nine-thirty Meret let herself into the front entry of the house and went straight through to the peristyle. This morning, like many others, Strand saw her enter the colonnade with an armload of documents and walk around to her office door, where she let herself in. While she was settling in, he stepped out into the courtyard and crossed to the other side to the kitchen. He prepared two cups of coffee and took them back around the colonnade to Meret's door. She was already standing there, holding it open for him.

"Perfect," she said, taking her cup at the door. "There are a few things you ought to deal with straightaway," she began. Meret was organized, and there were limits to the amount of time she would allow a loose end to remain loose. Strand increasingly took advantage of this, letting unessential details go unattended, knowing that if they were even potentially important, Meret would catch them and bring them to his attention.

"Such as . . ."

"Such as these," she said, snatching a pink Post-it off her desk and waving it at him. She kept "to do" things on the bright adhesive squares, and sometimes the whole left side of her desk blushed with ranks of reminders.

Strand settled into an armchair beside the sofa where Meret presided during their morning conversations. She sat down, her legs and feet together, and stuck the pink note on the hem of her skirt, which left more than half her leg exposed. Meret was not a petite young woman, but she knew instinctively how to dress to her best advantage. The stylish short skirts and revealing blouses that she favored were worn with a sexy intelligence that told you immediately that she knew what she was doing. Degas or Maillol would have asked her to take off her clothes in a minute. She would have done it, relishing the adventure and the humor of it, though she would have charged them by the quarter hour and wanted her payment in cash. On top of that, she would have had a highly educated opinion of the artist's efforts.

"Leaman Stannish," she began, holding her cup and saucer like a duchess. "The matter of his Gérome studies."

"What do you think?"

"I thought we'd agreed they were too weak."

"That's what I remembered."

"Then you have to let him know we're passing."

"I've been putting that off . . ."

Meret looked at him with her best "that's the point of this conversation" expression.

". . . but he's got those fine, those very fine, Carpeaux drawings, the sculpture studies . . ."

"And you don't want to piss him off," she said.

"Right."

"What he's saying is, You want my Carpeaux? Take my Gérome first."

"That's right."

"You shouldn't play that game."

Strand sipped his coffee. "I know. Write him and tell him we can't do it."

Meret stiffened. "*You've* got to write him, Harry. Stannish is a pain in the ass, but you can't afford to alienate the guy. He knows he's being unfair, and he's also very much aware of your reputation as an ethical dealer. He'd much rather operate under that cloak of respectability than work in the market without it. He'll come around."

Strand nodded. "I'll let him know." He had already decided what to do, but it was good to hear Meret's opinions coinciding with his. It had gotten to the point that he was no longer testing her to see how her judgment and instincts were maturing; now he was actually relying on her counsel to confirm his own instincts.

"I'll mail it this afternoon," Meret said pointedly, putting him on notice that he was expected to do it today.

Strand nodded again.

Meret glanced at her lap. "You got another fax late yesterday from Denise Yarrow in San Francisco. She wants to add the Eakins collection to her 'reconsider' list."

"She's going to wear me out."

"She always does this, but . . . she always comes through, too." Meret was consistently optimistic. She was upbeat. She did not believe in fate's negative side, and Strand found it surprising how many times she was rewarded for her bright expectations.

"First," she said, "Aldo Chiappini called yesterday and wants to know when you'll be coming to Rome. He wants a specific date. I think he's got someone else interested in the Fuselis." She raised her eyes at him expectantly. "They're worth the trip. That many together . . . . fine quality."

"You're right. I don't want to lose those. I'll check my calendar later this morning and give you a date. I'll call Aldo, too. Smooth his feathers."

"Next, this," Meret said, holding up the pink note by the tips of her tapered fingers. "A woman called yesterday who said she had a collection of drawings she wants to sell and wants to know if you would handle it. Said you were recommended to her by Reynolds Truscott in New York."

"Good old Reynolds."

"Says she has Maillol, Klimt, Delvaux, Ingres, Balthus."

Strand gave her a skeptical look.

Meret raised a testimonial hand, an eager expression on her face.

"That's an odd grouping. What's her name?"

"Mrs. Mitchell Reinhardt."

"First name?"

Meret shrugged, sipping her coffee.

"Did you look her up in the collector's catalog?"

Meret nodded. "Not listed."

"Did she say anything else?"

"Uh . . . as soon as possible." She leaned over and handed Strand a second piece of pink paper with the address on it.

"I'm going to call Reynolds first," he said. "Get some idea of what I'm getting into."

The prospect of seeing drawings by these artists whose works seldom came available on the market anymore prompted Strand to call Reynolds Truscott within the hour. But Truscott was of little help. He did not know the woman personally, he said, he had gotten her name from a dealer friend of his in London who specialized in twentieth-century British paintings. This man had mentioned her almost incidentally in a conversation, said he knew a woman who had recently moved to the United States, to Texas, who had an interesting little collection of drawings. Then one day Mrs. Reinhardt herself had called Truscott, using the British dealer as a reference, and asked if he knew any reputable dealers in her area. Thus Strand. That's all Truscott knew about her.

"There aren't that many of you concentrating on drawings," Truscott said. "She was surprised to find someone in Houston."

"If she's a collector, she should have known about me."

"Hello—modesty? Well, the fact is I don't think she is a collector," Truscott said, lowering his voice in a tone of confidentiality. "I think this is a divorce thing."

CHAPTER 4

When Strand called Mrs. Reinhardt to make an appointment, she gave him an address in Tanglewood, an upscale neighborhood near the posh Post Oak shopping district in West Houston. The address did not live up to the reputation of its environs. La Violetta Terrace was a cluster of old town houses tucked deep into a wood of dark pines and aged water oaks whose ponderous boughs were draped with verdigris beards of Spanish moss that hung limp in the warm spring air. The motley brick facades of the town houses had acquired a rusty patina of neglect, and the tight little meander of a lane that fronted the small gardens of each address had the faded air of a disregarded byway.

Strand parked in front of Mrs. Reinhardt's address and got out of the car. He followed a pathway of dun bricks through a tiny garden of ordinary shrubs, nandina and boxwood and wax ligustrum. The midmorning sun penetrated the thick overstory in broken amber streams and fell onto the crown of a small dogwood near the front door, the soft light illuminating the pale pink blossoms as if it were a theatrical spotlight.

He rang the doorbell and waited. All around him the dense woods dampened every sound to quietude, the constant rumble of city traffic seemed distant, and even a contentious blue jay sounded more disgruntled than raucous.

Strand was not a man who was often caught flat-footed, slapped in the face by surprise, but when the door opened and he found himself staring squarely into the unsuspecting eyes of Mara Song, he was caught off guard.

"I'm Harry Strand," he managed to say with deceptive equanimity. He wasn't sure his face was playing along.

"Mara Reinhardt," she said, smiling, a little wearily he thought. Her handshake was light, and he could feel her warmth and the slenderness of her body in the shape of her hand. He had to will his eyes to relax, not to gaze on her. "I appreciate your coming," she said, backing away from the door and letting him in.

She didn't have a trace of a foreign accent; she was one hundred percent American bred and born. Her eyes were just below level with his, which meant that she was a tall woman, certainly tall for an Asian. The mouth that he had seen with such effect through the moonstone water he now saw had a slight dimple to one side that gave her smile a suggestion of irony. Her dark hair was again pulled to one side and fell over the front of her shoulder. She was wearing a long saffron shirt-waist dress with short sleeves.

"I have the drawings in another room," she said, getting right to the point. "I've been working in here, and it's cluttered. Anyway, the light's bad."

She led Strand through a modest living room with an abundance of art books scattered about in rambling stacks. The furniture was pedestrian and told him nothing about her.

He guessed that it had been included with the town house lease. As they passed through the room he glimpsed some uncommon touches here and there, a small draped table with a collection of softly burnished black pottery and three white lilies lolling in one of the lean amphorae, a rich throw glinting with gold threads tossed over the corner of the dreary sofa, an expensive and beautiful Anatolian medallion rug with predominant colors of scarlet and pollen yellow. These, he imagined, were Mara Song.

In just a few steps they had crossed a hallway and entered a bright sunroom with tall windows looking out into a small enclosed courtyard filled with potted plants. The stones in the courtyard were still wet from the morning watering. There was another sofa here and several comfortable rattan armchairs. The drawings were mounted in archival folders and were arranged in an approximate semicircle on these pieces of furniture, propped up against the backs of the cushions.

"Here they are," she said. "They're in alphabetical order. Balthus . . . Delvaux . . . Ingres . . ." She stepped slowly past them in review, her right hand, wrist up, indicating each artist by flicking a long index finger at each drawing. "Klimt . . . and Maillol."

Then she stopped and turned around.

"Five men. Seven naked women," she said matter-of-factly.

There were indeed seven drawings, and Strand was delighted to see that they were very fine examples of the artists' work. In fact, the collection was superior, and as they talked about each drawing, he realized that even though she was not a "collector" she had an educated and discerning eye and that her appreciation for these drawings went far beyond their financial value. She had a genuine affection for them.

As he stood before the pictures, Strand's mind was divided between the images and the woman who owned them. He remembered Truscott saying that he thought the sale of the art was being prompted by a "divorce thing," and he assumed that also accounted for the discrepancy between her two names. The drawings were going to bring a handsome price; he guessed that a handsome price had been paid to acquire them. Since Mara Song was having to sell them, Strand surmised that she had not come out well in her divorce.

After they had talked for a while about the drawings, she took a step back, folded her arms, and looked at him.

"They're jewels, aren't they?" she said.

He noted the distance from her waist to the hem of her skirt, and he remembered the long legs slipping through the bright water.

"Have you owned these awhile?" he asked.

"Most of them about four years."

Strand scanned the drawings again, his hands in his pockets as he stepped back away from them, too, beside her, surveying the group of images.

"I'm guessing that you already know I won't have any trouble selling these," he said. "You seem to know very well what you're doing here. I'll be glad to go ahead and work up appraisals and all of that whenever you're ready."

She didn't say anything for a moment, and Strand turned his head slightly to observe her. She was thoughtful, but her expression was uncommunicative.

"You don't want to sell them," he said.

"I teach art," she said. "I know how . . . wonderful these

things are." She turned to him. "Before five years ago I never in my wildest dreams imagined that I would ever own art like this myself. Then, for a while, a small window of time, I could afford them." She shook her head. "I'm afraid if I get rid of them, I'll never ever be able to afford anything like them again."

Strand said nothing.

"I'm going through a divorce," she said. "I don't need the money, but the fact is, I'm not going to be in the same financial comfort zone that I was in while I was married. I just thought I ought to, sort of, take stock."

"These aren't easy choices," Strand said. "I've been a dealer and collector all my life, and I have to face these choices all the time. Can't keep them all, no matter how much you love them. I tell myself that the pleasure of just having them for a while is a value every bit as real as the profit I'll get when I sell them. It's a mind game. It's really the truth, too."

When he turned back to her she was looking at him, the beginning of a smile on her mouth. But it never quite developed. They looked at each other, and for a fleeting moment he thought he sensed in her expression a vague notion of having seen him before.

"Would you like a cup of coffee?" she asked. "I made a fresh pot about an hour ago."

"No, I'm fine. Thanks, though."

The filtered sun was gilding the plants in the garden behind her, outlining her gray silhouette with a thin seam of gold. She would not have been universally considered beautiful, for her features, when taken individually, could not have been described as classical. Her nose was a little more prominent than Asian features usually allowed, and there was a small rise in the bridge. She had high cheekbones, and her eyes were as much Caucasian as Eastern. But regarded as a whole, these attributes conspired to make Mara Song a striking woman. She sure as hell lived up to his memory of her from the swimming pool. She was still looking at him, her arms crossed again as before. Then with her middle fingers she lightly touched her full lower lip.

"How long have you been married?" she asked abruptly.

He frowned at her, and she tilted her left hand back and touched her ring finger with her thumb.

"Oh. It would have been four years . . . well, in July."

She didn't move her eyes or speak.

"She died in an automobile accident. Almost a year ago."

Her face fell. "I'm sorry." She was embarrassed.

"No, that's all right."

There was a pause. She was visibly uneasy.

"This divorce," she said. "I find myself wondering how long people have been married." She shrugged. "That's pretty strange, I think. But that's what I do." Her eyes fixed on him. "I am sorry about your wife. My first husband died suddenly also, an odd heart condition. So I know . . ."

"It happens to people all the time," Strand said, not wanting to talk about it anymore.

The sun had found an opening in the overstory now and was flooding the courtyard behind her in brightness. He could see the shadowy silhouettes of her long legs backlighted through the saffron summer dress, and again, in his mind, he saw her long body stretched out, in the opalescent water.

She obviously did not recognize him from those mornings at the pool a month earlier, and Strand decided to see how she would react to being reminded.

"You know," he said, "I think we've almost met before."

The phrasing was unnecessarily cryptic, and the instant he spoke he wished he had said it differently. Her reaction confirmed his mistake. She turned to him, a look of suspicion playing nervously at the corners of her eyes.

"What do you mean?"

"I swim every morning at the River Oaks Swimming Club. Five or six weeks ago I think you came there every morning for a couple of weeks and swam laps at the same time I was there. There were only the two of us."

She studied him, still tentative, her mind searching back for the connection, her eyes raking his features for a hint of recognition. For a moment Strand thought he had made a terrible mistake. She almost had the look of a woman who was slowly realizing that the man she was talking to had been stalking her.

"I remember that," she said in dismay. Then happy, relieved, she added, "Yeah, I *do* remember that. We swam together for about two weeks and never spoke a word."

Strand smiled.

She laughed, now even more relieved. "That was you?"

"Odd, isn't it?"

"Well, it *is* odd. Did you know who I was when you came here today?"

"Not until you opened the door. You used a different name."

Slightly suspicious again. "You knew the name I used at the swim club?"

"When you stopped coming, I asked about you."

"Why?"

"I wanted to know who you were."

There was a moment when her face registered the unpleasant possibilities that must have suddenly sprung into her
mind. Then in an instant she realized the innocence of it all,
and she began to laugh.

He grinned. "Why did you stop coming?"

"Oh, long story." She was still smiling.

They sat at her kitchen table next to the sunroom and
talked, the seven drawings still propped on the cushions of the
chairs and sofa, the reflected brightness of the sunny courtyard cheering the uncheerful sobriety of the tired town house.
With only a few gentle questions from Strand, she pliantly,
though not eagerly, talked a little more about herself.

She told him of her first marriage. She and her husband
both had been art teachers at the Farnese Academy in Rome,
and after his death she had stayed on there. In a few years she
had met and married Mitchell Reinhardt, and for four years
she had endured a marriage that from its consummation never
found its balance, wobbling on unsteadily until it had become
so shaky that no ballast could steady it, and she had filed for
divorce.

"It was a sorry end," she said, reaching over to a vase of
geraniums sitting to one side of the table. She picked an orange
red flower and toyed with its petals. The strong fragrance of
geranium spilled into the room when she broke the stem.

"I've tried to sort it out for four years," she added. "I take
some responsibility. He deserves some. It was so wrong it
could never have been right, and I do blame myself for not realizing that sooner." She shrugged. "I quit wailing and throwing sand and ashes in the air a long time ago. Self-indulgence
really isn't of major interest to me."

She stopped, looking at the flower, thinking of something. He watched her fingers as they felt the velvety petals and then plucked one and placed it alone on the tablecloth.

"Then you're living here now?" Strand asked.

She looked up. "Oh, no, I'm just here for a few months. Mitchell's lawyer—well, the one handling the divorce, anyway—is here. It's easier if I am, too. The papers are complicated."

"Where will you go, after it's all over?"

"Back to Rome."

"To teach."

"That's right." She hesitated. "The thing is, I got a good deal in the divorce. Mitchell's been wealthy all his life, and he's used to defending his net worth. I knew he was prepared for a battle. I didn't want a battle, and I didn't want his money, certainly not bad enough to make a career out of getting it. I just wanted it to be over. He did have one thing I wanted, a home in Sallustiano in Rome. I told him I'd walk away from the usual financial fracas if he'd give me the seven drawings and the Sallustiano house with enough money in a trust for its upkeep and to pay the taxes on it for the rest of my life. He could be free of me with just a couple of straight, flat-out transactions. No strings."

She sat back and looked at Strand. "He agreed."

Strand studied her. She was turned aside from the table, her legs crossed at the knees under the saffron skirt, leaning slightly forward, her arms crossed on her long thigh, hands dangling limp. Her expression was open, frank.

She leveled her dark eyes on him. "I still have the teaching job. I was getting along just fine financially before he came along, and I was paying rent." She smiled a little. "I sure as hell wasn't living in a villa."

Then she straightened her back, a gesture that said she had had enough of talking about herself.

"As for the drawings"—she looked over at them—"well, they just suddenly seem like such an extravagance now that I'm no longer in that league. I don't know." She puckered her mouth to one side as she looked at the drawings.

"My part of it will take some time," Strand said. "I don't know what kind of timetable you're expecting, but I'll need a few weeks at the very least to work up an appraisal. And then some more time to contact potential buyers. I expect they'll sell fairly quickly."

"I should be in Houston for another month or two," Mara said. Her hands were folded in her lap now, and she was looking into the courtyard, presenting her profile to Strand.

"And you want the drawings sold by the time you go back to Rome."

"I think so."

"Okay, then," Strand said, taking one of his cards out of his pocket and handing it to her. "Whenever you're ready. I'd like to have the drawings while I'm working up the appraisals. I have very good security. They'll be safe."

She swung her leg a few times, looking at his card as she touched her bottom lip with her middle fingers, thinking. She made no move to end their conversation, no subtle gesture to indicate they were through. She idly flicked the bottom corner of his card with the fingernail of her little finger.

She looked up. "When could you begin working on the appraisals?"

"Whenever you want."

She dropped her hand to her lap and laid the card on her long thigh, looking at it.

She looked up. "What about tomorrow?"

"Okay."

"I have some letters, bills of sale, other items of provenance on some of them. They're still in the bank. I'll pick them up and bring everything to you in the morning. What would be a good time?"

"Same as today? Ten o'clock?"

"Sure. That's perfect."

"Good, I'll look forward to it," he said, standing.

"This has been kind of you," she said. "I appreciate it very much."

"My pleasure." He smiled. "It's good to be reunited with a misplaced mirage."

CHAPTER 5

BRUSSELS, BELGIUM

Dennis Clymer had been in Brussels forty-eight hours. It was his third trip to the city in as many weeks, and it was his last stop before returning home. In the past month he had spent time in most of the capitals of Europe, carrying his black Hermès briefcase to meetings in glass office towers in London, to elegant old-world restaurants in Prague, to the shady terrace of a pale ocher villa overlooking Monaco and the hazy Mediterranean, to a stolid dacha deep in a forest outside St. Petersburg that smelled of woodsmoke and *shchi* and was filled with objets d'art.

Clymer was at home in all of these places. Unlike the stereotypical American, he was eminently adaptable. He was fluent in German and French, but he conducted business only in English. Four times a year he made these hectic trips, usually a two- or three-week period during which he shuttled from one European country to the next, crisscrossing his own path, doubling back, retracing routes he had traveled two days or ten days before. Though he routinely stayed in small, exclusive hotels, he rarely stayed in the same hotel in succession in any city in Europe, and only recently when he was in

Brussels did he ever make a predictable diversion from a schedule that was otherwise fast paced and seemingly random.

Dennis Clymer was forty-three years old, had a master's in economics from Stanford University and a law degree from UCLA. He lived in the tony Brentwood section of Los Angeles. He and his second wife had two children, daughters from her first marriage. Clymer had a son by his first wife who lived with his mother in the San Fernando Valley. He had visiting rights with the boy but often had to cancel his visitations because of his busy schedule. He paid little attention to his family. His business took up most of his time.

As Clymer walked out of the Métropole Hotel in the center of Brussels, he had come to the end of a hammering schedule. Mentally he suddenly shifted gears. He had two nights in Brussels before he returned to Los Angeles, and he planned to spend both of them in the same place.

After returning to his own rooms in the Copthorne Stéphanie on the fashionable Avenue Louise, he bathed and changed clothes. The long afternoon meeting in a suite at the Métropole was with a slow-speaking Londoner who smoked dark Honduran cigars and a woman from Lyons who favored a particularly nasty kind of cigarette. His California lungs were screaming for fresh air. Just as dusk was settling over the city, Clymer left his hotel and walked out onto the avenue.

The lights were coming on all over Brussels, and the spring air was crisp, the sky deepening from peach to amber. He turned right on Avenue Louise and headed toward a large boulevard that lay just ahead. He was in the heart of the city's most exclusive district, which exuded luxury in its public and private residences and sparkling shops.

At the Avenue de la Toison d'Or/Guldenvlieslaan, Clymer

crossed to the other side, where it became Boulevard Water-loo/Waterloolaan, and once again turned right, walking in the failing light past posh jewelry shops and art galleries and chic boutiques filled with designer clothing. Smartly dressed shoppers strolled unhurriedly along the boulevard, among them Dennis Clymer, feeling very much pleased with himself for having once again negotiated nearly a month's worth of complex transactions for his clients. He anticipated the evening with the satisfaction of a man who was using his considerable intellect to make tons of money. To him Brussels never seemed more charming, and his place in it never seemed more deserved or appropriate. Everything was just as he wanted it.

He turned into Rue du Pépin/Kernstraat and made his way past a string of boisterous nightclubs, entirely oblivious to their allures. Beyond these he turned left to the Place du Petit Sablon, a quiet square with a beautiful formal garden in its center, and to one side, its front door illuminated by the green glow of lamplight reflected off the boughs of a sheltering chestnut, was his favorite restaurant, Chez Marius en Provence.

Clymer had made reservations in the name of Paul Franck. He was shown to his table—he had asked for a quiet corner—and immediately ordered a bottle of Bordeaux, a Premier Grand Cru Classé from St.-Emilion. He had just finished his first glass when he saw her smiling at him past the shoulder of the maître d' as she allowed herself to be shown to the table.

Clymer beamed and stood as she approached. The maître d' withdrew, and Clymer took her hand and kissed her gently on the offered cheek, catching the familiar scent of sachet.

"It has been an endless week," she said, showing no hint

of being tired as she sat down. Dennis Clymer relished every accented syllable.

She was one of over five thousand translators employed by the European Commission, which had its headquarters buildings only a few kilometers away. Clymer had met her on his last trip to Europe two months earlier. In fact, his present trip could have waited another quarter, but the memory of her had made it seem more urgent. During the past three weeks, Clymer, whom she knew only as Paul Franck, had managed to spend one night of each week with her.

The affair was a surprise to Dennis Clymer. He was not the kind of man who had a roving eye, though his travels frequently put him in situations of opportunity. He was, primarily, interested only in business, and the clients he represented used him for precisely this reason. They did not indulge miscalculations, and though Clymer was reaping stunning profits for his services, which he wisely invested and did not squander, he was cognizant of the fact that a failure to perform could very well have more serious consequences than a loss of income.

In short, he was a man who was under a good deal of stress, though it was a point of importance with him never to show it. He was on a very fast track, and for a long time now the money he was making was the only seduction to which he allowed himself to succumb.

She was nothing like the women he usually met when he traveled. Some of his clients always had beautiful women hovering about, and any of them happily would have indulged Dennis Clymer's requests. But Clymer was wary. Not only did he not trust these gorgeous, tightly fleshed creatures, but he didn't want to appear to his clients as having a weakness that possibly could be exploited. He kept his mind on his business and his hands on his black Hermès briefcase.

He had met her, however, in a situation unrelated to his business and well away from the people he represented. The absolute unpredictability of their meeting was what made him comfortable with her. He had been walking through the chic Galerie Louise, one of the several elegant shopping arcades in the center of the city, when he impulsively stepped into a leather goods shop. The place smelled richly of oiled leather, and he wandered around a corner to the briefcases where a woman was trying to decide which attaché to buy for her boss, a busy man who had asked her to get one for him to replace an old one. Unable to decide among the dozens there, she saw Clymer standing nearby and asked him his opinion.

She was not a stunning beauty, though she was quite pretty in a fresh, uncalculating way. She did not have the sleek, self-aware figure of the women he studiously avoided: she was a little hippy, though pleasantly so. Her hair was butter blond, and she wore it pulled back in a practical style vaguely reminiscent of the 1940s. She wore a smart, working woman's suit. Clymer noted that she had a quick, genuine smile and a charming way of knitting her brow when he offered a bit of sensible advice about briefcases. After a few minutes she chose one of his recommendations. As she was paying they chatted. When he told her he was from Los Angeles, she brightened with curiosity and asked if he knew any movie stars.

They ate an early dinner together at a little sidewalk café a few doors from the leather shop, and he told a few movie star stories, embroidering a little on his personal familiarity with a few famous names. She told him about her work as translator with the European Commission, about how she had studied languages in Paris, how she had worked for a while for IBM in Berlin before coming back to Brussels.

She had an unassuming manner, and Clymer quickly felt comfortable being with her. They lingered for a long while over their meal and then coffee, and when it seemed time to go she surprised him by asking him if he would like to join her for a drink. She knew a quiet place nearby with tables in a garden.

They drank more than either intended, so much so that Clymer forgot his habitual cautiousness when she asked him if he would like to see where she lived, perhaps have a last drink with her. They walked down Avenue Louise underneath the overhanging chestnuts that bordered the boulevard and turned into a side street in a historical residential district dating from the 1890s. She rented the top floor of an old three-story home, and it was there, his head lightened by alcohol and his mind full of the scent of sachet, that he had sexual relations with her, eventually falling asleep against the softest, palest breasts he had ever imagined.

The affair was born full-blown and unhesitating, surprising them both. Clearly they were inexperienced in such adventure, and the swift pace was inflammatory. Clymer could not stay away from her. Still, he was a man habituated to discipline, and that did not change. Having reflexively invented Paul Franck in the leather shop, he stayed with it. He did not invite her to his rooms in the Stéphanie, and she never asked to go there. At night, as they lay in the quiet of her bed and talked about their lives, he discreetly re-created himself. He gave little thought to where all this was leading, and apparently, neither did she. The affair itself was its own reward.

They didn't think about the future. It was not that sort of affair. They merely were enjoying the thrill of unexpected sexual abandon. Somehow it seemed entirely benign because it was not calculated. It was as surprising as a snowfall in July.

He told her he had only tonight and the next before he had to return to Los Angeles. They had finished eating and were lingering over a second bottle of Bordeaux.

She considered this a moment, pensively.

"And tomorrow? What about tomorrow?"

"I don't have any more business here."

"Then stay with me. Tonight, tomorrow, tomorrow night." She raised her eyebrows, allowed a wry smile. "I will call my office and say to them that I am ill. It won't matter."

Her expression was anticipatory and hopeful. Clymer hesitated at the suggestion.

"I don't know," he said.

"You don't know?" She mocked surprise and leaned toward him gently, the small candle between them throwing a timid, flickering light over the tops of her breasts. "How could you *not* know?"

They walked arm in arm along Boulevard Waterloo/ Waterloolaan, a couple lost in an outdated gesture of romance, naive characters in an old movie. The wine had made them uncaring of such a simple demonstration of affection, and they were oblivious of the chic scene through which they strolled to Avenue Louise. Yet again they walked unhurriedly under the dark, looming chestnuts and soon turned into her street and followed the slow, descending curve, the globes of the street lamps lighting a pale beaded glow in front of them.

They must have passed the parked car, but Dennis

Clymer didn't remember seeing it. Two isolated images were embedded in his consciousness in those stunning last moments: first, one of the men who grabbed him and forced the drugged cloth over his nose and mouth smelled of a sickly cologne; second, in the confusion he saw her step back, unaccosted, unafraid. In the lamplight their eyes met: she was calm.

The Belgian police *judiciaire* did not identify Dennis Clymer's body for nearly three weeks, and only then because of a birthmark under his left arm. His head and hands were never found.

CHAPTER 6

When Mara Song arrived at Strand's house the next morning, Meret went to the front door to answer the bell. Strand was finishing a letter when he heard their voices. Through the windows near his desk he saw them coming out of the central hallway into the peristyle. Mara was carrying a single large portfolio, and Meret was leading her around to the library door.

Strand stood and walked into the library, meeting them at the door just as Meret was pushing it open. Her face turned away from Mara, she flashed a sly smile at him. She excused herself and retreated to her office.

Mara Song's hair was pulled back and knotted behind her neck, and she was wearing a loosely cut linen shirt tucked into tailored linen trousers. Her smile was relaxed.

"Beautiful place," she said, looking around the library as she laid her portfolio on the library table. "Would you mind showing me around a bit? Have you got time?"

"Sure," he said.

Though she was careful not to be too intrusive, Mara was nevertheless very interested in everything having to do with the house. She asked about its history, how long Strand had lived here, whether the garden was already designed as it was now. She asked about the furniture, much of which Strand and Romy had bought in antique shops in Europe, and she asked about his own collection of drawings, where he had bought them, and why.

Strand watched her as he talked. She was as curious about him now as he had been about her, but she was far less reserved in satisfying her curiosity. With every exchange in their conversation he learned as much about her as she did of him. She was proving to be complex, though he was reasonably sure that she would not have characterized herself in that way. He was slowly beginning to suspect that Mara Song's personality was like the clear, bright sliver of the new moon: what you saw was stunning, but by far the greater part of it was hidden in shadow and would emerge only slowly.

In a little while they came full circle to the library. They sat at the long table, both on the same side, and Mara opened the portfolio and took out a folder.

"I think I can help you a little and save you some time on the appraisal," she began, laying out several sheets of paper with densely typed lines. "I have a fair amount of data on the provenance of each drawing."

She put the pages between them, then began going through her documentation beginning with the Klimt drawing, citing its catalog references, a history of its sales, and a brief description of the work, whether it was a fully executed drawing or a study for a later work.

When she finished, she sat back and tucked a loose bit of hair behind an ear. "It's a beginning, anyway," she said.

"It's more than that." Strand was still looking at the last document. "You've saved me a lot of work. I appreciate it."

"The truth is," she said, "I was afraid of getting ripped off. I'd never paid that kind of money for anything before in my life. It made me uncharacteristically thorough."

Strand was skeptical about this last remark. He was quite sure that Mara was, in fact, a very methodical woman.

He paged through the portfolio, looking at the seven drawings once again. They were superb, all of them, each in its own special way.

"This last one," he said, "Delvaux's *Réticence*. He's a different kind of draftsman from the others. What were your thoughts behind this purchase?"

She smiled as if he had caught her in a deception.

"It was the most spontaneous purchase of them all," she said almost reluctantly. She mused on the drawing. "Delvaux tended to simplify his technique, which of course fits perfectly well with the psychological content of his eerie imagery." She reached out and touched the edge of the paper. "But here, in this drawing, it looks as if he is going to allow the classical draftsman in him to take over—and here and here—then he reins it in. Here, for instance. Then again it emerges here." She tapped the paper. "That sort of thing goes on all over this drawing. In that sense, it's a kind of schizophrenic image. I'm not sure he knew what the hell he was doing." She tilted her head, looking at the drawing. "But then there's the title . . . so . . . Anyway, when I saw this I thought I sensed a different kind of Delvaux psychology hiding here, which instantly appealed to me."

For a little while neither of them spoke. Strand concentrated on the drawings, appreciating her eye and her astute sense of what she valued. Then, uneasily, he became aware of her studying him.

Though he had done precisely the same thing to her the morning before, their proximity—he could easily have put an arm around her—made him self-conscious. When he looked up from the drawings, she was watching him with an expression of keen interest. Having been caught, she quickly altered her expression to one of benign, but uninformative, pleasance.

"How did you end up in Texas?" she asked.

"That seems odd to you?"

"Not odd, but . . . well, interesting."

"Why?"

She laughed. "Oh, come on," she said. "You know what I mean. I'll bet you haven't lived here very long. I mean, not many years, anyway. For one thing, your card: 'Paul Davies, Dealer in Fine Art.' Why not 'Harold Strand'? You bought someone's business."

"Harold?"

"Well, whatever."

"You didn't ask Truscott? He can be very informative about dealer gossip."

"I don't know Mr. Truscott. He was just a 'trustworthy' name a London dealer gave me." She paused. "You're being evasive."

"Okay," Strand conceded. He hated talking about himself and had several stock responses to such questions. "Here's a cheap version of how I got here. When I was just out of the university—Chapel Hill, University of North Carolina—I went to work for a jewelry importer in New Orleans. I'd gotten a liberal arts degree, which prepared me for nothing in particular and everything in general. The jewelry importer was stingy with his employees and generous with himself. Collected art. It was my first exposure to fine art, and I fell in love with everything about it. I went back to school and got a master's degree in art history. I worked for a gallery in San Francisco for a while. Learned the business. Opened my own gallery, but apparently I hadn't learned enough business. I went broke. Got a job with a private collector in New York, an old man who had recently developed a passion for drawings and was raiding Europe. By this time I'd already zeroed in on drawings, too. We continued to educate each other.

"One day he walked in and told me he was dying of cancer. He wanted me to oversee the liquidation of his holdings. He said he wanted to reward me for my services, and since I was putting myself out of a job I might as well get a commission on it. So I became his broker rather than his employee. It was a generous gift. In one form or another, that's what I've been doing ever since."

"You've spent most of your career in New York?"

"No. London. Rome. Paris. Geneva. Vienna. Those are the places where I'd built my connections when I was buying for the old man, so that's where I headed and stayed. The old guy was good to me. He knew what kind of education I was getting."

"Did you meet your wife in Europe?"

"My first wife?"

She nodded, but he saw immediately that she had actually meant Romy. He told her about his first wife. She had been the daughter of a British MP who was a promoter of the EC when it was even less popular in England than it was now and who had more money than his profligate daughter could spend even in her most irresponsible binges. He told her briefly of their life in London, of his wife's indiscretions, of her destructive addictions, of her hair-raising escapades in polite society, and of her attempts at suicide.

After all that, Mara didn't have the heart to ask about Romy. He knew she wouldn't.

"So you lived mostly in London."

"A lot over the years, but not mostly."

"Always as an art dealer?"

"Always."

"So . . ." She repeated her first question: "How did you end up in Texas?"

Strand reached out and closed the portfolio. Behind her the courtyard was losing its light as the Gulf clouds built up outside. It was beginning to look like rain. The contrast of light and shadow in the library was softening to a monochromatic gray.

"Paul Davies went to Europe every year to buy art," Strand said. "He was from California, but he'd married a woman from Houston and moved here nearly thirty years ago. He was a very fine dealer, and I'd known him most of that time. When he died five years ago, his wife called me and wanted to know if I would be interested in buying his business. Romy and I were feeling adventurous. We took her up on her offer and moved to Houston. Paul had built a respectable reputation in the U.S. Since I'd spent most of my time in Europe and was less well known here, it just seemed to make good business sense to retain his name." He opened his hands. "It was that simple."

"No ego involved? You didn't want to use your own name?"

"I have to make a living. Ego follows that."

Mara looked around at the library and the house. "Just how good does your living have to be before you can give your ego a little satisfaction?"

Strand shrugged. "I have a low-maintenance ego."

Mara stared at him, her head turned ever so slightly at an angle, almost as if she were listening for something. Her face was a study in thoughts that seemed to venture far beyond the present conversation.

"I wonder," she said, "if you'd be interested in going to an art exhibit with me this afternoon?"

"The Menil surrealist exhibit?"

"Yes . . . exactly."

"You know," he said, "I would."

CHAPTER 7

Strand asked her to stay for lunch, suggesting that they go to the Menil Museum immediately afterward. Though surprised by the invitation, she agreed. Strand called Meret to join them, and they went across the courtyard to the kitchen.

While the two women started a tuna salad, Strand began cutting potatoes into thin strips, which he then deep-fried until they were nut brown and crispy. When everything was ready, Meret put on a Wynton Marsalis CD, lowered the volume, and they sat at the long refectory table in the middle of the kitchen.

It was their usual custom that Strand and Meret lunched together in the kitchen. Sometimes she went out and sometimes he did, but generally they prepared casual lunches of sandwiches or salads in the kitchen nearly every day. They talked or didn't talk, read, listened to music. It was relaxed and without ceremony. On occasion one of Meret's girlfriends might join them, which Strand always enjoyed. Now and then another art dealer who was visiting Strand when lunchtime arrived might be asked to stay. But Strand's invitations were reserved for the few people with whom he felt especially comfortable.

The conversation never flagged, and the two women quickly established an easygoing rapport. They could easily have lingered at the table for the rest of the afternoon, but soon the telephone began to ring, and Meret excused herself. Strand and Mara put away the food, cleaned up the dishes, and then left for the museum.

The Menil's surrealist holdings were famous, and Strand had seen exhibitions from them as often as they had been presented over the four years he had been in Houston. The surrealists were always popular, and he was not surprised to find a crowd at the museum. Which suited him perfectly. He had come not to see the exhibit, but to see Mara Song.

When they entered the museum Strand stayed with Mara for the first fifteen or twenty minutes and then gradually moved to drawings on an adjacent wall, then to those on the other side of the room, periodically separating himself from her by allowing the ebb and flow of the crowd to come between them. At first she sometimes would glance around to find him, but eventually she became entirely absorbed in the drawings and forgot about him altogether. Carrying her bag over one shoulder and holding her sunglasses in her hand, Mara moved slowly from image to image, concentrating on each drawing as if she were trying to peer into the very fiber of the paper itself. She ignored the unavoidable jostling of the crowd, having eyes only for the individual pieces of art before her, often remaining so long in front of an image that she reminded Strand of one of those photographs in which the central image was the only thing in focus, while the crowds surrounding the subject appeared as a blurry swirl of movement.

He watched her from every angle as they moved

through the exhibition rooms, sometimes observing her from only a few feet away, sometimes through a doorway, sometimes glimpsing her through the movement of heads and bodies and limbs of the crowd. What he saw was a woman who was captivated by a form of art that, compared to other media, was an unobtrusive world apart. To genuinely appreciate drawings, one had to be attracted to their inherent subtlety, to their modesty and intimacy. Most collectors of drawings believed that in some elemental way a drawing was a direct link to the mind of the artist in a manner that other forms of expression could not be. When one peered closely enough at the accumulated lines of a drawn image, or even at a few solitary strokes, one could almost believe that one saw the intent of the artist, and sometimes his discipline and sometimes his abandon, in a way that was bracing in its immediacy.

In a world defined by an insatiable hunger to gorge its senses with explosions of color and fulmination of sound and unrelenting activity, looking intently at a drawing on a piece of paper was an almost ascetic act. Strand found it, in her, beguiling.

When there was only a single room of drawings left to see, he drifted back to her and they finished the exhibit together.

Outside the threat of rain had passed and the sun was bearing down through the heavy air. The humidity was so high that their sunglasses fogged over immediately when they put them on. Mara laughed about this and said she found the city's semitropical atmosphere a challenge to feminine grace. On the other hand, she added, wiping off her sunglasses on the hem of her dress, she thought there was something sexy about the heat.

They returned to Strand's house and sat for a few minutes in the air-conditioned library, sipping iced tea.

"Well, that was fun," Mara said. "It was, uh, it was comfortable being with you." Then, frowning, watching him closely, "I hope that doesn't sound . . . odd to you."

"No, not at all." He smiled. "I know what you mean."

Mara daubed at the sweat on her glass with her napkin, thinking.

"You don't know," she said tentatively, "how much I appreciate your asking me to have lunch here, with you and Meret. It's the first normal thing I've done in . . . ages."

"Normal?"

Her eyes roamed the bookshelves. "Well, maybe normal isn't the right word, but, I don't know . . . comfortable, normal . . ." She took a deep breath. "It felt . . . tranquil."

She looked up cautiously to see how that might strike him. He nodded.

"I'm just trying to say that it felt good to be included in something like that." She shook her head. "With this really absurd divorce grinding on, sometimes I feel an absence of context, as though I'm just not quite meshing with . . . anything." She stopped. "This is muddy water to you, isn't it? I'm not making myself very clear."

Strand nodded. "I've enjoyed today, too. It's been a good thing, for both of us."

She looked at her watch. "Well, the morning appointment has turned into most of the day." She stood. "It's been wonderful. Thank you very much, Harry Strand."

❖   ❖   ❖

The time of day that Harry Strand hated finally arrived. It used to be his favorite, the hour just before dusk when the sun was poised only a few degrees above the horizon and the sharp light of the southern spring relented to the inevitable demise of another day. In the garden of the courtyard, protected by the stone walls of the old house, shade had already enveloped the fountain and the palms, and the blue hues of evening were alchemizing the tropical greens of Romy's garden into deepening shadows.

Romy's garden. Romy's time of day. Sometimes Strand still kept their ritual, sitting in the quiet with a glass of ice-chilled Scotch. But it wasn't any good anymore. The companionship was gone, the exchanges of small concerns and expressions of small delights. The Scotch remained. More of it now than before, of course. It didn't replace what he had had, but for a little while every day it dulled the regret of having lost it.

Tonight, instead of taking his drink into the courtyard, Strand took it into the library, put on a CD of *Lucia di Lammermoor*, and took down all of his books on the five artists who had created Mara Song's drawings. He put all the books on the library table, pulled his chair close, took a sip of Scotch, and began searching through the books.

After nearly an hour, Strand went into the kitchen to pour another drink. He returned to the library, turned off all the lights except a small one, and kicked off his shoes, propping his feet on the seat of another chair. *Lucia di Lammermoor* was well into its tragic story as he let his eyes settle on the drawing illuminated by the dim light on the wall at the end of the library table. There, in a space especially created in the center of the bookshelves, was his own Maillol drawing, a conté study of a nude the artist had done in preparation for executing the lithographic illustrations for the French-language edition of Lucian of Samosota's *The Dialogues of the Courtesans*.

The image was of a woman who, in the process of walking away from the viewer, turns in midstride and looks back. It was the first drawing that Strand and Romy had bought together, shortly after she'd come to live with him while he was in Vienna. He had discovered it in the home of an old Austrian banker whose family had retained Strand to appraise his art collection prior to selling his estate. It was a lovely thing, and when he'd shown it to Romy she had reacted to it passionately. She had become intrigued by the tenuous message implied in the turn of the woman's hips, by the curiosity conveyed in the twist of her neck and her tilted shoulders, her head, bent slightly and turned to cast a sidelong glance at the viewer.

The number of hours Strand had sat here looking at this drawing during the last year was well into the hundreds. Or so it seemed. Though the house was full of art that they had collected during their years together, this single drawing held more of Romy's soul than any of them; when he was in its presence, he was in Romy's presence.

It was at this moment that Strand suddenly thought of Mara Song. She was the first woman since Romy who had worked her way unbidden into his thoughts. He was just superstitious enough to find that of significance, though he had no idea what significance to attach to it. Maybe it simply meant that it had been long enough, and Mara's appearance at this point in his life was nothing more than a gift of time and circumstance.

CHAPTER 8

Within a few days of receiving Mara's drawings, Strand finished his appraisal of her images and asked her to come over to review it. She came in the middle of the afternoon, and they talked about his conclusions and how he would approach the sale. Mara was still there when Meret left at five o'clock. They had drinks. They talked. Strand suggested they go to Chiara's for dinner.

A few days after that Mara called him to say she had received legal papers from Italy that represented yet another hurdle in her complex divorce proceedings. Would he like to celebrate—quietly? She had learned of a Thai restaurant that might be good. They ended the evening talking over drinks in the garden of Strand's house.

Gradually, with neither of them bringing attention to it, the subject of the sale of the drawings fell away. Mara returned the drawings to the bank vault. Strand didn't mention it because the sale of the drawings was a conclusion and introduced a connection to the end of something. He didn't ask Mara why she had dropped the subject.

The next few weeks passed quickly. Strand and Mara saw

a lot of each other, each of them growing increasingly at ease with calling the other to suggest dinner at a favorite restaurant or a movie or just to get together at either of their homes for a meal, which often ran late.

Mara came frequently enough to Strand's at the end of the day that she and Meret soon became good friends. Often when Mara was coming over for the evening she would show up a little early, before Meret left for the day, and the two of them would have an early glass of wine and visit while Strand finished whatever he was doing in his office.

Sometimes on weekends when Meret wasn't working, Mara would come over and spend the day, browsing in Harry's library or playing CDs from his collection while he worked at his desk. She would bring her sketchbooks and curl up in a chair somewhere and work quietly. They would have drinks in the garden and talk, a pastime of which neither of them seemed to tire, every conversation bringing to each of them an accumulative knowledge of the other that continued to stabilize their friendship.

And it remained a friendship, a close friendship, but nothing more than that. Mara always went home in the evenings, or Strand did when he was at her place. Increasingly, though, Strand's house became the place where they were most comfortable.

Strand thought a lot about what would happen if the relationship turned more intimate. In a way he yearned for it, but in another way he very much wanted to keep it just the way it was. He tried to make peace with his ambivalence, but in the end he couldn't bring himself to remove the boundary line that protected him from a level of complication that he still wanted to avoid.

For her part, Mara seemed at ease with this, and their
friendship settled into a routine in which they desired and
sought nothing more than simply to be in each other's company. But it quickly moved beyond that to the point where
they very much desired each other's presence, and the alacrity
with which this happened surprised both of them.

May and June passed from the calendar in this manner,
and the first anniversary of Romy's death slipped quietly past
in a single summer night, its hurt and heartache softened, at
least to the point of being bearable, by Mara's reassuring presence. July was almost gone when Strand told Mara that he was
going to have to start traveling.

"Really? For how long?" She was curled up in an armchair in his office, near the windows and his desk, sketching by
the oblique light that came in from the courtyard. She had
gathered her hair in a loose pile on her head to keep it out of
her face while she sketched, securing it in place with a couple
of pencils. She was barefoot, and she was eating a frozen lime
bar, a napkin in her lap.

"A few weeks." Strand put down his pen and pushed away
from his desk. He had kicked off his shoes under the desk and
propped his feet on an ottoman.

"Where are you going?"

"San Francisco, then Rome. I've got a collection of
Eakins portrait studies that I've been putting together for a
client in San Francisco, and a man in Rome has got a little
bunch of Fuseli drawings that I'd be a fool to pass up."

Mara finished her lime bar and wiped her mouth with the
napkin and then carefully wrapped the stick in the napkin.

"You've been working on these a long time?"

"Most of the year."

"Sounds like fun," she said, but she wasn't successful at hiding her disappointment at the prospect of his leaving. Strand was a little surprised, and gratified, at her reaction. "When are you leaving?"

"In a couple of days."

"Oh, that soon?"

She was pursing her lips slightly, her eyes diverted to her pencil as she doodled distractedly in the bottom corner of her sketchpad.

"I was wondering," he said, "when I get back from San Francisco if you'd like to go on to Rome with me."

Her pencil stopped. She didn't look up. She said, "Oh . . . well . . ."

He could see her mind working in her face, something he was beginning to appreciate about her. It was an unusually transparent behavior, a lack of calculation that he found refreshing. His entire professional life had been spent dealing with people under control. Spontaneity, apparent spontaneity, was rare.

"In a few days?" she asked, still not looking up.

"Right."

She nodded slightly, as if having confirmed something to herself, and then she looked up at him.

"I want to say something, Harry." Her face reflected just a hint of acknowledgment that she thought she was stepping into risky water. "I'm forty-two. I don't want to pretend that I'm in my twenties, and that I'm engaged in some sort of game here. One, I don't have the patience for it anymore. Two, I don't have the time for it anymore. I've wasted too much of it already. I must have thrown away five years in the last twelve months. Three, I want you to know, without having to be coy about it, that I like you very much, and, frankly, I don't want you to wander away before we get to know each other better. Really get to know each other."

She stopped, but not long enough for him to say anything before she went on.

"If you don't have the same . . . interest . . . in continuing this in a serious way, just tell me. I've been through quite a lot in the past couple of years, and I think I can handle honest answers if they've got honest feelings behind them. You don't strike me as the kind of man who'd be cruel about it if you didn't want this to go on."

She paused again, but again she didn't let him interrupt her train of thought.

"I guess what I'm trying to say is, well, I think I'm a romantic woman, but at this point in my life it seems to me that good common sense is just as important.

"I've been burned pretty badly with this marriage, Harry, despite my bravado about it. I just can't make that kind of mistake again." She stopped and looked down. "But we seem to have so much to offer each other. If this is a . . . possibility for us, well, I'd hate for us to miss an opportunity simply because we didn't know how to talk to each other about what we're really feeling." Again she confronted him with her eyes. "I don't want the rituals of . . . getting to know each other to confuse what we might be genuinely feeling. We can't mistake, or misrepresent, our feelings for each other, Harry. Either way." She paused. "I think . . . that would be a shame."

He couldn't answer her immediately. Though she had spoken haltingly, there was no misunderstanding the depth of her feelings, and Strand wanted to accord her the same considerate deliberation.

"I can't think of anything I'd like better than to continue this . . . as long as we can." He thought a moment, his arms crossed. "I don't know how far down the road I'm thinking. I don't know that I have 'plans.' . . ."

"No"—Mara sat up in her chair, putting the sketchpad down on the floor—"I didn't mean that you had to spell it out for me. I, it's just that, a trip like that, it could change things." She stopped, seemingly frustrated at her own inability to express precisely what she was thinking. "Harry, you know what I mean here. I'm so very grateful to you for our friendship . . . for you sharing your home, for Meret's friendship . . . for you including me in your life." She took a deep breath. "For me, it could easily go farther than this. It seems like we're at that point where this could become something else, something more."

"But you don't want to do that yet. Or maybe ever."

"It's not that I don't want to. It's that I'm afraid to if . . . Look, I don't want sex to complicate a friendship. If it's only going to be a friendship."

Strand stood, put his hands in his pockets, and leaned his shoulder against the window frame. He looked outside a moment and tried to straighten out his thoughts. When he turned back to her she was reaching up and taking the two pencils out of her hair. She tossed them onto the floor by her sketchpad, shook out her hair, and leaned back in the corner of the chair and looked at him.

"Do you think it's possible that you could be expecting too much from this?" Strand asked.

"Expecting too much? What do you think is out of proportion in what I've just said?"

"It sounds to me like you're wanting guarantees."

She frowned at him, waiting for him to go on.

"Guarantees," Strand said, "that you won't get hurt. Guarantees that I'm going to be the kind of person you want me to be. Guarantees that I'm not going to disappoint you."

For a moment neither of them said anything, and this time he had no perception whatsoever of what was going on in her mind. The silence went on longer than he imagined it would. She broke her gaze and looked away. She nodded slightly, as if to herself, her eyes finding and settling on a drawing on the wall near her chair.

"Okay, I see your point," she said. "Maybe I'm trying to be too careful." She shook her head, thinking. "Maybe I'm, I don't know, trying too hard to avoid the common little disasters that destroy a relationship, the kind of things that afterward, when it doesn't work out and it's over, you say to yourself, I should have seen that coming."

"I'd like to do that, too," Strand said. "But you can't take the risk out of being human. Especially the kind of risks that two people take when they're trying to feel their way into each other's lives."

She seemed embarrassed and at the same time a little sad, a reaction that puzzled him.

"Believe me," he said, trying to diffuse her confusion, "I didn't mean to push this. It was only a suggestion."

"Harry, I'd love to go to Rome with you. I would dearly love to." She smiled apologetically. "I don't know. I guess I thought I wanted it too much."

"Good," he said, smiling too.

CHAPTER 9

ROME

Ariana Kiriasis sat on a large, damask-upholstered divan in the upstairs sala of her home in a quiet street in the Aventino, the southernmost of Rome's seven hills. She was looking out to the view over her balcony, the double doors of which were thrown open to the pleasant morning air and to the sound of crows in the stone pines on the grounds of the nearby churches of Santi Bonifacio e Alessio and Santa Sabina. This single view was the reason she had bought the old house, as well as the reason it was grossly overpriced, considering its wretched plumbing and deteriorating stucco walls, which she had had to pay handsomely to have repaired.

Having an artistic and romantic eye, she had never regretted her decision. To the northwest, the view encompassed a long stretch of the Tiber and all of the district of Trastevere. On a day like today, with a slight haze in the summer air, the filtered light illuminated the dome of Saint Peter's with exquisite effect, as though it were a colossal pearl hurled from heaven onto the muddy banks of the Tiber.

This was the view Ariana stared at now, but it was not the view she was seeing. So intensely was her mind engaged that

she actually saw nothing at all. On the sofa beside her, and
scattered over the floor around her small slippered feet, were
the pages of the morning's *International Herald Tribune*,
which her maid brought to her every morning with her
espresso and pastry.

Ariana had been through every page of it. She had been
through every column . . . several times. She did not find, she
could not find, the item that she had depended upon seeing
every first week of the month for the past four years. It was
usually in the form of an advertisement, and usually the smallest one the newspaper would sell. The word "art" or "drawing"
always appeared in the advertisement, which might address
anything having to do with art, the sale of art supplies, an art
auction, an estate sale, an exhibition. Sometimes they were
fanciful. Corsier was like that. He could be droll. Within the
brief advertisement were two things meant for Ariana to read:
first, there was the name "Claude Corsier" in a coded form
and in one of five languages; and second, there was a coded
date on which the next month's advertisement would appear.

Her own advertisement, meeting similar criteria and intended for Corsier's eyes, had appeared two days earlier in the
same newspaper.

She had already gotten up and gone to the writing desk in
her bedroom to check Corsier's previous month's advertisement and to confirm today's date. She had already spent a lot
of time staring at the crumpled newspaper, leaning forward on
the sofa, her elbows on her thighs, the fingers of both hands
embedded deep into her wiry hair as her mind raced over the
possibilities for the advertisement's conspicuous absence. None
of the possibilities made any sense except the worst one. She
felt distinctly as she imagined a woman might feel who one

morning found that dreaded lump in her breast after a lifetime
of knowing that her family medical history and her own habits
had predisposed her to that inevitable discovery. It had finally
happened. Still, it was a shock.

Suddenly she dropped her gaze from the white dome of
Saint Peter's to the newspaper on the worn and faded Persian
carpet. The sudden change from bright to dark blinded her
momentarily. She waited. Her sight returned from the edges
inward. As the newspaper reappeared it struck her as really
quite odd that she and Claude Corsier had never discussed exactly what they would do in this situation. They had created a
system for mutual notification, but beyond that . . . Well, there
was nothing beyond that, and she was dumbfounded by the
shroud of isolation that had dropped over her in the last
twenty minutes. Before coffee she had a place in life. Friends.
Lovers. Companions. After a few bites of her *torta di mele* and
a demitasse of espresso, she was suddenly an alien in that same
world.

Actually, that wasn't quite right, either. She was no
longer in the same world that she had lived in before the torte
and espresso. She had been dragged backward in time into a
former life. When she thought about it now, it seemed so far
removed from her present life that it was as though it had all
happened to another person. Yet, strangely, certain events,
certain moments, faces, bits of conversation, the sound of a
voice, a betrayal, the touch of a lover, a death, a fragrance, all
of it was as immediate to her as the events of last night.

And that was what petrified her.

Ariana picked up the telephone.

VIENNA . . . FIVE DAYS LATER

The second-floor flat was in an old apartment building in a residential street in Wieden, the fourth district. The little street was shrouded by fat chestnut trees whose broad boughs reached all the way to the window where Ariana sat watching and waiting for him, a cool Austrian breeze carrying the smoke from her cigarette out into the dappled light of late afternoon. She could hear people passing by on the sidewalk below, and she could catch glimpses of them through leaves.

Even though she had never been to these rooms before, they were already familiar to her. For the better part of two decades she had met Harry Strand and others in countless rooms like these in Prague and Rome and Athens, in Budapest, Berlin, and Trieste, all over Europe. For security reasons they moved regularly to different streets in different cities, but eventually all the safe houses in all the cities became the same. Their differences were completely obscured because they were all used in the same way for the same reasons—a place to plot, a place to escape to, a place to tryst and to share secrets, a place to wait for the inevitable encrypted message to move on. This one reeked with the stale odors of former meetings. It was an odor she would forever associate with the taut business of bringing one's fears under control.

She heard the key working at the lock in the door, and she turned in her chair and watched as the door swung open and he walked into the room.

"Ariana," he said.

"Hello, Bill."

He closed the door and flipped the deadlock. When he turned around again he stood still a moment, looking at her from the denser shadows away from the windows. She couldn't see his face, but she knew he could see hers.

She mashed out the last of her cigarette and stood up. He moved away from the door, taking off his suit coat as he came into the center of the room. After taking a pack of cigarettes from the inner breast pocket of the coat, he folded the coat and draped it over the back of a chair. He tossed the cigarettes onto the sofa.

"What's it been?" he asked as she approached him. "Nearly five years?" He made no gesture of greeting. The intervening years were nothing.

She said, "Something like that."

They regarded each other awkwardly, and then Bill Howard sat on the sofa and crossed his legs. He picked up the cigarettes, took one for himself and then offered one to her. She took it from him and bent down for the tiny flame he held up to her. He had a handsome, old-fashioned gold lighter, heavily engraved and much worn. It was the only elegant thing about the man, and it didn't seem to fit him at all. She had always wondered how he came to have it. She wasn't surprised to see he was still using it.

Howard smelled of an American shaving lotion, the same lotion she remembered from the years before. She had seen a bottle of it once in his bathroom in a hotel in Salonika. It was emerald green. Nothing exotic, a cheap aftershave that could be purchased in any pharmacy.

Bill Howard had put on weight, but other than that he had not changed. He was still wearing suits in tones of brown, the same unremarkable hue as his thinning hair. He wore a white shirt and a tie—geometric patterns in burgundy and beige—that could have been one from those earlier years. As always he looked as if he had dressed without paying attention to what he was doing, as if he had had something else on his mind.

She pulled heavily on her cigarette and crossed her arms again. None of the lamps in the room were turned on, and the only light came from the window, tinted with green reflected off the broad leaves of the chestnuts. The apartment was dowdy with forty-year-old furniture that needed reupholstering. The place made her terribly sad.

"Still beautiful," Howard said, appraising her in the pale light. "Greek women, I remember, have a way of ignoring the passing years."

"I thought you weren't going to come," she said, disregarding his remark.

"I'm sorry it took so long." He looked around.

"I've been waiting in these damn rooms for five days," she said.

"I was traveling."

"They might have told me that."

"You've forgotten how it is."

"I haven't forgotten a single moment," she said.

Howard said nothing.

"Claude Corsier has disappeared," she said.

He didn't have much of a reaction, only a fleeting frown.

"What do you mean?"

She looked at him, tense, restless. "Which of those words don't you understand?"

"You've been keeping in touch with him?"

"Yes."

"Really. And with Strand, too?"

"No."

"Okay," he said, shifting his shoulders on the sofa, settling in, "go ahead and tell me what's going on."

Ariana nodded and took a long drag on her cigarette for support. She collected herself.

"After the FIS changed our mission to criminal intelligence, everything changed for us . . . who worked with Harry. Even before that we knew things were going to be different after the Berlin Wall came down and the Soviet Union disintegrated. The cold war was over. We knew we were living through the end of an era. Harry said the FIS was being forced to . . . you say, downsize. Even though we had been redirected"—she shrugged—"we saw how easily we could be thrown away when we were no longer useful in a certain way.

"Harry . . . well, all of us . . . the three of us made certain plans to, uh, 'improve' our retirement situation. It was late in the day for me," she continued. "I was approaching middle age, had no money to speak of and no pension waiting for me. No husband and no prospects of getting one—that's too high a price to pay for security. I decided to look after myself."

Howard's expression changed slightly, taking on the impassive rigidity one often saw in people who suddenly realized they were about to hear news that they expected would shock them. They reflexively prepared themselves with a kind of facial fortification.

"We developed a strategy to get away with some money, a scheme. It went on for exactly six months, until Harry closed it down nearly six months before he retired."

Howard's face fell. "Jesus . . . Christ . . . Wolf Schrade?"

She nodded. "Of course, everyone scattered after that. We never saw each other again. None of us."

Howard had forgotten to smoke his cigarette. It smoldered between his fingers.

"But Claude and I decided we wanted to stay in touch with

67

each other. We agreed on a secret way to communicate, a way to make sure that each of us knew the other was still alive. A warning system."

"He's missed his turn."

"Exactly." She smoked, her stomach aching from the tension.

Howard wasn't interested so much in Claude Corsier's disappearance. "How much did Schrade lose?" His voice betrayed a forced stoicism.

She hesitated. "Millions."

"How many?"

"I don't know. Quite a few."

Howard didn't react.

"The way it was set up," Ariana went on, "he didn't know. It was a very good operation. Very good. Extensive planning." She paused. "I think he has finally puzzled out what happened. And who did it."

"Shit." Howard remembered his cigarette, which had burned down to the filter and was stinking. He put it in the ashtray.

"The point is," she said, "I think this is going to get dirty. This is very complex."

"God . . . damn." Howard swallowed. "This was Harry's idea, wasn't it?"

Ariana looked at him. "We were all involved . . ."

"But it was Harry's idea."

"You've got to understand—"

Howard held up one hand to stop her. His face had grown red. He was furious. She knew the reality here. Bill Howard didn't give a damn that Ariana was afraid, that she believed she was going to be killed, and that she was desperate for protection.

What was coursing through his thoughts like a fever was that his twenty-three-year career in the Foreign Intelligence Service, a carefully shepherded career, was suddenly as unstable as the smoke wisping up from the end of her cigarette.

She smelled food cooking, a thick odor that she couldn't identify. It lacked the tangy sharpness she would have smelled in Salonika or Athens, or even Rome. She turned away from Howard's silence and moved back to the window. Below, a car purred by slowly in the street.

She wasn't sure where she stood legally on this, but the game was intricate from the point of view of international law. It had all taken place in the gray areas of the spying game, and it was her guess that it would unravel in the same sphere. Behind her she heard the flick and scratch of Howard's lighter. A pause while he inhaled.

"I can't believe you people thought you'd get by with this," he said, his voice husky with smoke. "Screw a guy like Schrade and just get slick away with it."

She turned around. "It was a lot of money. Harry, well, you know, he inspired a lot of confidence. We thought we had a good chance. You know better than I do that people like Schrade steal from each other all the time."

"And they get killed all the time. It's a violent vocation."

"Maybe, but then a lot of others get away with it, too, don't they? It happens. We thought it could happen to us."

She put out her cigarette in the ashtray she had left on the windowsill. Her heart was loping erratically. Below on the sidewalk a couple paused under the trees to talk in the fading light. She could see only the lower part of the woman's skirt and her legs.

She turned around and came back toward the sofa. She

avoided a heavy armchair with its loathsome upholstery worn bare in spots by the buttocks of spies and traitors and the women who slept with them. She pulled around a wooden dining chair and positioned it in front of him.

"Claude Corsier," Howard mused, "that son of a bitch would've picked the devil's pocket for spare change if he thought the extra pennies would help him buy another goddamned little scratchy drawing."

"He took a lot of risks for you, too, Bill. And you didn't pay him shit."

"I haven't forgotten that." He dropped his eyes to the dead cigarette butts in the ashtray beside him. He was lost in thought. Then he closed his eyes and slowly shook his head. "Jesus H. Christ," he said. He looked up at her. "And what did your cut come to?"

"A lot." She wasn't going to get into that until she knew if they were going to help her.

Howard swore again. "Strand knows about this, that Claude's disappeared?"

"I don't know." She knew he wasn't going to believe this. None of them had ever really understood Harry Strand.

"Our agreement," she said, "actually, it was Harry's stipulation, was that we would never contact him after this was over. Never even try. Ever. And I haven't."

Howard was already shaking his head. "I don't buy that, Ariana. You worked together too long, went through too much. You were like a family. He couldn't do that."

"Well, he did, Bill." She was finding it difficult to stay calm. Both of them were barely handling the tension. "None of you ever really understood what you were dealing with in Harry Strand. The reason you find this idea so confounding is that you never could have made that kind of decision yourself. It's too extreme, too radical. That's why Harry was so successful for you for so many years. He never let reality get in the way of possibility. That is why he is what he is . . . and why you are what you are."

Howard said nothing for a little while, and though she couldn't read his face, she sensed his agitation.

"How is this going to work?" she asked. It was time for blunt questions.

He shook his head. "I don't know." He sounded tired. "Anyway, it's not for me to decide, you know. It's them."

"It's the same thing."

"No. Big difference. I'm out here. They're back there. It's not the same thing at all."

Ariana felt a resurging nausea. "You tell them I want to talk," she said. "I'll tell them everything—but I want protection from Schrade. They need to know what happened."

"What about Harry? This can't be good for him."

She fixed her eyes on him. She felt near tears, but she fought it. "You tell me about Harry," she said coldly.

"What."

"Is he alive, Bill?"

"How the hell do I know?" He started to say something else but stopped.

Neither of them trusted the other, but Ariana was at a distinct disadvantage. They both knew it.

"I need to know what I'm dealing with here, Ariana," Howard said. "Give me some idea of where you're going with this. I've got to know where this is headed before I can take it back to the guys who call the shots."

She really had no choice.

71

CHAPTER 10

ROME

Mara's home near the Piazza Sallustio was a lovely place with a garden surrounded by high walls and well-kept grounds. In the 1950s and 1960s, when the nearby Via Veneto was the center of European *dolce vita*, the home was owned by a titled family from Monaco who put it to good use entertaining the glitterati of those heady days. Today the area had slipped into genteel quietude. The real estate was still choice and expensive.

Mara seemed most comfortable here; she had scattered throughout the house the myriad small personal items that one kept around simply because one liked something's shape or color or had fond remembrances associated with its acquisition.

Here, too, Harry Strand saw for the first time some of Mara's fully developed drawings, which she had framed and hung throughout the house. She had not told him that they were hers. They had been there nearly a week before he had enough leisure time to wander unhurriedly through the large rooms and examine all the paintings and drawings she had accumulated.

She was a far better artist than she had allowed him to see from the sketching she had been doing in Houston, having implied that her work was little more than academic. She had a very fine hand, a sound grounding in draftsmanship, and a genuinely original eye. She had a few figure studies, but most were studies of Roman architecture and city scenes.

When Strand looked at these pictures, Mara came into a clearer focus. It is inherent in an artist's work to be revelatory, and Mara's drawings were no exception. In the way she expressed the attitude of a seated nude, in the way she brought the light to a church or palazzo, or chose a perspective of one of Rome's countless small, winding streets, she revealed, incrementally, ever more of her mind and personality and gave him access to other dimensions of understanding her. He saw nothing in these works to lessen his growing affection for her. He saw everything to enhance it.

After he had finished the week-long process of acquiring the Fuseli drawings, he and Mara began showing each other "their" Rome. They were surprised to learn that in the past they had spent many months in Rome at the same time, and Mara found it intriguing to speculate that with their common interests they might very well have been in some of the same galleries or museums or restaurants at the same time. In reality, however, Strand knew that his Rome and Mara's Rome, despite all their common interests, had never had the remotest chance of overlapping. They had been, in fact, worlds apart.

None of that mattered, for in the Rome of the present they stopped pretending that the very thing each of them had desired, and each had believed was inevitable from their first meeting, was not going to happen.

They had been dining late at Toula, which had become

their favorite restaurant, an understated place at the throat of the tiny Via della Lupa in the center of the city. They lingered long over desserts and more wine, then walked awhile in the narrow streets near the Pantheon in the cool of an evening so rare that it seemed to have been conjured for them from antiquity. She leaned against him in the taxi, and he could smell her, not her perfume, but the fragrance of her skin, and the ride to Sallustiano took them through a Rome that had never seemed to Strand more beautiful or ancient.

There was no decision, no word spoken, as they climbed the stairs together. With Mara still holding to his arm, he simply walked past his own bedroom and followed her into hers.

He undressed her by the opened balcony doors above the palms, the late Roman breeze moving all about them like a vague memory he could never quite remember. She waited for his hands, head bowed, leaning into him slightly with a grace of controlled desire that he had never before experienced with a woman. When her dress fell away to the floor, she was naked. As he touched her waist, traced his fingers over the rise of her hips, and gently moved his hands up to cup her breasts, she leaned her head forward and put her lips lightly upon his neck. The feel of her was as new and erotic to him as the first moment he had ever felt a woman's naked breasts, that long lifetime ago as an astonished boy.

"I just got a call from an old friend," Mara said, approaching the door to the room where Strand had been spending the afternoon poring over half a dozen art books he had bought that afternoon in the Largo Chigi. "A woman I've known for years. We're going to have drinks at a little café near the bottom of Veneto. Want to go along?"

Strand looked at his watch and then outside to the court-yard, where the light was already softening in the late after-noon.

"You still want to have dinner at Toula's at nine?" he asked.

"Sure."

"Then I think I'll pass."

"She's going to be disappointed."

Strand shrugged. "I'll open a bottle of something here and think about you at dusk."

She came across the room to the sofa, where he sat among books and papers scattered about him, and leaned over the back of the sofa, put her arms around his neck, and kissed him.

"She's pretty," she whispered. "You'll be missing something."

"Well, that's enticing"—Strand scratched his temple with his pencil—"but I really don't want to stop in the middle of this. Tell her . . . it pained me to forgo the pleasure of her company."

"Yeah," Mara said, straightening up, "she'll swoon." She turned and headed for the door, grabbing her shoulder bag from a chair on the way out. "See you later."

Strand worked for nearly an hour more before he stopped, laid aside a folio volume of early Renaissance archi-tectural drawings, and rubbed his eyes. He hadn't even gotten up from the sofa since Mara left, and he needed to stretch his legs and go to the bathroom. First he turned on a few lamps, giving the room a soft amber glow.

This generous room had become Strand's favorite place in the house because of its antique furniture and broad doorways opening to the loggia and courtyard. Pictures hung every-where here, covering the high walls, hanging over the fire-place and over the doors. There were tall narrow paintings and horizontal drawings, some with elaborate frames, some with simple ones, square pictures, small oval ones; oils, pastels, pencil, charcoal, and metal point. One of Mara's rare large nudes hung on the north wall, a dominant piece that Strand liked very much. In one corner of the room was an easel and a small table cluttered with pencil and charcoal boxes with colorful French and Italian labels.

He went down the corridor to the bathroom, and when he returned he opened the French doors to the evening air, standing and looking out with his hands in his pockets. Some-where in another concealed garden a peacock cried. The city was all around him, yet the only evidence of it was a faraway and almost imperceptible hum of traffic.

Leaving the French doors open, he stepped outside and stood for a moment in the loggia. The east wall in the court-yard was rosy and deepening quickly as the sun fell behind the Janiculum across the Tiber. He stepped out onto the cinder path that followed the wall and began walking, his shoes mak-ing a crunching sound on the cinder. At the far end of the gar-den he stopped and listened to the peacock again and took a deep breath of the air. The air of Rome changed at dusk and acquired a special quality in the same way that the city's fa-mous light took on a unique character of its own at certain times of the year. At night the air was nearer to antiquity than in the day, and one could imagine with greater clarity the men and women of former ages.

He moved on, rounding the garden on his way back to the loggia. When he was nearly there he looked toward the

French doors, anticipating that the amber glow from the few lamps in the room would be even richer in color now with the greater darkness. Instead he saw a jarring, pale light, flickering against the panes of the French doors.

He stopped. The television? Was Mara home? She hadn't touched the television since they had arrived.

His heart began to lope, and all of his old reflexes roused themselves as he studied the pale light from the darkness where he stood. Then he walked on. He stepped up on the loggia and entered the villa through the French doors.

No one was there. He called out. Nothing. The house, his sixth sense told him, was empty.

Between the fireplace and the French doors was a small black statue, an admirable study of a Maillol nude. It sat on what must have been a narrow pedestal covered with a faded scarlet Renaissance damask with fleur-de-lis pattern in gold thread and a gold cord trim.

Next to it was a dark, heavy antique table upon which sat a black television and a VCR. On a shelf below were half a dozen cassettes, all of them labeled with Mara's handwriting: "Master drawings, the Uffizi"; "Drawing collection, Villa Borghese"; "Modern drawing exhibit, American Academy"; "Balthus exhibit, Accademia Valentino." Strand had looked at the labels before, but he had never watched the tapes.

The VCR was on, static dancing on the fluorescing screen. A cassette was half out of the slot.

Strand walked over to it and took it out. No label, no identification. He put it back into the slot and pushed it in. The slot door closed. The gears whirred. He stood, watching, as it began to play. The Balthus exhibit. Mara's voice narrating. The images were sharp and in color, and Mara was doing a good job, taking the exhibit slowly, coming in close on the paintings and drawings, narrating, reading the attributions on the labels below or to the side of each piece.

After fifteen or twenty seconds, Mara's narration was abruptly interrupted and a grainy black-and-white tape began to play. A timing counter showed up in the lower left corner of the screen. A gummy, hot feeling washed over him as he immediately recognized the characteristics of a surveillance tape. He stood, riveted, in front of the screen. There was no audio track, and the only sound in the room was the slight hiss of the tape whirring slowly on the spinner heads inside the player.

The camera seemed to be mounted on the dashboard of a car. It was night, and the headlights of the car picked up traffic traveling in the same direction on what appeared to be an expressway. Headlights from approaching traffic across a median flared in bright streams as they approached and disappeared. The car moved in and out of the general stream of traffic with no discernible purpose. After a few moments it became clear that only one car had been in front of them consistently through all the lane switching and the passing and being passed.

Strand tried in vain to identify the locale: highway markers and exit signs had been manipulated and deliberately blurred. The cars were American; that was all he could tell. The camera car stayed so far back behind its target that Strand couldn't tell anything about the driver or even how many people were in the car, and when the driver braked or switched lanes the tail and signal lights caused a halo effect that obscured its identifying marks even more.

What the hell was this?

The traffic grew thinner, then sparse. The car being taped

took an exit onto an access road, then turned onto what appeared to be a country road. The nighttime conditions and the relatively narrow field of vision afforded by the headlights did not allow Strand to gain any significant information from the terrain. Once or twice he thought he saw sand dunes.

The two cars then turned off onto a smaller road, which, though it was still paved, was most likely on private land. Suddenly the speed of the cars accelerated dramatically. The camera car quickly closed on the car in front of it, and in a sickening instant Strand recognized his old Land Rover. Before he had time to make his mind work around that realization, a spotlight came on in the camera car, lighting the back of the driver's head in the lead car just as she looked around.

It was Romy.

Strand's legs buckled, and he dropped to one knee. His eyes stayed locked on the video screen. He had no awareness of whether he was sitting or kneeling: he was cognizant only of the mind-numbing fact that he was watching Romy's last moments.

Romy's car careened wildly in the turns of the narrow paved lane, the chase car's headlights losing her just as she was sliding or skidding on the edges of the road. Marshland brush and sand dunes jumped in and out of the headlights, and then suddenly the chase car's lights were squarely on the Land Rover. Once, twice, three times the chase car accelerated and rammed into the rear of the Land Rover, the camera shuddering violently with the impact. In the illumination of the handheld spotlight, Strand could actually see Romy's head snap from the impact of each fierce jolt, and he could see her arms wildly fighting the steering wheel.

Abruptly the bridge railing was in front of her. The Land

Rover began to fishtail out of control and careened off the road, plunging into the tidal stream. Water shot up high above the headlights of the chase car, glittering like an explosion in the bright lights; the chase car itself barely managed to stay on the pavement and clear the railing as it skidded to a stop in the middle of the bridge.

The camera was snatched from the dash, and nothing was clear for a few moments. Then the spotlight snapped on again and the camera was looking down into the tidal stream, the Land Rover's rear end just scarcely visible out of the water, the brake lights burning steadily, then flickering out.

The camera stayed a long time on the rear end of the Rover. A long time.

When the tape finally played out and the machine clicked off, Strand fell over on his side. His face was wet. He felt partially paralyzed, as if a brain aneurysm had rendered him immobile. He coughed up bile, fought back nausea.

Romy's pale, horror-stricken face was fixed in his mind.

God. God. How could he have been so wrong about it all?

CHAPTER 11

"Ghosts," Darras said, looking at Strand across the table. "I never thought I would see 'Lawrence Vane' again." He spoke with the same indifference with which he expressed all emotions, from shock to boredom.

They were sitting in a trattoria on Via Famagosta in a working-class neighborhood north of the Vatican. Alain Darras was being predictably unpredictable. He did not eat in the same part of the city where he slept. He did not sleep in the same part of the city where he worked. Sleeping, eating, and working were the three habits of life. Habits were patterns. Patterns were reliable. Reliability enabled "others" to anticipate you. A bad thing.

Strand himself was still trying to staunch his adrenaline hemorrhage. He was forcibly making himself appear calm, but the stunning impact of discovering the video could not be diminished by will or wish.

"It took me an hour to find you," Strand said.

"Good." Darras's life was so outré that there was no intended irony in his response. He was drinking the cheapest wine in the trattoria, a light grape-juicy red that came in a bottle with a local label. He was eating olives, the slick, de-nuded pits lying beside the bottle like legless beige beetles. The doors of the trattoria were open to the street, where people from the neighborhood were coming out to linger in the cool Roman evening, young men lounging around the parked cars, children playing sidewalk games, old women watching life from the kitchen chairs they had brought outside where life was happening.

"You haven't been in Rome," Darras said.

Strand shook his head.

Darras slid a small glass toward Strand with the back of one hand in which he was holding a half-eaten olive, and with the other hand he poured some of the rosy wine into the glass.

Strand nodded thanks.

Alain Darras was in his late fifties. He was French, which was all that Strand knew about his past. Though his straight black hair was thinning, he still kept it combed back from his forehead with a high part. He was a little more jowly now, but the mustache on his long upper lip was still neatly trimmed, though grayer, and his handsome, sad eyes were still hand-some, though sadder.

"This is something of an emergency," Darras said. He had an olive in his mouth, and he was worrying the meat off of the pit. He always asked questions as though they were state-ments. They were more like assessments that he threw out for confirmation.

"I have a few names," Strand said.

"And you are in a very big hurry."

"I'm no longer in the business," Strand said.

Darras took the clean pit out of his mouth and placed it on the table with the others.

"Photographs."

"No."

"Photographs are a big thing these days," Darras said. "Digital capabilities. My business has changed more in the last four years than it changed in the entire twenty years before. With the computers it is getting pretty damn close to magic. Half the people working for me now are children. I want more children. They come out of the universities with brains like alchemists. They know chips and digital. They don't know shit about life, but they know 'virtual.' They think virtual *is* life. Damn, sometimes they can almost convince me that it's real, too." He shrugged. "We're raising a generation of completely fucked-up kids, you know." He dropped his eyes to his wineglass. "I like them." He picked up another olive.

"I need this tomorrow," Strand said. He knew he was being curt, but he didn't have the strength to finesse it.

"That is enormously expensive."

"If I thought it was physically possible, I would ask for it tonight."

Darras nodded slowly. "I see."

A few more people wandered into the trattoria. Romans ate late. A little girl about five or six years old came from the kitchen in the back and dawdled past their table, chewing on a crusty piece of bread, carrying half a hard loaf under her chubby arm. When she got out the front door, she broke off pieces for two little friends who were waiting for her on the sidewalk.

"Odd, isn't it, that it's like the Mafia," Darras said, "intelligence work. You never really get to leave it. It follows you to the last place you lie down." He regarded Strand with melancholy reserve. "I see it all the time."

Strand took a piece of paper out of his coat pocket and placed it on the table. With a flick of his fingers he spun it around so Darras could read the names written there. Darras dropped his eyes to the paper.

"Oh."

"I want to know how to get in touch with these four men. I need to get to them personally, without some ambitious lieutenant trying to get between us. I have to speak to these men themselves . . . no one else."

"I see. So you actually have been out of touch after all. And the lady?"

"Everything." Strand jabbed the end of a forefinger on the table. "Everything."

Darras bit into the olive. "The names below. She uses these, too."

"Yes, she might."

Darras sighed as he picked up the list and put it in his inside coat pocket. He regarded Strand as he ate the olive. Strand wanted to leave. He wanted to get the hell out of there and just be alone until he met Mara at Toula's. He needed to get his mind organized so he could make his body behave the way his mind knew it should. But Darras wanted to talk, and Darras was doing him a favor, even if it was a favor that Strand would have to pay for.

"You were always honest with me, Harry." Darras almost smiled. "If that word doesn't completely lose its meaning in this context. I'll have my kids go the extra mile for you." He minced the olive with his front teeth. "Why did you tell me you weren't in the business anymore?"

"So you'd know."

"Do I need to know?"

"I feel better that you know."

Darras was very still. He took the smooth pit out of his mouth and without even looking down added it to the pile of beetles.

"See. That's what I mean," he said. He drank his wine. When he put his glass on the table he shoved it around in a tight, idle circle, moving only his fingers, watching the wet snail smear of the glass on the tabletop. Then he looked up at Strand.

"When the Wall came down, when communism died its ignominious death, I thought I would starve for lack of work," he said. "In fact, just the opposite has happened. All of those intelligence services collapsed and disbanded and closed shop and shut down networks. The Eastern bloc, Soviets, you people. Suddenly Europe was drowning in unemployed secret service hacks and spies. Now they are all working again, much busier than ever, except this time they're working for criminals. I'm making a fortune, Harry. From criminals. Drug smugglers, counterfeiters, embezzlers, money launderers, car thieves, gunrunners, smugglers of illegal aliens. Assassins. They all need information. Reliable information."

He drank some more wine.

"I bought a ton of Stasi and KGB records—there are millions of tons of them, but I was specific about what I wanted— and my kids scanned them into the computers. I made so much money off the Russian Mafia in the early years after communism collapsed that I could afford to buy records from all the Eastern-bloc secret services. I bought Asian files. I bought South American files. Middle East. I have to admit, I was surprised that I could buy so much. Nobody has any loyalty anymore. The American dollar is more coveted than peace of mind. Anyway, for the last four years I have had nearly fifty people working day and night on computers I keep on two full floors of an office building here."

He sighed hugely.

"Only God has more names in His files than I do."

Strand was adept at the ruse of seeming to listen while letting his mind go elsewhere. It was not an easy thing to learn. Vacuity has a way of registering on a person's face the moment the mind begins to wander. But Strand had learned to do it well. It was a valuable deception, like hiding fear and panic.

". . . state of the art, of course," Darras droned on. "They're piranhas, these computers. So small, yet so voracious. You feed them and feed them and feed them. They digest everything you feed them."

Strand listened with his eyes, but his chest was tightening. It was the worst feeling in the world, and he had hoped never to experience it again. It was what the fleeing springbok felt when the pursuing cheetah seemed to read its mind—every feint was anticipated, with every dodge the cat was there . . . and there . . . and there.

Suddenly he said, "Alain, I need a couple of forged passports. U.S."

Darras regarded him. "I need a photograph."

"Use one of yours. I know you've got one."

"This is costly."

"I don't have any choice. And I need dossiers on two other names."

He took a notepad from his coat pocket and wrote down "Ariana Kiriasis" and "Claude Corsier." He tore out the piece of paper and put it on the table and again spun it around with his finger for Darras to read.

Darras dropped his eyes to the paper and then looked up. "You decided to cut yourself off from them."

"Yes."

"They don't know where to find you."

"No."

"That was your idea."

"Yes."

Darras was almost amused but conquered the impulse.

"You tried to slip away from your own shadow." Without looking he reached for an olive, but they were all gone. "That's what I was talking about," he said, wiping his fingers on a napkin. "The shadow of intelligence work. Once it attaches itself to you, it follows you around on the ground, on the water, up the sides of walls. You try to get rid of it at your own peril."

"Any problem with the other names?" Strand asked. He looked at his watch, just to let Darras know he had to leave.

"No."

"By tomorrow."

"If at all possible. Certainly as soon as possible."

Strand nodded. "Thank you."

He pushed back his chair to leave. Darras didn't move; he was staying. Strand stood, and Darras looked up at him.

"I like you, Strand," Darras said. "I always thought you were a decent fellow, which is a curse in this business."

CHAPTER 12

Strand parked the rental car in Largo Fontanella Borghese, a cobblestoned courtyard only a few steps from Toula. For a moment he sat in the car and watched the occasional nocturnal pedestrian drift toward Via Condotti and the Spanish Steps. The steps were a colossal magnet for the tourists, and if you were anywhere in the neighborhood, you were within the pull of that romantic flight of stairs and the pink place of John Keats's death that overlooked it.

He felt as though he were about to go onstage and had to give the performance of his life. He didn't know who Mara Song was, but he knew damn well what she might be. His proximity to danger, his sudden realization of his unknowing close association with it over the past several months in the person of this woman, made him light-headed. What had she done? What was she supposed to do? How close had he come—how close was he—to disaster?

He remembered too well the physiological symptoms of fear. It racked the body so thoroughly that hardly any organ remained unaffected. Everything reacted, everything threatened to fail under the stress of it. And in this case the metaphorical ache in the heart was by no means the least of Strand's anxiety. He had been a fool. Had he really been so out of touch with his benighted past as to believe that he could meet a woman like Mara, a woman who seemed so right to him in nearly every way, and she *wouldn't* be a player? Did he really believe that he could have a life apart from all those cryptic years? Jesus. He was getting old after all, wasn't he, and now he could add a deeply felt heartache to the rattling confusion of dread.

He guessed Darras was about right. Strand was like a man who had been a heavy drinker all his life and was now suffering from damaged organs. The past wasn't going to go away for that man, and it wasn't going to go away for Harry Strand, either. It would always be with him to threaten him, to despoil even his quiet moments, to remind him that what he had done for nearly twenty years had come at a high cost and that a large part of the debt was still outstanding.

Suddenly the image of Romy, her arms fighting to control the steering wheel, flashed into his mind. He saw her face as she looked back over her shoulder into the spotlight from the car behind her. How horrified she must have been. Had she thought of him in those last terror-stricken moments? Did it enter her mind that he somehow had failed her?

He swallowed the lump in his throat and got out of the car.

The restaurant was long, with a small bar just to the right of the entry with large armchairs and settees. To the left, one descended five steps to the main dining rooms, a series of three of them separated by an enfilade of arches that terminated in a pale terra-cotta wall. The rooms were lighted by lamps that made the stucco walls throw off a warm hazy light and caused the white linen tablecloths to phosphoresce like so many moonflowers scattered throughout the twilight of the rooms.

Mara waited for him in the center room at a table that he guessed she had requested specifically, since it afforded considerable privacy. She had quickly learned of Strand's demanding preference for a quiet table. She wore a simple black cocktail dress with thin straps and a low-cut neck. Her hair was pulled back in a chignon, and she wore black pearl earrings set in a crescent of diamonds.

He bent over and kissed her, surprised by her fragrance and by the ache for her that mixed so strangely with the grief. He sat down, his chest tightened to the point of collapsing his lungs.

"I'm glad you saw the note," he said, taking a napkin and unfolding it.

"Couldn't miss it," she said, smiling.

"At the last minute I needed a few more books," he said. The waiter appeared and poured wine for him from the bottle that Mara had already ordered.

They ate dinner slowly, Strand concentrating intensely on trying to pace himself so that he didn't betray even a hint of uneasiness or preoccupation. It was a greater burden even than he had anticipated, for every time he smiled or tried to make a lighthearted remark he saw Romy's face looking back over her shoulder at him. Trying to maintain a semblance of equanimity with that image flashing constantly into his mind was torture.

Halfway through the meal he was jolted by the sudden realization that he had made a terrible mistake. He should not have let the videotape out of his hands. After he had viewed the complete tape three times, after he had collected his un-raveled thoughts, he had immediately begun the necessary procedures to find Darras. When he'd finally found him, they had agreed on a meeting place and Strand had hurried out of the house—leaving the tape in the machine.

Now that seemed a tragic mistake. What if it wasn't there when he returned? What if he had let the only proof of Romy's murder get away from him? Aside from the evidence that it represented, it would be a betrayal of Romy to have let that documentation slip through his fingers. He feared that if he never saw the tape again, eventually, over time, he might begin to wonder if he had ever really seen it at all. Too easily those stark images of the crash might fade from reality into a vivid nightmare, and at some point in a future as yet unimagined he might awaken suddenly in the darkness, sweating, haunted by the question of whether he had only dreamed what had seemed so terrible and so real.

The rest of the meal was excruciating.

It seemed an eternity before Mara's breathing settled into the unmistakable rhythm of sound sleep. He lay in the dark beside her, exhausted. Though they had had sex—a truly schizophrenic experience for him—his fatigue was the result of nervous tension, not the sex. He really didn't know if he could do this. He was less resilient than he used to be. This would have been hard in the past, of course, but it wouldn't have taken so much out of him. It had been only seven hours since he had found the video, but every hour had seemed a full day in itself. The tension and the doubt and the lack of direc-tion had consumed him.

He had to admit that the three years with Romy had been disarming, and as those years had added up, Schrade had receded further and further into the past. After Romy's death—he was stunned that he had ever accepted her car crash as an accident—Schrade had faded off the screen entirely. Until tonight. Strand was feeling the full strain of the whiplash.

As he waited for Mara to fall asleep, her head on his chest, his arm around her naked shoulders, he replayed the evening minute by minute. Had he given himself away? He sifted through the vocabulary of their conversation and tried to remember her exact facial reactions to everything he had said. Were there subtleties that, in retrospect, were telltale signs of suspicion? Had her eyes lingered on him at any point, or had they turned away as she asked a question that might have been planted to elicit a revealing response? Had she been more reserved than before, or had she been too relaxed, pretending not to notice something in his behavior that had set her sensors tingling?

Then, later, there was the surreal sexual intercourse with her, she who was suddenly no longer Mara. His imagination careened from possibility to possibility. All of this piled on top of his own emotions about her, emotions that had grown and matured during the last three months so quickly and comfortably that he would never have imagined he could have been capable of it. His was a fool's dismay, precisely the thing he himself had relied on in the past to catch a fool. It was a bleak realization.

Mara's breathing had been consistent for half an hour. She had shifted in her sleep and rolled over on her stomach away from him, throwing back the sheet so that she was naked all the way down to the two dimples above her buttocks.

He eased out of bed and lifted his robe off a chair and went downstairs. A pale light from the city flooded the room in powder blue as it came in from the courtyard. He could easily make his way around the first large sofa, across the Persian carpet to the black Maillol statue.

The tape was gone.

His ears actually began ringing, and he almost lost his balance. He scrambled through the cassette boxes and put each one into the player, regardless of its label. No luck. He stood still, looking out to the courtyard where the palms were black silhouettes.

U.S. EMBASSY, VIENNA

Bill Howard sat alone in a room filled from floor to ceiling with electronic equipment: computer screens and keyboards, television screens, deck panels crowded with square and round buttons and toggle switches, red-and-green digital readouts, and black-and-white analogue dials. He sat at a built-in countertop with a notepad, a pencil, and a mug of coffee. Though the room was permeated with the odor of hot plastics and electrical wiring, he was freezing, the thermostat on the air-conditioning system having been turned down low to keep the equipment from overheating.

To Howard's left was a plate-glass window that looked into the next room, where two engineers worked in an environment almost identical to the one in which Howard was sitting. He had just put on a set of headphones with a pencil-thin microphone attached, leaving his hands free so that he could doodle on the notepad and sip coffee.

He heard a series of stereophonic clicks in the headphones and looked at the engineers through the plate glass. One of them looked at Howard and began counting down through the headphones and then pointed at Howard.

"Hello, Gene?"

Gene Payton was always very polite, and Howard impatiently endured a brief exchange of pleasantries. Then he said, "Well, it's just exactly what I goddamn thought, Gene. We've got a serious glitch in the Strand situation. Bad, bad timing. Kiriasis is afraid Schrade has discovered the embezzlement and is tracking them all down. She swears she hasn't been in touch with any of them except Corsier. She wants protection."

Howard stared at the blinking lights and listened.

"No, I acted shocked, stunned to hear what they'd done. If she's lying and really is in touch with Strand, or even if she isn't and he gets in touch with her, whatever, if they communicate, we don't want him to know we've known about this for over a year. If he knew that, his mind would go to work on it. We sure as hell don't want that."

Howard listened.

"Sure, she wants to know how we're going to handle it. What we're going to do with Strand."

Howard sipped his coffee. The mug was crazed and a thousand servings of coffee had permanently stained it. It should have been thrown away. It looked filthy.

"I told her the truth," he said. "I said it would depend on who ended up with the money . . . What?"

He listened.

"No, my hunch is Harry kept it strictly compartmentalized. She's not going to know much, but we need to find out what she does know. I have to find out if there's some way we can use her. If we can't use her, then we sure as hell have to keep her out of the way."

He doodled on the notepad and glanced up at the engineers in the next room. The one standing was telling the other one an animated story. They were both laughing. Howard tossed his pencil down in disgust.

"Well, we know he's killing them, for Christ's sake. I can't go knock on his door and ask him to please stop because he's screwing up our little program here. Schrade's tactics are a lot more persuasive than ours, Gene. I think we're trying to be too smart for our own good. It's hard to compete with brutality and goddamn hair-raising fear."

He listened.

"I know, I know. We haven't got any choice now but to go ahead and play it out, but I think we need to be flexible here. Schrade's scattering these people all the hell over the place. They're either dying or running. My bet is that his harebrained revenge program is eventually going to screw up our own operation. I don't care how much time and money and planning we've put into it."

He listened.

"Of course Schrade knows where he is. You kidding me?"

He listened.

"Look, let me get through another twenty-four hours here. Let's let our deal work. Give it another twenty-four . . ."

Howard clenched his teeth. Payton was talking to someone. He was, no doubt, getting advice from all the experts sitting behind their desks. They had no idea. They had read Strand's files, and they thought he was a character in a screenplay that they could just manipulate from where they sat, make him do this, make him do that. Harry Strand was the last person in the world you could manipulate, and they didn't have a clue about that. He had tried to tell them. He had gone over it and over it with them at Camp Peary. Yeah, yeah, they would say, but we've got to get him to . . .

"Fine, then," Howard said, his throat tight with anger. "I'll get back to you after I talk to her again."

He listened.

"No," he said, "I haven't heard anything."

He wanted to say, I told you so, but he didn't.

After the disconnect he stormed out of the communications room, leaving his pencil and pad and coffee sitting on the countertop. He was so pissed he didn't give a shit.

CHAPTER 13

HOUSTON

When Strand was out of town Meret Spier lived in his home until he returned. This was an arrangement that suited her enormously. Not only was Strand's place larger than her West-heimer condo, but it was just plain fun to be in a grand house, and she could "go to the office" dressed any way she wanted. When she knew there were to be no deliveries or appoint-ments, she often didn't bother putting on makeup, didn't bother with her hair, and, sometimes, didn't bother to dress in anything other than her underwear.

But Strand's absence didn't mean she didn't have to work. When he traveled he constantly called on collectors, visited dealers, and prowled galleries; and his curiosity about the art he encountered was wide-ranging and insatiable. It was not unusual for him to call her two or three times a day to ask her to look up something in his library, whether he was in San Francisco or New York or Geneva or Madrid or Warsaw. As far as Strand was concerned, the only time zone on earth was the one he was in.

So, given the fact that she was on call twenty-four hours

a day for weeks at a time while Strand was traveling, Meret decided that going to work in her underwear was a justified perk.

After Meret's initial astonishment at Strand's sudden developing relationship with Mara Song, she hardly had time to adjust to it before Strand was planning to follow up on the unfinished business with Aldo Chiappini and Denise Yarrow, energetically planning the trips to San Francisco and then to Rome.

In the two years Meret had known Harry Strand—she had been working for him only ten months when Romy died—she had come to admire him immensely.

Strand had dealt with the sudden disaster no differently than grieving men had always dealt with it, sometimes stoically, sometimes nearly childlike in his helplessness, sometimes pathological in his hopelessness. Since Meret had nothing to compare it to, she didn't know if Strand's behavior was what she should have expected. She knew only that it was a painful thing to watch as he passed through all the gates and passageways that opened and closed for him on his journey back from Romy's death.

What surprised Meret most of all, and what endeared Strand to her, was that he was as concerned for her as for himself. She had never been close to anyone who had died: though she had known Romy only ten months, the two women had worked practically in the same room for all that time, and she had grown fond of Romy's brightness and intelligence and affectionate nature. They had become very close in a short period of time.

Moreover, Meret had only narrowly missed being in the car with Romy. They had invited Meret to spend the weekend with them at their beach house near Galveston Island, and the two women had planned to drive out Thursday night, taking Friday off for a long weekend, and set the place in order before Strand's arrival late Friday. At the last minute Meret had decided to take her own car and run some errands first. They had decided that Romy should go on and Meret would follow shortly. Meret had found Romy's Land Rover in the tidewater stream. Death, such an alien idea to her in her youth, had stepped right in front of her face, so close that she could almost smell its breath.

Strand knew what a dreadful experience this had been for her and took especial care to help her absorb its impact. His response was simply and naturally to treat Meret as family, as Romy's sister. He talked with her a lot and nursed her emotions through those early awkward weeks when the void that is death's wake seemed so brutal in its banality. One evening when they had worked late—Strand worked ferociously in those early months—and she was lingering before going home, he asked her if she would like to stay for dinner.

In his usual manner he made her sit down and visit with him while he quickly made omelets and toast, which he served with apricot jam. It was the first of what became a once-a-week tradition with them, usually on Friday nights. Strand cooked, and sometimes Meret helped him, though mostly it was Strand's dinner, simple and sometimes offbeat. But it was the conversation that nourished them. During these meals Meret began to realize that Strand and Romy had had a rather more exotic life than she had first believed, from hints he dropped into the conversation, from references that he never followed up on. Once or twice she had asked him about them, but he was always evasive and dismissive. There were, Meret came to believe, dark places in Strand's past, and in Romy's, too. Without his saying so, Meret understood that there were closed doors on the far side of their yesterdays, and she was not welcome to approach them.

The small jet taxied onto a private strip of tarmac at Hobby Airport and proceeded toward a nest of isolated hangars, its night-lights winking from its wingtips and under-carriage, throwing smears of ruby and sapphire onto the wet pavement. The doors of one of the hangars glided open, and the aircraft entered into a clean, bright open space where a dark Cherokee was waiting.

He had been studying Houston city maps for two weeks. He knew it as well as his own neighborhood in Mexico City. The door of the sleek jet folded down, and he descended to the floor of the hangar and walked briskly to the Cherokee. He opened the door and got in. The wallet was on the car seat. He opened it, confirmed the identification he had required, Texas driver's license, insurance cards, credit cards. He put the wallet in his inside suit coat pocket, buckled his seat belt, and drove out of the hangar. He had seen no one in the hangar, and no one had seen him. In his rearview mirror he saw the hangar doors slide closed behind him.

The late-night traffic was sparse. He quickly found his way to the Gulf Freeway and headed northeast into the city. The Cherokee was fine. He knew where everything was. He had one exactly like it, down to every detail, waiting for him wherever he worked.

When the skyscrapers were looming over him, sparkling like pyrite, he turned south on the Southwest Freeway and then very shortly exited on Main. Soon he was turning onto Bissonnet. He picked up the telephone and dialed a number.

"Hello?"

"I am just turning onto Bissonnet." His accent was very slight.

"We're the blue Four Runner a block past the house."

"Everything is in place?"

"Two upstairs in number three."

He visualized the number three bedroom.

After turning off Bissonnet, he drove the Cherokee down the narrow lane without hesitation, dousing his headlights just before he approached the house. He pulled into the driveway, stopped under the porte cochere, and cut the engine. It was a quiet engine, with a customized muffler, softer than a sigh.

He opened the glove compartment of the car and took out a small automatic handgun with a short, blunt silencer permanently attached to the barrel. He checked the clip of hollow-point bullets and put the gun into his coat pocket. From the floor in front of the passenger seat he picked up an aluminum, vinyl-wrapped canister designed to look like a small fire extinguisher.

The alarm system had already been deactivated by the team in the Four Runner, so he had no hesitation about unlocking the door with the key on the ring. He set the canister on the floor just inside the door and took off his shoes. He moved quickly and carefully through the dining room and kitchen to the pantry, where he found the breaker box for the electricity. He threw the switch and then pulled the fuses just for good measure. He could not afford an electrical glitch. He went back through the rooms to the foyer and picked up the canister. Carrying it in one hand, the automatic in the other, he started up the stairs. He couldn't even hear himself moving.

Once on the second-floor landing he quietly put down

the canister and moved ahead with deliberation, walking briskly through the second-floor halls to the number three bedroom. The door was open. He stepped inside and went up to the bed. They were both naked, asleep, the girl curled in her boyfriend's arms. She was a pretty girl, blond and busty. He looked at her a moment, then shot her in the right temple. He shot her boyfriend before he could even stir out of his sleep at the sound of the silencer. He shot them both again, twice, in the head. The hollow-points made a mess, but he never had to wonder about the results.

He quickly retrieved the canister and returned to the bedroom. He opened the nozzle, released the lock, pointed the nozzle at the bed, and pressed the trigger. With a loud *whoosh* a broad stream of jet fuel shot out. He sprayed the bodies liberally and then hosed down the room, the highly pressurized canister enabling him to saturate the bodies and the room in only a moment. He sprayed the other upstairs rooms as well.

Downstairs he did the same thing, spraying, just for the hell of it, all the drawings hanging on the walls and giving a good shot into the library. By the time he made it through the other rooms the fumes from the jet fuel were almost unbearable.

He slipped on his shoes and took from his coat pocket a small plastic box the size of a pager. He peeled a piece of paper from an adhesive patch on the box and slapped the box on the wall. He pushed some buttons, and a green digital readout appeared on a screen. At the programmed time the box would produce nothing more than a series of electrical sparks, more than enough to ignite the fog of jet fuel now expanding throughout the house. He gave himself thirty-five minutes. He could almost be back at the airport by then. He would even have them circle the city so he could see the fire. On second thought, with an additional ten minutes he might even be able to see the explosion itself. He changed it to forty-five minutes. By then the fumes would be so dense that even the thought of a spark would set them off.

Carrying the canister, he went out the front door and dutifully locked it behind him.

CHAPTER 14

ROME

Harry Strand sat with his back to the stucco wall in a café in Testaccio and stared in stunned silence at the phlegmatic face of Alain Darras. It was midmorning in yet another working-class neighborhood south of the Aventine, and both men were leaning over cups of steaming cappuccino. The front doors of the café were open to the street, where trucks and *motorini* buzzed by like insects swarming in the warm morning sun. The bakery in the front of the café was a popular stop for a fast breakfast, and the tin-covered bar where most of the customers stood while they quickly devoured their espresso and roll had been busy since Strand arrived. But in the rear of the café he and Darras had a table to themselves in relative isolation.

"I told him nothing, of course," Darras said. "Not even that I had heard from you."

Strand felt weak and nauseated, as if he had been hit very hard and was struggling to stay conscious.

"They must have known that it was likely you would call me at some point." He stopped. "I don't like it that I was the one to tell you."

It was mind-boggling. What Schrade had done was horrible, incredible.

"Howard knows you've come to Rome with a woman. He knows her name."

Strand's face must have registered suspicion.

"No, no, they did not get this from me. From the flight information. They have her name from that. That's what Howard said, anyway. As for me, I couldn't find anything on her. If she's working with anyone, I can't find any trace of it. She doesn't show up with Schrade. There's nothing on her anywhere else. I don't think she is in the business, my friend. Or, if she is, she is very, very new to it."

Strand processed this. He had never had bad information from Darras. Ever. He was surprised, but it was difficult to believe, even though he wanted more than anything for it to be true. But if he was going to remain sane, he couldn't go on playing mind games about her. He had to trust the information he was getting. And he had to trust her. Then his mind went right back to the house and the explosion. The two bodies. God, what had he done?

"Of course, Howard wanted information on Mara Song, too," Darras added.

"You confirmed Howard's story about the explosion?"

"Yes, Harry, I did. The FBI is already involved. They are interested in the explosives, of course."

"What was it?"

"They think it was jet fuel. Probably spark ignition." He paused. "I understand . . . well, it was very bad. Almost total destruction. As for forensics, there's almost nothing to work with. The jet fuel . . . you know, it burns so hot. . . ."

Darras showed no emotion beyond the momentary hesitations. Strand noticed it and was pained.

"Do they have anything else?"

"I don't know what they have. It's moving too quickly. My sources are not good on breaking information."

Strand knew that Darras's sources were very good indeed, and he wondered if Darras was holding out on him. If he was, why?

He quickly calculated the progress of events. No records would be left. Nothing to start from. He was sure that aside from the fuel residue precious little would remain to guide investigators. They would go back to his old ties in Europe from four years before and start from there. Strand still dealt with some of the same people, though not as many since he'd retired. Those dealers and collectors would not know about Mara Song. The only person who would know about the house in Sallustiano would be Aldo Chiappini, and since he had become Strand's client after Strand left the FIS, his name would not be in agency records. So they would have to work their way to him through Strand's other contacts. The world of drawing collectors was a small world. It wouldn't be long. Strand didn't have that much time.

Schrade, of course, knew about the Sallustiano house. That was how the tape had gotten there.

"And Corsier?" Strand could hardly speak. He was forcing himself to be analytical. He didn't have the luxury to grieve about Meret now.

"He disappeared several weeks ago. The Bundespolizei in Zurich say he left one day to take some drawings to show a client and never returned. They didn't know anything. No flight information. No client name. They don't even know where he went."

"Ariana?"

"She lives here in Rome, actually. When I saw that, I sent someone to her home, but her housekeeper said she left quickly about three or four days ago. She doesn't know where she went. Ariana is still impetuous. When she wants to go, she goes. So the maid didn't see anything particularly suspicious about the way she left."

"Clymer?"

Darras told him about the lawyer's death, and Strand could only regret that he had not been more vigilant. How long had Schrade known? Since before Romy's death, obviously. How long before? Why hadn't he come after the rest of them immediately after Romy's execution? Why had he waited for over a year?

Whether it was Schrade's intention or not, he had effectively cut Strand off from Houston. His whole life had been in that house, all that was left of Romy, his library, his personal art collection, the new career he and Romy had carved out for themselves. He imagined it had been methodical; it had probably taken less than fifteen minutes. In and out. He was ashamed about Meret. Whatever in God's name had made him think he was not putting that young woman in danger? Once Schrade had found out what Strand and the others had done to him, from that moment on, everything that Strand cared about belonged to Schrade until Strand could have a conversation of understanding with Bill Howard.

"How do I get in touch with Howard?"

Darras took a manila envelope from the chair beside him and placed it on the table along with contact information for

Obando, Grachev, Lu, and Lodato. "It's all in here. Howard is in Vienna now."

Strand pulled the envelope over and put his left forearm on it. "The passports?"

"In there. And the latest on Schrade is in there, too," Darras said. "Do you know that he cut his ties to FIS about eighteen months ago?"

"Eighteen months ago?"

"Yes."

"But they were closing him down when they brought me back to the States. They were shutting him down then."

"No. They kept it alive."

"The same objectives?"

"As far as I know."

"Why did he break it off?"

Darras shook his head. "No one is saying anything about that."

Strand's thoughts raced ahead to the possibilities.

Darras studied Strand with his dispirited gaze. "You must have done something terrible to him, Harry."

Strand didn't answer for a moment. The manila envelope was hot under his arm. The smell of fresh espresso wafted from the front of the café and came to them thick and rich, riding on the warm fragrance of yeast. For a moment—an instant, really—he almost forgot Meret, but in a blink she was back. She had no idea what he had been; that he had kept it from her, that he had ever thought it wouldn't matter, was unforgivable.

Jet fuel. What a mad conflagration it must have caused on a shady little street that had never known anything more disturbing than the droning of cicadas in the summer heat.

Darras did not look away.

"When you think about what he's done," Strand said, "what he is, almost anything anyone did to him would be justified."

CHAPTER 15

By the time Strand returned to Sallustiano noon was approaching. He had replayed the explosion over and over and over in his mind until he was sick of it. Then he had concentrated on bringing his blood pressure and emotions under control.

Schrade wanted two things: revenge and the money. He was getting his revenge. Romy. Corsier. Probably Ariana. Clymer. Meret. Eventually he would get around to Strand himself. But first, the money.

By now, Schrade's accountants had discovered that his millions were not going to be easy to retrieve. That, Strand reasoned, was why he was still alive. Schrade wasn't sure he could get to it without him. Romy and Dennis Clymer had done an incredible job with those millions. Schrade had already made a tactical error by having killed them. He was giving too much of the credit to Strand, thinking that Strand was the only one he needed to gain access to his money. How in God's name had Schrade discovered the embezzlement, anyway? Maybe he shouldn't be surprised, but he was. He honest to God thought they had covered everything. All of them thought that. All of them had done their damnedest to ensure that not a single speck of a loose end remained after they closed down the operation.

When he arrived at the house in Sallustiano he went straight upstairs. Mara was just getting out of the shower when Strand walked into her bedroom. He startled her.

"Whoa," she said, "you scared me." She had stopped in the doorway of the large, white-tiled bathroom, still naked, drying her hair with a towel.

Smiling, she came over to him and gave him a wet kiss. Her mouth was cool. She smelled of shampoo.

"Now I feel better," she said.

Strand just stood there. On the way back from Testaccio his mind had been flying in every direction but this one. Until he'd climbed the stairs just now he hadn't given any thought to the way he was going to break this to Mara.

She saw instantly that something was wrong.

"What's the matter?" she asked, daubing her face as the water dripped off her hair.

"We've got to talk," Strand said.

She said nothing, but his manner and tone of voice caused her face to go rigid. Holding the towel bunched up at her waist in front of her, she braced herself, her eyes fixed on him.

Strand turned and walked to the windows. He sat in a chair and looked out over the rooftops of Rome toward the Palatine. The summer sky was cerulescent and flung with tufts of white clouds floating in from the Tyrrhenian Sea.

He turned to her. "Some terrible things have happened, Mara, things that have to do with my past. A past that's going to require some explanation. Right now I'm going to try to tell

you as much as I can as quickly as I can, because what has happened is going to turn my life inside out . . . starting now." He
paused. "I don't know how much this will affect you. We have
to talk about that. And we have some decisions to make. Fast."

She was stone.

"Everything you know about me, Mara, is the truth," he
began. "It's just that you don't know all the truth there is." He
paused. "For nearly twenty years I was an intelligence officer
with the U.S. State Department's Foreign Intelligence Service. I ran agents in Eastern and Western Europe using my art
business as a cover occupation. I bought and sold art under
several different business names over the years and used several different names myself whenever the circumstances
called for it. I retired four years ago, when I married Romy,
moved to Houston, and bought out Paul Davies's business,
keeping his name for obvious reasons."

Mara swallowed.

"All of that about how I got started, that's true, that's the
way it happened. After I was recruited into the FIS I continued dealing in art, only now my profession became my opera-
tional cover. I ran businesses out of London, here in Rome,
Vienna, Zurich . . . a number of places.

"I met my first wife while on assignment in London. She
knew nothing about my intelligence work. The marriage failed
largely because I hadn't yet learned how to handle the stresses
of a secret profession. She was the type of person who needed
a lot of attention, which I wasn't able to give her. I really do
feel responsible for much of the sadness that marked her life."

Mara was still holding the towel at her waist. She was
beautiful like that, unaware of herself, totally disarmed by
what she was hearing.

Strand turned away from her and looked back outside, letting his eyes settle on the horizon.

"My particular cell of agents relied mainly on two key people: Claude Corsier, an art dealer like myself, based in Geneva; and Ariana Kiriasis, a specialist in Hellenistic antiquities whom I'd met in Athens. From the mid-seventies through most of the eighties we were working the Soviet picture.

"In the late eighties the FIS decided to get serious about gathering information on a developing phenomenon: the increasing cooperation among the major players in international organized crime. Throughout the eighties we'd seen mounting evidence that these new collaborations were going to become a serious problem. It was like watching storm clouds building over the sea.

"In 1989 the FIS pulled my cell off of Soviet affairs just four months before the Berlin Wall came down. They put us on international crime; we spent the next year or so assessing the difficulties involved in launching an intelligence operation of this sort. One of our main sources in the Soviet operations was a German businessman named Wolfram Schrade, whose many commercial interests were spread widely over an international market.

"Because we worked so closely with Schrade we knew a lot about him, more than he thought we knew. We knew he was getting in on the front end of a variety of international crime operations through contacts he was making during his travels to foreign countries on legitimate business. Borders to people like Schrade were incidental, if not irrelevant. He knew that profits from illegal activities were as big in one country as in the next. He understood the potential.

"Soon, like all the big players, he had a cash problem. His

money managers were scrambling for new ways to wash the stuff."

Strand paused and watched the shadows from the clouds move across the cityscape, an ever changing scene where light, or its absence, illuminated an ancient landmark in one moment and then plunged it into darkness the next. It was a moving metaphor for history, played out on the surviving architecture of a perished empire.

"By 1991," he went on, "my international criminal intelligence operation was ready to go active. The Soviet Union was only months away from implosion, and the black marketeers, who had kept a corrupt Soviet system from collapsing for fifty years, were becoming the Russian Mafia right before our eyes. Russia was swallowed by criminals so fast it shocked everyone. One of the enterprises they were best at was laundering money through their financial institutions. Our man Schrade was using them and paying a high premium for the privilege. The Russians were taking twenty-five percent of everything they washed, with no guarantee that their cut wasn't going to go even higher.

"At the time Schrade had no choice but to pay up. He was moving enormous amounts of money, and they were the only ones who could handle it. But it burned him up. Schrade hated the Russians, even though he'd made a lot of money out of corrupt Russians over the years. He never forgave them for dividing Germany after World War Two. That decision had ruined a huge family manufacturing business by splitting it in half. Spying against them was his revenge."

Strand paused. "Wolf has a whole philosophy of revenge," he said. "He's a believer."

Mara still hadn't moved. Water was dripping from her body, from her hair, puddling on the tile floor.

"About this time my people learned that Schrade had had enough of shoveling money out to the Russians. To avoid the high laundering premiums, Schrade went to a great deal of time and expense to design and put in motion his own complex laundering operation that cut them out. We had an informant inside and followed the entire development.

"My immediate superior in the FIS at this time was a man named Bill Howard. He came up with a scheme to get Schrade to cooperate with us as a high-level informant. He drew up a secret engagement advance, proposing that we offer Schrade a negative incentive: The FIS would confront Schrade and show him that we knew all about his criminal connections with the Russians, the Chinese, Italians, the Yakuza, Uzbekistanis, Ukrainians. All of them. We'd show him we knew about his money laundering operation, inside out. We'd tell him that we'd overlook all of this—all of it—in exchange for information about his worldwide criminal associations. We would present him with a want list, and he would be expected to fill it. If he didn't cooperate, we would arrange to have his criminal involvement exposed.

"The legality of Howard's proposal was highly questionable, but the payoff was enticing. If Schrade was successful at fulfilling this list, we would have the most in-depth picture of global organized crime that any governmental agency had ever had. In the end someone in the FIS decided to take the risk. But it was a 'shrouded' operation—an FIS secret. Howard got the green light."

Mara was now sitting on the foot of the bed, the towel tied around her chest. He was reminded of the first time he had seen her, drying herself with a towel after getting out of the pool at the River Oaks Swimming Club. He leaned a shoulder against the window frame, facing her, and went on.

"I had a problem with it. It had nothing to do with the morality of what we were doing. Intelligence services cozy up to the worst people in the world. Always have; always will. Sometimes intelligence services get what they need by making compromises that would seem abhorrent in another context. There's no way around that. That's just the way it is. In Schrade's case, I was faced with other factors.

"First of all, every intelligence officer knows going into an operation like this that if it all unravels somehow, the lowest man in the pecking order is always the one who hangs. That was me. If the operation ever blew up in our faces, it would be a disaster for me personally. The legality of what we were doing would be challenged, and I would catch the full brunt of the investigation. I was very much at risk and knew it. So I had to assess that.

"Also troubling was the prospect of working with Wolfram Schrade. I detested the man. I'd learned too much about him when he was spying on the Russians for us."

Strand stopped, thinking of Schrade. "He was internationally powerful, but wielded all of his influence from behind the scenes. Shunned publicity. Reclusive. You never saw his name in *The Wall Street Journal* or *U.S. News & World Report* or *Fortune*. You never heard his name in the news at all. If his legitimate business involvements were buried in secrecy, his illegitimate relationships were hidden even deeper. Almost even beyond rumor.

"I was assigned to work with him because he was a passionate art collector and had a scholarly hunger for knowledge about it. Read constantly. Studied. That was our connection. Much of our communication occurred in that context. It was an efficient and useful cover. Unfortunately, Schrade pursued art as ruthlessly as he pursued everything else. It wasn't a pretty thing to see, and I hated that he was even remotely involved in something that meant so much to me."

Strand twisted his shoulders against the window frame, trying to alleviate the growing tension.

"What troubled me the most about what we were about to do was that we were turning a blind eye on too much crime. Considering the amount—and type—of criminal enterprises Schrade was involved in, by giving him a free hand, regardless of the kind of information he was feeding to us, I thought we were dangerously close to becoming part of the problem instead of part of the solution. I didn't like it at all."

Mara sat straight backed as a sphinx and just as silent, watching him. He could hardly blame her. God only knew what he would say next, where this was taking him and, by extension, her too.

He shook his head and looked outside again. Her total focus on him was understandable, but it was also disconcerting.

"God help me, I went ahead with it."

CHAPTER 16

VIENNA

"You know how much Harry hated Wolfram Schrade," Ariana said. "You must've known."

"Sure."

"He was never comfortable having to launder for him."

"Nobody was asking him to be comfortable with it."

She threw him an amused look. He could barely hide his intolerance of Strand, who had never been enough of a team player in his opinion. Howard used to keep a firmer grip on his biases. Things changed. Ariana ignored his testiness.

"It's too late to talk about scruples, too late to claim we had any"—she shook her head, remembering—"but Harry came the closest of any of us to agonizing over what we did for Schrade."

"Bullshit."

"No, Bill, it's true. Harry never believed in the 'percentages' argument, that official explanation that we all pretended was a genuine justification. Help one murderer kill a few people and use the information he gives us to prevent ten murderers from killing hundreds of people."

"Well, he may not have believed it, but he bloody well

spent nearly twenty years doing just exactly that," Howard said.

"Maybe, but he paid a terrible price."

"We all do. That's the cost of fighting a war. You sacrifice the few to save the many. The concept is as old as civilization."

"See," she said. "You have it all worked out, a little moral formula that sums it all up neatly so that we don't have to confront the terrible things that we do. If someone asks us how we could do such things, if, in the middle of the night, we ask ourselves how we could have done such things, we immediately hold up the formula, like a talisman. It makes everything justifiable, helps us look at ourselves in the mirror without turning away in shame." She stopped. "Harry refused to do that."

"Christ, you sound like you want to canonize him."

"I am just trying to help you understand what I am about to tell you, Bill. It may be more complex than it first appears to you."

In a way, she sympathized with Bill Howard. He had not advanced in the FIS the way he had wanted. He would end his career as a station chief, and although that in itself was an admirable accomplishment and Vienna was a plum assignment, it was not as good as having a headquarters position with division-level responsibilities in Washington. That was what Howard wanted and had wanted for a long time and would never get. Now this scandal. It had happened on his watch, and Howard knew that it had destroyed even the slightest little ray of hope that he might have been able to keep alive that maybe, someday, he would be called out of the dubious shadows and into the respectable light of a Washington directorate office.

"One day—it was May about five years ago—I got a message from Harry. I was in Prague. He was in Rome, soon to leave, and wanted to meet me as soon as possible. We agreed on Trieste. It was the next evening before we were able to meet, and a wet cold front was moving across the Adriatic. We sat in a small café in a side street a couple of blocks off the waterfront, and all during the meal I had no idea what the meeting was about.

"Finally, Harry told me he had a proposition. He said he wanted me to know that he was going to be retiring in a little over a year. He wanted me to know so I could be thinking about what I wanted to do."

She stopped. "Could I have another cigarette?"

Howard gave her one, lighted it, and she went on.

"Harry said, 'Before I leave, Ana, I want to burn Wolf.' I stared at him across the table. I couldn't believe my ears. He said he was going to give me and Claude a chance to get in on the operation if we wanted. If I was interested, he would arrange a meeting for all of us, probably the only meeting in which we would all be together at the same time. He said there would be a lot of money in it for all of us. Enough for us to protect ourselves from retaliation if we used our heads. Though he wouldn't tell me much more than that, he did answer enough questions for me to say that, yes, I was interested and I would like to be included in that meeting.

"Then Harry hesitated—just that, a hesitation. That little thing gave me some idea of the enormity of what he was planning. Harry never gave himself away like that. He was a master of opacity . . . the 'poker face,' you say." She smoked. "The first thing out of his mouth was, 'Marie is designing the plan.' "

"Good . . . God . . ." For a split second she thought Howard was going to smile.

"I don't know the details, of course I wouldn't," Ariana

went on, ignoring him, "but I know that she had a major role in putting it all together. Claude and I became couriers. For the next several months we traveled constantly. We carried legal documents and communications. Often we met in Brussels and Liechtenstein with the legal wizard they got to carry out Marie's scheme. On her advice, Strand himself went to Los Angeles and recruited this man. Dennis Clymer. I'm not sure what he did, but it was very complex and, eventually, legal. Or so I understood. It was through him that everything Marie diverted from Schrade's money laundering operations—or at least the part she handled—found its way into the legitimate marketplace. After six months Harry closed down the operation."

"Closed it down? What went wrong?"

"Nothing. Everything was running perfectly. Harry said that was the best time to quit, before we made any mistakes. Not only had we avoided mistakes, but if we quit then, we would have six months to take our time and carefully cover our tracks from every conceivable direction. We would have time to think, time to make sure."

Ariana drew long on her cigarette and exhaled the smoke slowly, lazily.

"It would take you a decade to extract that money now," she said. "Actually, I don't know that it can ever be done."

Howard stared at her, silent for a moment.

"How in the hell could Schrade let something like that get by him?"

"At some point in life everyone has to trust someone, Bill. Even people like Wolfram Schrade. It's not possible to live without doing that. Wolf kept a sharp eye on his money, at least on what the computers told him he had. And on what

Marie told him he had. That's the great leap of faith of modern finance. I even do that. I get a piece of paper from the bank in Cyprus that tells me how much money I have there. Is it *really* there?" She shrugged.

Howard had been concentrating on something.

"A moment ago . . . you used the word 'enormity.' " He was sober. "What kind of money are we talking about here?"

"Well, I don't know exactly," she said. "All I know is that I've been getting a percentage of part of it. You know, the interest thrown off by part of it."

"How much?"

She hesitated. "I get almost a million U.S. dollars annually."

Howard's face sagged. "Fuck."

Ariana had never heard Bill Howard say that word.

"In . . . credible," he said softly. "In . . . credible."

He dropped his face into his hands, his elbows resting on his knees. He rubbed his face. He rested his forehead in the palms of his hands.

"And you all shared in it."

Ariana nodded.

"This . . . Clymer, yourself . . ."

"Me and Claude and Clymer and Marie and Harry."

"Five of you."

"As far as I know."

"Goddamn." Howard's eyes rolled to the side as he calculated. "I suppose you all shared equally. You said the interest . . . that's, hell, that's five million in *interest*—just *interest*." He gaped at her. "I don't even . . . I don't even know how to calculate the principal on something like that." He stopped. "Are you *sure*?"

"What do you think, Bill?"

Howard spoke softly. "You stupid idiots. And you're surprised that Schrade wants to kill you?"

"Of course not, not after he found out what we had done. But I am surprised that he finally discovered it."

Howard was incensed but controlling it. "You've been talking interest here. What about the principal?"

"Harry stipulated that we never touch the principal. We've been splitting only the interest."

Howard's hand was in front of his mouth, holding the cigarette as he sucked on it. "And how does that work?"

"It just shows up in my account in Cyprus. Quarterly."

"Who's responsible for that?"

"I don't know."

"You're just trusting whoever."

"That's right." She smiled grimly. "I told you, that's how the world is today. Marie set it up."

Howard was still, brooding in the dull lamplight, the smoke from his cigarette rising in front of him, sometimes fogging around the lampshade before dissipating, adding another layer of acrid stench to the wallpaper in the room of conspiracies.

"Okay," he said after a minute or two, "okay, you don't know where Harry and Marie are."

"No."

"Claude's gone."

She nodded.

"Clymer?"

"I have no idea."

Howard smoked. Ariana had put out her cigarette a while

ago and wanted another, but she had already smoked far too much. What she wanted was a drink, but she didn't say so.

"I don't understand why you're not already dead," he grunted as he shifted on the sofa. His white shirt was growing more wrinkled by the hour. "He obviously found Claude."

"Maybe that was because Claude was still selling him drawings."

"*What?*"

"He signaled that in one of his advertisements."

"So he was sticking his head in the lion's mouth."

"Something like that."

"I didn't have any idea that mild-mannered bear had that kind of balls."

"There's a lot you didn't have any idea about, Bill."

Howard snorted, looked toward the green light of the window. "You people . . . I don't know." He turned back to her. "You don't know anything about how Schrade reacted to this? You don't know what he's doing? Do you know *anything* about him?"

"I heard he cut his ties with the FIS about eighteen months ago."

"No, damn it. I mean about this, about discovering what the hell you've done."

"All I know is that Claude did not put his advertisement in the *International Herald Tribune*. I know that means that he couldn't. I know that is the trigger that was supposed to warn me that something had broken loose." She paused for emphasis. "And I know Schrade's going to kill me if the FIS doesn't stop him."

Howard nodded impatiently, irritated at her persistence. "Okay, okay. They're going to want to hear more from you, that's for damn sure. I'll take it back to them. I'll do the best I can, but, hell, this is huge. This is a fucking disaster."

Ariana stared at him. She didn't like the way he was sounding. She had a bad feeling about it. Panic grew in her chest, and every beat of her heart became a labored struggle for breath and for self-control.

CHAPTER 17

Until now Mara's eyes had never left him, not even for a second, not even a glance away. As Strand moved from the window and began pacing, she got up from the bed and walked to the closet, tossing her towel over the back of a chair. She slipped on her dressing gown, tying the sash as she walked to the French doors to look outside. Strand stopped pacing and looked at her. She had folded her arms, and the light coming in from the balcony struck her across her chest and fell the full length of her to the floor. Her face was in the shadow.

He felt so terribly bad for her. He had presented himself to her as being stable and reliable and, if complex, at least straightforward. Strand knew very well how he came across to most people, and he had always used that knowledge to his advantage. If things had been different, she might never have known at all about the man within the man, even if she had lived with him for the rest of their lives.

All of this ran through Strand's mind as he paused before going on. He wanted her to put his deception into its proper context. Time, he knew, was growing short, but he needed to set things right between them if he could. He realized that whatever he salvaged out of this mess he salvaged for them, not just for himself. If he was going to have anything to live for when all of this was over, he had to redeem himself to Mara Song.

"Are you all right?" he asked.

There was a moment of silence as she continued looking out over the balcony. The peacock nearby cried several times, a wild, otherworldly sound.

"I don't have any idea how to answer such a question," she said.

"I know this sounds bizarre. . . ."

She nodded. "Yes, exactly. Bizarre." Her eyes were focused on the palms in the garden. "I want you to get to the point, Harry. You said something horrible had happened. I need for you to get to the point of all this." She paused. "Then I'll tell you if I'm all right."

Strand took a few steps, to the edge of the sunlight on the stone floor.

"Schrade, of course, accepted our offer. Soon the arrangement was working perfectly. Schrade was productive and had no scruples whatsoever about betraying the people he worked with, always shrewd and careful to cover his tracks. He was brilliant at it."

Mara turned around, her back leaning against the hinged edge of the French doors.

"You should know that the FIS is strictly an intelligence organization—it has no prosecutive role at all. It doesn't get involved with covert action. It gathers intelligence. That's all it does. This intelligence is passed on to policy makers. They use it however they want, whatever suits their purpose. Usually it gets caught up in politics. Intelligence is power, and

power is the ultimate political tool. An intelligence organization is its government's fly on the wall. The fly's job is to observe and then report what it saw. It may witness all manner
of crime and treachery, but it never gets involved, not even to
prevent something horrible.

"Anyway, Schrade's illicit profits were laundered by several money managers who worked for him. One of these was
a woman named Rosemarie Bienert. Her history with
Schrade was . . . complicated. She was brilliant, held university degrees in international economics and finance. He called
her Marie. I called her Romy."

Mara reacted briefly in surprise. Suddenly, unexpectedly,
taking Strand aback, her eyes glistened with tears. He quickly
looked away from her and then went on.

"I'd actually met Romy while Schrade was spying on the
Russians for us. I was his case officer, and Schrade was such
an arrogant bastard that he often demanded I go to him in secret at his villa on Schwanenwerder, an island in the Havel
River in the Nikolassee district of Berlin. I saw Romy there
many times and got to know her.

"When FIS took me off the Soviet project, the abrupt in-
terruption of my meetings with Schrade forced Romy and me
to acknowledge how strongly we felt about each other. We
arranged our first secret meeting in Geneva."

The memory of that rendezvous was still so vivid and
provocative that it actually disrupted Strand's train of thought.
How he would have liked to dwell on it, to have had the time
to indulge himself with the intense remembrance of it. But he
didn't.

"For nearly a year I evaluated the prospect of an intelligence operation focusing on international crime. It was a hec-

tic time for me. There were long, intense periods when the days and nights ran together. During all of this Romy and I would steal as many days together as we could manage, meeting at some out-of-the-way hotel or isolated cottage in Geneva, Lake Como, Paris, London, wherever we felt we could successfully elude Schrade and the FIS for a few days."

Strand ran his fingers through his hair and turned to look out the window. Over the Tiber a flock of birds wheeled in a moray of light and shadow, a living, shifting Escher pattern.

"When the criminal intelligence operation began, Schrade thought he'd landed in paradise. We watched in silence while he unabashedly went about making deals to smuggle illegal arms and illegal aliens all over the world, watched as he bought and sold drugs from Mexico to Macao, watched as he rubbed shoulders with terrorists, watched as his illegal profits soared. While we watched we listened. We listened while he eagerly betrayed to us all of these associations from which he had profited so richly. He was very thorough about it, very matter-of-fact. He had no compunction, and apparently no fear, about playing both sides to his own benefit.

"This went on for nearly a year," he said, glancing at his watch. He was taking too long. His neck and shoulders were aching with the tension of trying to remain calm in the face of the dazzling flight of time.

"Now that Romy and I were out of Schrade's orbit we could see each other more easily, though we were still scrupulous about concealing our affair from both sides."

Strand rubbed his face with his hands. "I've got to cut this short," he said.

She didn't react, and he went on.

"At the same time all of this was going on, the intelligence community was going through a sea change as the cold war ground to a halt. Internal blunders and scandals became public, and certain important people were calling for radical changes. All of us on the front lines knew there was going to be downsizing, some of us were going to be brought in and forced into early retirement. Romy and I decided that when that happened to me, she was going to break with Schrade and go with me."

Strand hesitated only slightly before plunging on. "One day I told Romy that before they shut us down I wanted to do some damage to Schrade. I wanted to hurt him, and I wanted it to be serious. I knew that Schrade didn't have any nerve endings at all unless they were connected to art or to money. I went with the money. Over the next several months we talked constantly about how to embezzle the money Romy was laundering for him. All forms of money are vulnerable to theft, but the most vulnerable is cash. Illicit cash is the most vulnerable of all. The people who have it, and need to launder it, usually possess ludicrously large amounts of it. And because of this they have to turn to unorthodox methods to move it. The same technology and the expertise required to steal from legitimate banks and institutions work just as well when they're turned around and applied in the other direction. Schrade was vulnerable.

"Eventually Romy designed an astonishingly complex system to divert some of the money she was laundering for Schrade, which the FIS was allowing him to launder in exchange for his skills in providing us with information." He hesitated. "Actually, she was able to divert huge amounts of it. Hundreds of millions."

"Oh, God." Mara gaped at him.

The Roman sunlight was creeping across the floor between them, receding toward the balcony, less and less of it as it steadily escaped through the French doors. Soon it would be visible only on the sill, and then it would vanish.

With his hands in his pockets Strand stood in front of Mara.

"The strategy that Romy devised was sophisticated and knotted. She had a lot of advantages. Aside from being brilliant, she was in a pivotal position inside the organization. She knew intimately how it worked and why it worked that way. The plan involved half a dozen people, all of them the very best at what they did. We all considered the risks. The weak spots in the scheme were examined and corrected. We worked at it until we were all exhausted, until we all agreed we couldn't do anything else to improve it. Then we went ahead with it. And it worked.

"We ran this thing for six months before I stopped it. It could have gone on much longer, some of them thought a lot longer, but I wanted to pull out of it while we still *knew* we were a long way from being discovered."

"You mean discovered by Schrade, or by the people you worked for?"

"Either."

"So, you and . . . your 'cell,' your people, were hiding this from the government, from FIS? This Howard, he didn't even know?"

"That's right."

"Harry—you really thought you could get by with this?"

"That's right. We had every reason to believe we would. At worst, if it was discovered, we thought it would be so far down the road, and so much more laundered cash would have passed through the system behind it, that the whole thing would be impossible to sort out. The key was stopping early, letting subsequent business flow over it, bury it. Every year that passed made us feel even more secure and convinced us that we had been successful."

Mara saw it coming. "But it didn't work out that way," she said.

Strand shook his head. "For nearly a year I've thought Romy's death was an accident. Last night I found out that it wasn't."

He told her what had happened with the videotape in her VCR.

"Oh . . . oh . . ."

He told her who Dennis Clymer was and what had happened to him. He saw her brace her back against the door frame.

Then he told her about Meret.

She gasped, a burst of breath that sounded as if she had been hit in the stomach. Her knees bent slowly and ever so slightly; Strand thought she was going to sink to the floor, but she didn't. Her arms crossed slowly over her abdomen, and she held herself, her shoulders slumped forward.

"Good God, Harry," she said hoarsely. "What . . . what have you done?"

Strand stepped toward her, but she quickly raised one hand, palm out, stopping him.

"No, don't . . . I've got to think . . ." Her expression betrayed her inability to absorb everything she had heard. "Meret is *dead*?"

Strand nodded. He wanted to go to her and put his arms

around her and talk it out with her, even if it took all day or several days or a week. Whatever it took. But that was impossible. He could feel sweat on his forehead. He could feel his nerves slowly beginning to throb, his adrenaline going to work.

"Mara, listen to me. There's a lot more you need to know, but we don't have the time for that right now," he said. "We've got to leave here—"

" 'We'?"

He spoke very deliberately. "That's right. For now, for the next twenty-four hours, you've got to stay with me. I can't be sure you're safe unless you're with me."

"Why *wouldn't* I be safe? I'm not involved here."

"If you're involved with me, you're involved with Schrade. I'm sorry, Mara, but that's the way it is."

He could see her thinking about this, thinking, he guessed, about Meret.

"The point is," he went on, "if you want, I can help you get away from all of this later. Right now we have to take care of right now. Okay?"

She nodded. She understood, and she believed him. Her face had changed, and he could see her mind beginning to grapple with the present reality, connecting to the moment.

"Yeah," she said, looking around. "Okay." She straightened up. "I'll throw some things in a suitcase. I'll pack some things." She turned away from him and started across the room.

U.S. EMBASSY, VIENNA

"Well, for openers, it's a hell of a lot more money than Schrade told us they'd taken," Howard said. Today the air conditioning was freezing, even for him. He was drumming the eraser end of the pencil on the notepad. "Well, hell, Gene, it's got to be *hundreds* of millions. I don't even *believe* this. No wonder Schrade didn't tell us the whole truth on this. I mean, there's a difference between being embezzled and being buggered. Schrade was buggered."

Howard listened and shrugged against the frigid air. Shit, he was going to get pneumonia.

"Yeah, damn right," he said. "That woman was not only a financial genius, but gutsy to the point of insanity. She must've been damn sure of herself. You just don't do something like this unless you think you've got it sewed up—tight. Hell, she knew everything from the inside. I mean, it was like stealing from your mother. Schrade wasn't double-checking on her, of all people."

He listened. He nodded.

"Yeah, and listen, I've got to admit, Gene, Harry might've been hard to handle, might've been a wild card sometimes, but he was always careful, methodical. He could throw in some surprises, but he never did anything half-assed. When he set up something you knew it was going to work. He was brilliant in that way. I'll give him that. Hell, maybe we *can't* get the money."

Howard suddenly picked up the notepad and threw it at the plate-glass window. When the engineers looked around at the noise, he hugged himself and scowled at them and pointed his thumb upward and jacked it up and down. One of the engineers got up from his chair as though it were a big chore and walked to the wall and diddled with the thermostat. Howard didn't believe it. The guy just pretended to diddle with it. Shit.

"Yeah, well, she'd *heard* that Schrade had left us, but she obviously doesn't know why."

He listened.

"I don't know. It's discouraging as hell. I mean, it took us four months to get you people over there to agree to do this, a couple of months to agree on how, and then eight months for training and planning, and just when we get ready to put it into gear Schrade decides to wade in and start killing off everybody." He rolled his eyes. "I don't know why the hell he waited so long. It's been eighteen months, you'd've thought he would've gone on a rampage when he discovered it. I guess he didn't want to do anything until his accountants had picked the bones of this thing clean."

He listened.

"You know what, to tell you the truth, now that we've got a better idea of how much money was involved in that scheme, I'm surprised that Schrade didn't do more than just accuse us of double-crossing him and breaking off our deal. I'm thinking maybe he decided, Don't get mad, get even."

He listened.

"What I'm saying is, we know he's working with the French, the Germans." He hesitated a beat. "Gene, I'm convinced every operation he was involved in with us has been compromised. He's spilled his guts about us to his new partners. I know, I fought that theory myself"—he shook his head—"but that was before I had a grip on how much money was involved here. Look, we've had our own financial people looking into this from the first day Schrade came to us boiling mad. After all this time they hadn't figured out that the numbers were this big. Even so, we thought they were big enough to justify this operation if the end results ended in a forfeiture situation. But now we know that this is an *incredible* amount of money. And I think Schrade will go to incredible lengths to get even for having had it stolen from him."

CHAPTER 18

They threw some clothes into a few suitcases and left Sallustiano in a cab that took them to Piazza Esquilino, where
Strand rented a car using one of the forged passports. Since
the car was leased on the spur of the moment, it would be
clean of any electronic surveillance. As for human surveillance, Strand had not stopped watching for it for a second
from the moment they stepped out of Mara's villa.

They drove west out of the city and then headed north
along the coastal autostrada, driving mostly in silence, their
preoccupation with their own closely held thoughts diverted
now and then by occasional glimpses of the breathtaking views
of the Tyrrhenian Sea.

After a while the autostrada turned inland for a while and
then fell back to the coast. The angle of the sun, which was
now well on its downward way to the horizon, had caused the
color of the water to deepen, the bright blue now tempered
with tones of brooding gray.

Strand was the first to break the silence.

"I know this is a shock to you. . . ."

"A *shock*," she said, her elbow propped on the windowsill,

her hand holding her forehead as she stared straight ahead. "It's goddamned grotesque, Harry." Her voice cracked with anger and alarm.

"I'm sorry," he said.

"You might've said something." She turned and looked hard at him. Her voice seethed. "I mean, you were a *spy*, for God's sake! Would it have made a difference to me? I don't know. But I could have had a choice, couldn't I, Harry? Only you never *gave* me a choice. Now I'm involved in this . . . this mess, and it's scary. It's frightening. I can't even . . . really, I can't even get my mind around this, it's so . . . so incredibly unreal."

She turned away from him and rested her head in her hand again, once more turning her attention to the autostrada. She started to say something else and then checked herself.

"I'm not going to make excuses, Mara. Not going to try to justify any of it, but I need to tell you that I didn't deliberately deceive you, if that makes any sense. It had been behind me for nearly five years. It wasn't deception, it was silence. We've talked about our pasts. Haven't there been things about your life you haven't told me? Is it because you're not ready to share it with me yet, or is it because you want to deceive me? There's a difference, and it's not that subtle. I didn't keep this from *you*. I keep it from everyone. In time it probably would have come out."

Mara did not respond. Strand glanced at her several times, but she remained silent. He thought he detected a change in her, a disturbance of another kind, but it was such a nebulous thing that he couldn't define it.

"Look," he said after a while. "We've got to talk this through at some point."

"Jesus," she snapped, "I've just got to think some more. That's all. I just need to think . . ."

They drove on in silence again.

By dusk, as the sea changed colors and the lights along the coast threw down their glitter against the darkening water, they reached Genoa. They ate a quick, tasteless dinner at a gasoline-and-quick-food stop on the autostrada and then continued north, turning inland.

In another hour they were skirting Milan, still headed north, and in another half hour they were in Como. By the time they started up the torturous eastern shoreline of the western leg of Lake Como, it was well after dark. Even in the blue night the famed beauty of the lake and its shores was plainly evident as the dark, forested shoulders of the hills rose steeply from the cobalt water, bespangled with the tiny lights of villas and villages.

Bellagio was a small village on a lake that had many villages more chic than this where the haute monde preferred to amuse themselves in one another's company. The little town was out of the way, which was the reason Strand had often retreated here, vanishing deliberately, his whereabouts unknown to anyone, whenever he had craved isolation from time to time over the years.

Perched on a heavily wooded promontory where the western and eastern legs of the lake met like the two branches of an inverted Y, Bellagio had stunning views of both sections of the lake, a visual perspective that rivaled any that Strand had ever seen for sheer beauty.

They checked into a suite of large rooms that Strand had reserved earlier—using yet another passport—at the old Hotel Villa Cosima.

In uncomfortable silence they put away their clothes and then took turns freshening up in the bathroom. When Strand came out, his hair slightly wet from throwing cold water on his aching neck, the suite was dark, but the doors were open to the balcony.

He stepped out and found Mara leaning on the balustrade, looking out over the lake. The cool blue darkness was still and silent except for the soft washing of the lake against the shore below, a movement like the shallow breathing of sleep. All of Bellagio was unconscious. He looked at the lights across the water, their sparkle blurred by the mist that was beginning to rise from the lake. It was an unreal beauty and a fitting sight for his state of mind. A water bird of some kind called from far along the shoreline, a solitary warbling, then ceased.

He went over and stood beside her. Neither of them spoke for a long time. And then she said:

"God help me, Harry, I believe you about all of this." She paused. "The thing is," she went on, "over these past three months, in my mind I'd gradually shifted from thinking of us as 'me and Harry Strand' to thinking of us as 'we.' That's a big shift. I didn't realize how big until . . . all of this."

"Now you can't do that anymore?"

She didn't answer immediately. "No, I still think of us as 'we,' Harry. But fear changes things."

"I know that," he said. He was feeling his way, as if the darkness had gotten into his mind. "I'm sorry that you've got caught up in this. I honestly thought all of it was behind me and that it would stay behind me. I'd done everything in my power to make sure that it would."

The quiet all around them seemed to absorb their voices.

The lake sounds lingered in the darkness, cushioned on the dampness rising from the water.

"Do you remember in Rome, when I was telling you about all this," Strand reminded her, "and I said you were going to have to make some decisions. This is what I meant."

Their arms were touching as they leaned on the railing. He felt her move, shifting her weight on her long legs.

"I know," she said. "I know it is." She paused, and he thought that she swallowed. "It's hard for me, Harry. It's very hard." She laced her arm through his and took his hand. "It's just that I've reached that moment when you're on the precipice and you're looking down at the water and you're very still. You know you're going to dive. There's no question of that. Still, you take a moment to gather yourself together. You concentrate. You resolve."

Again he thought she swallowed.

"That's where I am, Harry."

The next morning he told her he had to take a brief trip and that he would have to be away for a day and a night. When he returned, he promised, he would tell her as much as he could. They would take all the time she wanted, and he would answer anything she asked. But first, he had to make this one trip. He would tell her where he had gone when he returned.

He reminded her that Bellagio had always been his personal sanctuary, that he had kept his retreats here a secret from everyone. He was sure that no one knew they were here. But to be doubly cautious, he felt it would be best if she remained within the hotel grounds and environs until he returned.

CHAPTER 19

VIENNA

"Get a coat," Howard said abruptly, standing in the open doorway.

"What?" Ariana was caught off guard.

"We have a meeting."

The evening had turned overcast and dampish by the time they had walked two blocks up from the safe house to catch a cab. A mist had begun drifting down on the streets, which were already wet enough to cast reflections.

They didn't talk at all as the cab made its way to Margaretenstrasse and headed into the inner city. The mist grew heavier and stippled the windows. By the time they crossed the Ringstrasse Boulevard and made their way to Freyung Square, the streets were crowded with the glistening dark canopies of umbrellas.

They left the cab at Palais Ferstel and entered the Freyung Passage, a bright shopping arcade that kept them dry in palatial surroundings until they came out on the other side of the block onto Herrengasse. From there it was only a few steps to the corner entrance of Café Central.

The Central had been Vienna's most popular coffee-

house for over a hundred years, its grand ceiling supported
by massive pillars and lighted by chandeliers in the best tradition of old-world elegance. Wood-paneled wainscoting
added to the ambiance, as did the black-and-white attire of
the waiters and waitresses who tended the open tables and
booths and private corners with quiet and formal efficiency.
The inclement weather had driven people inside, and the
Central was full.

Howard paused and surveyed the crowd. Ariana had no
idea whom they were looking for as they slowly began to
penetrate the maze of tables. Her eyes instinctively roamed
the faces, scanning the crowd for something familiar, a hair-
cut, a way of sitting, the shape of a head. Then she saw him
and caught her breath. She felt hot. Sitting at a table in one
of the wood-paneled alcoves was Harry Strand, staring at
her.

He was sitting so that he saw them immediately as they
came through the doors of the Central. He had a few moments to deal with his surprise at seeing Ariana before she
spotted him and started toward him. Howard saw her
change course and followed her. Strand had no idea that
Howard had been in touch with her—or that she was even
in Vienna.

As they approached, Strand remained seated at his table,
a window looking out to Strauchgasse on his left. They sat
down without shaking hands. Ariana looked exactly the same
as the last day he had seen her four years earlier. No new lines
in her face, no more pounds on her hips. He wasn't sure why
that made him feel good.

"It's good to see you," he said to her.

Ariana smiled, but he noticed a nervous edge to it.

"Harry," Howard said, pulling his chair up to the table.

"Bill, welcome to Vienna." Neither of them smiled. Strand turned to Ariana. "I learned only yesterday that you were living in Rome. But you were gone. I was worried."

"I'm fine, Harry," she said. "Frightened," she added, "but fine."

Strand looked at Howard. "Not everyone is fine," he said pointedly.

"No."

A waiter took their orders, then left them alone.

"I'm sorry about Marie," Howard said immediately. "I didn't know about it, Harry."

Strand noticed Ariana cut her eyes at Howard. She didn't know what he was talking about.

Then Howard added, "Houston, too."

Ariana frowned, puzzled, but said nothing. She might be afraid, but she could still think quickly.

"First of all," Strand said, avoiding Howard's condolences, "what do you know about Claude?"

"We only know he's missing. That's all," Howard said.

Strand looked at Ariana. "What's your situation here?"

Ariana told him about her warning system arrangement with Claude Corsier and how he had failed to respond. She was convinced Schrade was on to them. Afraid, she'd gone to Howard, hoping FIS would intervene.

"It was my only choice, Harry. I had no way of knowing about you . . . or anyone." She paused. "I couldn't handle it alone. I don't apologize for it."

"You'll never owe me an apology for anything, Ana,"

Strand said. "You know that." He turned to Howard. "So where do we stand?"

"You know about Clymer?" Howard asked.

Strand nodded.

Again Ariana's eyes shifted quickly. Howard hadn't told her a damn thing. Again she checked herself. It couldn't have been easy.

"Okay, the big picture is this. Schrade is after you. Washington is furious. They want to seize the money under the forfeiture laws. They want your neck in a noose."

Strand grinned. "But . . ."

"You tell me, Harry."

The waiter arrived with their coffee, a Pharisäer with a small liqueur glass of rum for Howard and an Einspanner for Ariana. He left a tiny plate of the Central's chocolate wafers. Strand waited until he was well away.

"They don't know how to get at it without having me expose the Schrade operation. So they're in a quandary. They keep thinking about the money. They keep thinking forfeiture. They can't bear the thought of us getting away with that kind of money and not being able to either seize it or hang me for it."

"That's about it," Howard said, picking up his coffee and then sipping it. "The truth is, nobody in Washington has the balls to go after you on this. You stole a march on them, Harry." He nodded at Ariana. "All of you. So, what they want to do is, we all just walk away from it. It's a wash." He paused. "But you've got to keep your mouth closed. It's a real-life stalemate. That's it."

"No, that's not nearly it," Strand said.

Howard looked up from his coffee with an expression of mild, innocent surprise.

"Romy's death was no accident, Bill. I've seen proof."

Ariana gasped.

Howard stared at him. "Bullshit."

"I want you to call him off."

"Call him off? We've got nothing to do with the man anymore. We can't do that."

For a moment the two of them looked at each other across the table, hearing only the murmuring of conversations and the clinking of spoons and cups and saucers.

"Tell them to do it."

"Jesus, you're pushing them, Harry. That's dangerous."

"More dangerous than waiting for Schrade to get all of us? Am I going to have to look over my shoulder for my own people, too?"

"Your 'own' people? Don't get righteous with me, Harry. I mean, you took the goddamned money—you want to get righteous?"

"FIS was letting it go. If you'd seized it, it would have been yours by forfeiture, but you were *letting it go.*"

Howard fixed his eyes on Strand. Another silence.

Strand sat back in his chair. He was aware of Ariana's silent, waiting fear, a rare thing in a woman who had been willing to face it and fight it off for so many years. He looked out through the rain-stippled window to the glittering Strauchgasse. Who would have thought that this city, cleaned by a fresh July rain, could be freighted with so much menace.

He turned to Ariana, thoughtful a moment, then smiled.

"You've not changed," he said, "not even a little."

She was surprised at his sudden remark, having been concentrating on the growing tension between the two men.

"Do you remember Madame Sosotris, the famous clairvoyant in Athens?" he asked.

Ariana gaped, recovered, and forced a smile. She spoke hesitatingly.

"How could I forget her? She predicted everything exactly wrong." Her smile faded. "The last time I saw her it was winter in Athens. She had a terrible cold."

"Well, I saw Guy Parain in Geneva, almost a year ago. He told me she'd died."

They visited a few moments about her and other old friends, other times and other places, until Howard found the diversion too distracting to tolerate.

"For Christ's sake, Harry. I don't have time for this."

Strand turned on him abruptly, almost angrily.

"*You* don't have the time? What about the two of us, Bill? How much time do we have? That's a problem for us right now. Time."

"You want me to tell them to stop Schrade or you'll blow this thing apart? Jesus. Have you thought about what that means?"

Strand locked his eyes on Howard.

"Wolfram Schrade is conducting a scorched earth policy against me. Romy. Every physical thing I own on this earth was in that house in Houston. As well as most of my memories. Not to mention the two wasted lives." He paused. "What do people do, Bill, when something like this is happening to them?" He paused. "Have I *thought* about it? You impertinent son of a bitch."

Silence.

"This is it?" Howard clearly didn't want to take this back to Washington.

"I'm stripped down to my life and a suitcase," Strand said. "That's all I have left. Do you really think there's any question what I want you to do?"

Howard looked down at his Pharisäer, largely unconsumed, picked up the tiny fluted glass of rum, and sipped it. He put down the glass, watched his own fingers turn it this way and that.

"This implied threat . . ."

"It's an explicit promise."

Howard nodded, still looking at the tiny glass. "This is backed up . . ."

"After what we did to Schrade"—Strand had recovered a measure of self-control—"even though we were careful, even though we were thorough and we thought we had gotten away with it cleanly, and on top of that, covered our tracks, even with all that confidence, do you really think I wouldn't also have had the imagination to envision a day like this? Do you really think I wouldn't have a plan for such a development?"

Howard sighed and sat back. He looked at Ariana and shook his head. His expression was sober, even grim. Finally he looked at Strand.

"So this is one of those 'if anything happens to me' threats, I guess."

Strand said nothing.

"I don't know what they're going to do, Harry. I can't imagine . . . can't imagine."

"Just make it clear to them."

"Oh, I'll do that." He paused. "Harry, listen, the most dangerous thing you can do to these people is get the upper hand." He lifted the tiny fluted glass and drank the last of the rum, then put the glass on the table, upside-down. "It makes them desperate."

CHAPTER 20

PRAGUE

The two men dawdled along the center aisle of St. Vitus's Cathedral. They were dwarfed by the immense, soaring height of the cathedral ceiling, a vaulted work of intricately webbed Gothic tracery as high above them as heaven itself. Tourists walked quietly all about them in the massive nave, the hissing of whispers and the murmuring of lowered voices creating an aural undercurrent befitting the respect due hallowed stones.

The taller man was middle-aged and dressed impeccably in a dove gray suit. He wore a stiffly starched white shirt with a high, spread collar, cobalt blue striped tie knotted in a firm Windsor. There was a sparkling white pocket handkerchief in the breast pocket of his suit coat. He walked with his hands clasped behind his back in a dignified way that seemed befitting of another era when correctness of carriage in public places was a matter of manners. He was broad shouldered and wore a mustache and goatee, very neatly trimmed and peppered with gray.

As they strolled, he stooped slightly toward his companion in order to hear better what he was saying. The companion was a man perhaps twenty years younger, dressed casually in dark trousers, a faded striped dress shirt, olive sweater vest, and a flea market sport coat. The shorter man was stocky, with a round florid face, his tight cheeks beginning to show out-croppings of scarlet spider veins. He had pale eyes and a button nose, and though he might have been a little heavier than a doctor would have advised, he exuded an air of military efficiency and capability.

The taller man was concentrating on the remarks the shorter man was making about a document the latter was reading and which he held in his right hand.

Suddenly the shorter man stopped squarely in the center of the nave and closed the document and rolled it up in a tube. Holding it in his right hand, he turned and gestured with it toward the other man.

"This . . . this is very serious business," he said.

"Oh, without a doubt, Mr. Skerlic," an obviously bogus name, but since Claude Corsier was using the equally bogus name of Charles Rousset, he felt compelled to refer to him in some appropriate way.

Someone dropped one of the hinged prayer benches on the backs of the pews, and the slap of heavy wood against stone echoed throughout the enormous nave.

"He's not just any man," Skerlic said, beginning to construct the scaffolding of reasons that would support the high price he planned to quote.

"No."

"He has his own intelligence . . . his own agents . . ."

"Yes."

"Very difficult."

"Surely that, but a man can always be killed, can't he?"

Mr. Skerlic looked at Rousset with his most sober expression, and then a faint, almost cunning smile flickered across his mouth and then passed away.

Rousset moved to walk on, and Skerlic followed. Neither of them spoke for a while as they idled toward the side aisles of the cathedral and passed under the long enfilade of Gothic arches where a succession of chapels lined the walls on either side of the nave. The older man stopped in front of one of them and gazed up at the stained-glass window above it and with one hand stroked his mustache and goatee. He was silent. "A lovely thing, this window," he said.

"When do you want this done?" Skerlic was standing slightly behind his companion, not even interested enough in the window to approach the chapel railing.

Rousset did not answer immediately but continued gazing up at the brilliant Gothic illuminations of the window made all the more striking by its setting in the gloomy chapel.

Sighing, and allowing a small shake of his head, the gentlemanly Rousset turned with resignation to his impatient acquaintance. Clasping his hands once more behind him as he faced the brighter nave from the shadows of the side aisle, he said, "As soon as you can do it with certainty. Every hour we can add to his sentence in hell the better."

Skerlic nodded. He was tapping his right leg with the rolled-up papers. Maybe he should just go back to Belgrade. This didn't feel right. After all, the target was a man of some significance. And who was this guy?

"No, I don't care when, Mr. Skerlic. That is, the date is not critical, if that is what you mean. Though if it happened within the next instant it would not be soon enough."

He stopped. They were standing in front of the chapel, looking out at the milling, pacific wanderers in the dusk light

of the cathedral. They might have been two husbands waiting
for their tardy wives to read every last word of yet another in-
scription or to ogle the munificence of silver and gold in yet
another chapel.

"As to how it's done," Rousset said, "I do have some in-
sight into that. That is, I have some essential ideas about how
this man is to be approached. Crucial ideas."

Skerlic bridled slightly at this encroachment into his profession.

"Your man is nothing special," he said, risking the case he
had been building for a high price. "We've done plenty of men
who thought they were untouchable. He won't be the first in
line on that score."

"Oh, I'm not questioning your ability, Mr. Skerlic," Rousset said reassuringly. "I'm quite familiar with your résumé. No,
I mean merely to hand you an advantage."

Rousset watched Skerlic closely as the Serb's eyes looked
down the length of the cathedral toward the chancel, his attention distracted momentarily by the universe of gilded motes
that hung in the light penetrating the clerestory high above
them, the slanting rays plummeting a hundred feet to the
stone floor below. Rousset guessed the Serb knew little of
cathedrals or architecture or religion, yet was he somehow
moved by being in the midst of its beauty and immensity? The
Serb's eyes fixed on one of the mote-laden rays and followed it
down, down past the triforium, down through the base of
heaven, down past the Gothic arches, down past the bundled
stone pillars, and finally to the stone floor, where it shattered
like a glittering breath.

"I have the advantage already," Skerlic said, turning suddenly to Rousset with a sober expression, "just by virtue of setting out to do it."

"But surely you want all the advantages you can get."

"Of course I do. And I'll make sure I have them, or I won't do it."

Rousset nodded. The little Serb was a prickly bastard. But he was the man he wanted.

"If it were, say, a bomb," Rousset ventured again with polite persistence, "I could provide you with the place and opportunity. I have the wherewithal to do that. You would be responsible for doing it, of course, but . . . well, since I know him so well I could save you a great deal of time."

The Serb pondered the gentleman's demeanor and finicky manner of dress.

He nodded. "When the time is right, maybe we could use some of your ideas."

"Then you're confident," the tall man said.

"Oh . . ." Skerlic nodded with conviction, pulling down the corners of his small mouth in a shrug of assurance. The Balkan bitterness, the internecine struggles, the racial hatreds, the criminal enterprises that rushed into the vacuum created by incessant war, all of it had taught him that he had a knack for killing. The more he did it, the better he got and the less it bothered him. As far as he was concerned, everyone was ripe for dying, and he might as well be around to help them along and get paid for doing it. And with modern technology, it was so easy nowadays. Confident? "Oh, yes."

"Then you will do it?"

"Well"—Skerlic looked away smugly—"I will do it, but I'm not sure you will have me do it. It's a matter of money."

"What is your fee?"

"Two hundred thousand. Deutschmarks."

Rousset stared at the Serb. He was delighted. He was prepared to pay more than that, but he didn't want to appear as though that kind of money didn't hurt him. He swallowed deliberately, though there was no need. It was for the Serb.

Skerlic saw the reflex and raised his eyebrows and allowed his eyelids to sink lazily in a "take it or leave it" expression.

"I will agree to that," Rousset said, a hint of strain in his voice.

Skerlic slapped the side of his leg once with his rolled document. "I may have some need to get a message to you. Do you have an e-mail address?"

They exchanged addresses.

"That's that, then," Rousset said. "And the payment?"

"Don't worry about the payment." The little Serb looked at the older man. "When I'm ready for it, I'll want it all."

"Of course." Rousset hesitated. "I'll need proof, naturally, that you've done your job."

"That won't be a problem."

They didn't shake hands. Skerlic simply turned away and walked back out into the vast nave, moving through shafts of light, his own decisive and irreverent footsteps clearly distinguishable from among the shuffling soles of the tourists, until the last shadow swallowed him and he was gone, somewhere near the chapel of St. Wenceslas and the Golden Portal.

Claude Corsier, one hand behind his back, the other tugging pensively at the salt-and-pepper goatee, watched Skerlic leave. He didn't know exactly what he had expected, but he hadn't expected that. As a lover of art, he was naturally a little romantic as well, and the dark angel that he had imagined he would meet for this conspiracy had been quite other than this abrupt and testy little Serb with pale eyes and a deteriorating complexion. Still, he did have to admit, there was something of the smell of death about him.

CHAPTER 21

GENEVA

Strand flew to Geneva as early as he could the next morning, chartering a private plane out of Schwechat to avoid the paper trail of the commercial airlines. When he arrived he checked into the Beau-Rivage on the Quai du Mont-Blanc on Lake Geneva.

He called Mara. She was not happy to hear of his delay. He tried to be reassuring, but it was obvious she was not convinced. He couldn't blame her. Her situation was horrible, and she had very few options for extricating herself. She was largely dependent on him at this point, and he feared that sooner or later she would either find some other options or create some of her own. He was eager to get back to her to dispel the obscurities that were accumulating between them.

He told her to go to Milan and buy a specific kind of laptop. He gave her the e-mail address he wanted her to use and said that all further communication should be through the Internet. Once they made contact, he would give her information about the encryption key he wanted to use.

They talked a few minutes longer. Neither was satisfied with the way the conversation ended.

That afternoon he went to a computer store near the Place Bel-Air and bought the same computer he had told Mara to buy. Then he returned to his room and set it up.

He left the hotel well after dark and walked toward the Rhône on the Quai des Bergues, to Parain's, a restaurant on the quay overlooking the water with a clear, sparkling view of the lights on the left bank across the Rhône.

He gave the maître d' his name, and they started toward the tables next to the windows looking onto the lake. When Strand spotted her, sitting with her back to him, he touched the maître d' on the arm. The man retreated immediately. Strand approached the table and bent down and kissed her neck.

"Jesus Christ," she said, turning and taking his face with both hands and returning his kiss. "I don't believe we did it. I don't believe it!"

Strand sat down and looked across the table at Ariana Kiriasis, who had put her hand flat on her chest as if to still her pounding heart. He grinned at her. She still smelled of her own seductive mixture of smoke and perfume.

"You've got a hell of a memory," he said. "It's been five years at least since we've used that. I thought it was a long shot."

Ariana was still shaking her head, smiling in relief and disbelief. "I wasn't sure I'd got all the signals straight. When you mentioned Madame Sosotris, the 'famous clairvoyant,' my God, I almost fell over."

"I saw the recognition in your face. I just wasn't sure you'd remember the details."

"My God, yes, of course I remembered, I just hadn't expected it." She was laughing.

When they'd first begun working together they had devised a method of secretly arranging meetings when they were
in the presence of others. Strand would mention Madame
Sosotris, a Greek character from T. S. Eliot's *The Waste Land*.
Ariana would confirm that she was ready for him to go ahead
by referring to the woman's illness, also mentioned in the
poem. The city, place, and time of their next meeting would be
the next city, place, and time mentioned by Strand in the subsequent conversation, though these details would be interwo-
ven into varying contexts.

"I didn't know if you were free to leave Vienna," he said.
"I didn't know your arrangements with Howard."

She told him again, this time in more detail, of her failure
to hear from Corsier and of her subsequent approach to
Howard, and then of her debriefing.

"I was getting depressed," she said, reaching for her cigarette pack on the table, "and afraid. Howard wasn't inspiring
much confidence." She offered one to Strand, who shook his
head. She lighted her cigarette and went on. "When Bill
dropped me off after our meeting at the Central, we made
arrangements to meet again tomorrow morning. But I went
straight inside, packed my things, and took a late train out of
Vienna."

"You're ruined with them now, you know."

"I don't give a damn. I don't trust them," she said, blowing smoke up into the darkness of the restaurant. "I didn't like
it, but I didn't have anywhere else to go. I didn't even know
you were alive. He didn't tell me whom we were going to
meet—I was stunned to see you. I was so damned relieved. To
tell you the truth, I thought they would protect me, but I
thought they would seize my accounts, and I would end up

serving some time in prison. Harry, I don't know what you have on your mind, but whatever it is I'm going to take my chances with you."

"You didn't think you could hide from Schrade?"

"I did, but I didn't think I could stand the strain of having to live that way for the rest of my life."

Strand understood that. He had done his share of thinking about that, too.

"How did Howard take our conversation?"

"He was angry. Very angry."

"They're in a messy spot. It's not the first time."

Their dinner came, and they ate for a few minutes.

"He said you were with a woman." Ariana wiped her mouth with her napkin, a slight smile remaining on her lips.

Strand nodded.

"You know her . . . well?"

"She's not involved."

"And she's beautiful."

"I think so."

"You, of all men, would know. You have her tucked away?"

"Yeah."

"How is she taking all this?"

"She knows that Schrade knows about her. She's afraid, but she'll deal with it. She's gutsy."

"Then she's in for the duration."

Strand nodded. Ariana couldn't wait any longer.

"Okay, Harry, what was Bill talking about?"

He told her. Everything. In detail, from the strange appearance of the videotape of Romy's death up to the present moment. She listened, stunned, mesmerized, her own anguish rekindled and intensified as she grasped a new understanding of the dimension of hatred they were dealing with and of the immediacy of its threat.

Without speaking, she reached for the bottle of wine and poured some more into both their glasses. Her hand trembled. Her face was drawn. As she sipped her wine her eyes remained on him across the rim of the glass. When she spoke she had to clear her throat.

"What do you want to do?" she asked. "What do we have to do?"

"Okay," he said, pushing aside his plate and pulling his glass over in front of him. "I have some ideas. First, we know the FIS isn't going to walk away from this. Bill's talk about this being a stalemate was standard FIS bullshit. They don't see this as a stalemate at all. They see themselves as having lost. They can't, and won't, tolerate that. This is by no means the end of it for them. Plus, as long as Schrade's alive he'll be trying to find us. The FIS can't do anything about him. That's it. It's as much a fact as gravity."

"Harry, before you go any further . . ." She was hesitant. "Have you considered trading the money for our lives?"

"Who are you going to trust with that kind of arrangement? Wolf? The FIS? The money's our only protection. Take it away, we're dead."

"How in the hell are we going to keep it and live any kind of normal life?"

"We can't make the money go away, but maybe we can make Schrade and the FIS go away."

Ariana stared at him blankly. "Oh, I see. You are grasping at straws."

"No, we can do it."

Ariana shook her head. "Maybe you can, but I'm not going to be able to help you."

"What?"

"I don't believe in magic." She smiled ruefully. "I'm too practical. I told you, Madame Sosotris never made anything happen for me."

"Magic hasn't got anything to do with it," Strand said. "Cold, hard reality will make him disappear."

"Disappear. You make it sound easy."

"No, it sure as hell won't be easy. Let me give you some additional background. After we broke up our operation and we all scattered in different directions, Schrade continued working with the FIS for another three and a half years. Then he abruptly cut it off. The FIS claims it doesn't know why."

"That's right. Howard wouldn't talk about it."

"Here's what I think happened. About eighteen months ago Schrade discovered the money was missing. I can't imagine what must have gone wrong. I don't know. But he went crazy, thought the FIS was in on the scam, and broke off his longtime arrangement with them. I don't have any doubt that he probably went to work with someone else, the Germans, the British, the French. Maybe all three of them. In the meantime, he put his best computer and accounting brains to work trying to find out where it all went. They discovered who before they discovered how. The first thing he did was find Romy and me. He killed her.

"No one else died. Why did he wait another year before coming after the rest of us?" He stopped. "I didn't even suspect Schrade in Romy's death. That's incredible, I know. I just didn't."

Ariana hadn't moved. She didn't respond.

"After killing Romy in an initial burst of anger," Strand went on, "Schrade realized it was a terrible mistake. He may never get the money if he kills all of us. In fact, he probably killed his best prospect for ever getting it all back. He spent the next year trying to track it all down."

Strand stopped and sipped his wine.

Ariana slowly shook her head. "You lost me," she said.

"The fact of the matter is, he *can't* get it back. Any of it. It's impossible. When Schrade finally realized that, he turned his attention to dealing with the rest of us. He's swinging his scythe in a wider arc. Anyone near me, he kills. Anything I own, he destroys."

"Is that true? The money can't be recovered?"

"In a sense, yes," he said. "It's gone."

CHAPTER 22

"Explain it to me," Ariana said bluntly, lighting another ciga-rette. "Where the hell is my money coming from?"

Strand nodded. There was no reason to keep it to himself any longer, nothing to be gained from it, nothing to be lost by it. He was the only one left who knew how it had been done.

"The money we stole from Schrade was money that was in the process of being laundered, money that was being 'streamed' through a byzantine scheme of 'filters,' fake com-panies, banks, investment programs, markets, commodities, everything. Romy's job, as it had been for nearly four years, was to determine at what point Schrade's dirty money had passed through enough 'filter entities' to keep it from getting traced back to Schrade's enterprises. When it was clean, she had to move it into the mainstream.

"The dirty money was passing through the 'stream' at an erratic rate, but it was averaging about forty-four million a month. Romy's plan was to divert a portion of this money in midstream and move it into another set of filters that ultimately spat out the clean money into our own legitimate entities. Romy and Clymer got together and created a . . . I don't know, a financial labyrinth, a highly complex web of legal mechanisms. They worked furiously for nearly a month on it, after Romy had already spent over a month designing the concept. It was all done by computer and then backed up by tons of forged paperwork. That's what you and Claude were shuttling back and forth to Dennis Clymer.

"When the money came out of our filters, we had the problem of isolating it."

"Isolating it?"

"From Schrade. I wanted to make sure that if he ever discovered what we'd done, he could never actually get his hands on the money we'd taken away from him. Six hundred and two million. . . ."

Ariana's mouth dropped open, an involuntary hiss of astonishment escaping her throat. She had never known the exact amount. She had only calculated backward from her own income. It had *not* come up to $602 million.

"My God," she said, "my God."

"Well, that's a big hit," Strand acknowledged. "I knew how Wolf would react to that. He'd easily spend that much, and more, to get it back. Even if he couldn't get it back, he wouldn't want us to have it, either. The thought of having that kind of money stolen from him would be intolerable. Especially considering who was responsible for it.

"I wanted the money to be integrated into a legitimate legal framework subject to U.S. laws. I didn't trust an EU country to resist the kind of pressure that Schrade was capable of putting on them if it eventually came to that."

He paused for a drink and looked out the window. Lake Geneva reflected the lights of the city around the harbor, a double image of the glitter and fantasy of a Swiss dream. He turned back, looking first into his wineglass for a moment and then at Ariana.

"What did you do with it?" she asked.

"I told Clymer to open lots of accounts in various banks in Zurich and here in Geneva. Out of those accounts I arranged for us to begin receiving payments in equal amounts, an arbitrary figure I came up with to provide us incomes up until we stopped the operation. These payments were sent to our private accounts, your Cyprus account, Romy and me in our bank in Vienna, then Houston, Claude's bank here in Geneva, and Clymer's own bank in San Francisco.

"When it was all over, when we shut down the operation, we had taken a total of six hundred and two million from Schrade. I instructed Clymer to take twenty percent of the total. That came to one hundred and twenty million. I had him split it four ways and open four accounts at four separate banks in Zurich. That put thirty million in each of our four accounts. I say four because Romy and I shared a single account. I instructed the banks not to touch the principal. Every month I had them send to each of our private accounts the interest off the thirty million principal."

Ariana was listening closely, nodding. "That's right. I've been getting one million two hundred thousand every year."

"That's our hazard pay," Strand said.

"So," Ariana said, her glass paused halfway to her lips, "what happened to the other eighty percent, the four hundred and eighty-two million?"

"I set up a series of charitable trusts that established and administered schools and hospitals in the very countries where Schrade's drug and arms business have caused so much miserable hell."

He looked out at Lake Geneva again, this time focusing on the darkness rather than the lights.

"As each of us dies," he said, turning back to her, "the principal that's been throwing off the interest from our four accounts reverts back to the original amount until, when the last of us dies, the entire six hundred and two million will be back together again. Managed correctly, that money can do a lot of good in perpetuity. Romy and I spent a lot of time and thought researching this, putting it together. The trusts are sound. All the legal strings have been neatly tied. The trusts can't be dismantled, not by anyone, not at any time. Everything's in place . . . to stay."

Strand drank some of the Bordeaux. It was very good. He let it stay in his mouth a moment, then swallowed it. A smile slowly softened Ariana's mouth and eyes.

"This is some kind of atonement, is that it, Harry?"

"I didn't put a name on it," he said, shifting in his seat. "I just did it. I did have thoughts of poetic justice."

"Schrade can't get to this?"

"It's way past him now. It's gone."

Ariana shook her head. "My God. You get away with over half a billion dollars . . . and you give it all away."

Neither of them spoke for a moment. The crowd in the restaurant had diminished; only a few diners remained, quiet groups, talking softly, intimately.

Ariana ran her fingers through her hair and sighed. She looked tired.

"Okay. Then tell me this," she said, leaning forward on the table. "How the hell are we going to stay alive? Tell me how reality is going to make Schrade disappear."

"Yeah." Strand nodded. "We've got to talk about that."

But he was hesitant. "Look, it's been about three days now since the videotape turned up in Rome. Obviously Schrade knew where I was three days ago. I did everything I could think of to lose his people. I think I'm okay now." He paused. "What about you?"

She looked at him. "That's blunt."

"We're both going to have to do some traveling," he said. "We're going to be carrying documents, documents I can't afford to lose." He paused again. "I just need to know how you feel about it. If you have any question in your own mind that you aren't absolutely clean, I need to know. I can make other arrangements."

"Here's my thinking, Harry," she said, her voice a little strained. "If Schrade knew where you were in Rome, and if he wanted you dead, why didn't he kill you then? Apparently he *chose* not to kill you in Rome. So, it could be that he knows where you are now, too, and is still choosing not to kill you. Maybe your evasive capabilities aren't as expert as you would like to believe." She smoked. "Just a thought." She smoked again.

"Now, as for myself," she went on. "I have no reason to believe that Schrade would *not* kill me if he knew where I was. He didn't let Clymer live. Nor, I believe, Claude. I have no reason to think he would have different plans for me. So, if I'm alive now, perhaps it's because he *doesn't* know where I am. That, I would think, would speak well enough for my evasive skills."

By the time she had finished, Ariana's tone had grown decidedly testy. Strand had to concede that she had a point. He was glad to see that her Greek ire was still alive, that it hadn't been completely cowed, as he first had thought when he'd talked with her and Howard at the Café Central. He grinned at her.

"Touché," he said.

"Yes." She arched one eyebrow. "Indeed."

"Okay, look, tomorrow I'm going to a bank here where I've been keeping documents that I set aside during the years I worked with Schrade. We'll get together again, I'll give you the documents you'll need, and tell you then what I've got in mind."

"Fine. Where do we meet?"

"Not a public place this time. Your hotel or mine. We're going to need some time together, most of the day."

Ariana picked up her purse and began looking inside. She took out a key and laid it on the table, shoving it over to Strand.

"My hotel room. The Métropole."

"I'll call you when I leave the bank," he said, putting the key in his pocket. "Do you have an e-mail address?"

They exchanged addresses, repeating them for each other several times. They didn't dare write them down. She didn't even ask him where he was staying or where he would be when he left Geneva. She knew he wouldn't tell her.

"I probably won't get there until late in the afternoon," he said. "I've got to copy these documents . . . and there are photographs . . . and tapes that'll have to be duplicated. I'm sure I can get all of that done somewhere near the banking district, but it'll take most of the day." He paused. "If for some reason we get separated, if something happens and you aren't there when I come, or if I don't show up, leave Geneva. I'll do the same. We'll check in with each other on the Net."

Nothing remained to be said. Finally Strand smiled and

held up his glass in a silent toast. They drank the last of the wine, looking at each other.

"I was glad to see you, Harry," Ariana said, putting down her glass. "When I saw your face looking at me across that room of unfamiliar faces, everything seemed possible again. Christ, it was bleak before that."

"This'll work out," Strand said.

"It has to, doesn't it?"

Strand nodded. "Yeah. It has to."

They looked at each other for a moment longer, then Ariana reached for her purse and stood up. She put the strap over her shoulder, then leaned over and put her hand flat against the side of his face, holding it gently as she kissed him softly on the lips.

"Good-bye, Harry Strand," she said.

When he returned to the Beau-Rivage, Strand had an e-mail message from Mara.

Up and running. Waiting.
M.

CHAPTER 23

BANJA LUKA, BRITISH SECTOR, BOSNIA

The short, stocky Serb sat on an upturned gas tin under a thick poplar tree at a farmhouse on the southern edge of the city. A spring rain had soaked the countryside for the past week, and the Serb's shoes were caked with dark, gummy mud. So were the boots of his two companions, one of whom sat on the rim of a huge, cracking tractor tire while the other, standing, had propped one foot on the edge of a wooden trough as he leaned forward, his forearms crossed on his raised knee. Gnats hovered around them in humid air that was rich with the odors of damp earth and weeds.

The Serb's two companions were brothers in their late thirties, farmers who seemed to be making only a scrabbly living off their small acreage. Around them was a mud-spattered stucco farmhouse with tiles missing from its roof, a derelict barn that had not seen meaningful use in nearly five years, a rusted-out flatbed Soviet-era truck, a twenty-year-old Russian tractor that had not been able to run for seven years.

"It's the same stuff we used on the general in Bihać," the Serb said. "Almost the same. Treat it the same way. I want you to get it out of the British sector, into Croatia, to Split."

"Just the explosives. Not the detonators?" the standing man asked.

"Just the explosives."

"And how much of it?"

"It would fit in a lunch pail."

"Can we take it apart?"

"I don't care how you do it, so long as you deliver to the address in Split the exact amount that I give you here."

Both men nodded.

The short man reached into his shirt pocket and took out a piece of paper and handed it to the brother sitting on the tractor tire.

"That's the address in Split," he said. "Go there between two and three o'clock in the afternoon. Any even-numbered day. But only that hour. The woman there will take your package. She will open it and verify the amount. If all is fine, she will tell you where to go to get your money."

"That day? Then?"

"Yes, that very moment."

The two brothers exchanged looks. They had fought with the short man in Bihać and Mostar in 1992 and 1993 and had learned to trust him in a soldierly way before they were shipped to another front of the war. After they had all left the army, he had looked them up. This was the fourth smuggling job he had brought to them. So far, it was the most simple. And the most lucrative. And the most risky.

The brother standing with his leg on the trough turned to the short man.

"All right. When do we get the explosive?"

"Right now. I have it in the car." He stood up. "But I have

to know when you think you can deliver it. The woman has to know within one or two days."

"Three days. We can get it to Split in three days."

"Fine."

In the distance thunder rolled from one side of the horizon to the other. They all looked up at the overcast sky.

"Goddamn it," the older brother said, and took his foot down from the trough to follow the little Serb to his car.

GENEVA

The next morning Strand sent an e-mail to Mara. It was early, because he wanted to have breakfast and be at the bank as soon as it opened. He had a lot to do. He told her the trip was uneventful, that he was fine, and that he would let her know when he started "home." He also asked her to let him know how she was doing.

After breakfast he walked down to the Quai du Mont-Blanc and in a few moments entered a leather goods shop, where he bought a briefcase. Outside he hailed a taxi and rode the short distance down the stylish Quai des Bergues and across the Rhône to Place Bel-Air, the heart of the business and banking district. The Suisse Crédit Internationale was huge and modern, with sparkling bright interior architecture and an abundance of brushed chrome and glass and marble. Strand had not been in the bank in three years.

He presented the passport and identification papers for Georges Fouchet, requested access to his security box. After the usual paperwork and subdued formality involving several officers, he was led to a large room laid out in aisles and corridors. The walls of the aisles and corridors contained row upon row of brushed chrome drawers, each with a number, a recessed handle, and a keyhole.

They went through the ritual of the keys, Strand retrieved two chrome boxes, and the officer locked him in a small private room and left.

For the next fifty minutes Strand carefully searched through the two metal boxes, selecting the documents he had been thinking about ever since he'd left Rome. There were files of photographs and several dozen plastic cases of CDs, all labeled with dates and number codes he checked against a list in a notebook.

When Strand was escorted back to the main bank floor again, he asked one of the officers where he could go to duplicate documents, photographs, and CDs. The man reached into his desk and gave Strand a piece of paper with the names of two establishments.

Another short taxi ride, and he was there. It took an hour and a half to duplicate everything he wanted, and they were completely understanding that he wanted to watch every step in the process of duplicating each of the three formats.

He returned to the bank, replaced the original documents, photographs, and CDs in the deposit box, and left with two copies of everything.

It all had happened much more quickly than he had anticipated. It was almost noon, so he walked around the corner from the bank and ate lunch at a quiet restaurant that he remembered on the Quai de la Poste.

He finished earlier than he had expected and walked to Ariana's hotel. She was staying on the left bank in the old Métropole on Quai Général-Guisan. It looked across the narrow end of the lake near Pont du Mont-Blanc, where the lake

squeezed down to become the Rhône. It had an old-world feel
about it, something Ariana would seek out. A sophisticated
traveler, she abhorred what she called the clinical modernity
of anything built after the close of the nineteenth century.

As he entered the lobby he remembered that he hadn't
called Ariana as he had promised. It didn't matter. She was expecting him, and if she had gone out to lunch, he would wait
there for her.

He took the elevator to the fourth floor. As he followed
the numbers on the doors he was not surprised to see that she
had gotten a room with a lakeside view. Approaching her door,
he saw her "Do Not Disturb" sign and rang the doorbell. He
waited. No answer. He rang again. She must have gone out, as
he had expected. He thought about going downstairs to the
hotel's dining room to see if she was there, then changed his
mind, thinking he would use the time to go over his plan once
more before explaining it to her.

He let himself in. Of course, it was a suite, even though
she was alone. A small foyer opened up into a sitting room, and
from the door you could look through the sitting room to
French doors that opened up to the Quai Général-Guisan and
the glittering water of Lake Geneva. Strand closed the door
and called her name, but there was no answer.

After throwing the deadbolt behind him, he walked into
the sitting room and put the briefcase down beside a sofa and
then walked to the French doors. It was a beautiful view of the
promenades on the quayside, the lake, and the right bank just
across the narrow neck of water. The French doors were open,
and though the balcony was almost too small, Ariana had
pulled an armchair onto it, as well as a small table. On the

table was an ashtray filled with lipstick-marked butts and a hotel glass with a little melted ice in the bottom.

Strand walked back and stepped into the bedroom doorway. The bed was unmade. The bathroom door was open, and he walked over to it and looked in. Ariana was messy. The place was littered with cosmetics, nylons drying over the shower rod, a pair of shoes kicked to one side. On the marble countertop over the sink below the mirror, a toothbrush, earrings, half a pack of cigarettes, and her cigarette lighter. Damp towels in a pile by the toilet. The smell of perfume and soap and cigarettes.

On the other side of the unmade bed another set of French doors was open, the source of a nippy breeze during the night.

He turned and walked back into the sitting room, found a cart with bottles of liquor on it and some clean glasses. He poured himself a splash of cognac, went back to the sofa, and sat down, put the cognac on the table in front of him, and pulled the leather briefcase over to him. He snapped open the clasp and, in the same instant, looked up.

What he saw in his mind he saw in his eyes. He did not see the other side of the room. He saw the half pack of Ariana's cigarettes and the cigarette lighter on the marble shelf over the sink.

He could hardly breathe, and instantly he felt damp around his mouth and forehead. His hands were still on the briefcase. He snapped the clasp closed.

He stood, aware of the weakness in his legs. He wiped his forehead and walked back to the bedroom door. His eyes crawled over every object in the room. Nothing was disturbed. No struggle here. But he had missed something. He must have. He stared at the unmade bed. It was just an unmade bed. Nothing.

He stared at the rumpled sheets. Like the patterns of sand in an estuary, washed into drifts that belied the flow of the water that had moved it, the sheets, too, had a pattern. The folds all drifted to one side, the side of the bed opposite him, next to the opened French doors.

Strand walked around the end of the bed with a sense of dread so heavy that it almost prevented him from moving at all.

She was there, on her stomach, her head and upper torso stuffed under the bed, her naked buttocks exposed, her bare legs partly wrapped in the sheets that had been dragged off with her. And here was the blood. A lot of it, sneaking out from under the bed as though it had tried to escape the horrible moment.

Strand had to see her face. Trembling, he stepped over and knelt down and grabbed her waist above her hips. She had the remarkable weight of death, a phenomenon he hated, the oddness of how death seemed to add tens of pounds to a body that would have been so much lighter in life.

She was difficult to get out from under the bed, and he heard himself apologizing to her for the rough treatment, for the way he wrenched her body to free her from where they had wedged her. When she came free, her wonderful mane of wavy black hair was all around her head, gummy and caked with the grume of the end of her life.

He turned her over and with the tips of his fingers separated her hair away from her face. She had been all night in her own blood, which had long since begun to curdle. When he had rolled her over the sheet around her legs had wrapped with her and covered her pubic hair. Her exposed navel seemed so . . . risqué. With her wild hair swirling around her head, her body cocked oddly at the waist, she looked like a Greek belly dancer closing her eyes, caught up in the dance. *Danseuse du ventre*. One night in Salonika they had been going to bars, drinking. At a crazy place, almost out of control, she had made a joke. *Danseuse du ventre*.

He thought of Romy. And Meret.

And Mara.

CHAPTER 24

Strand did what he could to cut himself off from Geneva. With his stomach churning, he turned away from Ariana's body and went back into the living room, where he sat at a writing desk and plugged in his laptop. He sent an e-mail to Mara:

> Bad luck here—but I'm fine. I'll be home tonight.
> Be careful.

For just a moment he stared at the computer screen and thought about e-mailing Bill Howard. Then he decided to hell with it. Let them find out about it when they find out about it.

He logged off, folded up the laptop, put it in the briefcase with the papers from the bank, and walked out of the suite. He took the "Do Not Disturb" sign off the door handle. Goddamn it, she didn't need to lie there all day. He did not go back to the Beau-Rivage. There was nothing of him there. The only traces of his existence—the bogus passports and papers—he always carried with him.

Once again he chartered a private plane, leaving Cointrin

in Geneva in midafternoon and arriving at Malpensa outside Milan a couple of hours later. He rented a car at the airport and drove to Bellagio, arriving there around dusk. By the time he pulled into the courtyard of Hotel Villa Cosima his back was aching and his neck was taut with the beginnings of a headache.

When he walked through the door of their suite, Mara was there instantly, embracing him. She held him a long time without speaking, and he could feel the worry in her body and in her breath at his neck as they held each other.

She had been sitting with a drink in the main room of the suite. She had not turned on the lamps, letting a pale dusk deepen to the blue of evening as she watched the lights come on along the steep slopes of the opposite shore. He mixed a strong drink and joined her on the sofa, and for a little while they sat together in silence, looking out across the lake. Strand was grateful to her for not speaking right away, for allowing him to gather his thoughts. He knew she must have a swarm of questions, yet she didn't press him. That was gutsy. As soon as he had hit the "send" key on the e-mail from Ariana's suite, he was sorry he had mentioned "bad luck." He shouldn't have done that. Mara probably had imagined a thousand scenarios, created a thousand ghosts, feared a thousand harms.

He told her everything. As far as he was concerned, now they were inseparable. Their survival would depend on a symbiotic reliance. He hoped she would agree. If she left him now, there would be no way that he could protect her.

"How long had you known her?" Mara asked.

"Twelve years," Strand said. "But it was longer than that. The kind of work we did ... it alters time. Sometimes stretches it out, sometimes compresses it. It drains you and changes you in countless sad ways. And you're aware of it, even while it's happening."

"She must've been good at it."

"Yes." He raised the Scotch to his lips. "She was."

Mara waited a couple of beats. "That's what's happening now, isn't it? You're slipping back into that old life."

"I don't know," he lied.

"You do know, Harry. Don't do this. I've got to be able to believe you."

Strand turned his eyes away from the tiny sequins of light across the lake. He looked at her. It wasn't dark in the room; there was an ambient glow from the lights below on the promenade at the water's edge. They provided her with a small luminant speck just near the center of each eye.

"When Schrade changed his focus to global organized crime," Strand said, his voice almost husky, "he stepped into a far more dangerous world than the Russian spy game. It was one thing to spy on a derelict state, but it was quite another to inform against growing criminal enterprises. They were strong and fast and vicious.

"International crime has no ideology. It has no parameters, no borders, no lines to cross. It's a vast, horizonless galaxy: no rules beyond brutality, no values beyond greed. Drug profits alone—only one of many markets of international crime—exceed three hundred billion every year. *Every* year. That superabundance of money inspires a kind of madness that can be stunning in its savagery.

"When I got the idea to steal Schrade's money after he'd laundered it, I got a safety deposit box in a Geneva bank. I immediately started filling it with documentation. Without any of our people knowing it, I wired myself and taped nearly all of my conversations with Schrade. When he gave me information about the Lu Kee group out of Taipei doing contract hits in Germany for Matvei Grachev's Russian organization there, I got it on tape. When he told me about Sergio Lodato in Naples providing the Russians with counterfeit hundreds in exchange for armaments and Russian real estate and Russian bank ownerships, I taped it. When he told me that Mario Obando in Colombia was selling cocaine to the Chinese (who gave him heroin in return and which the Mexicans then smuggled into the U.S.) and to the Yakuza, who distributed it in Japan—and then everyone laundering their profits through the Italians in Eastern Europe—I taped it."

Strand shook his head and took another drink. The alcohol was beginning to loosen his knotted muscles.

"I even managed to photograph him with Bill Howard on four separate occasions when Schrade demanded face-to-face meetings to reassure himself that the FIS was following through. He was constantly afraid his sweet deal was going to fall apart."

A motor launch left the quayside below and started across the lake, the deep-throated mutter of its engines dying as it disappeared into the darkness.

"That's your insurance," Mara said.

Strand nodded. "Well, maybe insurance isn't quite the right word. It's more like having a contingency plan for a defensive maneuver. My idea was to divide the information up between myself and Ariana and take it to the concerned parties. I think the evidence would be convincing."

"In other words, when these people saw what Schrade had been doing to them, they would kill him. You'd be serving his death warrant."

"That's what I was hoping."

"Oh, Harry . . ." Mara shook her head but said nothing more.

"After I found Ariana's body this morning, I knew he was all over me. If he didn't know I was in Geneva . . . I don't know . . . maybe she'd been careless leaving Vienna. But she was in an FIS safe house there. She should have been clean. I think if he'd known I was there, he would've let me know about it."

"He did."

"No, not like that. I mean directly. He'd want to let me know he knew, just like he did with the tape in Rome." He drank the last of his Scotch. The ice had melted, watering down its smoky flavor. "I don't think he knew. It was just a fluke that I wasn't around when it happened."

"I don't understand this. Why wouldn't it still work, telling them . . . those people?" The urgency in her voice pained him. Her situation was unbelievable. At least he had spent a lifetime getting to this point.

"It's not that it won't work. It will. They'll kill him." He paused. "I just don't know how quickly they'll move."

Mara was still with him. "You mean," she said, "if they'll get him before he can get us."

Strand just looked at her.

"Oh, God. What are we talking about?" Her voice was soft with dismay. "I don't believe this is happening."

It was an awful moment for Strand, watching and listening to Mara gradually come to the realization of her appalling position. He felt the full weight and distress of his guilt. For all his audacity, for all his planning and good intentions and moments of hubris when he thought he could do the impossible, practically nothing of it was left except Mara.

"What about the FIS?" Mara's voice was edged with urgency. "They're not going to do anything?"

"They can't. Schrade thinks they're part of the embezzlement scheme. They don't have any leverage with the guy. I hadn't realized what was going on with Howard and Schrade until I was driving back from Vienna. Then it occurred to me that Schrade was holding the FIS responsible for the embezzlement, too. That's why Howard was telling me he couldn't call off Schrade. He was telling the truth about that. I just didn't see it at the time."

"Oh, come on. They could *expose* him. They could tell the whole world about him."

"It doesn't work that way. The common bond between people like Schrade and the intelligence agencies who use them is secrecy. He needs it to do what he does, they need it to do what they do. They use each other, knowing that if there's ever a falling-out between them, neither side will expose the other, because the relationship itself is illicit."

"What about this guy Howard? What's going to happen when he finds out Ariana is dead? Won't that change things? Are you going to let him know she's dead? How will this change what you were wanting him to do?"

"I'm not going to let him know anything," Strand said. "To tell you the truth, I don't think Ariana's death will affect anything one way or the other. A sad fact. Right now I don't want a goddamned thing from Bill Howard. He and I had a rocky career together. We didn't like each other much, and I didn't see anything in Vienna to change my opinion of him."

Mara said nothing. Through the balcony doors they could hear the faint voices of people walking along the promenade. Strand envied them. He knew it was irrational to do so. It was a human weakness in dire times to see others' lives as richer, more fortunate, than your own. At this moment the voices he heard were the voices of careless people, those fortunate strangers who did not have your cares, or your tragedies, or your bad luck. Strand always wondered about them. Who were they? What brought them to this village, to this promenade, at this moment? How incredible that they had no idea that only a few meters away from them a man and a woman were sitting in darkness, afraid, confused, desperate even to understand what they should do at the end of the night.

Without speaking Mara stood in the near darkness of the room and walked to the balcony doors and stepped outside. He watched her silhouette against the blue light of the night sky. He could not tell whether she was staring across to the black hills on the opposite shore of the lake or whether she was looking down toward the promenade.

He got up and followed her. She was leaning on the stone balustrade, looking out toward the dark water. He put his arm around her waist, and she took his hand.

"You can't imagine, really, how terrified I am, Harry," she said. Her voice quavered, and the sound of it broke his heart.

"This bears no resemblance to any reality I know," she went on. "I'm not a stupid woman. I know what I'm involved in here. It's bizarre, but it's happening and . . . I have to deal with it." There was a pause. "I'm going to tell you exactly the way it is, Harry. I'm on the verge of panic."

They were both looking out into the various darkness. He waited for her to go on, and then suddenly he was aware that she was crying. He would have given ten years of his life to be able to comfort her.

"It's going to take every bit of our concentration," Strand

said. "There's a balance here. We have to find it, and very carefully make it work for us."

She leaned into him, burying her face against his shoulder. He could feel the small shudders of her weeping.

"Do you understand what I'm talking about?" he asked.

There were a few moments while she gained control. Then she said, "Yes."

She didn't understand, of course, and they both knew it.

CHAPTER 25

They went to bed late, and Strand slept the dead, dreamless sleep of exhaustion. He woke early the next morning with a start, heavy headed yet wide awake. He carefully crawled out from under the covers, dressed, and went straight to the sitting room, closing the bedroom doors behind him.

He threw open the balcony doors to the cool morning, called room service for coffee, sat down at his laptop, and flipped on the switch.

Using the information that he had gotten from Alain Darras, he began the complex series of contacts over the Internet that would eventually lead him to a face-to-face interview with the first of the four crime lords.

He had no idea how long the process would take, but the procedures he had obtained from Darras were supposed to cut through the red tape that the new, increasingly sophisticated criminal organizations put into place. As in all corporate structures, illicit or legal, the men at the top isolated themselves with multiple layers of intermediaries.

He had been working for nearly an hour when Mara came out of the bedroom.

They walked up the hill to a little café near the center of the village and had a quiet cup of coffee with pastries. When they started back through the narrow, cobbled streets that fell steeply to the waterfront, Mara laced her arm through Strand's and they meandered down, catching glimpses of the lake through the linden trees as they turned corners on their descent.

"Okay, Harry," she said, "why don't you tell me what's going on."

He hardly knew where to begin.

"Not a lot yet," he said. "This morning I started the process of contacting the first of the four men Schrade was betraying to the FIS. My first thought was to approach all of them at the same time, just turn them loose on Schrade all at once. But then, considering all that I don't know about the details of Schrade's involvements with each of them, I was afraid that I might trigger a bloodbath. That's not the way this needs to be done."

"Who are you contacting first?"

"A Taiwan Chinese named Lu Kee. Lu is our best first meeting because he's the most civilized of the four. Talking to him will give us a less jarring sample of the meetings to come. He'll be like a wise old uncle. He personally dislikes harshness. He pays people to be harsh for him.

"I've given Lu three crucial bits of information. First, proof that I have inside knowledge of one of his failed enterprises, a scheme that cost him hundreds of millions of dollars when it fell apart. He never found out why it happened. Second, the fact that I'm a former U.S. intelligence officer. Third, a promise that I'll reveal a traitor.

"The first of these three is going to shock him. That

probably would be enough to get me the interview. The third bit of information will seem like a scam without the first. The second bit of information will be expected to be proven at the meeting."

"This could take days, couldn't it?" Mara asked.

"Could. But I doubt if it will. I suspect it'll happen very quickly."

"If he's in Taiwan . . ."

"He's not. Darras's information puts him in Zurich now. He has a home there."

They stopped at a turn of the street that gave them a wide view of the lake. The sun was well into the eastern sky, throwing shadows to the west along the shoreline and strewing a shatter of brilliance across the surface of the water. Farther to their left, on the western leg of the lake, a single sailboat was tacking back toward the villas of Tremezzo. Down on the waterfront a tour boat pulled away from the quay and headed out across the lake.

"We just have to wait."

The back-and-forth with Lu's intermediaries dragged on past lunch. Strand had received from them three e-mail messages that, through a series of precise questions, were intended to determine the legitimacy of his request. He was patient with this, having expected nothing less. He answered the queries as fully as possible, while being careful not to reveal more than the circumstances required. Midafternoon brought another delay, another long wait.

"He's not going to do it," Mara said. She had tried to sketch but couldn't concentrate. She had stared at the glistening lake, but even the incredible beauty of Como could not distract her. Strand watched her and worried. The waiting, the slow pace of negotiations, was wearing on both of them. Time dragged.

"He's just cautious." Strand rubbed his face. "He'll do it." He looked out through the balcony doors at the sailboats on the lake, the geometric shapes of their white sails passing smoothly back and forth within the view framed by the French doors.

By four o'clock in the afternoon, as the light on the lake began to soften, Lu Kee was still silent.

Shortly after five o'clock, four beeps signaled a message, and the words appeared like magic writing on the screen.

JL wishes to speak to HS.

This is HS.

Sir, I would like to arrange a meeting. Where are you?

Europe.

I am in Zurich. Is that near you?

Relatively.

I would like to meet tomorrow night. Is that possible?

Strand quickly flipped through Lu's file. He had a large French-made LaSalle jet. Strand hesitated and looked at Mara. He began typing.

*May I suggest Lake Como. I can
be there by eight o'clock in the
evening.*

Do you know Villa d'Este? I can
arrange a suite there. Will you be
alone?

Strand stared at the screen. He turned and looked at
Mara. "I think it could help if you went along. How would you
feel about it?"

Mara swallowed. "Well, you don't think that'll be just a
little obvious? You bringing along your token Chinese to show
him how simpatico you'll be."

"Maybe. But something tells me that a token Chinese is
better than no Chinese at all."

"I'll do it if you want." She hesitated. "I'm going to assume I don't have to be 'prepped' for this. I go along; I look
good, follow my instincts on the light conversation, and keep
my mouth shut when the serious stuff starts."

"That's about it."

"I can do that."

Strand turned back to the computer screen.

No, there will be two of us.

Then I will see you both at
eight o'clock.

Agreed.

Strand stood up from the computer. "That's it," he said. He turned his stiff neck to one side and then to the other and rolled his shoulders forward. He stopped. "What's bothering you?" he asked.

She shrugged and cocked her head. "Isn't that just an extraordinary . . . coincidence, him being, of all the places on the globe, just a couple of hours away?"

Strand nodded. "You're right to be suspicious," he said, "but it's not unusual for Lu to be in Zurich. He has a lot of money there. He keeps tabs on it. And he likes the city. It's clean. It's orderly. Sometimes Latin Europe frustrates him. I doubt if he'd ever set foot in Italy at all if he didn't need Lodato's organization to move his China white."

"How do you know all this? Have you met him?"

"No. How about you? You feel okay about this?"

Mara swung around in the chair, holding her sketchpad in her lap. She thought a moment before answering.

"This is your business, Harry. You know what you're doing. You know what I can do and can't do. If you're willing to have me do this, I'll do it."

"I honestly think it would help to have you with me," Strand said. "You'll be all right."

He put one hand in his trousers pocket and walked toward the balcony but stopped before he got there. He looked out a moment, then turned and came back and reached for the chair sitting in front of the computer. He turned it around to face her and sat down.

"Tomorrow morning I'll make arrangements for getting us there tomorrow night. Lu's people may try to follow us afterward. I don't want to take a car to the hotel because they'll tag it while we're talking. And we're going to need it." He paused. "Tomorrow night when we leave here for the Villa d'Este we have to leave here packed. Three days is long enough to stay in one spot."

"Where are we going?"

"I'm still thinking about that."

Mara frowned. "And this moving, we're going to have to keep it up until . . . something happens, with Schrade."

"We'll know more after we talk to Lu."

CHAPTER 26

SPLIT, CROATIA

The old woman was seventy-four years old. Her left leg had been blown off just above the knee in a little town called Lijeska in Bosnia Herzegovina, late in the war. She was taken away to Gorazde to a grim little hospital, where she waited out the remainder of the fighting. Her husband had been killed early in the conflict, one daughter had disappeared, and the second daughter had fled to Split, where she had friends.

When the fighting had been over several months, her daughter from Split had shown up at the hospital one day and taken her away to live with her. Now, thanks to French doctors, she had had three operations on her leg and had been fitted with a prosthesis that she kept under her bed in her daughter's house.

The mother and daughter waited patiently in line at the ferry quay. The daughter was very thin, with lifeless, dusty brown hair that hung to her shoulders. Her face portrayed no expression at all, and she seemed resigned to waiting, in silence. The old woman was sitting in a battery-powered wheelchair, also provided by French relief programs. Unfortunately the batteries had lost their charge a week earlier, and the daughter had not had the time—she worked the night shift in a small laundry—to have the battery recharged. During the last week the daughter had had to push the wheelchair wherever the old woman needed to go. The old woman was carrying a small suitcase in her lap. Her daughter was taking her to visit her sister, who had fled the former Yugoslavia well before the war and now lived in London.

The ferry left very early in the morning, passing through the Split channel and heading out into the open Adriatic. The old woman sat at the observation rail near the front of the ferry, staring across the hazy sea toward Italy. After an hour she opened her suitcase and took out a plastic bag from which she withdrew a loaf of bread, a large wedge of cheese, and a bundle of little green onions. The two women proceeded to eat, watching the blue gray coast of Italy grow larger in the approaching distance.

When the ferry arrived at Pescara, the two women disembarked and took a taxi to the Stazione Centrale, where they boarded a train for Rome. A bus would have been much quicker, but the wheelchair presented a problem. In silence they watched out the window of their compartment as the train wound across the middle of Italy from sea to sea, from the Adriatic to the Tyrrhenian.

The train finally pulled into the Stazione Termini near the center of Rome late in the afternoon. Tired now, the two women took another taxi to the Leonardo da Vinci International Airport. After half an hour of waiting in lines the daughter finally purchased two budget tickets to London. But the flight didn't leave for two hours. They settled down in one of the terminals. Again the plastic bag came out of the old suitcase, and the rest of the bread and cheese and onions were consumed as the two women watched the milling crowds with the weary but fascinated eyes of two provincials waiting on the brink of the twenty-first century.

When it came time for their departure, the old woman was told that she would have to be taken out of her personal wheelchair and put into one of the airline's wheelchairs to be boarded. She panicked. That wheelchair was the only way she could move. The French doctors had given it to her. It was hers to keep. She could not leave her wheelchair, no, under no circumstances could she leave it. Where would she get another one in England? The French doctors . . .

She was assured that her wheelchair would be folded up and put in the cargo bins in the belly of the plane, and she would be able to return to it in London. To placate her, they let her watch them put a tag on the chair that said it belonged to her and put it on the conveyor belt that would take it to the luggage carts that would carry it to the plane.

She boarded first, was installed in the first row in the cabin—there were no first-class seats on this economy flight—and her daughter showed her out the window how the little electric carts were loading the baggage into the plane. Strangest of luck, they even saw her very own wheelchair itself being loaded into the plane. The old woman settled back restlessly, leaned forward several times to check the progress of the loading, and, finally, resigned herself to having to trust the blind promises of absolute strangers.

There was a thunderstorm on the flight to London. Twice the passengers all gasped in unison as the plane dropped suddenly into the rainy darkness. The old woman and her daughter grasped each other's hands in the dim cabin gloom, staring

unblinkingly at the flight attendants, who had strapped themselves into their tiny seats against the back wall of the cockpit.

The Alitalia flight finally landed at London Heathrow, the
last flight from Italy for the night. The daughter followed
meekly as the old woman was wheeled off the plane and was
put on one of the courtesy trams. Together they rode swiftly
through the concourse, the tram beeping to part the crowds as
they sped past the fluorescent-lighted gift shops, through the
invisible but distinct odors of the quick-food eateries, past the
lounges and the pubs and the gateway waiting areas filled with
bleary-eyed travelers.

The tram waited until their wheelchair arrived on the
conveyor, and the old woman was helped into it and her
daughter pushed her along the way to the customs stations.
Their papers were examined, and they were questioned. Two
customs officers came out of a back room and told the daughter, who spoke a modest amount of heavily accented English,
that they would have to ask her mother to sit in the waiting
area for a few moments while they examined her wheelchair.

Once again she was helped into one of the chairs to one
side in the waiting area. She watched as the two customs officers examined her wheelchair in detail, using an odd kind of
metal rod to tap-tap-tap on every inch of the tubular steel
frame. They pulled off the cushions and put them through the
X-ray machines. They unscrewed the black plastic armrests,
looked at them, and put them back again.

They tested the wheelchair's motor. Why wouldn't it
work?

The daughter explained.

The two officers unscrewed the battery from its brackets
and took it off the wheelchair. They told the daughter they

were sorry, but they would have to keep the battery. Her eyes grew large, and the old woman began to protest.

Please, please understand, the officer said. Electrical batteries were lined with lead and could not be X-rayed to check for explosives. To make sure there was nothing in it, they would have to dismantle it, which would ruin it. The old woman began to tell them that the French doctor had given it to her. She said she would not be able to get around, couldn't shop, couldn't go to the market without her wheelchair. She waved her arms, protesting vociferously to her daughter.

The daughter tried to placate her, but she began to wail. The English were ruining her French wheelchair. Finally one of the officers left and returned with a piece of paper that he called a voucher, a check for the approximate amount of the cost of a new battery. They were sorry, but this would have to do. It would be quite easy to get a new battery in the morning.

The daughter comforted the old woman and helped her back into her French wheelchair. The customs officers put the battery on a cart and took it away to be dismantled.

The old woman was finally able to lie down on a lumpy, swaybacked bed in a dowdy flat on the outer edges of Basildon on London's east side. She was asleep in moments. Her daughter made a telephone call.

At two o'clock the old woman was awakened. Her daughter told her that the people had come for the package.

The old woman pulled herself up on one elbow and looked at the young woman with wiry red hair who was standing at the foot of the bed.

"We'll just have a look, ma'am," the girl said.

The old woman said something to her daughter. The daughter looked at the redheaded girl.

"She wants her money first."

The redheaded girl smiled and took a small bundle out of her purse. She gave it to the old woman. The old woman gave it to her daughter, who unwrapped it and counted the money. The daughter nodded, said it was the right amount, and then gave it back to the old woman. The old woman eyed the redheaded girl, put the money in her lap, and raised her dress on one side, exposing the stump of her leg.

The girl sat on the edge of the bed and pulled an elastic stocking off the leg. A cotton sock covered the stump. The girl removed the sock, revealing a packet attached to the stump by wide bands of a flesh-colored adhesive. The packet was the same diameter as the stump and molded to appear to be the end part of it. It added about ten centimeters to the length of the stump.

The girl began undoing the adhesive and in just a few moments removed the packet, which was wrapped in heavy plastic. The material in the packet was dense, doughy.

"Thank you very much," the redheaded girl said.

The old woman nodded and lay back on the lumpy bed, looking at the girl with uncaring eyes, clutching the bundle of bank notes to her stomach.

The redheaded girl took the packet and left.

CHAPTER 27

Mara walked up one of the narrow streets that led into the village, its steep grade pulling at the muscles in the backs of her legs. She wore a light sweater thrown over her shoulders, for it was still early enough in the morning that the air had a lingering sense of dampness to it. She carried one of her large sketchpads and a packet of pencils. The sun had not yet cleared the low eastern ranges, and the shadows in the small serpentine streets were still tinged with purple. She met only an occasional solitary figure, though the shop owners in some of the lanes were beginning to stir, their subdued morning voices punctuated by the sharp rattle of an iron grille rolling up to open the front of a shop.

She made several more turns, entering an even narrower lane, and loosened the button at the neck of her sweater. Even in the cool of the morning she was growing warm from the effort of walking on the continuous incline. She came to the walled grounds of a private estate and soon to its double-winged wrought-iron gates, which were locked. To one side was another iron gate, a pedestrian entry. She turned the latch and went through, closing it behind her.

Following a winding cinder path, she continued under old cypresses and linden trees to a small chapel on a promontory overlooking the lakes. In front of the chapel facing the lake was a stone courtyard flanked by hedges and terra-cotta urns filled with bright, orange red geraniums.

On a stone bench to one side of the chapel door a man was waiting, his legs crossed at the knee, a thermos sitting next to him with two coffee cups.

As she approached him he stood, but she gave him no opening to make a gesture of greeting before she sat down.

He hesitated only slightly, as if deciding not to say anything, and sat down again beside her.

Mara leaned her sketchpad against the bench, poured herself a cup of coffee, and picked up the cup. She looked at him.

"You're a son of a bitch," she said.

Bill Howard's face was heavy with the strain of the past week. He looked tired. She had no idea how much trouble it had taken him to get here, and she didn't care.

"How did you manage to leave him?" he asked

"He had to go down to Como. I told him I'd walk up the hill to sketch."

"What's he doing in Como?"

"I don't know."

Howard's mouth tightened with impatience. "What's he *been* doing?"

"He's been on the Internet. He's got the information Alain Darras gave him. He's contacting somebody, or several somebodies, in that file."

"You *still* haven't looked at that?"

"How am I going to do that, Bill? He took it with him to

Vienna and Geneva. When he's here I can't just walk over and say, 'What's this?' "

"When he's asleep, for Christ's sake," Howard pressed. "When he goes to the bathroom . . . damn."

She gave him a withering look. "You've been watching too much television."

"Goddamn it," he said, looking away in anger, "that's what you were put in place to *do*. We need to know what names he got from Alain Darras. And why. You're supposed to find out what he's planning to do. You're supposed to find out if there's any way to pry the money out of those shelters. You're supposed to find the key to his trick, goddamn it."

"Ariana Kiriasis is dead."

Howard's head snapped around.

"He found her in her hotel suite in the Métropole in Geneva," Mara said, "around noon yesterday." She went on to tell Howard about her conversation with Strand the previous evening after he had returned from Geneva. She told him everything except what Strand was planning to do. She did not reveal his files in the Geneva bank vault, nor did she mention the four crime figures.

Howard leaned back against the front of the chapel, and both of them looked out to the lake. The heavy shoulders of the hills were still green black in the rising light, but they were only minutes away from attaining their full color. The opposite shoreline was skirted in a trail of fog that had not yet lifted. In the far distance the highest Alps were just catching the first light on their snow-powdered peaks.

"This has gotten out of hand, hasn't it, Bill?"

"No."

"Are you going to sit there and tell me that I'm not in any kind of danger?"

Howard's effort to remain calm was almost palpable. It took him a moment to get his frustration under control before he spoke.

"You knew it could get dicey," he said. "That's why you went through the training, to prepare you for just this kind of thing. You were well informed about the possibility of being drawn in near the heat. But you personally? No one's going to kill you, for God's sake."

"That's not the picture I'm getting from Harry."

" 'The picture you're getting from *Harry.*' That's good, Mara. Christ. He's messing with you. You've got to recognize when he's messing with you."

"You ever work undercover, Bill?"

He rolled his head to one side, knowing what was coming.

"You know a lot about it, then, don't you?"

"Look, I've run people undercover all my career," Howard fired back. "I've run *Harry Strand* undercover, for Christ's sake. Tell me you're experiencing something I haven't seen before, something all new. That's good, Mara. You're such an old hand at it."

"If FIS isn't going to get into this, then I'm getting out."

"You don't get out," Howard said.

Mara wheeled around and flung her coffee past Howard's head, splashing it against the stone wall of the chapel. It was a deliberate near miss, and they both knew it, but Howard hadn't flinched. They stared stiffly at each other. Mara's anger was so tightly wound within her that she knew Howard could feel it, too.

"What makes you think I don't see through you, Bill?

What is it about me that makes you think I would walk head-first into a firestorm just because you told me to do it?"

Howard didn't speak. Their faces were close enough to each other for her to see the quivering in the soft pouches beneath his eyes that told her he would like to slap her off the bench. But he didn't speak, and he didn't move. He didn't take his eyes off her.

"Shit." She stood up, leaving her empty cup on the bench beside the thermos. She crossed her arms and walked a few feet toward the promontory. She was beginning to despise Bill Howard. She was beginning to think she was on the wrong side of the moral situation here. She was beginning to think . . . a lot of things.

Howard pretended her flash of anger hadn't happened.

"You haven't been able to talk to him about the money," he said.

"I sent it to you, what he told me."

"But we need specifics. What are the names of the charities? Where are they established? Who administers them? How many are there?" Howard stood, too, and put his hands in his pockets. "Our legal people need *some*thing to get them started. This situation is developing very quickly, very quickly. If Strand dies with this information . . . Christ."

"Why the hell don't you just pick him up?"

"That was answered in Briefing Mara 101. You were supposed to be our response to that answer. You were supposed to be the solution."

She turned around. "Bad faith, Bill. That's what that training was, that's what this exercise is. You misrepresented Harry Strand to me. You didn't tell me his wife had been *murdered*."

"We didn't know that."

"But you suspected . . . in your damned black heart you knew it because you knew Schrade had discovered the embezzlement. You should have gone to Harry, you should have told him."

"You don't know what the shit you're talking about, Mara."

"I know you misrepresented this operation to me. You misrepresented the threat to me. You misrepresented the risk to me."

Howard stood with his feet planted firmly, his shoulders slumped, his depressing brown suit beginning to show its unimaginative hue as the sun was just now touching the crest of the dark hills on the opposite shoreline. He ignored her remarks.

"At the very least," he said, "you could goddamn well find out what he plans to *do.*"

"You know the man—how easy do you think it's going to be to get him to give that up?"

"Who the hell ever said anything about easy? Just *get* it."

They faced each other. Silence.

"Maybe things have changed, Mara," he said. Still he hadn't moved. "Tell me plainly what you want to tell me. What do you mean 'if FIS doesn't get into this'?"

They stared at each other.

"If Harry Strand is killed, I'm going to blow the whistle on this whole thing."

He looked at her and shook his head slowly, his mouth forming a faint, sour smile as though he pitied her predictable and disappointing performance.

"God . . . damn." He snorted. Now he moved, taking a

few steps to one side. "You know what? I'm going to tell you something. Four of us were involved in signing off on your training. We met almost every day to compare notes on the progress you were making. Almost every day. When it came time to say you were ready to roll, I was the only dissenting voice. I was overruled by the other three members of the task force." He paused and shook his head again. "I told them . . . I told them this is what you'd do. I told them you were not a professional, that you would fuck it up in the end. I said, 'The woman won't be able to stick it out if it gets scary.' I knew you didn't have it in you."

"Pat yourself on the back, Bill," Mara said, "then tighten your ass, because if you think you know me so well that you think I won't follow through with my threat, you're going to soil your pants when I do it."

"Let me give you something to think about," Howard said, moving again, going the other way, arms folded and head down as he gave some thought to what he was about to say.

"You may be right, up to a point, about our bad faith. We didn't tell you absolutely everything. For instance, here's a fact we didn't tell you about Harry Strand: He's a dead man." He squared around on her. "There's nothing we can do about it."

Mara frowned at him.

"No, that's the honest to God truth," Howard insisted. "Harry's right about the FIS having no influence over Wolf Schrade anymore. In fact, not only do we not have any influence, but Schrade knows that the assassination of one of our former officers would be the ultimate insult to us, one which we would suffer in total silence. He knows. That's just one more reason why he'll see to it that it happens. What's more, Mara, Harry knows this better than anyone."

"So you're just going to stand by and watch it happen, with your arms folded, shaking your head at the shame of it all, trying to snatch the money out of Harry's hands before he stops breathing?"

"He could come to us for help, Mara. Did you ever think of that?"

"He did."

"No, he didn't. He came to us and threatened us."

"You don't buckle to threats."

"No, we can't."

"But you'll 'help' him. If he comes in . . . with the money . . . you'll cut a deal."

"Yes. That's right."

She looked at him. "I'll bet it'll be a sweet deal, too."

Howard didn't respond.

"What if . . ." She stopped.

Howard tilted his head, waiting.

Mara turned away from him and faced the lake. Howard hesitated and then walked over and stood close to her. In front of them the morning was rising against the Alps. Below, the waterfront was beginning to come alive. An early sailor moved out from the harbor, well before the morning breeze, his boat chugging slowly under its own power toward the open lake. No doubt there was a romantic at the helm, yearning to be the first to raise his canvas, to sail quietly, and alone, into the rising sun.

"Let me be clear about something," Howard said. "We're not going to give you a hell of a lot more time. They're weighing their options again back in Washington. My guess is that they're going to be coming after the money. *It's over half a billion dollars,* Mara."

She shot him a look. They had never told her how much money was involved. She just knew it was millions.

"They'll probably prosecute," Howard went on. "Do you understand what I'm saying here? For that kind of money they'll go for his throat. As for his 'insurance,' we'll argue that he's an intelligence officer, for God's sake. He knows how to doctor films, tapes, recordings, documents. That's his trade. No, he's not a righteous man, he's a rogue officer, a greedy rogue officer just like dozens of others who have shamed U.S. intelligence agencies over the years. He's got to be taken down. We'll crucify him. By the time it's over, if he doesn't go to prison, he won't have any kind of a life left at all. For that kind of money—I don't care how he's invested it to protect it—for that kind of money we'll pull every string we can get our hands on."

Howard turned to her. "Mara, get him to give it up. Look, he miscalculated. Hell, it happens. Convince him to walk away from it. He can keep the interest he's made during the past four years. It's a goddamn lot of money."

Howard's voice changed. When he spoke again it was flat, clinical.

"If Schrade's people don't kill him, our people are going to make him wish they had. Convince him to give it up. He'll get a life out of it."

It was late afternoon, and they were still several hours away from leaving for the Villa d'Este to meet Lu. They un-dressed and lay on the bed, their balcony doors open to the afternoon warmth and the faint sounds of the harbor. Every-thing in Bellagio was languorous. Here even the black kites that scavenged the shoreline and the alpine swifts that skimmed the surface of the lake for insects did so in an un-hurried manner that was at once graceful and serene. Strand could smell the water and the cypresses on the hillsides and the faint sweetness of Mara's body.

The idyllic setting was in sharp contrast with the reality of their situation and with the roiling emotions that he struggled to temper. There were treacherous days ahead, and a sense of ever shortening time wore and tore at him like a debilitating fever. He had been enormously relieved that Mara had chosen to stay with him, not only because it confirmed how much they meant to each other, but also because he could not in good conscience have allowed her to go. If she had fled, she would have lost even the dubious protection he was able to give her. Schrade would have found her in days.

In watching her come to this decision, Strand observed yet another dimension of her personality. She was not simply giving up, yielding to his wishes. Rather, her decision was the result of her sensible assessment of her circumstances. She must have reasoned that her best chances of survival lay in trusting him, even though, despite her personal feelings about him, she must have found it difficult to do. It was this calm common sense that he had been slow to appreciate. In most people a talent for balanced judgment was not an attribute that advertised itself. But in an attractive woman it was even less readily apparent. Beauty was too often an unintended di-version, a distraction that seduced one's attention away from the essential qualities of the person who possessed it.

"Where is Wolfram Schrade?" she asked, breaking the si-lence. Her head was on his shoulder, her long legs running alongside his, her breasts against his side.

"What do you mean?" He was surprised at the sudden question.

"Do you really think he doesn't know where we are, or does he know and he's just . . . waiting?"

Strand decided not to finesse the answer. "I've asked myself that a thousand times," he said. "I honestly think that when we left Rome, the way we left Rome, we slipped his surveillance. And I think we're still clean."

"What makes you believe that?"

"I told you last night, if he knew where we were, I think he would've let me know that he knew. Just like he did in Rome with the videotape."

"You don't think Ariana's death was a similar notice?"

"Maybe you're right . . . but I don't think so. If that's the way he's working and if he knows where we are . . . why are you still alive?"

Mara said nothing, but she grew very still, her breathing momentarily interrupted. He felt a pang of conscience. God, that must have sounded raw to her, grim evidence that his theory was sound. In truth, he was talking with far greater confidence than he was feeling. A pall of anxiety lay upon him that acquired a denser gravity with each shocking death.

As for the FIS surveillance, he was even less sure about having eluded that than he was of having escaped Schrade's private intelligence operatives. He knew what the FIS was capable of doing, but he also knew that excellence in surveillance required planning, and planning took time. He was beginning to have doubts about how long they had been on to him. If they had known about the embezzlement scheme before Ariana went to them—if they had had time to actually target him for a surveillance operation—it would be a serious challenge to hide from them.

So in part his argument was specious, an attempt to portray a confidence in their safety that he really did not feel. Moreover, he guessed that she knew what he was doing. He thought he felt her body gradually tense against him.

"What about you?" she asked.

"He wants to kill me. And maybe he will—eventually. But not until he gets his money. I'm okay until he either gets it or knows once and for all that he can't get it."

A murmur of voices wafted in from the balcony, a man's laughter, a shout, and then they subsided and were gone. He could almost feel her thinking. And he could feel the impulse to speak rising from her abdomen against his hip, rising until it emerged on her breath, almost apologetically.

"Why don't you just give him the money, Harry?"

He had anticipated that question since the moment in her bedroom in Rome when he had told her what he had done. She had waited far longer to ask it than he had guessed.

"I can't," he said.

Pause. "What do you mean?"

"It's not possible."

"You've spent it?"

"No. I haven't spent any of it."

She was silent, but again he could sense the turmoil of her disquiet. She didn't move. There was no caressing hand, no tucking into him to be closer than close. She didn't ask him what he meant, and she didn't press him further on his questionable assessment of the danger they were in. It was an unexpected and unusual display of restraint, and Strand found himself as curious about the reasons for her reticence as about her ability to deal with her fear in a manner that seemed extraordinarily controlled. The extremity of their circumstances was becoming a foil for revealing the complexity of Mara's personality. It was yet another shifting, unstable element in a kaleidoscope of shadows.

Then her hand, which had been resting on his chest, moved around to his side, and she drew herself closer. They lay that way for a long time, floating away in their own thoughts as the afternoon grew balmy. After a while he stopped trying to feel her thinking, concentrating instead on the hum of the cicadas in the cypresses. Her breathing grew steady and shallow as she slipped into sleep. Against his intentions, he too grew light-headed and drifted away.

CHAPTER 28

CÔTE d'AZUR, NEAR ST. RAPHAËL

The little village had no name, which was even better, but not something he had planned. It was not really a village, either, but some houses clustered in the hills above the Mediterranean. The only reason anyone knew about it at all, and many did, the reason the narrow little road was paved rather than dusty gravel like most of the others in the area, was because of the old villa that had been turned into a wonderful restaurant. The restaurant was open only in the evenings, and even though the prices were high—the haute monde expected it— the place was a losing proposition if one looked strictly at the bookkeeping aspect of it. Yet it flourished, in an understated, very elegant sort of way.

The large, bearish figure of Charles Rousset was easily recognizable on the terrace. He was dressed in a linen suit that was designed and tailored with the Cap d'Antibes in mind, and he was here because he knew the owner of the villa. The owner was very wealthy—of vague resources—and a longtime friend of Rousset's, who therefore enjoyed special privileges, such as having the shady terrace all to himself, overlooking the beryl waters of the Corniche de l'Estérel, for this special meet-

THE COLOUR OF NIGHT

ing. He and his companion were not disturbed. They came and went unobserved.

Mr. Skerlic was uneasy. The elegant surroundings did not impress him as much as they pissed him off. Rousset knew the little Serb thought him irritating and a poser, but he didn't care. He knew also, however, that Skerlic appreciated Rousset's discretion and was beginning to be comfortable with that, which was important. Rousset doubted that Skerlic would ever be able to find his way here again because the countryman who drove him here from St. Raphaël, and whom Skerlic considered the village idiot, had never stopped talking so that Skerlic could concentrate on where he was being taken.

"So, how are we doing?" Rousset asked when they were finally settled on the terrace. "Progress, I hope." They sat alone at a sturdy wrought-iron table with a granite top, enjoying a view that normally cost handsomely to appreciate. Skerlic was not dressed for the Côte d'Azur. He was perspiring a little.

"Everything I need is in London," he said, and he tried the wine, which, Rousset noted, he seemed to dislike. It was expensive and superb, but it might as well have been a local beer as far as Skerlic was concerned.

"Oh, very good."

"You said you had some ideas about 'how,' " the Serb said. "Before I go any further I want to hear what you have to say along those lines."

"Yes." Rousset grew serious and sat forward in his chair. He took off his straw hat and set it on the table and looked at Skerlic. He stroked his mustache and goatee. "I've given it a lot of thought," he added, prefacing his presentation with an expression of calculation. "Wolfram Schrade is a passionate collector of certain kinds of art," he began. "Passionate. He pursues it. He is a collector of the first order and readily spends a great deal of money for what he wants. And he wants an awful lot. It happens that I know his habits in this regard, in an intimate way. I know his desires. I know his unfulfilled desires, things he wants but cannot have, for one reason or another. I know the honey to which this bee will come."

Rousset liked the metaphor. Skerlic didn't even seem to notice. Talking to this wicked little beast was like talking to a cultural tabula rasa. It was astonishing the things of which Skerlic was unaware. Like the wild boy of Avignon, raised by wolves, he knew nothing but the tricks of survival.

"An art dealer in London sells work to Schrade very often, more often than any other dealer with whom Schrade trades," Rousset continued. "He happens to specialize in the kinds of things that appeal to Schrade, and he is deeply knowledgeable about them. Schrade trusts him. Schrade will listen to him if he comes up with something unusual, just because this man has found it."

Warming to his subject, he leaned forward and took a pear from the bowl of fruit beside the wine bottle. He took a small knife from the bowl and began cutting the pear into thick slices.

"I propose to offer this particular dealer—he has one of those names that is all surnames, Carrington Hartwell Knight, and that's the name of his business: Carrington, Hartwell, and Knight." Rousset smiled. "Clever, really. Anyway, I'm going to offer Carrington a piece of art that I know Schrade wants very much. Now, Carrington is . . . well, a peculiar fellow in his own right. He deals in only the very best, even the best of the best. He's odd and has been doing business the same way for thirty-five years. This man has an office in Mayfair. The same address for twenty-two years. He dresses very modern, but his business is carried on in a very traditional way. Electric locks, but no videocameras. A security guard who acts as doorman and decoration. But his wealthy clients can come and go quietly, without attracting attention, unobserved."

Rousset had cut the pear into a dozen slices, which now lay on the table fanned out in a semicircle. He took one and put it in his mouth and chewed it, savoring its ripe freshness. Then he ate another, and as he chewed he looked at Skerlic and nodded at the slices. "Please, have one. They're delicious." The Serb didn't respond at all. Rousset swallowed the bite he was chewing and went on.

"He lives above, in the same building, and he keeps a fortune in fine art there. This is known, but it is not well known. Those who need to know, do know. This man is a rather flamboyant personality, but he is a very subtle dealer.

"Most important, among his numerous personal peculiarities is his attachment to this residence of twenty-two years. He will do business nowhere else. If you want to sell him something, you go there. If you want to buy something from him, you go there. That is all there is to it. There are no exceptions. The delivery boy goes. The art-loving mogul goes. The wealthiest men in the world go to this address in Mayfair."

Rousset paused, then smiled softly again.

"Well, as it happens, this is an interesting analogy," he said. "This odd man, this good fellow, is very much like death itself. To him, all men are the same, and he treats them all the same. Eventually all men come to him, prince and pauper alike. He is indiscriminate."

Skerlic did not appreciate the comparison. He pushed away the wine. He had no idea why rich people came here so they could sweat on this hot fucking coast. He took off his sport coat, which was so pedestrian as to be almost indescribable. In fact, Skerlic himself was so unremarkable as to be almost indescribable.

Rousset reached for another slice of pear.

"That's the best place to kill Wolf Schrade."

"Can you get to the point?"

Rousset took a small bite of the slice of pear and chewed it a moment, thinking. Then he went on.

"Schrade will go to Carrington's to inspect the art." He paused to emphasize the self-evident point. "We ourselves can prescribe the exact place," he said, "and the exact time and thereby minimize the chance of any missteps."

Skerlic studied Rousset. "What about this art dealer?"

"What about him?"

"You have a plan to avoid blowing up his ass in the process?"

"I have a plan, yes. It will require some very precise timing." He looked at Skerlic's scorned wine. "Would you like something else?"

"What's the plan?"

"The plan? That is the plan, my part of it. I can make sure of the delivery. You have to make sure of the execution . . . so to speak."

Skerlic used the side of his thumb to wipe the perspiration that had gathered on his brow like beads of warm dew. Then he reached for the bowl of fruit and broke off the long stem of an apple, stripped off the leaf, and rolled the stem between his fingers to remove the rough spots. Then he put the twig into his ear and began probing, tilting his head slightly.

"This is a sure thing?" Skerlic asked. "I can count on this, as of this moment?"

"Oh, most assuredly. I've only to negotiate the time. It might take as long as five days, however. I'll try to hurry it up."

"I see."

"Does it suit you? This plan?"

Skerlic pulled something from his ear, looked at it, then flicked it toward the Mediterranean.

"I don't mind it," he said. "It could work."

"It's ingenious. Very precise."

"If we do this, there's no going back. I have to concentrate on the delivery mechanism, and once I get started on it I don't want you to come to me and tell me you have changed your mind or that it can't be done. What we settle here, we settle for good. The decision is final."

"Well, that is good with me," Rousset observed cautiously, "but, well, this is a bit rigid, isn't it? I thought one had to be flexible . . . you know, the value of resilience."

"You are not so sure, then, after all."

"You need to be certain that your 'delivery mechanism' is realistic, given the context of the situation. You understand? I mean, for instance, what if you've thought of a brilliant way to work the explosive into, say, a pat of butter . . . but butter has no place in an art dealer's shop. Do you see?"

Skerlic looked as if the comment were so stupid that he didn't know how to respond to it. But he summoned his patience. The money was so extraordinarily good.

"We will have to meet again, Mr. Rousset, to work out the logistics of the situation. Then you can see for yourself."

"One more thing," Rousset added. "About the explosive device. I want to stress that Mr. Schrade is the target. I don't want . . . there mustn't be . . . a conflagration, an apocalyptic event. You understand?"

Skerlic regarded him with a blank expression. Rousset suspected him of playing dumb.

"The term required is 'surgical,' Mr. Skerlic. I don't want anyone to die except Mr. Schrade. That's a *firm* stipulation. I am making the opportunity very accommodating to you. *You* have to make sure the explosion is precise. Do you understand?" Rousset asked.

"I understand what you want," Skerlic said.

"That's good, wonderful." Pause. "Can you do it?"

"Yes, I can do it. Okay?"

"Very good. That's important to me. Precision. One can't just throw a stick of dynamite into the room."

CHAPTER 29

Strand and Mara drove out of Bellagio at dusk and headed along the east side of the western leg of the lake, driving nearly halfway to Como on one of the most torturous stretches of mountainside roadway in Europe before Strand turned off the pavement outside a small unnamed village perched above the lake. He maneuvered the rental car down a long drive shrouded by the heavy canopies of ancient trees, to the front of a large, gloomy villa resting on the breast of the shore.

Just as Strand cut the headlights and the motor, a figure appeared at the edge of the cinder courtyard, walking toward them. They followed the figure through a portico into an inner courtyard and out again to a curving path that took them in a slow decline to a boathouse on the water.

Inside the boathouse a thirty-foot Abbate speedboat sat in its slip, black, low against the water, glistening in the dim light. Its nose faced out to the lake.

Within moments the boat's powerful engines came to life, and they eased slowly out of the boathouse, away from the tree-draped shore and into the open lake. It was a clear night, the darkness crazed by the blue light of the stars and the amber lights of the villas along the dark swells of the hilly shoreline.

The Abbate made the ride down the lake an easy endeavor. Soon its engine cut back to a mutter, and the boat slipped toward the Villa d'Este's boat docks and its floating swimming pool that jutted out into the lake, ringed with lights. Other boats were arriving and departing along the docks, and they had to wait a moment before the long Abbate was able to pull up to the dock and let them off onto the cork-covered landing.

The brightly lighted sixteenth-century Villa d'Este loomed up into the trees above them. They made their way through the formal gardens, passing the hotel's guests coming and going through the lamp-lighted evening, some in swimsuits and some in formal dress. There were also lakeside residents who, in the summer evenings, boated in from their villas up and down Como's shores to dine at the hotel's famous restaurant, a gathering place for those who had acquired a large measure of international wealth and fame.

Strand left Mara in the center of the elegant main hall surrounded by white marble columns and grained ceilings and announced at the reception desk that he was here to meet Lu Kee. Then he turned and watched Mara, who wore a simple black dress. No jewelry—the flight from Rome had not allowed time for that.

"Mr. H.S.?"

Strand turned to see a slim young Chinese whom he guessed to be in his late twenties, dressed in a fine white linen summer suit, looking at him.

"Yes," Strand said.

"Mr. Lu is waiting."

❖   ❖   ❖

Lu's suite was lavish, with a stunning view of the shores of Como. The old man appeared immediately, dressed nattily in ecru linen trousers, a black linen shirt open at the neck, and a mocha silk jacket with a black kerchief in its breast pocket. He wore light beige espadrilles. His hair was white and very thick. His manner was relaxed and gracious.

Strand introduced himself and then introduced Mara Song. The old man made no pretense of taking her beauty for granted. He bowed to her first and then reached out and took her hand. He did not shake it but simply held it a moment, smiling at her appreciatively. Then he said:

"Very lovely." He turned to Strand. "Well, it seems that I have a lot to learn from you, Mr. Strand. So why don't we begin."

Lu's English was fluent and was spoken with a soft British accent. They walked to a sitting area of several sofas and armchairs, and Lu gestured for them to sit down.

"I was rather startled to receive your message," Lu smiled, sitting down after them. "My people became very excited." He raised both opened hands, wagging them lazily in imitation of his flustered subordinates. Without further niceties, he held out his hands to Strand, palms up in a gesture of invitation. "Please proceed."

"For many years I was an American intelligence officer living and operating out of Europe," Strand began. He quickly moved into a detailed but concise recounting of what he knew about Lu's international criminal involvements and then focused on the spectacular series of failures that he had mentioned earlier to Mara. Lu listened closely, his elbows resting on the arms of his chair, the fingers of his hands interlaced, the tips of his thumbs touching and resting against his chest.

"In short," Strand concluded, "this betrayal set back your European operations by about three years."

Lu dropped his head forward slightly and looked at Strand as though over the top of a pair of glasses.

"All of this was brought about by one man," Strand added, "with whom you are still working. He no longer works for the Americans, but I'm reasonably sure he's now informing for the German Bundeskriminalamt and the French Sous-Direction des Affaires Criminelles."

"You are going to tell me his name?" he said.

"Yes."

"And give me documented proof of this betrayal?"

"Yes."

Lu nodded pensively. He thought a moment, looking at a place on the floor in front of him. Then he looked at Strand.

"Mr. Strand, I find it difficult to believe that someone who works for me could cause me that much damage and I would not yet have found him out. This is very disturbing."

"He doesn't work *for* you, Mr. Lu. He works *with* you."

Lu's head came up. "I see," he said, and his eyes regarded Strand differently now, as though he was reexamining everything Strand had said in a different light. Strand watched as the old man reordered his thoughts, recalibrated his mental instruments to adjust for a new kind of measurement and calculation.

"This will be interesting," Lu said finally. "But first, before we hear this name"—he cut his eyes at Mara and allowed a polite, almost timid, smile—"which you have so cleverly withheld up to now"—he came back to Strand, his smile fading—"what wicked thing do you want done in return for this . . . kindness?"

The note of irony in Lu's voice was not lost on Strand. He did not want to respond too readily. He did not know what influenced him in this decision to be hesitant, but he gave in to it. He looked at Lu and tried to appear as guileless and straightforward as possible.

"I will be satisfied having done this," he said.

Lu raised his eyebrows. He studied Strand. And then slowly, very slowly, a smile returned to his face.

"Oh, Mr. Strand," he said, "that is a most revealing answer."

Strand waited.

Now Lu adjusted his position in his chair, turning his body slightly toward Strand. He was still smiling, as though he were enjoying the game they were playing and he had just anticipated Strand's next move.

"You must believe that you know me very well, Mr. Strand. Having brought this . . . valuable . . . information to me, you have already envisioned my response to it. You are satisfied that this response will suit you. And that is enough."

He paused.

"Certainly, my reaction to such a traitorous association cannot be a happy one for the person under discussion. He may come to a bad end. Which will suit you. So. You betray him out of revenge. Or from a desire to be rid of a burden. Or from a deep-seated hatred. Or, perhaps, greed: you would benefit financially from his demise."

He waited with an anticipatory expression, his eyes on Strand.

Strand met his gaze candidly. "I have many faults, Mr. Lu, but greed is not one of them. It doesn't suit me." And he left it at that.

Lu Kee continued looking at Strand for a moment and then stood up and walked a few steps to the tall windows that provided the fairy-tale view of Lake Como. He clasped his hands behind his back and looked out. He said nothing.

Strand glanced at Mara whose attention was fixed on Lu.

Lu turned around.

"Okay," he said. "Who is it?"

"Wolfram Schrade."

Lu's face did not change. Then he tucked up his chin and turned down the corners on his mouth dismissively and shook his head.

"Well," he said finally, "that's very interesting." Unhurriedly he sat down in his chair. He sat forward, closer to the coffee table between him and Strand. "Let me see what you have."

Strand opened his briefcase and laid out on the table all the material he had prepared for Lu. The old man listened to him, looked at the photographs, read the documents, and let Strand explain to him what was on the recordings and the CD. Lu asked a few questions, which Strand answered while the old man listened carefully, pensively.

When Lu finally sat back in his chair, he shook his head again, thinking. He smiled at Mara as if to say he hadn't forgotten she was there. He said to her:

"Do you know anything about the Song dynasty, Ms. Song?"

"A little . . ."

"Can you give me a single important fact about it?"

Mara, surprised by his question, smiled, embarrassed. She hesitated. "The Song were the first to provide a recipe for gunpowder, I believe, and they were the inventors of the true cannon used in warfare."

Lu grinned, surprised and delighted. "Good. Can you name any famous historical figures of the Song?"

"I remember a famous outsider: Chinggis Khan, who over-ran most of the northern Song dynasty in 1215." She paused. "Mmmm . . . I remember Su Shih, known as Su Dongpo, per-haps the greatest essayist and poet in the Chinese tradition. There is Zhu Xi, the dynasty's greatest educator, who established many academies and revived Confucianism."

Lu laughed softly, nodding. "Good, good, very good. Okay, one last question: What was the Song's greatest accomplish-ment?"

Mara did not hesitate. "In my opinion . . ." She looked at him and tilted her head for permission.

Lu nodded.

"Its greatest accomplishment is that in its three-hundred-and-nineteen-year history, there was not a single tyrant among the Song emperors."

Lu continued to beam at her. Then, slowly, he lifted his hands just above his head and applauded silently while inclining his head in a bow to her.

"I applaud your knowledge . . . and your sound good judg-ment. And I applaud your father's intelligence and sense of re-sponsibility."

"Thank you, Mr. Lu, but it was my mother, not my father, who taught me the history of the Song. As well as the history of Abraham and his people."

"Then I commend your mother even more. Her daughter has honored her." He looked at Strand. "Would either of you care for something to drink? I would like a few more words with you, and then you may go."

They both declined Lu's offer for refreshment, and the old man went on.

"Mr. Strand, the information you have brought me poses

an interesting situation for me. You see, it seems that Wolfram Schrade has been committing adultery with both the wife . . . and the husband."

Strand frowned.

Lu put his short legs out in front of him and crossed them at the ankles. Even in his casual clothes, he was elegant. Strand expected that he still went to Savile Row for everything he wore. He was clearly an Anglophile at heart. Lu went on.

"It must have been shortly after you retired from the service that Mr. Schrade came to me with a proposition. He said that he had had the good fortune to make the acquaintance of an intelligence officer in the United States Foreign Intelligence Service. He said that this man, who was very well placed, would be retiring in a few years, and he was interested in building a retirement fund for himself."

Strand's pulse quickened.

"I began making payments. Strategic bits of intelligence began coming my way. I benefited greatly from this. I gathered from a few remarks by Mr. Schrade that I was not the only one receiving helpful . . . information. Nor was I the only one whose enterprises profited, literally, from this arrangement."

"You're still paying?"

"No." He smiled. "That's why I can tell you. Mr. Schrade stopped it about eighteen months ago. He said something had happened: he could no longer trust his source."

"So, you received information from this man, via Schrade, for about three and a half years."

"About three years." He looked at Strand steadily, trying to see the effect of this surprising information. Strand gave him no satisfaction.

Strand said, "Why have you told me this?"

"Because, sir, I am afraid my reaction to the news you have brought me will not be suitable to you."

Strand's stomach tightened.

"I am skeptical that I can . . . affect . . . Wolfram Schrade's life in any way."

Strand's disappointment was sudden and complete.

Lu nodded at the coffee table and the papers and photographs, the audiotape and CD.

"I trust your information, Mr. Strand. I believe it. If circumstances were different, I would act upon it as you anticipated that I would. But . . . they are as they are. As matters stand now, I can do nothing to help you. I really cannot say any more than that." He shrugged. "I thought, in some way, for you to know about the man in the Foreign Intelligence Service would be of benefit to you. I thought you might be able to use it somehow."

It was the end of the conversation.

"I understand," Strand said. He sat forward in his chair and began gathering up his documents.

"Please," Lu said. "I assume these are not originals."

"No, they're not. If anything changes, I hope you'll use the same lines of communication to get in touch with me."

"I will do that."

They all stood, and Lu offered his hand to Strand.

"I like you, Mr. Strand. I am sorry."

The Abbate moved slowly away from the glitter at the dock of the Villa d'Este. Lanterns dotted the night along the shore as they eased past the floating pool, away from the voices and sounds of careless opulence. The craft picked up speed gradually, meandering up the western side of the lake rather than the middle as they had done before. Then the speed increased a bit, and then more, and then more until the Abbate was screaming northward, skirting the shoreline, the lights of the villas flickering through the trees.

The speed of the craft seemed almost wild for a boat. Suddenly the engines throttled down, the steering lights went off, and the captain turned out into the open water, the engines almost silent, purring. They drifted.

On the bow and stern two men stood and surveyed the lake behind them with binoculars.

"You suspect Lu?" Mara asked.

"Anyone. We have to be clean when we get to the car."

The Abbate, its lights still out, continued to purr as it steered eastward. The two men exchanged words in Italian with the captain, who cut the engine altogether and turned the rudder so that the boat faced roughly back toward the Villa d'Este. The boat sat heavily in the water, hardly rocking. Now all the noises were small and distant, and the boat became one with the water. Far in the distance they could hear other boats, but they remained far away.

Again the men exchanged words, their voices sounding dull and mysterious against the water. The engine started again, and slowly the Abbate turned toward the east and headed across the lake, toward the villa where they had first emerged from the boathouse.

Strand sat with Mara tucked in against him. She was silent, but he knew her mind was not quiet. As they moved across the water he looked toward the Villa d'Este. It glowed on the shore far in the distance, a sad and magical place.

CHAPTER 30

LAKE COMO

Strand and Mara got into their car and started up the drive to the main road, the gravel crunching underneath the tires as the headlights illuminated the close walls of pines crowding either side.

The route south along the lake was even more dangerous in the darkness. They rode most of the way in silence, both of them staring out from behind the flailing headlights that raked wildly across the constantly changing view: a wall of rock, a short stretch crowded with woods, darkness as the lights swung out over the lake on a sharp turn, the surprise appearance of a hamlet of a few houses, suddenly another rock wall, another gap of darkness on an outside turn, a short stretch of woods.

Finally Mara said, "There's a *spy* inside the FIS? Isn't that what he said, Harry?"

"Yeah, that's what he was saying."

"God, what are you going to do? Don't you have to tell somebody?"

"I'm going to think about it."

She turned and looked at him. "Do you think you know who it is?"

Strand hesitated. "Bill Howard."

"Why do you think it's him?"

"The timing was right. The opportunity was right. And I know damn well the money was right. Howard hasn't been happy with his career, and he's near the end of it. It was his chance to get even for all the disappointments. They must've come to some kind of agreement shortly after I retired. After Schrade discovered the embezzlement scheme and broke off with the FIS, Howard must've stayed with him, selling him FIS intelligence that Schrade then passed on to Lu. And others."

Secrets. They accumulated in men's lives like spiderwebs in lightless corners, one upon the other until they were festooned into a thick and dusty drapery that obscured the turns and, ultimately, hid the way entirely.

"You seem awfully sure of this. What if you're wrong?"

"I wouldn't have said it if I thought I was wrong."

Mara was quiet again.

"I was surprised by Lu's response," Strand said. "Obviously Schrade's providing him with intelligence from other sources now—the Germans, the French maybe. And it must be paying off in big numbers. Whatever Schrade's past betrayal must have cost Lu, he's willing to overlook it for now."

"For now?"

"Schrade hurt him very badly. The old man won't forget that. Lu takes the long view. For now Schrade is useful, but he won't be always. No one ever is. Time passes. Things change. Revenge is a demon with a long memory and abundant patience. Schrade's day will come."

Strand glanced at Mara. She was facing forward, lost in her own thoughts, embracing herself as if she were chilled. Her face and the front of her black dress were washed in a pale jade light from the dials on the dashboard.

He couldn't imagine what she must be thinking.

After a few moments she said, "What are we going to do now, Harry?"

"We're going to contact Mario Obando. We'll set that in motion, and then keep on going."

"Where?"

"France, I think."

When they entered the outskirts of Como, Strand turned away from the center and stayed on the outer edges of the city. Mara said nothing as he drove deeper into the working-class neighborhoods, where the silk factories that supplied the famous designers of Milan toiled in a gray sameness. Occasionally he glanced at her. She had leaned her head against the window and was watching the city grow darker and grimmer.

Their room was on the second floor of a begrimed hotel overlooking a dreary piazza. It was filthy.

Strand took off his suit coat and quickly set up his computer on the gritty surface of a small, wobbly table. Getting down on his knees at the baseboard, he took off the cover of the telephone jack. With a pair of wire strippers he kept in his laptop case, he bared a small section of several colored wires and connected color-coded alligator clips to them. The clips led to a hand-size black box that plugged into his laptop. Within half a minute the laptop was up and

231

running. He logged on to the Internet and began the laborious approach to Mario Obando.

Mara pushed aside the lace curtains stiff with dirt, opened the window, and looked down at the café across the street. There was a scattering of tables and a few people drinking, talking quietly, and smoking in the jaundiced light. She turned around one of the two chairs and sat down, lifting the skirt of her dress and putting it in her lap. She gathered her hair and twisted it and piled it on her head, holding it with one hand to let air to the back of her neck. She leaned on the windowsill and looked down at the café.

When the computer began beeping Strand looked at his watch. It had been only forty minutes since the last communication. Immediately the words began scrolling up on the screen.

Where do you want to meet and when?

Strand typed:

As soon as possible. Europe.

Five minutes passed. Ten. Then words began reappearing on the screen again.

France. Will give you time and place
four hours from now.

✳   ✳   ✳

They bypassed Milan and headed west, soon crossing the Ticino River into the flat landscape of the rice fields that dominated the terrain from Novara to beyond Vercelli. The highway was straight and unremarkable. A low half-moon illumined the cloudless night and the highway, its monotony interrupted only occasionally by the dark clumps of villages or solitary farmhouses.

At Santhia the highway turned northward slightly and began a slow ascent out of the plain. The foothills of the Alps began to punch up out of the landscape, and in the near distance he caught the dim silhouette of the Alps themselves, dark and hulking, blacker than the half-moon night.

At Aosta they stopped for gasoline and two cups of strong coffee and pushed on. The air had grown cool and crisp. In half an hour they entered the Mont Blanc tunnel at Entreves, and when they emerged eleven and a half kilometers later they were in France. Strand turned away from the ski resort of Chamonix and started toward Geneva, half an hour away.

"It's almost time to check in with Obando," Strand said. "We might as well stop for the night."

At the first small road sign advertising lodging, Strand pulled off the main highway and followed a narrow alpine road for a few kilometers into the foothills. They came to a collection of kitschy little "Swiss chalets." Strand roused the concierge, paid an outrageous price, and got the keys to one of the cottages near the edge of the compound.

Mara insisted on bathing, and while she did Strand tapped into the telephone wires again and logged on to one of the French service providers. Within twenty minutes he had an answer from Obando: Paris. The day after tomorrow. Café Martineau, Blvd. des Capucines. 4:00 P.M.

It was not until they were ready to collapse in bed and Mara threw back the curtains in the bedroom that they understood why they had paid so much for the room. The little cottage was perched on a small promontory above a shallow valley. In the wan light they could see the downward-sloping hillside falling toward a broad alpine meadow and a valley that ran to the left and right. On the opposite side of the valley the land rose up quickly, then fell back and rose again. A mountain range emerged, and almost immediately the gargantuan dark mass of Mont Blanc towered above them in the night sky like another planet that had drifted too close and was rising toward them over the edge of the earth.

"My God," Mara said. "Look at that." She stood at the window a moment and then came back and crawled onto the bed. She sat there, embracing her knees, staring at the mountain, a dark behemoth anchored against the cobalt night. At the top, the frail light of the half-moon reflected off the legendary snowy crown.

As Strand lay on the bed beside Mara, looking at her naked silhouette highlighted by the moon glow between her and the mountain, it was not the mountain's beauty that he saw, but its menace. In the light of day the massive landmark's brooding gray body was a stunning foil for its majestic, snowy cap. But now, by the beguiling light of the half-moon, Strand sensed something altogether different. Now he felt an ominous pull, something like a beckoning, and the mountain became the physical presence of the Father of Darkness.

He reached out and touched Mara's bare skin. She turned and looked at him, but he could not see her eyes. Then, without speaking, she lay down beside him, her face turned toward the mountain.

CHAPTER 31

BERLIN, SCHWANENWERDER

The villa sat on the island like a stone outcropping emerging from the deep emerald of the German woods. A nineteenth-century residence in the neoclassical style, it was made of gray limestone. From its high elevation it commanded a panoramic view that took in the exclusive villa district of Nikolassee on the opposite shore as well as the broad waist of the Havel River. In the distance the river narrowed as it neared Pichels-dorf, the densely wooded banks closing in and gradually swallowing the water in a throat of green.

A Mercedes motored slowly across the bridge from the mainland and proceeded to make its way along the narrow drive to the gates below the villa. Here the Mercedes stopped while Bill Howard presented his identification at the gatehouse, then continued up a serpentine lane to a motor court in front of the villa.

The view from here was stunning in the summer sunshine, but Howard did not bother to stop and look at it. He was welcomed by a young man dressed in a business suit and carrying a clipboard who led him into the villa and up several flights of wide stone stairways whose steps were so shallow that the climb was hardly noticeable at all. At every turn Howard caught sight of the Havel from windows that perfectly framed different views and brought him to the top of the stairs and an anteroom.

If he had known what he was looking at, which he did not, he would have found himself surrounded by works of art by some of the finest French, German, and Flemish artists of the late Gothic period: van Eyck, da Fabriano, Bosch, Fouquet, and Wiertz. Careful thought had gone into the manner in which the works were displayed, their sequence, their visual impact, their dominant color schemes, subtleties completely lost on Bill Howard. In fact, he had mused privately that the overall effect of this curious collection of paintings was rather grim and severe. He also assumed that the art in the anteroom had cost a fortune. This time he was closer to the mark.

Though several doorways exited off this anteroom, he was ushered toward the one straight in front of him. The room he entered was perhaps four times as long as its width and terminated at the far end with a huge window that once again provided a spectacular view of the heavily bowered Havel. More paintings and drawings hung along the high walls of the room, and down the center of its entire length was a series of waist-high lime wood cabinets with narrow horizontal shelves that contained scores of leather-bound portfolio boxes. Each box had gilt stamping on its face and spine, identifying a specific collection of drawings. One portfolio lay open on the slanted top of each cabinet, its contents ready for perusal. Farther toward the windows was a sitting area, and beyond that, just in front of the window itself, was a massive antique desk at which sat Wolfram Schrade.

Howard had been here many times before, and he knew

the routine. Schrade was busy at his desk, so Howard did not speak to him but took a seat in one of the armchairs in the sitting area. Schrade ignored him. Howard let his eyes wander around the room. The place was a goddamn museum. It gave him the creeps.

After about ten minutes Howard heard some shuffling at the desk. He looked around to see Schrade standing, taking off his reading glasses as he came round the side of his desk. He was buttoning a double-breasted navy blue suit, which he wore over a tailor-made white shirt with medium-width crimson stripes. No tie. He was tall and lean, his face angular with a straight nose. His hair was thick, the color of sun-bleached flax.

"What about the woman?" Schrade asked, as if they were picking up a conversation of a few minutes earlier. His accent was not subtle, but neither was it distracting. His voice was unconcerned, his manner relaxed. Howard had never seen him otherwise.

Howard explained that the hunch he had had about her from the beginning was proving to be right. He thought she had become sympathetic with Strand. He no longer considered her reliable.

"Have you told this to Payton?"

"No."

"I see. Well, I am finished fucking with them, then," Schrade said. "I want her put away."

There it was, Schrade's peculiar phrase that Howard always found so jarring. In his own experience the phrase was veterinary, and he wondered how Schrade had come by it in English. Howard, who did not consider himself squeamish, found it a particularly brutal expression.

He whistled softly under his breath. "You're talking about an FIS agent now. That's going to get a response . . ."

"They are not going to respond to anything," Schrade said with indifferent disdain. "Strand knows the thing is finished. Besides that, she obviously means something to him. Where are they?"

"Bellagio. My tech people said this morning the signal hadn't moved. . . ."

"Oh, your 'tech people.'" Despite his languid manner, Schrade was expert at conveying frigid sarcasm. He was standing in front of Howard in his distinctive manner, erect posture, though not rigid, with his unoccupied arms hanging straight down by his sides. He appeared to be very comfortable that way, feeling no need to cross his arms or put his hands in his pockets or otherwise engage himself in some type of self-conscious body language that most other people could hardly avoid.

"You ought to reconsider what you're doing to Strand," Howard said.

"No."

"No, shit. I'm going to tell you, you kill that woman he's with now, and he'll never let go of a single goddamn Deutschmark of what he took from you. Hell, he's got to think he can save her life by giving it up." He paused. "Most people, Wolf, respond to pressure when they have some reason to. You take away a man's reason to live—"

"Nothing is going to save her life."

"Fine. Whatever." Howard glared at him. Vicious fucker. Howard always walked a narrow line with Schrade. He had to exhibit a certain amount of brazen aggression. Schrade understood and appreciated that. But he couldn't push it too far.

Fear and fortune were closely aligned in Schrade's orbit. Right now the guy was as serene as a nun. Howard couldn't figure it out. He always looked as though he were wearing new clothes. His shirts and suits were unfailingly fresh and crisp. His damn pants were never even wrinkled at the crotch after he had been sitting behind his desk all day. Did he have some kind of fetish about putting on new clothes every day? That would be weird, even for Schrade.

"I have to tell you . . ." Howard started out carefully; he didn't want to provoke the goose until he'd put one more golden egg in his own Liechtenstein account, but he had to conduct some business here. "The FIS is pretty damn hot about the way you handled the Houston hit. That was over the top."

"The man responsible for that fiasco has been put away," Schrade said. "That was regrettable."

"They're trying to contain the investigation, but, Jesus . . ." Howard hesitated, again wanting to be careful. "It's thrown us into an emergency situation back in the States."

Schrade's clear eyes picked up the faintest hint of a pale glacial blue from his navy suit.

"Yes, I imagine it has. You realize, of course, I don't give a damn. If the FIS had not been so feeble, this would not be happening. You understand, if it had not been for the very"— here his voice allowed a tonal change of nearly imperceptible difference—"*thinnest margin* of chance, I would never have known about this disaster in the first place. If Dennis Clymer had not made the mistake of using the same tactics to embezzle for one of Lodato's clients, if that client's accountant hadn't bungled the plan, if I hadn't agreed to launder a certain sum for Lodato, and if *my* accountants hadn't seen a curious familiar pattern in Clymer's Lodato scheme . . ." Schrade paused and approached to the very edge of Howard's chair. "If all of that had not happened, none of this would have been discovered at all."

Howard was looking up at him, a perspective he didn't like. These had become Schrade's mantras: the thinnest margin, the stupidity of the FIS, his terrible financial losses.

"That, Mr. Howard, is too many ifs," Schrade concluded. "The FIS should not have sent you with this little complaint." Pause. "Considering our relationship, you should not have even passed it on to me."

"I still have to work for them."

"That is no concern of mine." Schrade turned away and walked to the nearest of the lime wood cabinets, where he began idly paging through the drawings displayed there.

Finally he was doing something with his hands, Howard thought.

"It ought to be," Howard said. "You're making a fortune off the intelligence I'm still passing along to you."

"No, it ought not to be," Schrade disagreed with a mild finality, still studying the drawings. "My only concern regarding you is whether you are useful to me." He looked at Howard. "Everyone is always 'making a fortune' off of something or someone. I hear that hyperbole all the time."

The starched young man who had escorted Howard into the house entered the room. Schrade turned his head.

"The two representatives from Christie's and the woman from the Galerie Séverine are here."

Schrade gave a dismissive nod to the young man, then looked back at Howard.

"I want to see you again tomorrow. Same time. There are

some additional concerns on this issue. Aside from that, I have several client requests for intelligence. Very important. Lucrative. For both of us."

Howard began to get up out of the overstuffed armchair, but Schrade was through and had already turned toward his desk, unfolding his reading glasses as he went. By the time Howard had gained his feet, Schrade was sitting in his chair, already absorbed in his reading. Howard paused and looked at him a moment. The impertinent son of a bitch. Never said hello, never said good-bye. Those were transitional niceties of human communication that, over the years, Schrade had gradually abridged, and then completely eliminated, from his dealings with people. At the exact moment he was through with you, you ceased to exist. The man had no soul; he really had no need for one. The only time Howard had ever seen him behave with anything resembling an actual human emotion was when he encountered new pieces of art that he wanted to buy. Only then, in the presence of oil and canvas, when his pale, pellucid eyes fell on sheets of paper scrabbled and scratched with pen or pencil or chalk, did he appear to want to interact with something outside his own intellect. Such an absence of human needs was frightening.

Howard turned and walked out of the long museum of Schrade's mind, accompanied only by the sound of his own footsteps and a sour taste in his mouth.

CHAPTER 32

ANTIBES, FRENCH RIVIERA

Charles Rousset cautiously made his way along the stone path that for a few meters clung to the curve of the precipice above the Cap d'Antibes like a swallow's nest glued to a cliff before it gained solid ground again and ascended toward the old house. He paused a moment and turned to enjoy the view of the Mediterranean. There was a haze over the water today, an impressionist's interpretation. How could one help but be romantic about such a stunning perspective?

Reluctantly he turned back again to the path, which, like the house to which it led, was in a state of neglect, not from indifference, but from a lack of the proper funds to maintain it. At one time it had been a pristine piece of real estate. In the 1950s it had been purchased by a London banker who lavished a great deal of his fortune on it. In those days the footpath had been lined with brilliant bowers of saffron sepiara and the blindingly bright cerise bracts of the bougainvillea. Exotic flowering cycas marked each turning of the way, and pastel perennials of every color snuggled in among the crevices and corners.

Those were former days. The banker and his wife were

long since gone, as were the flowers and the blooming trees. Common cactus and weeds had now overgrown the edges of the footpath, and unforgiving rocks gouged up through the flat stones to make walking a precarious effort.

The house was large but could not be called a proper villa. It was sited handsomely above the blue-and-green bay, and though its stucco was cracked and stained, though the stones of its courtyard and terrace were loosened and hosted sprays of dried native grass, and though some of its terra-cotta roof tiles were slipping and askew, the style and beauty of the house still gave Rousset a thrill as he rounded the last turn in the footpath and came upon it, silhouetted against the ageless Mediterranean.

Edith Vernon was the only child of the banker who had built the house, and when her father died, in much reduced circumstances, the house was the only thing he left her. Though it was debt free, Edie, who was now in her early sixties, was hard-pressed to keep it up and pay the proper taxes. When her father was in his financial heyday, Edie was in hers as well. An art student in her university years, she fully partook of Rome's *dolce vita*, and her beauty opened what few doors her father's money would not. Though the memories of those days remained, they were all that remained, and Edie had scratched out a poor living during the last two decades, trying to live off her art. Like many artists, she was a better copier of others' work than she was a creator of her own. At this she was brilliant.

"Good God!" she exclaimed. She was standing solidly in the kitchen doorway, her hands on her hips, looking out at him. "Claude?"

"Indeed."

She gaped at him.

"And"—he tipped his head forward in a polite bow, smiling—"Charles Rousset."

"My Gahhhhd! I don't *believe* it!"

"Oh, do, Edie. You really must." Corsier laughed as Edie stepped outside and embraced him. She was wearing a long peasant skirt and a cotton blouse hanging loose to distract from the fact that she no longer had much of a definable waist. Her long honey-colored hair was shot through with gray, and she had it pulled back and piled in a rough chignon. She was thicker now, but even so there was something undeniably sensual about her that made hugging her a pleasure. She smelled of lavender and the musk of oil paints.

She stepped back and put the palm of one hand against his goatee. "This becomes you, dear. Very fetching." He smiled. "The Schieles," she said. "I did these . . . these darlings for you?"

"Indeed."

"Oh, Claude!" She clapped her hands together. *"Quelle intrigue!"*

They had tea on the frumpy terrace and brought each other up-to-date on the gossipy parts of their lives in the intervening five years since they had seen each other. Corsier, of course, left out almost everything, and he supposed that Edie did also.

"Well," she said finally, setting aside the tiny wicker tea table and putting her hands on her knees, which were spread apart underneath the long skirt, "let's get down to business."

She got up and returned in a moment with two drawing boards with butcher's paper covering the image on each. She propped them against the legs of the tea table and went out again, returning instantly with two thin easels, which she set up with their backs to the house so that the pictures would catch the light from the sea. She put a board on each easel and removed the papers. Then she stepped back beside Corsier so that they could look at the pictures together.

Corsier smiled. He was thrilled.

"You like them, then," she said.

"They're perfect." He got up from his chair and went over to look at each of them more closely. "Edie," he said, his face glued to the pictures, "these are exquisite."

"Schiele," she said, "the man's a freak. Insane." She came up beside Corsier. "You were very precise, as usual, Claude. I confess, I wasn't always sure I was doing the right thing. You said to have her arms thus, as in this picture. Her legs thus. Her hair thus, but opposite, as in that picture. Her eyes looking directly at you, but vacant."

"I left the color to you."

"I knew them. I remember the originals that I've seen as though I had owned them myself."

She pondered her drawings. "Despite your assurances to the contrary, I had a friend in Berlin send me some old drawing paper he had salvaged from a prewar paper mill near Munich. It'll pass close examination, but not a chemical analysis. The pencil wasn't a problem. Getting the right shade on the watercolor was a little tough."

Corsier stepped back again from the two pictures, each of them roughly twenty-one inches high by fourteen inches wide. Both of them were unabashed exhibitionist portrayals of the female body, the distinctive mark of Egon Schiele. The first was a pencil drawing of a nude woman standing, looking at herself in the mirror. The back of the woman was nearest the viewer, and then another, smaller image of the woman was seen from the front, behind the first image, this one being the actual reflection. She was vamping for the artist, wearing only black stockings pulled up to midthigh. She had short bobbed hair and thin, horizontal eyes encircled by smoky shading.

The second picture was of two nude young women, done in pencil and watercolor. The two women lounged on a dark amethyst drapery. One of them had bobbed hair, the other long raven tresses. Their pubic hair was as jet as their ringlets, and there were pale splotches of lilac on their cheeks and nipples. Both of them were looking at the artist, one of them from the corners of her eyes as though she were just in the beginning movements of looking away.

"Nineteen eleven," Corsier said. "I wanted them to precede his harsh, ectomorphic later works. You've done a wonderful job, Edie, of making them sensual while hinting at the meanness that was soon to dominate his style."

"Those rather prissy mouths," Edie said. "I liked doing them. I liked doing the eyes." She paused. "But the pelvis on this one"—she pointed to one of the figures—"was difficult . . . maddening. Those explicit crotches on them were *problems.*" She laughed at herself.

"Good use of the amethyst"—Corsier came in closer to the dual portrait—"on the drapery, darker at the edges. Mmmmmm. I like this horizontal line above her stomach." He perused the drawings for a long time.

Finally he straightened up. *"Les splendides!"*

Edie laughed. "God," she said, "I can't believe I've done this." She stepped back and leaned on a stone pillar. "I don't know what's going on here, Claude," she said, her voice a little more sober, "but frankly, at my age prison doesn't suit me at all."

Corsier turned around, his bearish body seeming even more formidable in his dapper linen suit. He came over to her and leaned on the other side of the pillar.

"Edie, just take the money, my dear, and forget about the drawings. They are destined to be short-lived."

"Really."

"Indeed."

"What does that mean?"

"Destroyed."

"Bloody hell," she said.

They were both looking at the pictures.

"I suppose one is better off ignorant," she mused.

"As far as you are concerned, I love Schiele, couldn't afford them, and you made copies for me."

"Except there are no originals."

"Even better. You imagined Schiele for me."

They said nothing for a moment.

"I need the money," she said by way of explanation.

"You didn't have to say that."

"Odd," she said. "I'm proud of them. Just as Schiele must have been proud when he did something like them."

"You should be proud," Corsier said. "No one would ever know the difference. Ever. Schiele would receive kudos for them. Why should it be any different for you?"

"Because they came from my cold intellect, Claude, not from a searing fire in my gut." She sighed. "Credit where credit's due. Come on. Let's box them up for you."

CHAPTER 33

PARIS

The hotel was small. Another of Strand's former haunts, it opened onto one of the narrow streets in the Quatre Septembre, a short walk from the Boulevard des Capucines.

"Harry." Mara's voice intruded into his dream, the illogical plot of which quickly began rearranging itself to accommodate her. "Harry." The second time she spoke, the sound was different, and he began to wake. "Harry, wake up."

When he finally roused himself, he saw her standing at the foot of the bed. She reached down and put a hand on his foot. Behind her the windows of their room were open, the curtains pulled aside to let in the morning sounds of the neighborhood. He could see the sun on the buildings across the street.

Whenever it was possible, Strand always insisted on a room that faced out from the front of the hotel. It was usually louder, but the sound of the city provided him with an aural orientation to the rhythm of his surroundings. Because he had traveled a great deal, crossing time zones as readily as he crossed the street, and because he more often than not stayed in small, neighborhood hotels, such a synchronization helped

him adjust his body clock to the meter of his new environment. Mara didn't seem to mind.

"Is something wrong?" The attitude of her body told him
there was.

"I just didn't want you to sleep late. I'm nervous about
this afternoon."

"Go ahead and bathe," he said. "I'll order some coffee."

"I've already bathed," she said. "You slept right through
it. The coffee's on its way."

Something *was* wrong.

"I'm sorry," she said. "I just couldn't sleep. I want to talk
to you."

"Okay," he said. He threw back the covers. "Let me
shower, wake up." He got out of bed, stiff from the long hours
behind the steering wheel. His stomach was already tightening
as he went into the bathroom to bathe.

"Harry," she said, leaning forward, her elbows on her
thighs, her hands twisting a napkin. "This . . . is very hard for
me. It's almost *impossible* for me . . ."

Mara was sitting on a small sofa, he was in an armchair.
The coffee and pastries were between them. He had managed
to quickly choke down a croissant while she was making some
preliminary remarks, circling around to get to the real substance of her concern, which was not, he soon realized, the afternoon meeting with Obando.

This was going to be bad. Stepping back mentally, he
tried to gain some distance from the condensed emotion that
was building between them. He watched himself in the armchair; it was as if he already knew the change of direction that
the plot was going to take, as if he could see what the duped

protagonist—Strand himself—could not yet see, that his world was about to encounter yet another upheaval.

"Harry, I love you," she blurted suddenly, "I didn't know that I was going to. I . . . it . . . Harry, it caught me off guard. How the *hell* could I have known?"

She looked at him, her head tilted to one side in suppliance. There were no tears, but he was jarred by the expression in her eyes. In a breath he understood that her emotion came from those arid places that waited inside everyone, places to which one was driven unwillingly, when there were no alternatives, and from which no one returned without a translation of the heart.

"God," he heard himself say. "Not Schrade."

"No, Harry, no, no. It's Bill Howard. I work for the FIS. Harry, I didn't know you. How could I have known that this would happen to me . . . to us?"

She stopped, searching for the right words, unable to find them.

"Harry . . . my God, you've got to understand how this is killing me, how wrong it all has become for me. Everything changed after I got to know you, everything turned inside out, it all went wrong."

When she stopped again, beside herself with inexpressible feelings, she quickly turned away, and Strand had a few heartbeats in which to become aware of his own emotions. He was numb. How incredibly stupid he had been, how completely he had misread her. How wrong he had been about Romy's death. How irresponsible he had been about Meret. If he could be so thoroughly deceived in these matters, what other delusions lay behind him? What other failures of discernment lay ahead? He thought of how much he hated Bill

Howard for doing this. He thought of how much he loved Mara in spite of it.

He stood and walked around the coffee table and sat beside her on the sofa. He put his arms around her and pulled her to him as she bowed her face against his chest. He felt like a fool, but he was too old, and not fool enough, to believe that he should walk away from her. Christ, this was a savage business.

"Mara, listen to me," he said. "Listen to me. We've got to talk this out. We've got to figure out where we stand, how we feel, what we're going to do."

He felt her shudder, but he didn't think she was crying. Neither of them spoke. Outside, the Quatre Septembre had worked its way to midday.

Finally Mara pulled away from him, averting her face, and stood. "Let me wash up," she said, and walked out of the room.

He waited, stunned, listening to the running water. She could have been sent by Schrade, and he would have behaved the same way. He would have fallen in love with her anyway. It could have been tragic. That it hadn't been was no credit to him. It took his breath away.

When she returned, her eyes swollen and red—she had not allowed him to see even a single tear—she was still composing herself. She didn't come back to him on the sofa, but rather walked to the armchair where he had been sitting before and sat down. Holding a damp washcloth, she stared at it, kneading it as she gathered her thoughts. She was in control again and determined to stay that way.

"You know how it works," she said, finally looking up at him. "They recruit for something like this. I'm not FIS. In

Rome, after my husband died, we had a friend who worked at the American embassy. He and his wife were very kind to me. At a party at their house one night I met one of the FBI's legats. When he found out I had lived in Rome for so many years, he was very interested. I got to know him. One night I got a call from him. He asked if I was familiar with a certain part of the city. I was. He said he was looking for someone in that area, and would I mind riding along with him as a kind of neighborhood guide. We spent most of the afternoon together, and I know now, after some experience, that he was evaluating me.

"Little by little over the next six months, he exposed me to more and more of the FBI's responsibilities, the kinds of things they were involved in. Never anything really confidential, just overview stuff. All the while they were doing background checks on me.

"Anyway, a little surveillance situation here, a stakeout there . . . I liked it. I liked it a lot. And they liked what I did. After a year or so I became, essentially, the equivalent of a special support group member, a civilian used as support personnel in surveillance operations."

She sighed heavily, still recovering, catching her breath. She looked toward the windows, kneading the washcloth. Her eyes began to redden again, but she cleared her throat and looked directly at him.

"When the FIS initiated this operation, they created a profile of the kind of woman they wanted. They went to the FBI first because of their large SSG pool. Not being FBI agents, SSGs weren't in any of the computer files, wouldn't be picked up by the private international clearinghouses. That's why Darras didn't find me. They knew you'd check me out.

Everything else is true that you know about me. The screwed-up marriage. All of it. All of that was perfect background as far as they were concerned.

"They sent me through a crash course at the training center at Camp Peary, and when they thought I was ready they put me out there on a very long tether. They had a high respect for your counterintelligence abilities. For your sixth sense. The 'dangle' was a very cautious one. I showed up at the pool, then disappeared for a month. They were willing to take it very slowly, very carefully." She looked down at her coffee. "They wanted to make sure that the hook set when you took it."

Strand felt his face flush.

"I wasn't any good at it, Harry," she said. "They didn't want me to make any contact with them while we were getting to know each other. They were afraid of you. So I was just let go. On my own. I was completely separated from them, as if I'd never known them."

Again she sighed, a kind of jerky catch of breath.

"I didn't hear from them at all until you went to San Francisco. A guy named Richard Nathan was my handler as long as we stayed in the States. If the situation moved to Europe, as they expected it would, I would work with Bill Howard."

"So what were you supposed to do?"

"The money." She was trying to be dispassionate, trying to be succinct, professional. "I was supposed to find out how much, where it was. How you had taken care of it. Once they had some basic information they were confident they could move on it. Seize it. There was so much, they were willing to go to great lengths."

"What about me?"

"They just wanted the money."

Strand looked at her. Did she really believe that? Was she lying to him, or was she kidding herself? She must have seen something in his face.

"I know," she said. "Yeah, I did believe it. I had no reason not to. Of course, as I learned more as I got into it . . ." She let her voice trail off.

"So they've always known where we were?"

She nodded.

"Now, too?"

"No. Not now. I had a tag. A fountain pen I kept in my purse. I left it in the hotel in Bellagio. They don't even know that we crossed over the lake to see Lu. As far as I know, the pen's still in the hotel."

"Then they know what I'm doing."

"No. They don't know that, either. I've been holding out on them for a long time, Harry. There's so much I haven't told them. Almost everything. Howard's all over me now. I'm sure he knows what I'm doing. He's furious."

Strand tried to regain his balance, trying to factor in and absorb all the readjustments to the reality of his situation.

"What about the tape of Romy?" he asked suddenly, almost without thinking.

"No, Harry. I didn't know anything about that. I don't think they did, either, to tell you the truth."

"When did you last speak to Bill Howard?"

She told him everything about their conversation in Bellagio two days earlier.

"I don't believe him," Strand said when she was through. "You're right about him being suspicious of you. Howard's been around too long not to recognize a miscarriage. He knows you're not going to stay with it. He knows this conversation we're having right now is inevitable. He knew it before you did. And if he knew it, and if he was telling the truth about Washington going after me, he should have brought you in and had me picked up. But he hasn't done that." Strand looked toward the windows. "I don't think he's gone back to Washington with this. Something's wrong with this."

Mara cleared her throat. He watched her as she held the cool, damp washcloth to her eyes for a moment. His mind was flying over the possibilities. There was so much to think about, it made him queasy. It occurred to him—shot into his mind like a bright spark—that she might be lying. Just as quickly he decided that if she was, if all of this doubled back on him again, they could have him. If she wasn't who he thought she was, whatever was left was nothing he wanted. He could understand what she had done. God help him, it wasn't all that different from what had happened with Romy. If he had learned anything at all from her, it was that if he was ever going to redeem himself from the years of lies, he was going to have to learn how to forgive. It was really the only way. If he was going to manage to stagger toward something better than what he was now, he was going to have to do it with damaged people like himself who were also looking for a way out. If they wanted to climb out of the darkness, if they genuinely desired it, he would gladly extend a hand. No one would be required to have a clean conscience. That kind of hypocrisy was no longer good enough.

CHAPTER 34

She didn't understand, and he really couldn't have expected her to. As they talked into the afternoon, he watched her closely. Sometimes her eyes would slide away from him, slippery, lubricated by guilt. Deception was so insidiously destructive; and the first rule of survival for those who made it a profession was that you must never care about the people you deceived. It was the difference between dropping bombs on people from twenty thousand feet and going into their bedrooms at night and cutting their throats. The closer you were to them, the harder it was to live with what you did to them.

When you worked undercover, you had to learn not only how to wear a mask successfully, but also how to put a mask on whomever you were lying to. If they became real to you, if they became human, deserving of compassion or of any kind of consideration, you were ruined. So you had to lie to yourself in order to live with the lies you were living. It got to be tricky, and not everyone was made to live in that kind of labyrinth. It took its toll on everyone, but some people were completely destroyed by it. If you wanted to endure, you had to learn how to keep your deceit from becoming a vortex and sucking you down into its darkness.

The strangest part of it was that the damage that was done, the hurt that was inflicted, all happened within. Within the mind. Within the psyche. And, most grievous of all, within the heart.

"Are you nervous?" she asked.

Mara was standing at the windows, looking down at the street. She was sipping a glass of water, shifting her weight from one hip to the other.

They had gone out for a late lunch at a café not far from the Bibliothèque Nationale and had returned to the hotel arm in arm among the crowds on the sidewalks.

"Not nervous," he said. "Anxious."

He was sitting on the edge of the armchair, examining the documents he was about to put into his briefcase.

"That's a distinction lost on me."

"Obando is a far different man from Lu," Strand said. "I'll have to play him differently. I'm just trying to work it out."

"*I'm* nervous about it," she said.

Strand slouched back in the chair and put his hands together, elbows on the fat upholstered arms of the chair.

"I'd like you to do something for me."

She hesitated a moment, then turned to him, her back against the edge of the window frame.

"I can't imagine how you could possibly justify my presence at that meeting," she said.

"No, it's not that."

She waited.

❖   ❖   ❖

Strand approached the Café Martineau from the opposite side of the Boulevard des Capucines. He walked past it several times, glancing across to assess its location, to get a feel for the kind of place it was. In the short time he watched the café, he saw no one enter or leave. Its name was written on the front window in gold letters against a black band, and a black border with gold trim framed the window itself. A black awning with a dark beige trim protected the entrance. It was a very smart address.

Finally, moving with the pedestrian flow, he crossed to the other side and approached the café from the direction of the Boulevard de la Madeleine. He saw nothing amiss. He opened the front door and went in.

"Yes, sir. May I help you?"

A young woman met him immediately, speaking in English. But her accent was not French. She had short dark hair that implied a businesslike mind underneath it. She wore a mandarin red suit and a black, open-necked blouse tucked in firmly to a thin waist. She was not the hostess, but she was working; it was no mistake that she allowed Strand to see the automatic pistol tucked slightly to one side into the waistband of her short skirt.

"I have an appointment with Mr. Obando."

"Okay," she said. "This is the right place." Two men came up behind her. "Put the briefcase down there," she said, indicating a small marble-topped bistro table next to the reception podium.

Strand did as he was told and raised his arms as the two men checked him for whatever they didn't want to find. Strand took the opportunity to glance farther into the café, empty except for a few more of Obando's assistants scattered here and there. He thought he saw Obando halfway back, sitting alone at a table. Apparently the Colombian had bought the exclusive use of the café for a few hours.

After the men were finished the woman approached him again with an electronic wand with a digital readout and began going over him. Up and down his sides, between his legs— strictly efficient, nothing cute—over his back. She asked him to take off his suit coat. He did, and she went through the arms, through the pockets, over the seams.

"You're very thorough," he said.

"Yes," she said. The two men were busy doing the same thing to the briefcase.

When she was finished, she held his suit coat for him and helped him put it on. She smiled.

"Thank you for being so patient," she said. As if on cue, the two men finished with his briefcase. "Please"—she tilted her head for him to follow her—"Mr. Obando is waiting."

It was odd to see the café empty. The staff was nowhere in sight. Only Obando's silent bodyguards stood politely against the walls of the long, narrow establishment. Each of them looked as if he could have been the café's owner or a very subtle maître d'.

As Strand and the woman approached Obando's table, she stopped and Strand stepped past her. Obando had been watching him approach, but he did not get up or offer his hand. He motioned to the only other seat at the table. Strand sat down.

"Harry Strand," he said, introducing himself.

Obando nodded. "Harry Strand," he repeated. His hair was a natural light caramel, parted on the left, wavy, beautifully barbered. He was forty-two years old but looked younger. "Well, Harry, lay it all out for me."

Strand had heard recordings of Mario Obando that had been made in Tel Aviv while he was doing business with an Israeli drug dealer. The dealer was the one who sounded like the foreigner. Obando sounded as though he'd been born and raised in the San Fernando Valley. You could have spent an evening with him and never known he was Colombian. Obando's files recorded how he had hated to be pegged by his accent. He hated the stereotype. So he had worked on it. It had disappeared.

So Strand laid it all out for him. From his briefcase he withdrew all the material he had copied from the Geneva bank vault on the two Obando operations—an arms smuggling conduit and a European drug distribution channel—that had been closed down because of Schrade's information. He placed a packet of photographs on the table along with a CD, several cassettes, and fifty-seven pages of documentation. He laid them out like a fortune-teller with a deck of cards. He outlined the two failed operations, told him how they had failed, then told him why they had failed.

Obando kept his eyes on Strand. At his elbow was an empty glass with a last sip of a grenadine *sirop à l'eau* remaining in the bottom, an ashtray with one butt in it, an opened pack of cigarettes, and a gold Dunhill lighter.

As he had done with Lu, Strand told Obando who he was and gave him some background on his career in the intelligence profession. By the time he had finished, Obando understood that Strand knew things about his organization that Obando had thought were secure. He also understood that the information inside the material on the table before him would confirm everything that Strand had said. As with Lu, when Strand finally stopped he had not yet given Obando the name of the traitor who had been responsible for creating so much havoc for Obando's enterprises.

Obando stared at him. His face portrayed no tics, no indication of what he was thinking or how he was feeling about what he had heard. He was simply a businessman listening to business talk.

He took his eyes off Strand and raised a hand. One of his men came over.

"Harry, would you like something to drink?"

He ordered Scotch and ice.

"I'll have the same damn thing," Obando said. As the man turned away Obando picked up the cigarettes, offered one to Strand. Strand shook his head, and Obando lighted one for himself and sat back.

"You know, I'm *still* pissed about that business in Amsterdam," he said, blowing smoke to one side. "On that one deal, that one deal alone, I lost—" He stopped himself. "I took a *very* big hit. Not just the money. It destroyed an arms conduit that I'd invested more than a year putting together." He paused. "You worked on that?"

"I was in charge of the intelligence on it. I was the one who finally took it to the Netherlands' Centrale Recherche Informatiedienst and worked with them until they closed you down."

Obando grinned and shook his head. "Goddamn."

The two drinks appeared. Obando raised his, said, "Prosit," and took a sip.

He pointed at the material Strand had put on the table. "This is my man, huh?"

"That's right."

Obando looked at Strand, saying nothing. Strand's back

was to the light that came in through the front window. Being oblique, the light diminished quickly inside the café, so that Obando was softly illuminated, but the surrounding furnishings were quickly lost in a dusky haze. Here and there the edge of a picture frame or the corner of a gilt-framed mirror glinted from the shadows.

"Why?"

"I worked with this man a long time," Strand said. "There are personal reasons . . ."

"Like what?"

Strand waited a beat. "The reasons are personal," he said. "I won't discuss them with you."

Obando was very good at keeping his thoughts to himself; neither his body language nor his face gave a hint of what was going on in his mind.

While keeping his eyes on Strand, he drank from his Scotch and took a last drag on his cigarette before mashing it out in the ashtray. Strand noticed that although Obando was a stocky man, not heavy but thick chested, his hands were the hands of a thin man, with long, narrow fingers.

Obando finished putting out the cigarette and opened the manila envelope of photographs. He looked at them one at a time. After he had finished looking at the last one, he reached for his cigarettes again. He lighted one.

"Wolfram Schrade," he said. He swallowed a mouthful of Scotch, then another. "Life is full of surprises," he said.

Strand said nothing.

"I didn't expect it to be him. Never would have."

"That's why I've provided so much documentation."

"You worked with him closely, then."

"I did."

"How long?"

"Almost a decade."

"That's fascinating." He studied Strand. "But that's over. You're out. And Schrade broke off with FIS . . ."

"Right."

"Okay. What about now? Anything else along those lines?"

"Probably."

Obando jerked his head. "Ah."

"I suspect he's working with either the British or the French now. Maybe even the Germans."

"You suspect."

"I no longer have the ability to get proof of that. But I'd bet money on it."

"Would you bet your life on it, Harry?"

Strand didn't hesitate. "There's nothing in this world that I'd bet my life on, Mr. Obando. Certainly not anything having to do with Wolfram Schrade."

Obando picked up the last photograph and looked at it again, considering it.

"This is a far from perfect world, Harry." Pause. "What if I told you this piece of shit lives a charmed life?"

"Which means," Strand said, "that Wolf Schrade is making himself so valuable to you at this time that, for now, you are obliged to overlook his past injuries."

"That's pretty good, Harry. Bottom line: I can't be your dark angel."

"Can you expand on that a little?" Strand asked.

Obando shook his head slowly. "It's personal," he said soberly and without a hint of irony. "I won't discuss it with you."

CHAPTER 35

It was a fine piece of one-upmanship, the sort of thing that was second nature to men in Mario Obando's line of work. The world of legitimate business provided a warm and fertile environment for male strutting, but it was nothing compared to the showy displays of male ego that occurred in the crime world. In Obando's milieu, no available opportunity to squirt a few cc's of testosterone in your adversary's direction was allowed to pass. For the younger ones, like Obando, a smart mouth was the extra edge that made them feel just that much more clever than their opponents. They had to be smart, look smart, and sound smart. And, of course, they had to be brutal.

"Even if I can't help you directly,"-Obando went on, having made his point, "perhaps I can give you something in return. I know you didn't do this from the impulse of a warm heart, Harry, but regardless, you did me a favor."

He dropped his eyes to Strand's glass. The Scotch was gone, the ice was melting. He looked toward one of his men and held up two fingers and then flicked his wrist downward, pointing at the empty glasses. He dropped his arm and looked again at Strand. He put out his cigarette, turned slightly to one side, and crossed one leg over the other.

"As for the other business, even though Schrade is being very useful to me right now, eventually the crows will return from Amsterdam and Naples. They'll come home to Berlin to roost."

Obando was not being clever. He was pissed. Cool, but pissed.

"Aside from that, it galls me—a lot—that Schrade's been able to play both sides of the game for so long. I have to admit, he's got huge balls. I've got to admire that. As far as it goes."

The two drinks arrived. Obando picked up his glass, raised it to Strand, said, "Prosit," and drank his first sip.

"But I think it's gone far enough," he said. "Obviously, so do you."

Strand had no idea where this was going.

"You want him killed," Obando said matter-of-factly, dismissing Schrade with a wave of his hand. For an instant the gold oval of his cuff link caught the light coming from behind Strand's back and made it glint far brighter than anything else in the room.

"What happened, Harry?" Obando went on, "You're a government man, were. You've been out of it several years now. By this time Schrade should have been just so much past business. An old war story. Yet here you are, right back in the middle of it. You've kept these files—" He nodded at the table. "Schrade was never past business with you, was he? And you never expected him to be." Obando tilted his head a little. "That's interesting to me."

He stopped and regarded Strand.

"Listen," he said, "I was raised in a religious family. Went to Catholic schools in Bogotá. Elementary and then high school. Two years in a Catholic *college* before I went to UCLA. I've read lots of Bible. Lots of it."

Obando lounged in his chair, one arm resting on the table, enjoying the conversation now. "You've heard the story of King David."

Strand just looked at him.

"I'll take that as a yes. And the story of Bathsheba."

Strand was silent.

"Another yes. And the story of Uriah."

Strand waited.

"Well, you get the point, Harry." Without looking at it, his long fingers found the gold cigarette lighter. He set it on its edge. "Actually, it was something of an understatement when you said this was personal, wasn't it?"

Obando smiled knowingly. Strand had the queasy feeling that he was about to encounter something he had not anticipated.

"I'll have to tell you a story," Obando said, shifting in his chair. "I know a little bit about you, but I didn't know it was you until today." He touched the lighter as if adjusting its position. "A couple of years ago Schrade came to me with a new proposition. I'd had these two big failures in Europe—which, thanks to you, I now know that son of a bitch caused—and he came to me and said, 'Look, I know we've had these setbacks, terrible luck, but I've got a connection in a certain place that'll allow us to develop some Mexican operations with almost zero risk.' I was listening.

" 'I've got a brother-in-law,' Schrade said, 'who is an officer in the U.S. Foreign Intelligence Service. The guy's in a position to open and shut doors. He can offer us a conduit for heroin and designer product *and* laundered money—through Mexico, in and out of the States.' I told him to give my people a proposal. We'd study it, get back to him. He did. We made some preliminary inquiries. We went over it in detail. Everything was good. I got back to Schrade, and we made a deal.

"I was cautious at first. Gave him small projects while we continued to do background. Then larger and larger commitments as all of this has proved to be sound and lucrative. It's been very nice, Harry. When the FIS stationed you to Houston the timing couldn't have been better. Mexico was just coming into its own in a very big way. Shit, the money I've made through you has already offset what that son of a bitch Schrade made me lose on those other two projects."

Obando closed his eyes halfway.

"So you see, Harry, after this long collaboration—even though we'd never met—I was already curious about you. And then you contact my people. You come here, give me this documentation on Wolf, and you want me to kill your own brother-in-law." Obando raised his eyebrows. "See what I mean? You say, 'It's personal, I won't talk about it.' I'm wondering, What the fuck's going on here?"

Strand was almost dizzy. What did he expect? Why was he surprised? Did he not think that Schrade's obsession with him was everything that defined an obsession? Did he think that Schrade's attention to revenge would be anything less than excessive? For two years this man sitting across the table from him had thought that Strand was still an FIS officer and the *éminence grise* behind a very successful money laundering and drug smuggling operation in which Obando was a participant and major beneficiary. He had believed this because his own intelligence people had "verified" Schrade's information through "independent" information brokers.

Strand hardly knew where to begin. The same senseless technology that had enabled him to steal millions from Schrade had allowed Schrade to steal his identity from him. In certain parts of the world, at least, Strand was a garbled concoction of Schrade's devising. Strand was appalled that when he had been gathering files on Mara and Ariana and Claude and Schrade, he had not had the foresight to have Alain Darras pull a file on himself as well. He guessed that Darras had done that to satisfy his own curiosity, and he guessed that Darras had wondered why Strand had "lied" to him about still being in the intelligence business.

"Harry." Mario Obando's voice brought Strand back to the moment. "Harry, you have been listening to me for a long time. I would like very much to hear a word from you now."

Strand decided simply to tell the truth to this most unlikely of men, who, having been raised a good Catholic, could still remember Bible stories though he had decided long ago not to believe them.

"I'm afraid Schrade's deceived you again," Strand said. He circled the ice around in his glass with his forefinger, chilling the amber Scotch.

Obando waited.

"Almost all of it is a lie."

"Tell me."

"I've been retired for four years. I wasn't your Mexico man. Couldn't have been. I've been living in Houston, but I've been an art dealer there. Not an FIS officer. It's that simple."

Obando nodded.

"I can give you the names of people with the Foreign Intelligence Service in Washington who can confirm that."

"I've already confirmed it with the FIS."

"In Washington?"

Obando's hesitation was almost imperceptible. "No. Here in Europe. It was confirmed at a very high level."

"High level," Strand said. "Let me guess: you talked to Bill Howard."

Obando's expression lost its composed confidence, a subtlety toward qualmish uncertainty.

"How did you know to talk to him?" Strand pressed. "Who gave you his name?"

Obando stared back at Strand in smoldering silence. Though he was far too sophisticated to let his embarrassment show, he could not so easily hide his aggravation. He seemed to be receding farther into the margins of the shadows as the light coming in from the Boulevard des Capucines grew more oblique and wan.

Strand broke the silence, "Don't feel bad about it, Mario. I've only recently learned about Howard myself."

"I don't know why Schrade lied to me about this, Harry," Obando said, "but I'm inclined not to give a fuck. Whatever's going on between you and him is your business. I'm still making a fortune from him, and I don't want anything to happen to that situation."

"I'm sure you don't," Strand said.

Obando's eyes were fixed on Strand, but his fingers again found the gold lighter and he began spinning it absently on the surface of the table, suddenly stopping it with his fingers. Spin . . . stop. Spin . . . stop. Spin . . . The lighter caught the dull light in its whirling, throwing off soft, rhythmic glimmers.

"Of course, I understand your own thinking, Harry . . ."

"No," Strand interjected, "you don't."

"Well, not exactly, maybe, but I understand revenge. I recognize it when I see it, even if the man who seeks it doesn't recognize it himself. Some men don't want to admit to it. They're embarrassed by feeling such a primitive emotion. They call it something else."

Strand closed his briefcase, leaving the documents on the table. He no longer had any use for them.

"One question," Obando said, still twirling the gold lighter. "You said almost everything Schrade had told me about you was a lie. What about that 'almost'?"

Strand studied Obando's face in the bruised light, studied the effect the swelling shadows had on the Colombian's coloring, on his features, on, it seemed, the very nature of the man himself.

"I married his sister," Strand said. "A year ago, in Houston, Schrade had her killed."

CHAPTER 36

LONDON, BAYSWATER

Claude Corsier sat in the rental car at the entrance to Harley Mews and craned his head over the steering wheel, watching for the light to come on in the garage at the end of the turn. He was uncomfortable sitting in the dark, a rather obvious, curiosity-provoking behavior, he thought. People walked by on their way to evening dinners in the cafés and pubs a few streets over, or just coming and going to God knew where. Sometimes they would spot him in the dark interior, and after they had passed they would turn and look back at him. Besides, he wasn't a lurk-about sort of man. Not that he hadn't done it before, but he never thought he did it particularly well.

The lights suddenly came on, clearly visible through the windows at the top of the wide doors that swung open to give access to the double-car interior. As he started his car, a curtain or some kind of drape was pulled across the windows, creating a glow through the cloth.

Having put the car in gear, Corsier turned on the parking lights and idled around the corner and into the mews, moving past the other garages and doorways before pulling to a stop outside the address at which he had an appointment.

He cut the car's motor, reached over into the rear seat, and picked up the two Schiele forgeries, which were carefully wrapped for protection. He locked the car and walked around to the doorway slightly recessed into the wall beside the garage doors and rang the bell. The door was poorly lighted by a single lamp on a curved bar coming down from the wall above, and Corsier could see vines of some sort growing all around the doorway and over his head.

Waiting for an answer, he looked around the mews. It was not exactly an upscale neighborhood, not ratty, but solidly lower middle class. He smelled curry cooking and tried to identify from which of the open second-story windows it might be wafting. His heart began tripping rapidly when a motor scooter entered the opposite end of the L-shaped mews and pulled up to a doorway several removed from where he was standing. He turned away, took a firmer grip on the forgeries, and then flinched when the door opened suddenly.

"Okay, come in," Skerlic said, backing away, opening the door wider. He was wearing an undershirt and a pair of baggy trousers. He smelled of gin and cigarettes.

They immediately turned into the garage area, but not before the curious Corsier got a glimpse into the kitchen, where an old woman with her head covered Islamic fashion sat spraddle legged in a plastic chair, watching a tiny television that flickered pale light into her face.

"In here," Skerlic said, gripping his arm, hurrying him on.

Inside the garage a workbench made of a thick piece of plywood placed across sawhorses sat in the center of the space, lighted by two light bulbs partially covered with improvised pasteboard shades. Woodworking tools were scattered about on the bench, which was littered with wood shavings, an electric drill, and various gadgets that Corsier did not recognize. In the middle of all this, resting front down on a ragged towel to protect their surfaces, were the two picture frames that Corsier had sent from France to an address other than this one.

Standing on the other side of the bench was a very pregnant woman who appeared to be somewhere in her middle thirties. She also was wearing the traditional Islamic women's headscarf, but her misshapen dress was Western and clearly not designed as a maternity garment. Its hem was hiked up in front to compensate for the additional volume it was so awkwardly covering. She had dusky, Middle Eastern coloring and features. Her left hand, which was gripping some sort of wood-carving tool, rested on the rounded shelf of her protruding stomach. Her right hand, holding a smoldering cigarette, rested on the edge of the bench. She was staring at Corsier as though she could pierce his mind and discern any disingenuity he might utter in the next few moments. It was an oddly tense situation, almost a confrontation.

Skerlic said, "Those are the pictures?"

"Yes . . . yes," Corsier said quickly, pulling his eyes away from the woman.

Skerlic held out a thick hand, and Corsier gave him the drawings.

"Be careful with them," Corsier managed to say. He felt as if he had risked the dark woman's wrath, but the drawings were invaluable.

Skerlic nodded, unimpressed, and turned and leaned the

drawings up against the garage wall. He gestured to the woman.

"Tell him how it works."

The woman flicked her hot eyes at Skerlic, then turned them on Corsier.

"Move up to the table," she said. "I'll go over it step by step."

Corsier was astonished. Her English had no Mediterranean accent. It was American.

She turned slightly and leaned the side of her tight belly against the edge of the plywood. She gestured with the hand that held the cigarette, strewing ashes among the wood shavings. Huge damp splotches of perspiration stained the underarms of her dress and the material between her distended breasts.

"Your two frames," she said. "They're good, thick and heavy like we needed. In each of them I've routed out a groove an inch wide, an inch deep." She ran the middle finger of the hand holding the cigarette around the edges of the nearest frame. "It's cut to within a half a centimeter of the carved surface on the front of the frame."

She reached into the junk on the table and picked up a scrap of metal channeling as shiny as chrome.

"I made a frame of this stuff," she said, holding up the piece of metal to one eye and looking at him through the U-shaped channeling, "just slightly smaller than the groove so that it would fit snugly inside. Okay?" She tossed the scrap into a pile of shavings. "That shit right there," she said, pointing to the channeling, "has special properties. The little bit that we got cost us more than anything else in this operation. That special."

275

With her middle finger, the remaining stump of cigarette smoldering next to it, she scratched her belly at the point where Corsier imagined her navel must be, taking into consideration its substantial displacement due to her condition.

"Then I took the plastic explosive and rolled it into a fat noodle," the woman went on. "I laid it into the channeling and smoothed it out, pressing it in, packing it in until the metal groove was completely full, no air pockets, just metal to plastic contact, hundred percent. Then I laid the packed channeling into the groove, facedown, so that the explosive is jammed up to the wood just under the gilded surface of the front of the frame. Okay?"

Without even paying attention to what she was doing, out of habit, she field stripped the cigarette, rolling it between her fingers until the ash, the few remaining grains of tobacco, and the bit of paper were all disintegrated. All the while she was looking at the picture frames.

"This is a cool deal," she said. She straightened and pressed her fists into her lower back as she leaned forward and backward. She looked at Corsier, and with her right hand she pressed the material of her dress down between her breasts, daubing the perspiration. "Ever been pregnant?" She didn't grin. She asked it as though it were a straight, legitimate question. Her dark eyes waited for an answer.

Corsier felt the beginnings of a nervous smile, but her somber expression stopped him.

"Uh . . . no."

"Don't ever do it," she said. "That little shiver you get from the sex is a good thing, but it's *definitely* not worth nine months of complete biological upheaval."

Corsier glanced at Skerlic. The little Serb was perspiring

also. He lifted a fat hand and drank some gin from an absurdly filthy glass.

The woman leaned against the table again, this time gesturing with the wood-carving tool.

"Here and here," she said, getting back to her explanation, "detonators. Radio-operated. Okay? And here"—she jabbed at two points on either side of the center of the frame—"little mikes. They're going to look like some kind of bracket pieces when I get through with them. From the front they're just going to be a deep groove in the ornate carving. That's why I had to have this kind of frame."

"Microphones?"

She raised her eyebrows. "Got to know when to detonate," she explained. "I was under the impression that this is a no-margin-for-error, no-fuck-up situation here. Very serious."

Corsier nodded.

"Well, then, you want to be able to identify your target. The way this is designed, when you hear his voice in focus, at a particular decibel level"—she flicked her eyes at Skerlic—"he'll have the audio equipment to determine when that happens—then your target's head is right in the center of the frame, the right distance, presenting you with maximum exposure. He's up close, examining the drawing . . . asking for it." She jerked her head at Skerlic. "He presses the button. The explosion's going to take the guy's head clean off his shoulders."

She straightened up, obviously miserable.

"What you've got here is a humane hit," she said, groping around in the wood shavings for her cigarettes. She took one out of the pack and lighted it with a plastic turquoise lighter, which she then tossed back into the wood shavings. "The channeling, like I said, is special shit, a metal alloy that will control the direction of the blast out the front of the frame in a concentrated pattern. Minimal, if any, collateral damage. However, woe to the target." She raised a flattened hand and kissed it front and back. "Praise be to Allah."

Claude Corsier stared at the woman. The accumulative effect of her manner and her lethal monologue froze his spine. This woman was a living, waking nightmare.

She leaned against the garage wall and looked at Corsier with the same dark expression she had turned on him when he had walked into the room. She was through.

Corsier looked at the perspiring Skerlic. "What next?" he asked.

"We will finish the frames—the microphones will take some fine tuning. The radio frequencies are very precise, very important. Then we will put in the drawings."

"They are easily damaged," Corsier reminded. "I can't stress that enough."

"I know this," Skerlic said impatiently. "I know this." He took another drink of gin.

Corsier wondered how well the gin and explosives mixed. For a jarring second he had the irrational fear that the garage might explode spontaneously, ignited by the fumes on Skerlic's breath.

"What next?" Corsier repeated.

"You will have to set a date with the dealer," Skerlic said. "I want you to get a room at the Connaught Hotel. I want to work from there. It's a perfect location. Perfect."

"Christ. The Connaught." Because of its convenient location, Corsier had stayed there many times before when dealing with Carrington Knight. It struck him as bizarre to use this grand old place as a staging point for Schrade's assassination. But if that was what it took . . . At least the hotel staff were well acquainted with him. It was not always easy to get a room at the Connaught. Prior familiarity was always an advantage, and an absolute necessity if one wanted a room on short notice.

"You have to go," Skerlic said. "We have to finish."

"Yes . . . yes," Corsier said. He looked at the woman. It seemed grotesque to thank her, but he felt compelled to say something. "Good . . . good," he said, nodding. "Good," he repeated as he turned to go. She was staring at him out of floating coils of smoke, a dark Medusa.

CHAPTER 37

PARIS

Strand walked to the end of the Boulevard des Capucines, continued on to the Boulevard des Italiens and then to Boulevard Montmartre. The sidewalks were crowded, and the end-of-the-day traffic was heavy, which was good. He went into the Passage des Panoramas and stayed in its narrow corridors for some time, wandering, waiting, watching, before he was back on the streets, following Rue St. Marc to Richelieu and then on to the Métro station at Rue Drouot, where he descended, allowing himself to be caught up and swept along with the crowds. He got onto a train and then got off again just before it pulled away.

With his mind replaying Obando's revelations, he watched the faces closely, monitoring the pedestrian flow, looking for another body that might suddenly turn against the grain as he did. The cynical Colombian had inadvertently confirmed Lu's report of Howard's treachery. Strand wondered how long it had been going on, if it had been going on when Strand was still with the FIS.

As he moved through the crowds, dawdling and reversing, his thoughts never left the conversation he had just had with Mario Obando. It was time to face up to the fact that his scheme was failing miserably.

Finally, satisfied that he was not being followed, he headed back to the Quatre Septembre.

There was a brasserie near the hotel, a medium-size, bustling place a few steps below street level. Large windows across the front afforded a view through a wrought-iron grille on the sidewalk. After dark, the lights from the street played crazily upon the murky panes of the windows like sparks flying up from a fire.

They went there immediately, in the dusk. There was an early crowd, young people from the couture shops and studios not far away, but they were not loud.

After the waiter came and took their orders, Strand looked at Mara and took a deep breath.

"Damn," he said, shaking his head slowly.

"You want to go first?" she asked. She was wearing a one-piece cotton knit dress of navy blue. With her black hair and carmine lips she was a striking figure.

He told her everything, even of Romy's relationship to Schrade. She was shocked and several times looked away as if trying to comprehend it all.

"I don't know why I didn't tell you before," he said. "It doesn't make any difference, except that it makes everything even more horrible."

"I'm so sorry," she said.

"That was another reason she was able to pull off the embezzlement so well. He trusted her more than the other money managers he had working for him. She stretched his confidence in her to the limit. It bought us a lot of time, gave us more room to maneuver."

Mara stared at him. He knew what she was going to say.

"She must have hated him," she said. "I know she loved you, that she would have done anything for you, but . . . she must have hated him so much."

Strand looked away. Even getting close to that subject made him suddenly empty, as if the marrow were being withdrawn from his bones by the sheer gravity of the sadness of that story.

Mara reached out and put her hand on his. "Harry"—she squeezed his hand until he turned and looked at her—"thank you for telling me. I'm grateful that you felt you could tell me."

For a moment they said nothing as they looked at each other, then Mara took her hand away from his.

"You want to hear about Howard?"

Strand nodded.

"I got him on the Internet," she said, swallowing. "I told him I was confused, scared, didn't know what to do. I confessed that I'd fallen in love with you, but I didn't know if I could just turn my back on the FIS, the U.S., all that. I didn't want to be a traitor. If that was the logical extension of what I was doing, if that was the way it was going to be interpreted, I didn't know if I could handle it."

"How did he take it?"

"I don't think he was buying it at first. I couldn't get a real good feel for nuance on the Internet."

"How did you leave it?"

"He wants to meet. I said I'd get back to him. I kept it open, just as you said." She hesitated. "But Harry, how in the hell could you ever do anything with him again?"

Strand knew what she was thinking.

"We just don't want to cut him off, that's all," he said. "We don't want to cut off anybody. We need as much flexibility as possible."

Their sandwiches came, and they stopped talking for a few minutes while they ate, each of them pursuing separate thoughts. The sounds of the brasserie returned to Strand's consciousness: the low gabble of the couture crowd, the clink of china and flatware, the hum of indistinguishable conversations.

After a while Mara wiped her mouth, took a drink of her coffee, and looked at him.

"Then who's next? Lodato or Grachev?"

Strand thought a moment. He might as well tell her straight out.

"I'm not going to waste my time with either one of them," he said. "They're going to give me the same reasons for not going after Schrade as the other two did. Schrade's way out ahead of me on this. He's made sure that all of them are finding him to be very useful right now. I've told you, he understands the psychology of revenge. Money, enough of it, will even buy off hate. As long as it keeps coming in."

Mara leaned toward him. "Harry, go to the FIS. They can get between you and Schrade. I know they can."

"It would never happen."

"You can hand them a *mole,* for God's sake!"

"And I worked for that mole for a dozen years. What kinds of questions does that raise, Mara? After stealing millions from Schrade, what kind of credibility do I have? You want to know the truth? They'd rather have the money I took from Schrade than the mole. Exposing Howard would mean tons of bad publicity for them. Getting the money would mean tons of good publicity. They can retire Howard and sweep him under the carpet. He can be made to go away very easily."

"Then you expose him. Threaten to go public if they don't give you—us—protection."

"Going public is character suicide. It wouldn't take much at all for the FIS to provide 'proof' to the media that I was part of Howard's rogue operations. Don't forget, I was already one step in that direction by agreeing to run Schrade in the first place."

She looked at him steadily across the table. "You're making a lot of assumptions again," she said.

"I worked for them for twenty years."

She paused. "Then . . . what, Harry?"

"I'm working on a couple of ideas."

"Like what?"

"Mara, I've really got to sort some things out in my mind, okay? Give me some breathing room."

Her dark eyes searched his. As they looked at each other he had the feeling that she knew exactly where he was going with this. She knew, but she didn't press him on it. She was giving him room, giving him time to get his mind around an unthinkable alternative. She knew what he was dealing with, and he guessed that it frightened her as much as it did him. It had to. But she waited.

"I love you, Harry."

It wasn't what he had expected.

They lay together, awake, in the dark, listening to the sounds of the Quatre Septembre. They each drifted off to sleep at different times and then stirred again, reassuring each other that they were there.

Once during the night he awoke and heard her whispering to him. He missed what she was saying, except the last part, "I love you." He thought he answered her with the same words, or maybe he dreamed it.

CHAPTER 38

BERLIN, SCHWANENWERDER

Howard was summoned to Schrade's villa just after nightfall, and he already knew that it was going to be a tense meeting. A lot had happened during the day and not much of it any good.

When he arrived, chauffeured as always, in one of Schrade's Mercedes, he was not surprised to see a number of cars in the motor court. Schrade's surveillance and intelligence apparatus was good everywhere, but in Berlin it was an absolute ghost machine. Howard never had to worry that any other intelligence operatives—even the FIS—would detect him doing business with Schrade.

Howard had been at the villa at night before, and he did not find it a pleasant experience. Mainly because Schrade, for all his self-restraint and detachment and understatement, treated his nighttime villa with a good deal more drama than Howard could stand. Tonight, as in times before, the place was not lighted in the normal way, in which rooms were provided a generalized lighting with visibility being pretty much consistent throughout. In Schrade's villa every room and corridor and stairway was lighted by dappled luminescence. There were only pockets of light, and one moved through the large spaces of the villa as through pervasive shadow, negotiating one's way to random areas of soft illumination. And these islands of light were not static, for Howard had seen them shift slowly, rearranging the mottled patterns of glow and murk.

And there was another attribute in the villa at night that Howard disliked: There was constant movement, though Howard rarely saw anyone. As evidenced by the cars in the motor court, there were always more people here at night than during the day. But he never saw anyone. He heard doors open and close. He heard voices, sometimes murmurs, sometimes sharp ejaculations. He heard footsteps. He heard movement. And sometimes, as the snappily dressed young man ushered him through this dim netherworld, he thought he sensed activity suddenly stop, waiting until he had passed.

Tonight was no different, and by the time Howard was shown into the long salon of Schrade's work space, he felt as though he had journeyed through a landscape of secrets and had arrived in a sorcerer's castle.

Schrade was at his desk and did not get up. The large hall was dark except for the pools of glow that hung over each lime wood cabinet and lighted the way down the long approach to Schrade's presence. The seating area was not lighted, which meant Howard was supposed to go to one of the large chairs anchored in front of Schrade's heavily carved baroque desk, which seemed to levitate in a slightly brighter spill of incandescence. He sat down and waited for Schrade to acknowledge him.

Schrade, dressed in a dark, formal suit with a sparkling white shirt and a dark tie that seemed to have been finely embroidered with gold threads, was reading. Stacked on either side of him were red leather folders bulging with documents that protruded from them, each folder tied closed with a broad crimson ribbon. Computer screens winked and glowed behind him. Beyond, through the wide window, the Havel River, bathed in the blue of night, stretched away, flanked by glittering cinders of light that receded into invisibility.

Schrade closed the red leather folder from which he had been reading.

"It is difficult to articulate how stupid the United States Foreign Intelligence Service can be," he said placidly, removing his reading glasses and clasping his hands together, his forearms resting on his desk, white French cuffs extending precisely from beneath the dark coat sleeves. The light sifting down from above him made his pale hair appear to iridesce. Howard had the horrible sense of being able to actually see through Schrade's clear eyes into the abyss of his head.

"But we know damn well your people have been looking over our shoulders this whole time," Howard said. "We've picked them up. I wouldn't feel too superior. When Mara left the homing device in Bellagio, why didn't your elite cadre of operatives intercept them? I've always had enough sense not to let another intelligence group do my work for me. They might not do it right."

"Obviously. They are lost?"

"We don't know where they are," Howard admitted, "but I'm in communication with Mara Song." He told Schrade about the Internet exchanges, of Mara's ambivalence, her desire to stay in touch.

Schrade was motionless. This interested him.

"The e-mail's encrypted, so there's no way to trace it, but if I keep talking to her, if I can keep it up, we'll find them. You know Harry, he'll keep moving, moving, moving. I think he's very worried. I think you can expect to hear from him pretty soon."

Schrade waited.

"Song is completely lost to us as an agent. Despite her communication she has no intention of leaving him, she has no angst or ambivalence. This is Strand. He's using her to keep the FIS on hold. He doesn't want to be cut off from us. He's up to something."

"Washington knows of Song's desertion?"

"Of course."

"And this theory of yours?"

"Yeah."

Schrade was thinking.

"Look," Howard said, "you've waited this long. Let me play this out. I'll concede your goddamn siege technique against Strand is probably working. He's not going to want to lose this woman. You can't kill her, Wolf," he added quickly. "Okay? You've applied just the right amount of mayhem, just the right amount of madness. Don't overplay it. He's got nothing left he cares about except her. So, we stop. Right here. He'll come around. He'll negotiate. You're going to hear from him."

"When?"

"Goddamn, I don't know *when*. But Strand's running. Running's exhausting. Covering your ass all the time's exhausting. You're after him. We're after him. He's afraid for her. Pressure. Pressure." Howard paused. "Soon. The running, the constant moving's going to wear him out."

"How much time? Days? Weeks? . . ."

"No, no. Days."

Schrade regarded Howard with opaque dispassion.

Really, the only thing that seriously bothered Howard about
the man, despite his shitload of psychopathologies, was his
clear eyes. Sometimes Howard found himself wondering—
irrationally, he knew, but wondering anyway—whether
Schrade could see things other people couldn't see because of
those damn eyes.

"I want to find Claude Corsier," Schrade said.

Done. They would do the Strand thing Howard's way.
Schrade was moving on to other things.

"We don't have a clue," Howard said. "We've tried to find
him. The thing is, we're dealing here with very well-trained
operatives. They know the tricks of the trade . . ."

"I found Clymer. I found Kiriasis."

Howard noted that he left out Marie, the sick son of a
bitch. He couldn't resist asking, "How the hell did that happen, anyway? The thing with Claude?"

Schrade ignored him. "Just be aware that I would make it
financially worthwhile for the man who finds him."

Schrade was going to get them all, sooner or later.

"You are returning to Vienna tomorrow, then?"

"That's right."

Schrade turned to one side and selected one of the red
leather folders from the stacks of them at his elbow. He placed
the folder in front of him, untied its crimson ribbon, and
opened it. He looked at some of the documents, perusing
them carefully. Howard guessed that they were about to move
on to another subject. Schrade sat in the pool of pale light like
a medieval alchemist, dealing in mysteries and arcana, comfortable with secrets and fog and the realm of mottled shadows. It was true that Howard himself and Harry Strand and all
of them in this quickly moving story were creatures in that

realm of shifting realities, too. That was true. But Schrade was different from them in that he was not simply a sojourner in the mist; he was not merely passing through. Rather, he was a part of it. It was his milieu, yes, but more than that, he was of its very nature and substance.

Schrade laid down the piece of paper from which he was reading and again folded his hands on top of the desk, covering the opened red folder.

Looking at Bill Howard, he began to talk, his voice modulated, his manner quiet, his wretched limpid eyes holding Howard's attention despite their unnerving effect. For ten minutes, then fifteen, then twenty, he outlined intelligence he wanted Howard to glean from the records available to him in the FIS computers.

It was always this way. Schrade provided him with no documents of any kind, and Howard took no notes. Neither of them ever forgot even the smallest detail of what was said at these sessions, even if the intelligence was difficult to come by and months passed before Howard made another secret trip to Schwanenwerder to deliver what Schrade had requested. Within twenty-four hours of his report, Howard's numbered account in Liechtenstein received another deposit.

"So, that is the sum of it," Schrade concluded, regarding Howard from across the surface of his desk. "Do you have any questions?"

"None."

Schrade gave a single nod. Done. He closed the red leather folder and tied the ribbon. He set it aside. He picked up his reading glasses and put them on and opened the red leather folder from which he had been reading when Howard arrived. He began to read.

Howard watched him. This was always an intriguing moment. He often wondered what would happen if he just sat there and didn't leave. How long would it take before Schrade looked up? When he did, how would he react? What would happen if someone actually called this man's inflexible hand? Howard's imagination answered his own question. He saw the face of Marie Bienert. Of Dennis Clymer. Of Ariana Kiriasis. Of Claude Corsier. Mara Song. Harry Strand. He saw the faceless silhouettes of dozens, of countless, unknown others.

Howard had managed thus far to work with this one-man pestilence and not succumb to his indiscriminate fever. He wanted to keep it that way, and no amount of idle curiosity would make him risk losing what he had managed to extract from the very heart of the plague.

He rose from his chair, turned away from the massive desk, and started to the door at the other end of the salon. As he passed through pools of dusty light hanging over the cabinets, he thought he could feel the intermittent shadows brushing at his clothes like spiders' webs, each web stronger, each dragging at him with more resistance than the previous one. The very fact that he was imagining this gave him the creeps, and it took all the nerve he had not to quicken his pace. He did not look back.

CHAPTER 39

By midafternoon of the next day they had rented a new car and were on the road again. Picking up Autoroute A1 outside Paris, they drove three hours to Calais, where they caught one of the numerous Sealink ferries to Dover.

They could have taken the Channel tunnel train from Paris and been in London in just over three hours, but Strand had grown increasingly edgy about evading Schrade's intelligence. Now that he knew Schrade had probably had continuous access to their whereabouts through Howard, via Mara's signal pen, up until they left Bellagio, his determination to remain hidden from all of them was reinvigorated, and his anxiety at the absence of any signs of surveillance whatsoever was heightened. The Channel tunnel train was too popular and its traffic too easy to monitor, whereas the multiplicity of ferry routes and timetables was more in their favor.

The drive from Paris had been quiet. Once they had driven onto the ferry and started across the Channel, Strand decided to broach with Mara the subject of his plans.

They made their way up the interior stairs of the ferry and walked out on the second-level observation deck on the stern. The coast of Calais was already drifting away, and the seagulls that would follow the ferry most of the way across the Channel were shrilling and hovering above them, diving now and then into the foam and the wake created by the huge propellers. The breeze was warm and salty, but there was a feel of hopefulness in it, too.

They leaned their forearms on the railing and stood there a moment, feeling the throb of the powerful engines and the gentle buoyancy of the ferry.

"I'm going to have to talk to Schrade," he said. Out of the corner of his eye he saw Mara's head jerk around. She was staring at him from behind her sunglasses. "But I want to catch him off guard, and that's important. I need to meet with him in a way that the meeting will be a surprise. I don't want him to know he's going to encounter me until the last moment. There's a dealer in London who's been selling art to Schrade for nearly fifteen years. Schrade trusts him. When Carrington Knight says he's got something worth seeing, Schrade listens. The thing of it is, if you want to buy art from Carrington, you have to go to Carrington. He rarely buys, and never sells, except in his own gallery."

Strand spent several minutes telling Mara about Knight's peculiar personality and habits, making it clear how he worked with his clients and why it was important to have him making the offer to Schrade. It would mean that Schrade would come to a certain place at a certain time to see what Knight had to offer.

"So it can be done," Strand said. "Schrade can be summoned." He watched a seagull plunge into the ferry's foamy wake and come up again with something churned up by the propellers. Three or four other gulls followed him into the water, with varying success.

"What I need, however, is something to offer."

"You mean art," Mara said.

"I had pieces he would've wanted, but they're gone now. Besides, he would have known where they were coming from."

Mara was staring straight out across the water. The ferry was fast, and France was rapidly becoming the horizon rather than the coast, the haze from the Channel turning it into a slate blue ribbon.

"Maillol. Klimt. Delvaux. Ingres. Balthus," she said.

"They *are* your drawings?"

"Yes, they're mine."

"What about Howard?"

"He doesn't know anything about them. I mean, the specifics of the art. I 'had art,' that's all he knew."

Strand waited.

"Would I lose them?" she asked.

"I can't guarantee that you wouldn't," he said.

"I wasn't asking for guarantees," she said, not looking at him.

It seemed that in no time at all they were disembarking at Dover, and by early evening they had made their way into London and checked into another small hotel, this one in Mayfair, not far from Berkeley Square.

The evening was mild. Strollers drifted through the small streets of Mayfair, and the large houses that were usually closed against the chill were thrown open to summer's tranquility. Occasionally, on a corner or in a mews, Strand and

Mara came upon a pub so crowded that its patrons spilled out into the street, knots of young people sitting at wooden tables or simply standing in the street, nursing pint glasses of stout or lager or ale as they talked, laughing, smoking, their voices lingering in the evening air.

On the west side of Berkeley Square, they turned up Hill Street and continued to South Audley, where they ate a light dinner at a café before starting back to the hotel. On the way back Strand took them onto Mount Street, an elegant stretch of Georgian residences and smart shops, and headed toward the sedate Connaught Hotel. They paused at an occasional shop window to peer in a moment before moving on. Until now their conversation had, by tacit mutual avoidance, steered clear of the business at hand. It was almost as if they had agreed to pretend, for an hour, at least, that the harrowing events of the last few days hadn't happened at all. It was Mara who brought them back to reality.

She looked at her watch. "When we get back to the hotel I'll call the bank in Houston. They can arrange for the drawings to be shipped here."

"Not here," Strand said. "I know a dealer in Paris who will receive them for us. I'll call him, make the arrangements. We can take the tunnel train to Paris to pick them up. There and back in half a day."

"Do we have to offer all the drawings?"

"He's more likely to come immediately to see a collection like this, rather than just one or two drawings. A collection, a jewel like this one, that comes on the market suddenly usually is sold quietly by a few well-placed telephone calls. The serious dealers and collectors know it will be sold quickly, never even come to the public's attention. This will happen fast."

"How do we handle the dealer?"

Strand noted the use of the plural pronoun.

Long afterward, in thinking about the whole complex affair again, as he would often do, Strand would be stunned anew at what had been decided between them that night. More precisely, he was stunned at his own behavior. Mara had decided to cast her lot with him, and she had done it calmly and deliberately. It was a decision of considerable courage. But what Strand had done in response to her commitment was far less admirable and unquestionably selfish: he did not try to talk her out of it.

"I need you to do something," Strand said. "I need to get Bill Howard to London. I think he's completely sold out to Schrade, keeping him abreast of everything that's developing here. I'm guessing he'll be a direct line to Schrade. I need you to e-mail him and tell him I want to talk. I'll give you the details for arranging the meeting."

"Tonight?"

"As soon as we get back to the hotel. It's important that you make him believe that I have to have time to get to London. He's got to believe we're somewhere in Europe."

"Why?"

"Axioms for countersurveillance."

"Keep moving. Multiple identities, multiple addresses."

"That's what they're going to be expecting us to do, and that's what I want them to think we're doing. The FIS and Schrade's people are going to be all over the travel connections, air, train, rentals, buses. So we're not going to travel. We're going to become London residents. Tomorrow, first thing, I want you to go to the estate agents here in Mayfair and lease a town house. Six months, a year, two years, I don't care.

Stay in Mayfair. Keep it close to everything we're doing. I want this to be all 'wrong' as far as intelligence expectations are concerned."

Strand paused on the sidewalk across the street from the Connaught Hotel. The clean gray and black cars that seemed always to be waiting at the curb in front of the hotel and along the Mount Street side glinted in the dull glow of the street lamps, adding a luster of the modern to a famous old landmark that still maintained the staid and subdued manner of British propriety.

In front of the hotel was a triangular traffic island where Carlos Place forked and went in opposite directions onto Mount Street. The near side of the island was usually lined with black cabs quietly biding their time until a Connaught guest emerged from the old residence. There was a cluster of plane trees on the island as well as a few stone benches and, in its very center, a dark bronze statue of a nude woman in a shrugging, crouching posture.

On the other side of the island was a five-storied Victorian building of terraced row houses made of bright red orange brick and having bay window facades with white stone and wood trim. The front of the building swept in a gentle arc from Carlos Place to Mount Street.

"He lives there," Strand said, lifting his chin toward the row houses. "Number Four."

"You're kidding."

"No. A discreet brass plate beside the front door says 'Carrington, Hartwell and Knight. Private Dealers in Fine Art.' "

"There's a light," Mara said. "Second floor."

Strand took a few steps to get a better line of sight through the trees.

"That's where he does most of his work," he said. "There's a large room with an ornately carved library table near the windows. Opposite that, there's a walk-in vault with narrow vertical bays for storing canvases. The drawings are kept in stacked rows of shallow drawers. There are bookcases along the walls below which are cabinets with countertops about waist high. He uses the countertops to display his canvases and drawings. Where there are no bookcases, the walls are covered in crimson silk. There's a sitting area furnished with rosewood and ebony antiques."

They crossed Mount Street to the island and stood under the plane trees, looking up at Carlos Place, Number Four.

"The first floor," Strand continued, leaning against one of the trees, "is a reception area. There's a gallery to the right to exhibit drawings. Here the walls are done in indigo silk. Usually some small, first-rate sculpture scattered about. All the woodwork is mahogany. Down a short hall there's a generous bathroom for clients. Marble. Linen washcloths. Complimentary flacons of cologne and perfume. There are little silver boxes with handmade tortoiseshell combs with a tissue band around them. Complimentary."

"Good Lord," Mara said.

"It's intended to convey a sense of elegant wealth. A client understands that the very best art is traded here. They can expect to be treated like royalty—and to pay royal prices." He went on with the description. "The stairs leading from this first floor to the second are wide and turn slowly back upon themselves. Mahogany banister and railing. A truly stunning Persian carpet covers the treads all the way up."

"Why are you telling me all this?"

"Carrington is going to play a very big role in our plans," Strand said. "You need to know what he's like, and what to expect from him. A young man usually stays at a desk in the foyer. He's a sort of security person, doorman, factotum. He takes care of the electric lock on the door and monitors people who come in to browse around the downstairs gallery."

"What does Knight look like?"

"He's just shy of six feet. Stocky, a little puffy. His hair is prematurely gray, white really. He wears it longish, like an artiste. Very stylish. He likes to wear black clothes to offset his hair. Sometimes he wears thin black wire-rimmed eyeglasses."

"Sounds foppish."

"Yeah, it sounds that way, but he's thoroughly masculine. Somehow it all balances out."

"What about his education?"

"Oxbridge."

"Really? What else about him?" She drew closer to him, putting her arm through his, lacing their fingers together.

"He understands Wolfram Schrade."

"Understands him?"

"The only thing that fascinates Carrington more than the art that he buys and sells are the people from whom he buys it and the people to whom he sells it. He's a collector of psychological minutiae."

"What do you mean?"

"Carrington believes that people who buy art, who care enough about it to want to own it, are an anomaly in the general scheme of modern life. In today's world, which so values speed and the quick result, the immediate feedback, the quick payback, the person who turns to art—something that re-

THE COLOUR OF NIGHT

quires a meditative discipline to create and to appreciate—is a
rower against the tide. Everything modern militates against
it." Strand paused. "Nothing fascinates Carrington more than
a rower against the tide."

"Even if he's Wolf Schrade."

"It doesn't have anything to do with morality. Besides,
Carrington doesn't know anything about Schrade's criminal
side. The connection is purely an artistic one. Carrington simply recognizes a fellow rower."

CHAPTER 40

Claude Corsier sat at a small square table with a starched linen cloth. It was set with Victorian china and sterling silver and Dutch crystal. Carrington Hartwell Knight sat across from him, each man enthroned in an elaborately carved, high-backed Spanish chair several hundred years old. Knight's elbow rested on the damask-upholstered arm of his chair, his wan face resting in his hand, an index finger lying close to one pale eye. His longish wavy white hair was carefully coifed, a full dandy's wave sweeping back in undulations from his temples.

The two men were eating a late brunch in Knight's second-floor library. The food was prepared upstairs in Knight's well-appointed kitchen by a French cook whom he retained three days a week. It was brought down in a small elevator by the chef's niece, who also served the two men. They had begun with a modest mixed-leaf salad with small medallions of grilled goat's cheese and then had gone on to *noisettes d'agneau* garnished with potato *galettes*. They had followed that with little plates of fresh fruit and slices of *brie de meaux*. Dessert and coffee were declined in favor of finishing off a very good bottle of Pouilly-Fumé.

Knight laughed richly at Corsier's third or fourth anecdote of the meal and poured himself a full glass of the vaguely smoky white wine, adding some to Corsier's glass. He sat back in his chair, smiling. Corsier recognized his moment.

"Carrington, the food was wonderful, as always," he said, lifting his glass. "My compliments."

Knight smirked pleasantly, accepting the praise.

"I told you I had something special," Corsier went on, "and I do, something that I am sure will delight you." He reached down beside his chair, where he had leaned a wafer-thin, royal blue leather portfolio. "I have photographs of two drawings in my possession."

He opened the portfolio and took out two eight-by-ten color photographs and handed them across the table to Knight, who put down his glass and sat up in his baroque chair, hand outstretched.

He looked at the first photograph. Frowned. Looked quickly at the second. Frowned. His attention still glued to the images, he moved aside the few things in front of him and laid the pictures side by side on the linen cloth. He leaned over them. Without removing his eyes from them, he reached into the breast pocket of his jacket and took from behind his gray linen handkerchief a pair of eyeglasses with perfectly round, black wire frames. He put them on, continuing to stare at the photographs. The frown disappeared. He began to shake his head slowly.

"*Good* God . . . extraordinary." He closed his mouth and swallowed, his eyes squinting, his head thrust forward.

He looked up at Corsier. "Where did you get *these*?"

"Long story."

"I've never seen them."

"Nor have I."

Knight tilted his head, looking at Corsier like a handsome if exotic owl. "Claude, are these cataloged?"

"No."

Knight gasped. "They're not authenticated?"

"Carrington"—Corsier leaned toward the flamboyant dealer—"I've only just discovered them!"

"How many people have seen these?"

"Only me."

"What?"

"And, soon, you."

Knight tucked in his chin skeptically, trying to hide his excitement at being in on the beginning of such an event.

"How the hell did you come up with these?"

Corsier relished the question.

"How many times have you heard this?" he began. "An estate discovery. But it's true. Two weeks ago a middle-aged British woman came to my gallery in Geneva. She had been visiting friends to whom she had told the following story, and they had urged her to come to me. An elderly aunt had died. The old woman had been very much of a rounder in her day and had flounced around with artists in Berlin and other places Germanic and had lived so bohemian a life as to have made herself an outcast from the rest of the family. Or at least a thoroughgoing black sheep. She lived a hermit in Bedford. She died. Left her little cottage and its contents to this niece.

"The niece dragged herself to Bedford, girded for the chore of cleaning out this dirty little cottage and its junk. She found scores and scores of drawings of every sort, all kept in boxes, one on top of the other. She also found seven framed drawings on the walls of the old woman's bedroom, where she spent the last four years of her life. Thinking the art might be worth something, the niece photographed it and sent the photographs to her friends in Geneva.

"When my assistant saw the photographs, she called me immediately. I was in Zurich. I flew home that night. The next day I visited the woman, saw the photographs, and made an appointment three days later to visit her home here in London." Corsier opened his eyes wide. "I found two little Kokoschkas, a rather nice Czeschka, a very good Kubin, two Broschs, and"—he paused for effect—"two Schieles."

"And you *have* the drawings?"

"I own them."

"You bought them yourself?"

"I bought the lot."

"You didn't tell her what she had?"

"Well, I wasn't sure," Corsier said coyly. "I'm still not sure."

Knight returned his eyes to the photographs, studying them. As he bent his head forward, a white lock dangled over his forehead rakishly. His fingers rested on the edge of the table as if he were at a piano keyboard, wrists down. He examined every line, every stroke, delved into the colors at their deepest and out to their lighter edges. He squinted at the expressions on the faces of the subjects and followed the intentions of the lines, where they broke or continued unexpectedly, where they hesitated, repeated, and confidently pressed on to unusual conclusions.

"Early ones, I'd say," Knight murmured to himself. "Before he grew so harsh, so cruel."

"Exactly."

"Mmmmm . . . mmmm." Knight was unaware of his audible voice. Suddenly he looked up. "Schiele." He wiped his mouth with his napkin and sat back once again. "Sure as hell looks like Schiele to me." He picked up his glass, paused. "Until I get to see the paper itself, anyway." He drank, rather quickly now.

"What do you think of them?" Corsier asked. He stroked his mustache and goatee.

Knight sighed and savored the lingering, smoky aftertaste of the wine. He raised his white eyebrows. "Well, they're sublime, Claude." His eyes grew heavy-lidded. "Why are you showing them to me?"

"I want you to authenticate them. Then I want you to broker them."

"What's the matter? Why don't you do it?"

"I can't."

Knight sipped his Pouilly-Fumé. "Explain."

"I know who will give the highest price for these two beauties," Corsier said. "Unfortunately, he and I had a serious falling-out recently, and if he knows I'm connected with these drawings, he will not buy. And we will not get the highest possible price."

"You're talking about Wolfram Schrade?"

"That's right."

"Really?" Knight's voice rose and fell.

"We've exchanged words. Angry words. Legal threats all around. So, you see . . ."

"Of course."

"It's imperative that I remain out of the picture here. Entirely. You mustn't mention me at all."

"Why should I?"

Corsier smiled to himself. Carrington Knight was already counting his crowns and pounds and guineas.

"Are you interested, then?"

"Christ. Of course." He paused, calculating while pretending not to be as he looked at the photographs over the top of his glass. "You don't want to be connected with the sale in any way?"

"Absolutely not."

Knight frowned abruptly and cut his eyes at Corsier.

"All this excessive secrecy, not wanting my man Jeffrey here when you come—all that has to do with your anonymity?"

"Precisely. I don't want anyone other than you to know who's offering these. You know Schrade. He snoops around."

"Oh, yes, yes." Knight nodded, thinking. "It will be of importance to the media."

Knight was understating it. Egon Schiele was one of the most collectible moderns. His output had not been enormous, and none of the known works could be said to be available. Everyone who had them was hanging on to them.

"You can have all the cream and all of the credit for the discovery," Corsier said.

"You want to be mentioned after the sale?"

"No."

"You'd just as soon the attribution remained 'the Property of a Gentleman.' "

"Forever, as far as I'm concerned."

"Fine. What's the commission?"

"Standard."

"Can't argue with that. What are you asking for them?"

"If they're authentic, I have an idea of what they're worth. But you've sold Schrade far more art than I have. I think you'll know best what he will put on the table."

"Yes, yes, of course." Knight was sitting forward in his small throne again, elbows on the arms, hands holding the wineglass. His eyes returned to the two photographs. "It's extraordinary, really, to come up with two unknown Schieles. Extraordinary."

"I have a suggestion about Schrade."

Knight looked up at Corsier from under his brows.

"A greater egoist never walked," Corsier said. "I actually think you could enhance the asking price if he were allowed to be part of the discovery."

"Explain."

"Tell him you think you have discovered a couple of lost Schieles. Briefly describe the background. Tell him that you are going to authenticate them. You knew he would want first look at actual Schieles. Would he be interested in being present for the 'discovery' itself? If they are Schieles, he will literally have first look. If they are not . . ." Corsier shrugged.

Corsier could see Carrington Knight's mind wheeling, his imagination foreseeing the drama . . . and the value of the drama. Corsier went on.

"If Schrade could share in the *thrill* of discovering a Schiele," he enthused gently, reaching out with his hand and closing it into a fist, his white French cuffs extending from the sleeves of his dark suit as he turned his fist and drew it back toward himself to connote the compelling effect of his argument. "Schiele the iconized." His voice softened to a whisper. "Schiele the harsh magician of nervous sexuality. Schiele the disturbed light of modern concupiscence."

He let his hand return softly to the linen tablecloth.

"I think that even the cold Mr. Schrade could be enthused, as it were, by the drama of seeing these drawings still encased in the frames that have held them since, say, the nineteen thirties, or twenties. The two frames, incidentally, are monstrosities, heavy, ornately carved, gold leaf. Who knows what one might find behind those drawings. Another sketch? A scrawled annotation in Schiele's own hand that would shed some light into his psyche?"

Carrington Knight was motionless, his face blank. For a moment Corsier was afraid he had overdone it. But no, Knight was seeing a vision. He blinked a couple of times.

"Jesus Christ, Claude," he said, "have you always been this calculating, and I have simply overlooked it?"

Corsier smiled kindly. "To tell you the truth," he said, picking up his wineglass, "I think these damn drawings are authentic. I suspect they will be on the market for only the few moments following Schrade's realization of this. Think of it. They have been lost for three generations, and then they come to light. For only a moment. Schrade will buy them and lock them away until he dies . . . another generation until his estate is sold. This, my dear Carrington, is a flickering moment of opportunity. It will not come again to either of us."

CHAPTER 41

Harry Strand sat on one of the wooden benches in Mount Street Gardens, a small, cloistered common of irregular shape enclosed on its various sides by the Gothic Revival Church of the Immaculate Conception, St. George's Primary School, Grosvenor Chapel, and the rear entrances to the elegant row houses that faced Mount Street.

The afternoon air was fresh as the sun filtered down through the bowers of the ponderous plane trees that dominated the gardens, their hand-size leaves rustling in the light breeze like rushing water. Pigeons sailed into the quiet close, skittering through the dappled light to land on the grass, where they strutted about in addled curiosity before finally settling into a meditative squat to warm themselves in the random puddles of sun.

Strand listened to the intermittent echoes of the voices of children playing behind the tall windows of St. George's and to the occasional quick step of a solitary pedestrian taking a shortcut through the gardens. He liked the feel of the air on his face and the distant rumble of London traffic that was all but dampened into silence by the surrounding walls of brick and stone.

Bill Howard came into the gardens from the Mount Street entrance, walking through the opened wrought iron gates at a slow, deliberate pace. He stopped at the intersection of the main path and lighted a cigarette, the gesture giving him time to scan the benches along the pathways to find Strand. Without indicating that he had seen him, he turned onto the main footpath. He was wearing a suit that seemed particularly stylish for him, a double-breasted one of chocolate summer wool. He passed through several shafts of sunlight as he approached Strand's bench. He sat down without saying a word.

They watched the pigeons in silence for a few moments and then Strand said, "Bill, I want to make a deal."

"A deal."

"That's right."

Howard shook his head slowly. "I don't know, Harry, you may have gone too far. I don't know if they want to deal anymore."

Silence.

"I sent Mara away," Strand said.

Howard just looked at him. He was trying to decide how to react.

"She told me everything," Strand said.

Howard smoked, then, slowly, a sarcastic grin twisted his mouth, and he shook his head, looking away.

"She was pretty good," Strand said.

"No, she wasn't any good at all." Howard looked around. "I knew damned well . . ."

"I know. She told me."

Howard snorted. "It may be too late for her, too. I don't think they're going to—"

"I don't want to make a deal with the FIS, Bill. I want to make a deal with Schrade."

Howard managed to hide his surprise. He frowned and leaned back into the corner against the arm of the bench. Like Strand, he crossed one leg over the other and pulled once more on the cigarette.

"What do you mean?" he asked.

Two women pushing baby carriages entered from Archibald Mews together and sat on a bench just inside the entrance. They turned their carriages a little to take best advantage of the warming sun. One of them produced a thermos, the other a packet of biscuits.

"I've had it," Strand said. "I'm not up to this anymore."

"You've thought it through?" Howard's voice was flat, his face sober with restrained emotion, like a physician whose terminally ill patient had just told him he wanted to pull the plug.

"Yeah. I've thought it through. I've pushed it as far as it's going to go."

Howard didn't move. He took another drag on his cigarette and tossed the butt onto the path. It smoldered there, burning the last bit of tobacco.

"What made you change your mind?"

Strand hesitated a moment. "It's just the accumulative toll. I don't want to lose what little I've got left."

"Why are you coming to me? I told you before, it's all over with the FIS and this guy. There's no communication channel."

"I've been out of the business for a while, Bill, and I may

THE COLOUR OF NIGHT

be a bit rusty. But I'm willing to bet that you still have access to Schrade, some kind of access."

Howard looked at him blankly, his best poker face. His "no comment" facade.

"I don't give a damn how," Strand added. "I don't care. I just think you're my best bet for getting this to him."

"This what?"

"My offer. A deal."

"Which is?"

"I'll give it all back. The principal. The interest. Every-thing."

"Bullshit. You can't do that."

"Why?"

"Hell, it's tied up in charities and all that."

"Where did you get that information?"

"Don't forget who you're talking to, Harry. Look, even if the FIS didn't have the best goddamn intelligence in the world, you know damn well Schrade's looked into it with a mi-croscope—right up through the ass of all those foundations you set up. He came to us stomping mad, before he left us with our mouths open and our pants down. He showed us what you'd done with the money." Howard's neck was swelling in anger.

"He couldn't have."

"Okay, he showed us *how* it was done . . . the system, the way."

Strand wanted desperately to know how Schrade had dis-covered their scheme, but he wouldn't give Howard the satis-faction of asking. Apparently Schrade's accountants really hadn't found the actual charities.

"Somehow nobody really believes that money is out of

313

their reach, do they, Bill?" Strand retorted. "I mean, why is everybody still hanging around? Why'd the FIS go to the trouble—the considerable trouble—of training Mara? Because you still think you can get the money. Why hasn't Schrade killed me? Because, despite what he 'showed' you, he, too, thinks he can still get his hands on the money—through me. It hasn't stopped him from cutting me off from everything but my arms. But I'm still alive. Everybody thinks they can still get their hands on the money somehow, some way, eventually."

"Christ, Harry." Howard didn't know what to believe.

"I hid that money behind a lot of doors, Bill, but not all of them were locked. No one's found them because they weren't supposed to. There wouldn't have been any point if people could find them. I think you know that already."

Howard gave him a sour look. He was thinking. Finally he asked, "What's the 'deal' you're talking about?"

"We just want a life."

"You want to turn back the clock."

"No." Strand handed Howard a piece of paper. "I just don't want Schrade to stop it."

"What's this?"

"An Internet address. This is where you can get me."

Howard looked at the address. "This is the way you want to work this out?"

"No. This is the way I want you to arrange the meeting."

"What meeting?"

"It's part of the deal. I want to talk with Wolf face to face."

"Oh, for Christ's sake . . ."

"It's a deal breaker, Bill. It's got to be this way."

"What the fuck do you mean it's a deal breaker? 'Deal breaker.' You're in no goddamn position to talk 'deal breaker,'

Harry. What're you talking about? Shit. You don't do the deal, he kills you. There's no *deal* here. I mean, even if you give him the money, all of it. The interest. The whole shitload. How're you going to get him to hold up his end of the 'deal'?" Howard shook his head, looking at the e-mail address. "This is insanity."

Strand was surprised. He had thought that Howard would take his offer and run to Schrade as soon as the words were out of his mouth. Instead he was pointing out that the offer was absurd, an act of desperation. A deal in which the "deal" would surely be violated. In Howard's mind, Strand was already a dead man.

"I'll make sure he holds up his end of the arrangement," Strand said.

"What, 'anything happens to me and the *New York Times* will get an envelope'? Harry, you poor fucking stump."

"I wouldn't have come to you with this if I didn't have it covered."

"Sure, that's good." Howard rolled his head. "You've got it covered. Great."

From the Audley gates an elderly couple entered the gardens with a short-haired dog, an animal of no discernible breed, on a leash. The three of them ambled along the main walk as the dog snuffled busily at the grassy margins, ferreting excitedly among the green clumps. Entrusted with the leash, the woman watched the dog with critical attention, while the man, hands behind his back, gazed about the close with a mild, bifocaled curiosity.

"Why should I do this for you, Harry?"

"Two reasons. First, I can keep the FIS from getting it. I can tie it up for decades. This was not a shoddy operation, Bill.

Some very intelligent people put a lot of thought and sweat into this before we even started. Dennis Clymer was a genius. We ran it for six months, fine-tuning it as we went along, addressing potential problem areas that might crop up farther down the road. We shut it down and took another six months to stabilize what we'd done. So if the FIS wants to try to get it, fine, but my guess is, if they're going to try to get it through the legal system, the Justice Department's going to take a closer look at this and tell them to forget it. Everyone you know in the FIS will have retired by the time they finally realize it's a goose hunt.

"Second, you'd want to do it for the three million dollars I'm going to put in a Belgium account for you. It's properly sheltered, safe to access."

"That's goddamn blunt," Howard said.

"If I remember, you're impatient with finesse."

"Yeah."

It was a crucial moment, but Strand never doubted how it would end.

"Three million dollars . . ." Howard's eyes were fixed on the bit of paper, which he had now folded and unfolded so many times that it was getting limp. Then, to Strand's surprise, Bill Howard seemed to grow angry. Strand could actually see him trying to control his temper, tucking in his chin, tightening his nostrils, his face flushing.

"I'll see what I can do," Howard said abruptly after a little thinking. "So, when I have something, if I have something, I contact you?" He raised the piece of paper and waggled it.

"Yeah. One other thing. I'm leaving London tonight. If you want to talk to me personally after tonight, it won't be easy. It'll take a little time to arrange."

"Where are you going?"

"I'm not staying anywhere very long," Strand said.

"I'll see what I can do. Shit."

"It's not something he really has to ponder, Bill."

"Harry, for Christ's sake . . . Okay, look, how complicated is the money end of this situation?"

"Not too complicated."

"Well, shit, that clarifies it."

"What do you want to know?"

"What do I tell him? A week? Days?"

"Hours."

Howard perked up. "Hours?"

"Yeah."

Howard studied him. "Where do you want to meet him?"

"I'll get to that."

"When?"

"When I see how he reacts to the offer."

Howard folded the paper one last time and put it in the side pocket of his suit coat. As the elderly couple passed by he held his next comment, watching the dog disapprovingly. When they were out of earshot he went on.

"What's the time frame here?"

"We'll work it out."

"The sooner the better?"

"That's right."

Howard was feeling better. He was trying to cover all the bases.

"What if he turns you down, Harry? What then?"

"Eventually he'll get me. I know that." He paused. "But I'll have the satisfaction of seeing half a billion dollars of his laundered cash do some good for a change."

"But you'd cough it all up to save your ass."

Strand looked at him. "I tried to do what I thought would be a good thing," he said. "I guess I've found out that I don't have the guts to give my life for it. Or Mara's. I've already lost everything but her. That's what I was telling you at the beginning, Bill. None of this is very pretty, any way you slice it."

CHAPTER 42

Howard walked away toward the Audley gates. From years of experience, Strand knew that he wouldn't look back. The meeting had left Strand drained and anxious. He couldn't decide whether Howard had been entirely satisfied with Strand's story or whether he harbored a lingering suspicion that Strand was setting him up.

Leaving Mount Street Gardens, Strand made his way through Mayfair to Piccadilly, emerging on Berkeley Street just down from the Green Park underground station.

He rode the underground all the way to Knightsbridge and then all the way back to Piccadilly Circus. He spent some time milling in the crowds there and then walked up the Burlington Arcade, where he drifted in and out of the shops. He worked his way back to Half Moon Street, which he followed to Curzon, stopping in at George Trumper to buy a tube of sandalwood shaving cream.

He turned up Curzon, stopping to look at the film posters on the front of the Curzon Cinema before turning back and following Curzon to Fitzmaurice Place. Half a dozen telephone booths lined the sidewalk just at the Charles Street corner. He stepped into the second one from the right, closed the door, and checked his watch. For seven minutes he stared at the poster advertisements that prostitutes had stuck to the walls of the booth, exposing their wares in black-and-white photographs of steamy vamping.

At precisely five o'clock, the telephone rang. He picked up the receiver.

"You're going to like this place, Harry," Mara said, giving him the address. "I'll leave the front door open."

The town house was close. He turned into Charles Street and started up the hill. Just past Queen Street he turned into Chesterfield Hill, and there, nearly halfway up the first block and across the street, was the red-brick Edwardian town house, newly refurbished, that Mara had leased.

He crossed the street and was pleased to see the "Available" sign still attached to the wrought-iron fence that enclosed the front garden. Upon entering the gate, he walked up the steps and let himself in through the moss green front door, shiny with layers of paint.

When he closed the door behind him the hollow sound echoed through the unfurnished rooms, which smelled of fresh paint and wallpaper paste. On the second floor a large reception fronted the street. To the left was a broad bay window overlooking Chesterfield Hill. Centered between the arms of the windows was a box spring and mattress on the floor, scattered with plastic packets of new linen. Mara walked in from the kitchen, drying her hands on a dish towel.

"Welcome home," she said.

At the other end of the long room, on the wall opposite the bay window, were stacked painters' supplies, five-gallon paint buckets and painters' canvases and scaffolding boards and ladders.

"I convinced the estate agent to leave everything as it was," Mara explained.

"The 'Available' sign is a good touch."

"Yeah, I asked him to leave it for another week. He thought it was an odd request but shrugged it off."

Mara had scavenged together the rough scaffolding boards and paint buckets to make a long table, which she covered with the paint-flecked canvas dropcloths. There was a telephone on the table and books stacked beside it, and a little farther over sat one of the laptops, the screen already lighted. A cobalt blue vase with fresh flowers in it sat on the far end of the table.

"The telephone was a lucky stroke," she said. "The estate agency had it installed to communicate with the workers who were doing the refurbishing work. We just transferred over the names."

Strand looked at her and smiled. "You're right, this is perfect. It's close to everything."

"I got it fairly early this morning," she said, walking over to him, folding her arms, the dish towel dangling from her hands. "It was the third place they showed me. I really had to fork over the money to speed up the paperwork"—she turned and gestured to the bed—"paid extra to get the furniture store to have the bedding delivered within a few hours. It's taken all day."

Strand walked over to the bed and tossed the shaving cream on the new mattress, then took off his coat and tossed it down, too.

Mara waited, her arms folded, her weight shifted to one leg. "Well, how did it go?" she asked.

"I think it's going to work. He's taking it to Schrade. He's supposed to get back to me as soon as possible."

"Then you feel good about it?"

"Yeah, I think so."

Mara thought a moment. "God, it's just so hard to *believe* what Howard's doing. You'd think the FIS would have *some* suspicions about him."

"I just hope he's swallowing this, that they both swallow it. Of course, Schrade's psychology is in our favor. He *wants* to believe. Greed's giving us a leg up here. None of them can stand the thought that the money's really out of reach. The longer we can make them believe it isn't, the longer Schrade's going to put off coming after us."

Strand looked around. "We're going to need something for the windows." He rolled his head from side to side, trying to limber up his stiff neck as he unbuttoned his collar and loosened his tie.

"I've got extra sheets for that. Do you think Howard believed you when you told him you'd sent me away?"

"I didn't get a feeling that he was suspicious," Strand said.

Mara went over to the bed and began taking everything off it.

"I was just as concerned that he not get the impression I was staying in London," Strand said. "I tried to make him think this was just a stopover for me. But I don't know . . ."

Mara opened the packets of new sheets and shook them out. Strand went over to help her.

"While the estate agent was drawing up the papers for me to sign," Mara said, putting down the first sheet, "I took a

cab to a Grosvenor Square. The agent recommended a solici-
tor there. I got the papers authorized that the Houston bank
wanted in order to release the drawings and faxed them to
Houston. About an hour ago I called them and they said everything was in order. They'd already called in the fine arts museum conservator to do the packing. I gave them Léon
Gautier's name and address on the Rue des Saints-Pères.
They'll get the drawings on a flight tonight. I'm to call him tomorrow for the flight number and arrival time in Paris."

They tucked in the last sheet, and Mara threw a bed-
spread over the bed. Strand straightened it from his side and
then sat on the bed while Mara put pillowcases on the pillows.

"When is Bill going to get back to you?" she asked.

Strand shook his head. "I don't know. I told him I was
leaving London tonight. After that it would be more difficult
to arrange a meeting."

"So we just wait."

"That's right."

Mara looked out the window. It was near dusk, and street
lamps were coming on all over Mayfair. The room was growing gloomy as the light outside slipped away.

"Come on," she said, "we've got to put up one of these
sheets before we turn on the lights."

Using the painters' ladder and thumbtacks—Mara had
overlooked nothing—they tacked the top of one of the sheets
to the ceiling, following the angle of the bay window, hanging
the sheet a couple of feet away from the windows themselves.
This created a luminous effect, softening and expanding the
glow from the street lamps.

"I hate to say this," Mara said as Strand was putting away

the ladder, "but I'm starving. My day was frantic, and I skipped lunch. I've got to have something to eat."

They went around the corner to Charles Street and walked to the top of the hill to a little pub that served meals in two rooms in the back. The rooms were small and intimate, and most of the other tables were occupied, which meant that they had no opportunity to talk about their plans. So the dinner was perfunctory, and by the time they had finished and pushed their way through the pub crowd to the front door and the yard outside, it was well after dark.

As Mara took his arm and they started down the hill, Strand realized the weather was beginning to change. Though it was still warm, the air was growing heavy, and the night sky was gauzy with humidity, hazing the street lamps in the distance.

"I've got to leave for a couple of hours," Strand said.

"Really? To do what?"

"I'd rather explain it to you after I get back," he demurred. "It'll be easier that way."

She said nothing for a moment, then she stopped and turned to him.

"Look, Harry," she said, "I want to remind you of something: You are not running an intelligence operation here. We're dealing with our *lives* now, and conceivably, mine is more at risk than yours at this point. So quit acting like you're a case officer. Stop compartmentalizing. If you don't think I have every right to all the information you have, to all the planning you're doing, to all the possibilities that affect *me* directly, then you'd better explain to me why that is. Either you trust me all the way on this, Harry, or you don't. If you don't,

I may want to rethink what the hell I'm taking all these risks for."

She was standing with her back to the brick row houses along the sidewalk, the spill of a street lamp softly lighting her stern expression.

"It's not a matter of trust, Mara. Not trust." He hesitated. "You're right about my reserve, and I know it. Old habits. I'm sorry. But give me a couple of hours here . . . just a couple of hours."

CHAPTER 43

He gazed out the cab window at the London streets. A light fog encircled the street lamps with bright halos.

Knightsbridge.

Mara had been right to call his hand. He couldn't do that to her anymore, even though all of his years of experience running agents made him resist revealing his plans to her. Under the circumstances, however, it actually would be foolish of him to continue to keep his intentions from her. But in this present instance, what he was about to do definitely took their conspiracy to another level. It would provoke some serious discussion, and Strand knew they hadn't had time for that before he left.

Hammersmith.

He had to admit that he found making decisions far more complex now that he was making them for the two of them rather than for himself alone. He found himself second-guessing his instincts, double-checking his gut reactions. His responses to developments were slower. Worst of all, his doubts were more profound. He actually began to fear them.

King Street.

In all the years he had been involved in intelligence operations, never had so much been at stake. If an operation went to hell, seldom did his own life risk a mortal wound. Failures were disappointments, not tragedies. Not for him personally. For others? Yes, but he dealt with that. Perhaps what he was going through now was retribution for all those tragedies in other people's lives that he had managed to "deal with." It wasn't the same at all now. In those days he told himself that if he suffered with everyone who suffered, he wouldn't be able to go on. And that was true, of course. But he wasn't sure it was moral to have been so stoic, to have repressed so much compassion in the name of emotional self-preservation.

Chiswick High Road.

The Terrier pub was on a street of darkness. Chiswick was littered with pockets of urban moribundity, and the Terrier, it seemed, was the last living thing on this street. Brick row houses on either side disappeared into the fog. The inhabitants seemed to be gone, swallowed up by the maw of Disappointment, the last mythical creature of the modern age in which people still actually believed.

He asked the cab to wait for him, and he got out on a wet, gritty sidewalk in front of the pub. The front door of the pub was open, but there was no rollicking on the inside, none of the gay, unruly laughter that he had seen in Mayfair. Here it was silent and grim and smelled of stale lager and piss.

Strand stepped through the door but did not have time to adjust his vision to the darkness before he heard a scratchy voice wheeze his name.

"Harry. Over here."

He turned toward the booths along the wall and made

out a solitary, sallow face looking at him through the smutty gloom. Strand moved to the booth and sat down.

"Jeeeezz-us." The word came from a raw, wounded throat. "Here you are, the real fuckin' thing."

Strand reached across the sticky table and shook hands with the man whose head hunkered down between his bony shoulders. Even in the twilight of the pub Strand could see a wasted man.

"You have a real knack for 'out of the way,' Hodge," Strand said.

The laugh was raspy and without strength.

"Hell, this isn't out of the way, Harry. This is where I live. My part of town."

Strand was embarrassed.

"Well, I appreciate your help, Mack. I didn't even know you were still here."

"Till I die," Mack Hodge said.

It was a deliberate reference to his situation. Strand had already realized that the man was in serious trouble. As his eyes adjusted to the low light, Hodge's face emerged as unrecognizable. Strand was appalled. The flush, boisterous face of memory was gone. The old familiar voice, spookily altered, issued from a papier-mâché visage.

"You're sick, Mack?" Strand asked. He had to. The man wanted him to.

"Dying."

Strand hesitated. "How long has this been going on?"

"Too fuckin' long."

Strand was shocked to see him lift a cigarette and puff on it, the end glowing mean and red between them.

"But not much longer," Hodge added.

"I'm sorry," Strand said.

"Shit." Hodge shook his knobby and emaciated head dismissively, the few remaining wisps of hair on top of it floating aimlessly. "It comes to all of us."

A mug of some kind of beer was clunked down in front of Strand. He sipped it. It was the last thing he wanted to do. And then he sipped again. Smoke floated up from the drawn and sunken mouth across from him and hung in the fetid air between them.

"Even in this dark, godforsaken place I can see you're still handsome, Harry."

It was the strangest remark that Strand could imagine. It was not a Mack Hodge remark. Strand didn't say anything. Nothing, nothing at all seemed appropriate.

Hodge's laugh squeezed from his throat in intermittent gasps.

"Some kind of thing to say, huh, Harry?" Hodge's bony head smoked. "You know what, Harry? It is absolutely true that imminent death gives the lie to life's stupidities. I always thought you were a handsome man. But would I have ever told you that? Hell, I hardly even wanted to think it."

Raspy grunts.

Strand had to summon all of his willpower not to break and run from this sepulchral pub. He could get what he needed elsewhere, surely.

"Quit squirming, Harry. I was just trying to convey to you a little of what it's like . . ." His voice gave out in a prolonged whiffle.

"You caught me off guard, Mack."

"Well, that's something. You always being so goddamn controlled. Macky scores a point, huh?"

Strand could only nod. He drank the warm beer and fought the gagging reflex. He wouldn't be able to take another sip.

"Speaking of death," Hodge whispered, and his scrawny hand floated out of the murk, holding a wadded paper sack. He placed it on the table between them. "I believe you have need of this."

Strand didn't move to pick it up.

"It's exactly what you asked for. Only better. You were never much on keeping up with the latest technology. Every ninety days there are improvements in the application of scientific knowledge to practical purposes. It's a natural law of some sort."

Hodge's mug rose up to his hollow face, and he drank some beer. The cigarette followed. Glowed. Smoke leaked up through the wisps of hair.

"Do I have to know anything particular?"

"You?" Hodge paused. "This is for you *personally*?"

Strand didn't respond.

Hodge didn't speak for a moment, but Strand could hear him breathing.

"Shit, Harry. . . ." His tone was sympathetic, even compassionate. "Shit." There was another awkward hesitation, and then he went on with the business. "Nothing special to know, buddy. It's a disposable weapon. Will not be detected by X-ray or metal detectors—there's no metal in it. I wouldn't rely on its accuracy past thirty feet. It's basically a contact delivery device. The ammunition is special, though. When you're through with it, throw the crap into the sea. For the hit, just break the skin with the bullet. The saxitoxin will do the rest."

He tried to cough but didn't seem to have the energy for it. His hard-drawn breath clattered in his throat, forcing its way past the phlegm. Hodge seemed not to have anything to do with it, as if he just had to wait passively while his body did what it had to do.

"About the pellets—they're a neurotoxin, will drop him on the spot, so you have to give some thought to that. Might make it a brush-by. Could have used ricin, but the target would've had time to run around awhile, call for help, go to the hospital, whatever. Doesn't matter, no antidote for either one of these. It's a can't miss weapon. Only downside is you've got to get in close to deliver it."

"The ammunition?"

"The bullets—pellets—are hard-cast plastic, like the gun. They come in a clip of six, the casings linked, insepara-ble. They're not delicate, but I'd treat them with the utmost respect."

"The sound?"

"About like slapping the side of your face."

"Will it penetrate clothing?"

"A business suit, probably not much more."

"It's automatic?"

"You bet. That's a recent improvement. Didn't used to be. Made the thing a little bulkier, but it's a welcome im-provement."

Hodge smoked and drank.

Strand withdrew an envelope from the inside pocket of his suit and laid it in front of Hodge.

"Thanks," Strand said.

"Lot of money for a dying man," Hodge said. "But I've

got expenses." He paused. "And, like everybody else, I know people who can use it."

Strand reached across and shook Mack Hodge's hand. The first time he had not noticed how the hand felt, but now he was aware of the brittle, parchment texture of the skin and of the sharp ridges of the individual bones.

"It was good to see you, Harry," Hodge said. "I hope this ends well for you."

"I appreciate it, Mack." Strand tried to think of something promising to say, a positive good-bye, but it didn't come to him. Hodge sensed his struggle.

"It's supposed to rain tonight," he said, and Strand was stricken to hear his frail voice crack with unexpected emotion.

"I've got to go," Strand said.

The skull nodded, and the hand came up and the mean glare of the cigarette flared dully one last time on the wasted face.

CHAPTER 44

The rain hammered down on the car in the darkness of Harley Mews. Claude Corsier sat behind the steering wheel of his rental car and looked at Skerlic. The way the Serb's hair was plastered to his forehead reminded Corsier of a dead dog he had once seen in the rain. Skerlic's face was wet, and his raincoat crackled as it worked against the leather seats. He smelled rancid, of cigarettes and sweat.

Corsier looked over into the rear seat. The cumbersome picture frames were wrapped in plastic bubble-wrap. He cringed to see the rain droplets on the plastic, the dry forgeries barely visible through the thick layers of clear wrapping.

"You mounted them as I instructed?" Corsier asked, worried.

"Exactly as you said."

"They weren't damaged? Even a scratch?"

"I'll keep the radio equipment with me," Skerlic said, again ignoring Corsier's fretting. "Give them to the dealer, work out a time for Schrade to come look at them. Contact me. Then we can work out the rest of it."

"Okay." Corsier couldn't take his eyes off the pictures.

"The moment you put them in the agent's possession, I want to be in the hotel," Skerlic said.

Corsier had worried about that. He could not imagine how this odoriferous and coarse creature could stay in the Connaught even for two days without attracting more attention than anyone would want, even if they weren't planning an assassination.

"Is there a problem with the rooms?" Skerlic asked, his glistening forehead wrinkling in suspicion at Corsier's silence. Water beaded on his upper lip.

"No . . . no, I've already reserved the suite. It's ready . . . You know, collectors, especially someone who is presented with a discovery such as this, will examine the frames closely. Curiosity. Everything about these drawings, even the frame in which they are set, will receive careful scrutiny."

"Yes, we thought so." Skerlic nodded quickly. "The job is very well hidden. As a matter of fact, after some concern, we decided to laminate the back of the frame, the part under the paper. We stained it with tea. The paper, too. Damp stain. He would actually have to lift off a rather good layer of laminate—which looks like solid wood—to discover the explosives and the microphones. He would have to take tools to it. It would not be easy."

Corsier felt a little better.

"But," Skerlic added, "you must not leave them with him the whole time. He will prowl. He will prod at it. I agree about the curiosity."

"I won't leave it," Corsier said, "but I will have to let him see the drawings, and give him time to peruse them, before he will agree to call Schrade. And, of course, he will have to have them the day before Schrade arrives. Twenty-four hours."

"That is not a problem. The frames will stand up to that."

"How . . . uh, how stable . . . ?" Corsier glanced over into the rear seat again.

"You have to have the electronics."

"And how easy is it to detonate?"

"Turn a switch. Push a button."

Corsier nodded. It occurred to him that the pictures were facing out, now, in the rear seat. He made a note to turn them the other way as soon as he got around the corner out of Skerlic's sight.

"Okay," Corsier said, turning back to the Serb. "Then that's it. I will call you about the hotel, about the date."

"You, of course, will be with me," Skerlic reminded him. "You have to identify the voice. Once you do that, then it will be up to me to pick the right moment."

"Then that is that," Corsier said.

"Yes," Skerlic said. He was studying Corsier. "Okay."

He turned quickly, his raincoat creaking loudly against the seats, and opened the car door and got out. The sound of rain swelled, and then the car door slammed. The Serb ran around in front of the car and ducked into the vine-covered doorway.

Corsier started the car and eased around the corner of the mews. He stopped and reached into the back and turned the two pictures facing away from him. God. He released the brake and drove out of the mews.

He drove through the rain with single-minded preoccupation until he arrived at a large house on a small street in South Kensington. He stopped at the curb, cut the motor, and looked at the white Georgian facade elevated several steps above the street and flanked by two great beech trees, whose broad leaves were shedding a thousand steady streamlets onto the stone-paved front garden. The windows of the lower floor glowed cheerily in the gloomy darkness, and Corsier could see someone moving about on the other side of the rain-spattered windows. No London residence ever looked cozier.

He got out of the car, locked it, and went to the door and rang the shiny black bell. It was opened immediately, and Corsier was let into a small foyer and then into the front room he had seen from the street. A tall, thin man was waiting for him.

"Ah, Claude, you've grown whiskers," the man said, reaching out to shake Corsier's hand.

Cory Fain was six and a half feet tall, with narrow shoulders, a long face with deep-set eyes, bushy eyebrows, a hawk nose, and a neatly trimmed salt-and-pepper mustache. He was a handsome man in a severe kind of way, with a distinguished bearing and a manner of moving and speaking that conveyed a genuine kindness of character. He was, and had been for the twenty-six years Corsier had known him, an actor, though he had never appeared an hour on a stage or a minute in front of a camera. He was completely unknown in the world of actors and directors, but he enjoyed a fame of another kind in a much smaller arena, where obscurity was held in far greater esteem than celebrity.

They sat in comfortably worn armchairs in slight need of cleaning and exchanged a few minutes of polite conversation, each carefully taking the other's measure to make sure there had been no dramatic changes in profession or position or loyalties.

Corsier paused and asked, "Cory, do you still have an office?"

Fain nodded. "Several, actually. Whatever suits."

"I find myself in need of a barrister."

Fain listened carefully with sober concern, as if Corsier were consulting, well, a barrister.

"This barrister represents a client who is selling several pieces of art anonymously, 'the Property of a Gentleman.' Normally, this is not a problem in the art world, as you may remember. This time, however, I suspect that the buyer will want to verify the identity of the seller. Just to make sure that someone other, namely myself, is not behind the sale."

Fain understood.

"Though you would be representing the gentleman in question, when pushed for an identity—I suspect the buyer will not buy unless he 'knows' that I am not behind the sale—you will be forced to reveal that the seller is, in fact, a woman, not a man. You know her personally, have been representing her family for twenty years or more, and you most certainly will not reveal her identity. Damn the sale. These are discreet people. The tradition of anonymity in art dealings is a long tradition and a tradition you and the lady in question take seriously and honor."

"I see," Fain said. "Exactly."

"Along those lines," Corsier said, "this buyer knows as well as we do that none of this can be ascertained without a reasonable doubt, but what he will be doing is sending a representative to get a feel for the authenticity of the situation. To assess the genuineness of the enterprise."

"Yes," Fain said.

"I would think," Corsier went on, "that the whole exchange would take less than an hour, but it has to be convincing. You'll need to read the reaction. They must be convinced. I would think that an adamant refusal at first, followed by the revelation that the seller is a lady rather than a gentleman, followed by a grudging capitulation, would do the job. And, of course, the agreement to draw up any legal documents required."

"Of course."

"Do you think this could be of interest to you?"

Fain studied the pattern in the rug for a moment, his bushy, brooding eyebrows obscuring the exact direction of his gaze. He looked up. "Is this government related?"

"No."

"Ah, private."

"Yes."

"Well, a barrister . . . that's a serious role, a criminal offense if this isn't government related."

"I understand."

"Expensive."

Corsier did not comment.

"Because . . . well, you know."

"I do."

Cory Fain brooded on the carpet design a little longer. "Would I be expected to produce the woman?" he asked.

"The buyer, or more probably his representative, has to be convinced, so whatever it takes . . ."

Fain raised his head slowly, looking at Corsier down the bridge of his nose. "I'll give you an estimate," he said at last. "Then you give me the details, your exact expectations. Then I'll give you a specific price. Then you decide."

"Very well," Corsier said.

They sat in the cozy front room of Fain's home and talked for another hour. Outside, the rain continued to drench the beeches, whose leaves spilled onto the old paving stones countless rivulets that disappeared into their aging joints.

CHAPTER 45

Hodge was right. It was already raining when Strand came out of the Terrier, and he rode back to Mayfair through a wet, sad London. He felt guilty for being glad to be away from the dying man. Hodge had made a career of selling clever devices for delivering death in a businesslike way to anonymous others. Now the time had come to Hodge himself. Death did not care so much about clever devices and used whatever lay close at hand. In Hodge's case it was nothing fancy, but it was brutally personal.

Strand had the cab drop him off on Queen Street and then hurried through the drizzle the short distance to Chesterfield Hill.

"You hadn't been gone five minutes when an e-mail from Howard came in," Mara said as he walked into the room. "He wants a meeting as soon as possible."

Strand went straight to the computer, sat on a paint bucket, tapped out Howard's address, and then the question:

Can you meet tonight?

Strand stared at the screen. He could feel rain on the sleeves of his jacket, on the legs of his trousers. Mara was behind him, silent. Then suddenly the words were there.

Okay. Tonight. When? Where?

The Running Footman pub on Charles Street, near Berkeley Square. 10 o'clock. Wait at the bar.

I'll be there.

When he got downstairs he put the pistol on the shelf in the coat closet, all the way to the back, out of sight.

Strand sat in a black cab on Charles Street, watching the doors of the Running Footman. Though the rain was keeping the customers inside, he could see from the movement behind the windows, and from the people coming and going, that the pub was busy. He knew Howard would not come by cab, rain or no rain, and since most of the people came in pairs or groups, the solitary figure would be easier to identify. There was no reason for Howard to wait on Strand. In other circumstances he might have been wary, but in this case he had nothing to fear. Rather, it was the other way around. So Strand would let Howard arrive first. Besides, his e-mail had told Howard where to wait. The assumption was that Howard would precede him.

Eight minutes after nine o'clock Howard emerged from around the corner on Fitzmaurice Place, his umbrella held low over his head. Strand recognized his walk. Howard immediately crossed the street and made his way to the pub. He had to wait at the door for a couple who were coming out, fumbled momentarily with his umbrella, then disappeared inside.

"Okay," Strand said, sitting forward in his seat, talking through the window to the cabdriver, "that's him."

The cabdriver held a flashlight in his lap and turned it on a photograph he was holding in his hand.

"Right. I'll recognize him."

"The photograph," Strand said.

The driver handed it back through the window.

"His name is Howard," the driver rehearsed. "I say to him, 'Mr. Strand would like you to come with me, please.' " He looked back over his shoulder. "That's it? He'll come along?"

"He knows the routine."

"But he's not expecting it?"

"No. But when you say that to him he'll know what's up."

"Right."

The cabdriver didn't sound convinced, but he sounded game. The money was more than he was going to earn in the next five nights.

"You have the route down?" Strand asked.

"Right. I do."

"Fine." Strand got out and hurried back to another cab waiting at the curb a few cars back and got inside.

The cab in front crossed into Hays Mews and stopped at the curb. The driver got out and went into the side door of the Running Footman.

Strand concentrated on the door. The rain suddenly became heavier, drumming loudly on the roof of the cab.

The cabdriver emerged from the side door of the pub and

ran to his cab, jerking open the rear door. Howard darted out of the pub and quickly crawled into the back of the cab. The driver slammed the door, got into the front, and turned on the headlights, and the cab lurched and disappeared around the corner.

Knowing the route, Strand's driver was able to lag behind several blocks, sometimes passing the first cab, covering the route like a net. They went as far north as Oxford Street and over to Regent Street and Piccadilly before working their way back to Berkeley Square, where the two cabs pulled into a tiny, dark lane on the northeast corner of the square and stopped in front of a place called the Guinea Grill.

The two men got out of the cabs at the same time and quickly ducked through the door in the vine-laden facade of the pub.

"That was a goddamn waste of time," Howard complained, folding his umbrella impatiently and tossing it toward a corner.

"Not for me." Strand wiped his face with a handkerchief and leaned his umbrella against the wall. The Guinea Grill was a restaurant with a small pub proper at the very front of the establishment set off from the entry by a wood screen with a narrow door in it. The screen was open at the top, and the conversation from the tiny pub was audible as one waited to be seated in the restaurant.

Strand gave his name, and they were quickly taken to a table in an oddly shaped alcove that comfortably contained three tables. All three of the tables had "Reserved" signs on them. Strand and Howard were seated at the center one, farthest from the entry.

"You bought the other two," Howard said.

"Yes."

"Hang the expense."

Strand ignored the sarcasm. They ordered drinks, and Howard wiped his hair and brushed at the sleeves of his coat, pissed at having gotten wet and pissed at having been wheeled around Mayfair because of Strand's scrupulosity.

"What did he say?" Strand asked.

"Shit . . ." Howard fussed, flexing his arm to straighten out his coat. Using his linen napkin, he wiped his face again, dried his hands. "He says, Okay. Get everything together, bring it to Berlin. He's willing to—"

"No."

Howard stopped. He gave Strand a cold, tight-lipped stare.

"None of this will be done according to anything he says. I'll spell it all out. How it's done, when it's done, all of it."

"Bullshit."

"I don't trust him, Bill. Everything having to do with this exchange is predicated on that."

"You think you're in a position to dictate this?"

"If he wants the money, yes. If he doesn't, then I guess not, and none of it matters anyway."

They sat in silence, looking at each other. Strand had nothing else to say, and if Schrade really wasn't going to cooperate, then the conversation was over and Howard could go back out into the rain. He suspected that Howard's instructions were far more flexible than this. He was just engaging in his own little pleasures of prologue.

Their drinks arrived, gin and tonic for Howard, Scotch for Strand. They each drank.

"Okay," Howard said, "what's for openers?"

"Is he going to meet with me or not?"

"Yes."

"Fine. Then I'll arrange a meeting place where he'll be safe."

"What does that mean?"

"He'll be familiar with it. He'll be comfortable with it."

"Okay, where?"

"My main concern is meeting with him alone, without his security. And I have to *know* we're alone."

"Okay, okay, okay." Howard wasn't interested in finessing his irritation. "Where?"

"I'll e-mail you a date and an e-mail address. On that date Schrade has to be ready to travel."

"Ohhh, bullshit, Harry. He's not going to—"

"I'll let him know where to go. He plugs in there and gets another e-mail message."

"This is stupid."

"It's the only way I'll do it."

"Okay, so you do a treasure hunt. Then what?"

"When I know he's clean, I'll give him the meeting place."

"Then?"

"I'll bring everything in a briefcase. The CDs with all the accounts, detailed instructions about transferring them . . ."

Howard started to laugh. "Jeee-zus. He said you'd do that, that you'd say you'd give him the instructions. Wow." He took a drink. "Well, Schrade says go fuck yourself."

Strand waited.

"You told me this morning that the transactions could be done in *minutes*. Schrade says, fine, then you do them in minutes, right there. The two of you. When his people tell him he's got the money, then he's got the money."

Strand waited again. He couldn't relent too easily, he couldn't say, "Fine, it's a deal," just like that.

"I don't know. . . ."

"Okay, you're so damn fond of giving ultimatums, here's one for you to deal with: You do it right there, in front of Schrade, or you forget it. Period."

Silence. Finally Strand said, "Okay. We'll do it right there."

Howard laughed again. "You really did a hard ass negotiation on that one, Harry. You drove me right down to the wire, up against the wall, made me sweat."

Howard was feeling cocky.

"But this is going to cause a delay."

Howard tried to hold his grin, as if Strand's last remark were of no consequence. "Oh, a delay. Why's that?"

"If I'm going to move that kind of money electronically, in just a few minutes, I'll have to give written notification signed in the presence of a designated bank officer that on a certain date, at a certain hour, I'll be making these transfers by wire. They're not going to do it just because they get a computer message that says I want them to do it. Even if I give authorized code numbers. I'll have to make arrangements ahead of time, and I'll have to do it in person, face-to-face."

"You told me minutes."

"That was if I handed over everything to Schrade. I would've had time to do that. But if you want it done this way, you've got to give me time to arrange it."

Howard studied him. He was trying hard not to let his exasperation show. "How long?"

"The money's in six banks in six different countries. It's going to take me a day and a half—minimum—to fly to each of them, get the authorization, and move on to the next. That's nine days. Banks are closed weekends." He fixed his eyes on Howard. "Two weeks."

Howard couldn't argue. He really had no choice. "I've got to go back to Schrade with this."

"Fine."

"Let's agree, right now, when and where."

Strand nodded. He let his eyes slip to the side as if making mental calculations.

"Okay. Zurich. Two weeks from today. I'll use your e-mail address to notify you of the exact time and location."

"That's it, then," Howard said.

"That's it."

Howard downed the last of his gin. He had to recover. Strand could see his mind working. Howard was over the hill, even worse than Strand. He screwed up as much testosterone as he could muster for one closing gesture of bravado. He smiled thinly.

"You know what, Harry?" Howard said, his voice low, his tone almost pensive. "All these years, I thought you were better than average as an officer. Not the best by a long shot, but a good bit better than average." He pursed his lips thoughtfully. "But I would never have guessed that you had the brains—or the stomach—for something like this. Never."

Strand had nothing to say to that. What Howard had or had not thought about him all those years was of no interest to him in the least. Everything he cared about now was in front of him. Everything behind him was dead and gone.

Strand looked at his watch. "I've got to go," he said, and raised his hand to get the waiter's attention.

CHAPTER 46

As Strand rounded the corner to Chesterfield Hill the drizzle had turned to a drenching mist intermingled with a light fog, a concoction so thick you could almost reach out and grab a handful of it. He had walked all the way from the Guinea Grill, his collar turned up uselessly against the moisture. Leaning into the incline, he looked toward their town house. There was a soft glow behind the sheets over the bay window.

By the time he had climbed the stairs to the reception, Mara had heard him and was standing in the middle of the room, waiting. She had been sitting on the bed, drawing: she had left her sketchpad there, and a lamp was sitting on the floor beside the mattress.

Strand had taken off his raincoat as he came up, and without speaking she came over and took it from him and laid it over one end of the scaffolding. Then she turned around and faced him.

"Well?"

"It looks like Schrade's willing to deal," he said.

Mara gasped as if she had been holding her breath.

"But I had to make a quick decision that I hope will look as good tomorrow as it did tonight."

"What?"

Strand sat on one of the paint buckets and started untying the laces of his waterlogged shoes.

"Schrade's totally focused on getting this money back," Strand said, tugging at one of the shoes. "Maybe it's the most important thing in his life right now. And that's the problem. We've got two parallel plans going here, and the first one was getting in the way of the second. First, we're holding out the prospect of giving him the money to keep him at arm's length, to keep him from coming after us. On the other hand, we're trying to lure him to London. With the money exchange imminent, I was afraid Schrade wasn't going to give a damn about the drawings. They can't compete with six hundred million dollars. So I changed the date when I said I could deliver the money—two weeks."

He tossed one shoe on the floor and started on the second one as he told Mara about the proposition he had given Howard.

"And Howard seemed to have the authority to accept it," he concluded, "which he did." He tossed the second shoe on the floor, took out his handkerchief, and began wiping the rain off his face.

Mara had sat on the scaffolding. "So," she said, "the idea is that with the money transfer not a possibility for another two weeks, if Schrade gets a call from Knight in a few days saying he's got this spectacular small collection he needs to look at, he's more likely to fly over and look at it."

"That's the idea."

Mara thought a moment. "Then as soon as the drawings

get to Paris, we've got to pick them up immediately and get to Carrington Knight."

"That's right. And I've got some ideas about that, too. We're going to have to be very good at approaching Knight."

Strand looked at the lower legs of his soaked trousers. "Damn."

"Where did you go the first time, Harry?"

There was no use pretending about this any longer. He waited a second and then looked at her.

"I went to buy a gun," he said. "A special kind of gun, to kill Schrade."

They stared at each other.

"Well," Mara said, her voice flat, without inflection, "it's a relief not to have to call it 'the meeting' any longer. Lying about it to each other, talking around it with euphemisms, made it even nastier."

He looked at her. With the pale light coming from behind her, he knew she could see his eyes. But for him, her face was shadowed in the lee side of the light, and he could see nothing of her expression. He didn't need to see her eyes to know she was disturbed.

"Harry, unless you're withholding something very serious from me," Mara said, and he could tell she was trying to control her voice, "you don't have any training in this stuff, in operations."

"I've never murdered anyone, if that's what you mean."

"Well . . . *God* . . . what are you *thinking*, Harry?"

"What would you do, Mara?"

"Run. Run like hell."

"For the rest of your life?"

"If that's what it took."

Strand was weary, and he spoke slowly. "What do you think that would be like? Every time you bought a tube of oils or a sketchpad or a box of pastels in some art supply store—anywhere in the world—you'd have to wonder if someday someone's going to walk into that store and show a photograph of you to the clerks and ask, 'Have you ever seen this woman?'" He looked at her silhouette. "You're not an easy woman to forget, Mara."

"I don't know, Harry. But it's got to be bearable. Everything is."

"Yeah, it would be bearable right up to the moment our car or our house blew up, or until we woke up in the middle of the night with a gun in our faces or a knife at our throats, or—"

"Harry—"

"Listen," he said, "why is running and living in constant fear the only moral response we have here?"

Again she was silent, but this time he felt terrible about it. Not only for Mara, but for himself. These were questions he had dwelled on endlessly. They were questions he had lain awake at night trying to answer in a new and different way, trying to find some light in a nuanced reply that, in its devising, he hoped would give him a little room to maneuver around either his conscience or the inflexible parameters of reality. Had he thought of all the possible answers to these questions? Were there no *other* answers than the ones he had already turned away from?

"So we murder him, Harry? That's the best answer that two intelligent people can come up with?"

"Give me some alternatives. Realistic alternatives."

She was silent.

"Self-defense," he said. "That's the way I think of it. I have to." He paused. "It's ironic, really, that in a world where everything is instantaneous, it is the absence of immediacy that puts us on the wrong side of this dilemma. If Schrade were to burst into this room right now, intent on killing us, we could kill him in self-defense free of moral taint. But if he takes longer than that, if he drags it out for days or weeks or months, even though we *know* he's trying to kill us, then we have to run and hide for the rest of our lives to sustain a moral position. We're only justified in defending ourselves when we do it just before the moment of death. If we can. If we don't see it coming . . . well . . ."

"I thought self-defense was only justified if you didn't have time to call someone else for help, or to ask for the protection of the law," she said.

Strand shook his head. "Look, the only people who know that Schrade is capable of this kind of stalking are the criminals he works with and the intelligence agencies who use him. How the hell are we going to justify a request for protection from him? To the business world he's a very successful international businessman. We'd sound like the worst kind of conspiracy nuts. Even if they took us seriously, think of the legal struggle we'd be facing trying to pull classified information from intelligence agencies to back up our claim. You know how effective that's been in the past. That would initiate a complex of legal maneuverings that would consume all of our energy for the rest of our lives."

"But we'd be alive, wouldn't we? He wouldn't dare kill us with that kind of media attention on us."

"That's right, Mara. But we'd die of natural causes. An inexplicable car wreck . . . it happens. One of us would contract

a rare virus, a seldom seen bacteria . . . those are not so unusual anymore. A heart attack, even though the autopsy would
show no signs of heart disease . . . it could happen to anyone.
Or we'd be found dead in our bedroom, needles and drug
paraphernalia scattered around us . . . you never really know
about people, what they're really like in the privacy of their
own homes."

Mara didn't respond. Suddenly Strand couldn't stand the
wet clothes any longer.

"Look, I'm going to shower. We can finish this later."

She nodded. "Sure," she said.

When he got out of the shower, he wrapped a towel
around his waist and took another to dry his hair and walked
back into the reception. Mara had turned out the lights and
had moved aside the sheets covering the bay windows. The
city lights reflecting off the overcast sky threw a glow through
the windows as bright as a full moon. She had taken off her
clothes and was lying on the mattress in her underwear. She
was on her stomach, propped up on her elbows, watching
him, waiting. He went over and sat on the bed, the towel he
was drying his hair with draped around his neck. He was
weary.

It began raining again. He was dissatisfied. He should
have defended himself better, in a more thoughtful way, less
stridently. The truth was, not only was he operating out of
fear—and was unable to find a satisfactory way to rid himself
of it—but also he was wrestling with the discovery that at the
back of his heart there was a wound that had begun to fester.
He had tried to ignore it, but it was no longer possible to do
so. It ached for a healing remedy that was as disturbing to him

as the discovery of the wound itself: it ached for the balm of revenge.

"What's on your mind?" she asked, looking up at him.

"Just about everything."

"Yeah, I know. But we can work this out," she said. "I'm not pessimistic about it."

"Everything's going to have to click. The timing. Everybody has to buy into the story. We have to be good, and we have to be lucky."

For a moment they thought their own thoughts, and then Mara reached over and put her hand on his bare leg.

"It's strange," she said softly, breaking the silence, "that we met like this, isn't it, Harry?"

"I don't know," he said. He really didn't. They had met, discovered something in common, fallen in love.

"It is," she said, "because this is a strange business, and we're strange people to be in it."

He ran his fingers through his hair. Jesus, what a world of confusion. How could he have been through so much and learned so little? How could he be where he was and be at a loss for what to do? Mara was right. For all their sophistication, for all the complexity of their situation, the solution he had arrived at was shockingly primitive.

"Harry, come on. Lie down." She moved over as Strand took off the damp towels and put them aside on the floor. He lay down, and she moved over to him and curled her back into him. He turned to accommodate the shape of her, and then both of them were facing the rain. He put his arm around her, and she took it and pulled it to her breasts, drawing him closer still. They watched the rain, listened to the sound of it streaking the windows, like no other sound in the world.

Strand was comforted by the motion of her breathing within his embrace, with the way she felt. He wanted to be able to touch more of her than was physically possible. He wanted to be absorbed into her.

CHAPTER 47

When Strand woke to the gray morning light, his limbs were leaden, his mind unrested. He had awakened repeatedly during the night and had lain awake, staring at the luminous London night sky. He had worried about everything all at once, each concern leading into the next one, forming a long chain of solicitude. He had resolved nothing.

Outside the bay window the rain had stopped, but the day was thick with mist. He looked at Mara. She was sleeping on her stomach, the covers pulled down to her hips, her long hair fanned out across her bare skin in a filigree of black.

Carefully laying back the covers, he got up stiffly from the bed. He picked up the two towels and walked out of the room, past the kitchen to the next room, where Mara had put their clothes in a closet. He dressed and went into the bathroom and washed up, deciding not to shave just then. Then he went into the kitchen and started the coffee.

Folding his arms, he leaned against the countertop and watched the nut brown coffee dribbling into the glass pot. The town house was quiet, but in an odd auditory deceit its empty rooms seemed to echo the silence.

"How much do you think you slept?" Mara was in the doorway, still in her underwear, holding her dress.

"Did I keep you awake?"

"You helped, but I managed to be restless all on my own. I'm going to bathe. There are pastries in that paper bag over there," she said, and went into the bathroom to shower.

Strand walked back into the main room and got the two tea mugs off the floor, then took them back to the kitchen and washed them. When the coffee was finished, he poured a cup and went over to the scaffold table. He sat on a paint bucket in front of the computer and clicked it on. There was e-mail from Howard.

HS . . . FYI
The new arrangements are acceptable. And
  firm. No changes. He said: "Impress upon
  him the gravity of the consequences that
  will quickly follow should he fail to make this
  meeting."
There it is. Take it seriously.
BH

Strand stared at the monitor: "the gravity of the consequences that will quickly follow." He had no doubt in his mind that the grave consequences were his ineluctable future regardless of whether or not Schrade got his money. If Schrade thought for a second that Strand believed he could avoid Schrade's wrath by handing over the money, there was no end to the self-delusion that plagued all of them. Schrade's menace blurred all other influences affecting Strand's motivation.

He flipped off the switch and stood up.

It was difficult not to feel paralyzed by the knowledge that Schrade's intelligence apparatus was as good as those of most governments. On the other hand, Strand had been in intelligence work all his life, and he knew that no intelligence organization was ever as good as it needed to be. He reminded himself of all the times he had not been able to find his targets, of all the times they had evaporated when he was most sure of their whereabouts, of all the times they had maneuvered themselves away from his agents and disappeared into an oblivion from which they had never again returned.

Remembering these old failures brought back into realistic focus the truth of Schrade's reach, a truth that was all too easily thrown out of focus by the swelling fear that one felt in the face of his rampant violence. No one, however, not even Wolfram Schrade, was omniscient. If you had enough money and reasonable good luck, you could evade the surveillance of even the best organizations. Sometimes for a long time. Strand's professional experience gave him an edge. He just had to keep reminding himself.

He took a sip of coffee. It was time to start working out the procedures that would propel them into Schrade's orbit.

"You're going to have to take the drawings to Carrington Knight yourself," Strand said. They were sitting on paint buckets, facing each other from either side of the makeshift table. Mara had finished bathing and was still wearing a white dressing gown, her wet hair wrapped tightly in a towel. Her coffee mug sat next to her half-eaten croissant.

"I obviously can't do it," he said. "You can use the identity on one of the passports I got from Darras. Carrington will be thrilled with the collection. And with you."

Mara flicked her eyes at him.

"There won't be any problem with Carrington," Strand added. "He can smell the real thing all the way across Mayfair."

"And what's the odor of the real thing?"

"Carrington knows. It's as distinctive as a pheromone to him."

"A pheromone."

"Do you have any problem with this?" Strand asked. "We could think of other ways to do it. But this would be best."

"No, I don't think I have any problem. It's just a straightforward offer to sell, right?"

"More or less."

"Oh. Well, let's talk about that."

"There will be two difficulties," Strand said. "One, to make sure that the offer for the drawings will be made first to Wolf Schrade. We want Schrade to come to London to look at them. Period. Other collectors would quickly buy them as a lot. We don't want Carrington to do the easy thing and offer them to the first available client. The second thing: You have to convince Carrington to keep you, the seller, anonymous. If he makes the mistake of describing you to Schrade . . ."

Mara nodded. "Okay." She thought a moment. "Maybe we can resolve both of these problems by the way I present myself to Knight." She stared off toward the bay window, toward the ashen light. Then she turned back to him. "Let me think about it. We don't have to decide right this moment, do we?"

"No, of course not. But there's another problem. All your documentation for the provenance of the drawings was still at my place."

"Oh, God."

"Yeah. I've got to come up with some forgeries to replace them. Carrington's not going to offer these to Schrade without documentation. I would've had to do this anyway, even if they hadn't been destroyed, because we've got to make sure the paper trail is obscure enough that Carrington can't easily confirm any of it. If the time is short, if the sale is dependent on a quick negotiation, he'll forgo his own provenance check and just rely on the documentation rather than risk losing the sale. Also, this way it won't lead back to you. We have to come up with a new owner for the drawings."

Mara sipped her coffee. Then she put down the mug and stood and took the towel off her head. Bending over, she fluffed her hair with the towel, then quickly straightened up, flinging her hair back out of her face. Preoccupied, she walked toward the bed, folding the damp towel, matching the corners precisely.

Strand said nothing. She had a lot to think about. He had no doubt she could play the role, run the scam. After all, she had already proven her abilities in that regard. Nearly their entire relationship had revolved around a scenario in which she had expertly demonstrated how capable she was at deception. Her thoughtfulness now was interesting. He guessed that after Mara had been pressed into service by the FIS, she'd been surprised to discover that she had a considerable ability—and liking—for undercover work. He also guessed that, in her innermost being, she must be confused by this. Maybe she had been more insightful than either of them had realized last night when she'd said that this was a strange business and they were strange people to be in it.

She came back to the scaffolding table and sat down. "We have a lot to do and not much time," she said.

"That's right."

"Can you get the forgeries done, if we come up with the right background? I mean, do you have time?"

"Yes. I know the people here in London who can do it. If I pay enough money, I can probably get it done in two days."

"Okay, then I have some ideas for the woman who's going to see Carrington Knight. If we get that settled this morning, can you get started?"

Strand nodded.

"I'll go to Paris for the drawings," she said. "Is that what you're thinking?"

"It is, yes."

"There's not going to be a problem with Léon Gautier releasing them to me?"

"None."

"Okay. While I'm there I'm going to have to buy some clothes. I don't have the kind of clothes in my suitcase that this woman wears."

"There's another consideration that we might as well address right now," Strand said. "We want all of this to happen as quickly as possible. I think we ought to put that kind of constraint on the sale if we can, press Carrington to make this happen fast. The point being to get Schrade to London immediately."

"Knight's going to want to keep the drawings."

"That's right. I would too in his situation. Any dealer at this level would. He's going to have to examine them closely. He can't offer them to Schrade—arguably his best client—on a cursory examination. They'll be safe there. He has the best facilities."

Mara nodded.

"But," Strand went on, "we don't want to leave the forged documentation with him. We can't risk the possibility that he'll discover they're not authentic."

"Then why have the forgeries worked up?"

"If he asks to see them, you'd better have them. You just can't leave them with him." He paused. "You'll have to play it by ear. See what feels right and play it out."

CHAPTER 48

The rain roared outside. Corsier stood at the windows and looked across at the Connaught Hotel through the downpour and the dull afternoon light. He saw the windows that he thought were in the suite from which he would identify Schrade's voice and then watch the explosion. The afternoon was so dark, the street lamps had come on and the street below was glistening with rain and glitter from the lamps, the rain running along the curbs like liquid light.

"All right all right all right," Carrington Knight chirruped, hustling back into the viewing room with a bottle of champagne and two tall, thin glasses.

Corsier turned around, his heart slamming against his ribs. Knight, dressed in black, was wearing a Tyrian purple necktie and a simpering smile that had a hint of collusion about it. He set the champagne and the two glasses on the library table on a Victorian silver tray. Then he grinned at Corsier, a gray ferret's grin, and opened his hands to Corsier, inviting him to proceed.

Corsier turned to the table and began undoing the first of two leather carrying cases he had had made in France when this moment was only a glorious anticipation in his mind's eye. He had ordered the cases the same day he'd bought the frames, measuring them right there and then. They were lined with a chocolate velvet that complemented the leather cases. He knew Knight would notice this. He knew Knight would appreciate it.

Asking Knight to hold the leather case, Corsier reached inside and slowly withdrew the first frame, face up, turning it so that Knight could see it upright from the other side of the table. It was the drawing of the two reclining women.

Corsier's eyes were fixed on Knight's face. Knight's mouth was slack. His eyes darted all over the picture, tonguelike, tasting every line, every stroke of the pencil, every blush of lilac, the slanted glance, the proud pudenda, his eyes greedy and glittering.

"Ohhhh . . . hhhhhh . . . *Claude*! Oh! My! God!"

Corsier let him revel.

"Schiele! Can you believe this?? *Look* at this . . ."

Knight raised his round black eyeglasses, resting them on his forehead, and stepped back. He shook his head. He came forward, picked up the heavy frame, and took it to the countertop, where he leaned it against the bookshelves.

Even Corsier's breast thrilled. In the special lighting in which Carrington placed the drawing, the very soul of Egon Schiele burst into view. The goddamn thing looked—authentic!

Knight whirled around. "The other one!" he said quickly.

They went through the same procedures to remove the second drawing from its leather case, and Knight immediately marched it over to the countertop and leaned it against the bookcases beside the other.

He put one arm across his stomach, rested the elbow of the other on top of its wrist, and put his chin in his hand as he studied them both. He stepped forward, leaned in close, his eyes vacuuming the surface of first one drawing and then the other. He reached up and lowered his eyeglasses to the bridge of his small nose and stepped back, pacing from side to side in front of the pictures, viewing them from different angles. He struck a pose, one leg stretched in front of the other, arms crossed, shaking his head slowly as he marveled, a silver lock of hair falling down over his forehead.

"Well," he said finally, raising his eyebrows and turning to Corsier with a look of theatrical amazement, "these are really quite beautiful. Convincing. *I* certainly have no hesitation to bring Wolf into this. The things just look like Schiele. I mean, it's a hell of a thing to discover Schieles, for God's sake, isn't it?"

"I could hardly believe my eyes," Corsier said.

He decided to grow serious instead of joyous. Knight had always to be tempered. If he were morose or skeptical, one had to pick him up. If he were ebullient, one had to portray studious sagacity. Knight appreciated a certain amount of tension, a certain *équilibre*.

"To be honest, Carrington, I find I'm a bit humbled by this discovery," Corsier said. He walked around to join his flamboyant associate. "Can you imagine these things hanging in obscurity for something like eighty years? Can you imagine how easily they might have disappeared?" He put his hands behind his back, a big, studious bear of a man, and stood before the drawings. "This hausfrau brings them in the back of her Volvo, and she knows nothing of what she has."

Knight said nothing. He turned and stepped to the table,

uncorked the champagne, and filled the two flutes. He handed one to Corsier, and the two men faced each other.

"To Schiele."

They clinked their glasses and drank, then simultaneously turned to the drawings. They looked at them.

"They haven't names?" Knight asked.

"Not that I know." Corsier stroked his goatee.

"They must."

"What do you suggest?"

"This one," Knight said, gesturing with his glass to the two girls, "should be *Two Lovers Reclining.*" He was emphatic. He stepped to the second drawing. "God, I love the way he's done the bottom of the buttocks here. And the *reflection* of that dark pudenda." He was pensive. "This one should be *Model Regarding Herself in a Mirror.*" He raised his eyebrows quizzically.

"Oh, I wouldn't change either name," Corsier said. "They are perfect. Schielean titles."

"Then there we have it." Knight drank. "You'll need to prepare a statement of provenance. You've got to get them from Schiele's studio to here."

"Easily."

"I'll need a letter from a lawyer stating that he is representing an anonymous owner and that the drawings, 'the Property of a Gentleman,' can be legally represented by him."

"Yes," Corsier said. "Here is the name of the barrister who will issue the letter." He handed Knight a card. "If by some off chance Schrade should balk at the proposition of anonymity, you may tell him that he is welcome to contact this man. He will keep my identity completely secure and at the same time be able to allay any doubts Schrade may have about provenance. I urge you to give the barrister's name only as a last resort."

"I doubt this will be necessary," Knight said, glancing at the card and putting it aside. "Schrade has bought anonymously from me before. Never was a problem."

"That would be the best possible situation."

"Now"—Knight continued looking at the drawings as he spoke—"it seems to me that the energy of discovery can best be sustained if I call Schrade immediately, *announce* the discovery, and urge him to act quickly. This is a momentous event, after all, and he can't expect me to linger with these. He will get first look, but he will not have a lot of time." He turned to Corsier. "When do you place them?"

"As you mentioned before, early. I'm going to think . . . 1911. His sister Gertrude was still posing nude for him then. I rather think the mirror one looks like Gertrude in the mouth and the eyes."

"Damned if I don't agree with you, Claude. Exactly."

They stood, regarding the drawings.

"When did you say you were going to call Schrade?" Corsier asked.

"Tomorrow."

CHAPTER 49

TWO DAYS LATER

The woman had called the day before and wanted an appointment to see him. Carrington Knight had no openings in his calendar for that day. She persisted. She said that she understood he was one of the leading authorities on the drawings of these five particular artists. She named them. Was this true?

Knight modestly agreed. He detected an American accent.

Well then, she had drawings by these artists. Seven drawings, which she wanted to sell for a client.

Knight was suddenly alert. These artists did not come on the market every day. In fact, they were rare. Highly collectible. She had seven of them?

These were actual drawings? Documented?

Oh, yes. Every one. Documented.

Maybe they should meet after all. What about tomorrow? he asked. That would be fine, she said, and they arranged a meeting late in the afternoon.

So here he was now, balancing a cup of Lapsang souchong and looking out the windows at the brooding day. On the countertop nearby he had propped up the two

photographs of the Schiele drawings. For the past two hours
he had paced his second-floor showroom, casting a bright eye
at the rain one moment and an avaricious eye at the Schieles
the next. The previous day he had e-mailed his news of the
Schiele discoveries to Wolfram Schrade at a special number
reserved for his art business in Berlin. The woman who handled the paperwork for his acquisitions had responded immediately. She was quite excited at his news, but, she said, Mr.
Schrade could not be contacted until that evening. She would
communicate the news to him as soon as possible. She was
sure she could get back to him the next day.

Today. But she hadn't. Yet.

Knight looked at his watch. Urgency was very important
in these situations. It created a fire in the clients. Urgency
begat urgency, and the greater the urgency about a particular
piece of art, the greater its importance. Therefore urgency was
a valuable psychological tool, and once urgency had been introduced, it was a terrible thing to let it subside. It was like an
erotic moment. One did not want to be distracted by the
plumber or by a delivery from the grocer. Sustained urgency
usually could be stoked up to a really satisfying financial cli-
max.

So Knight looked at his watch again. He sipped the smoky
tea, which he particularly enjoyed on rainy days. A rich tea for
a rich moment.

He was thinking of this as his eyes made regular sweeps
from the photographs of the Schiele drawings to the telephone
at the end of the library table and down to the rainy street—
unlike most Londoners, he relished the rain, liked watching it,
always had, and summer rain was the best—when the black

Jaguar Vanden Plas pulled up to the curb in Carlos Place and stopped.

After a moment a uniformed driver got out of the front door, put up an umbrella, and opened the back door of the car. For a flicker of a moment two long legs, almost entirely exposed beneath a short black dress, swung out of the car and onto the sidewalk; the chauffeur's umbrella blocked his line of sight and hid the woman's face. As she was helped out of the car, Knight saw the drape of an ankle-length raincoat descend to cover her long legs, and then the chauffeur and the woman hurried up the steps to the front door of Carrington, Hartwell & Knight.

Knight's preoccupation was momentarily arrested. What an elegant arrival. He loved it. It was a fine day.

He watched as the chauffeur returned to the car with Jeffrey, Knight's receptionist/security guard. While the chauffeur held the umbrella, Jeffrey removed a package from the rear seat, and the two of them hurried up the steps and out of the rain. Ms. Paille and her seven drawings had arrived.

Jeffrey had been given instructions to show her up straightaway upon her arrival, so Knight stood beside his library table and waited for the woman who belonged to the long legs to ascend the staircase, her high heels silent on the Persian-carpeted treads.

As she made the last graceful turn of the staircase, she arose slowly from within the winding tracery of the mahogany balustrade like Venus from the sea. Knight's heart stalled. Ms. Paille, dressed in black, was a most exotic mixture of Asian and European: tall, trim, her beautiful proportions clothed in a short two-piece affair of snug, fine silk. Her jet hair spilled generously over her shoulders, its highlights glistening in the soft spotlights of the showroom. Her dusky eyes were deep enough to swim in—swim naked, Knight thought—and her olive complexion was stunningly set off by rich carmine lips, which, as fate would have it, were the exact color of the scarlet silk walls of the library in front of which she now stood.

"My dear Ms. Paille," Knight said. The word of endearment surprised even him, but it just seemed so appropriate.

"Mr. Knight . . ." She extended a long arm, and he took her hand . . . and kissed it.

By God, if ever a woman wanted to have her hand kissed . . . The surprised smile she gave him was worth the extravagance of the gesture, and—should he not have guessed?—so was the fragrance of her wrist.

Jeffrey emerged from behind her and put the wrapped package on the library table, then disappeared silently down the staircase.

"I do appreciate your taking the time for this," she said.

"My pleasure, I assure you," Knight beamed. He turned to the package. "These, apparently, are the drawings?"

"Yes."

"And these are your own personal drawings?"

"No, I represent the owner, a gentleman from Hong Kong."

"Hong Kong? Really?"

"I'm Chinese American," she said, smiling. "Mr. Cao Pei is Hong Kong Chinese. I've worked for him for eleven years. Mr. Cao is not an art collector, but he acquired all of these drawings during the last fifteen years from a variety of sources, mostly Englishmen living in Hong Kong. Now he wants to sell them. He believes he can get better prices here than in Hong Kong. That's my purpose for being here."

"How interesting." He looked at her. "Then, your background is not in art?"

"No, not at all."

"Oh?"

"International economics."

"Then, uh, this is just an assignment for you. Art is not particularly an interest of yours."

"Not particularly."

What, Knight wondered, did impassion her? He couldn't imagine, but he would love to know. He would love to *see* her impassioned.

"Well, then, do you have documentation that this belongs to Mr. Cao? That's a very important part of my business, you know, provenance. A work of art, especially an important work of art, has to have, as it were, a genealogy of ownership."

"I have that in a bank box."

"I see." He looked at her breasts, their contours revealed to him in relief, black upon black, their actual shape apparent beneath the capillary attraction of the watery silk. "Then, let's take a look at what you have."

The double entendre was out of his mouth too quickly to stop. He smiled at her. She smiled back. Did they understand each other? He wasn't sure.

She stepped up to the library table, undid the clasps on the case, which was bound in heavy wheat buckram, and opened it. Inside the case a cover page preceded the actual drawings and was closed with a bow of silk. She untied the bow and folded back the cover leaf.

He was silent.

He leaned over the portfolio and carefully put his finger-
tips on the edge of the table. The first drawing was a Balthus.
A fine, a very, very fine Balthus. My God, he thought. A surprise. He turned the leaf. On both the left and the right were
two Delvauxs. Rare Delvauxs. Both deliberate drawings, not
studies. Knight's stomach quivered. He turned the leaf. On the
left was an Ingres. On the right, Klimt. Both impeccable. Im-
pec-cable. Good God. Either alone would have been a wonderful sale. He turned the last leaf. Maillol, left and right.
Mother of God. He steadied himself. He squinted as if to see
better, but he saw well enough. He saw damn well. He bent
closer and pushed up his eyeglasses to the top of his head.

It was extraordinary.

When you were in the art business a long time, as he had
been, you experienced over the years many exciting discoveries, you lived through many exciting deals, near misses, achieve-
ments. All of these accumulated in the course of one's career
until, eventually, the best dealers were in possession of a colorful oeuvre of anecdotes, stories of art and artists, dealers and
collectors, of happenstance and serendipity, of good luck and
bad, stories of people who were eccentric and feckless and
passionate and ignorant. By far the best stories of all were
those of discovery of great works of art and of serendipity. Carrington Hartwell Knight was staring down at a portfolio that
represented a second great opportunity in as many days, which
together would make one of the best anecdotes of serendipity
and discovery that he would ever have to tell. It was passing
odd how incidents of good (and, unfortunately, sometimes
bad) luck often came in clusters.

Jesus. Mary. And Joseph.

"Ms. Paille," he said, pulling out a chair for her, "please sit down." He held the chair for her. He pulled out another for himself and sat down, each of them turned half toward the other, the unbelievable portfolio between them on the table.

He concentrated on bringing himself under control. Ms. Paille—how the hell did she get that name?—was, it was obvious, a most sensible woman. She would not react well to flighty excitement.

"This is a very fine collection," he began. "Really, it is superb. A singular collection." He hesitated, but only a heartbeat or so. "Does Mr. Cao have any idea of the collection's worth?"

She looked down at the two Maillols. Knight studied her profile, appreciating the little dimple at the corner of her mouth that gave her smile a slightly askew expression.

"I have looked into this a little," she said. "It's my responsibility to be somewhat informed. But I would rather you told me."

"I would say, surely, a minimum of three million pounds."

Slowly, ever so slowly, as slow as the minute hand, her mouth formed a soft, pensive smile.

"Well," she said, "what do we do now?"

"If you want me to sell them for you, I shall need all the documentation you can give me about their provenance. You mentioned that you had considerable documentation."

"Yes."

"I'll need some time to examine that. I will also need to spend time with the drawings themselves, outside of the portfolio. I'll want to examine the paper, and the medium . . . whether it's pencil, crayon, graphite, chalk, etc."

"I understand," she said. "But they must not leave here."

"Oh, of course not. They remain here."

"Now, I would like to discuss some of the business aspects of the sale."

Knight nodded.

"What is your fee for brokering these?"

He told her.

"Will you sell them as a lot or separately?"

"I think as a lot."

"As I understand it," she said, "the drawings market is distinctive, quite different from, say, paintings."

"Exactly."

"Those collectors—individual collectors, that is, excepting institutions, who consistently pay the highest prices for the finest-quality works—are a rather small group. Some of them, those at the top, are passionate."

"Exactly."

"I looked into this," she said, "and I would like you to offer Mr. Cao's drawings to three different collectors. I understand that they are especially ardent collectors, and therefore pay the highest prices."

She suddenly produced a small card of cream paper with deckled edges and put it on the table between them.

"I'd like you to offer the drawings to these persons, one at a time, in this order."

What an extraordinary turn of events. Carrington Knight picked up the card and read the names. He looked at Ms. Paille.

Her eyes were fixed on his. Suddenly, unexpectedly, he realized that he had underestimated her.

"Well," he began, momentarily at a loss for words, "you have indeed done your homework. How did you arrive at these names?"

374

She smiled. "The same way I arrived at yours. It is my job to research well whatever Mr. Cao asks me to research. Mr. Cao does not tolerate mistakes. Would you disagree with the list?"

"I should say not."

"Not even the order?"

"Absolutely not."

"Then that is what you will do?"

He hesitated, though he didn't know why. She was absolutely right. For some reason he could not fully put his finger on, she seemed suddenly more astute. He felt a little odd about it.

"Yes," he said, "I will."

"Good. Mr. Cao has one stipulation."

A stipulation? What would an eccentric collector be without a stipulation? In this rarefied business prerequisites were a common expression of a special clientele.

"Mr. Cao wishes to remain anonymous in this sale."

"Very well." This was not out of the ordinary.

"Nor does he want you to reveal the seller's ethnic identity. Or mine, his representative."

This was out of the ordinary. But not a problem, just odd. "Very well," he said. He loved it.

"Then we have an agreement?"

"Yes, indeed, we have."

CHAPTER 50

Carrington Knight stood at the window and looked down at the street. In a moment she emerged with her chauffeur, the black umbrella hiding her head and shoulders, and quickly disappeared into the back of the black Jaguar. Silently the car pulled into the traffic of Carlos Place and disappeared into the rain.

He smiled. She was a very shrewd woman. A lovely woman. A woman who might even be dangerous to know. Dangerous in a nonlethal sense. Dangerous in the sense that she was capable of enthralling. He did not have the impression that she would take a man places he did not want to go, but, rather, that she could seduce a man into wanting to go places he normally would have the common sense to avoid. In fact, she had just taken Knight there.

It was his policy to be scrupulous about not identifying his clients. Especially those clients like Schrade who were reclusive—and big spenders.

He was also scrupulous about veiling his methods of selling expensive works. He had learned long, long ago that however colorful he himself might enjoy being, when it came to money, and to the buying and selling of fine art, far more profit was to be made from discretion than from flamboyance. He actually bought most of the artwork he sold, but when he did agree to broker something, he never revealed to a seller the potential buyers he might approach.

Ms. Paille had smoothly relieved him of these two long-standing rules of operation. She had done it in such a way that he had relinquished these long-established principles without protest. He had even enjoyed it.

He looked at the portfolio still open on the library table. It hardly mattered in this instance. Besides, the end result was that he was going to broker one of the sweetest little collections of drawings that he had come across in a long while.

She would bring round the documentation later. Jeffrey had quickly typed up a brief description of the seven drawings, which they all had signed, affirming that she was leaving such items in his safekeeping.

She had been most insistent that the sale take place as quickly as possible. She had given reasons, all having to do with her eccentric employer, Mr. Cao. They had agreed that she would call the next day to make an appointment to bring by the documentation.

All in all a very exciting hour.

He turned back to the library table, relishing the idea of a leisurely examination of the drawings.

The telephone rang.

Knight flinched. He'd forgotten. Quickly he walked to the telephone. He let it ring one more time, then lifted the receiver.

"Carrington."

"This is Wolf."

"Yes, Wolf, good of you to call." Knight was alert, ready, suddenly onstage.

"Helene told me about the Schieles." Schrade's baritone conveyed a languid self-confidence that was entirely peculiar to this man. "What do you think?"

"It would be easy to rhapsodize about them, Wolf, but just let me say this: They are first-rate. They are *solid*. I have never felt more sure of the quality of a Schiele. They're stunning."

"Mmmmmm. Good. They are genuine Schieles?"

"As I told Helene, I don't have any doubts about them being Schieles, but I've still got to open them up."

"When can I see them?"

"The sooner the better. I've been retained by the owner to authenticate them."

"Who is the seller?"

"I'm afraid they wish to remain anonymous. I can tell you this, the drawings are not coming from a collector's holdings. They were actually unearthed in the estate of a recently deceased family member."

"Where?"

"Where? Here, in Britain. They didn't even know what they had. That's why I was retained. I called you when I realized what we were dealing with. You and I would be the first ones to verify this discovery. Essentially it would be *our* discovery. A truly significant moment in modern art. To unearth new Schieles, never seen before. That's why I thought you would want to be here."

"This time, Carrington," Schrade said bluntly, cutting through the confection of Knight's verbal enticements, "I must know the seller, or I won't consider the purchase."

Knight was stunned. Good Lord, Claude had been pre-
scient. How freakish.

"But, Wolf, you know that we never—"

"This time, Carrington, I must know."

"But this just isn't . . ."

Silence.

Knight sensed he was pushing his position to the point
of effrontery. He thought of the money. The prestige. The
deal.

"Very well," he said. "I have the name and address of
the barrister who is representing the seller."

"Let me have them," Schrade said.

Knight gave them to him.

"I will call you back," Schrade said. "Good-bye, Carrington."

"Wait—" Schrade was gone.

Good Lord! Knight's hand was trembling as he put
down the telephone. Oh, hell, it didn't matter. Simply to
have the seven drawings in his possession when Schrade arrived would be remarkable enough. Knight would relish
working up to the surprise.

BROMPTON

He sat at his desk and gazed out at the park across the road
from his office, waiting. The telephone call had come just an
hour earlier. The caller, who identified himself as a lawyer
named Kevin Drenner, had been urgent in his request: to
meet with him immediately regarding the anonymous offering for sale of two unauthenticated works reputed to have
been done by the artist Egon Schiele. The man had an

American accent. Fain, using the name Edward Purchas, told him to come immediately.

So here he was arriving by cab, pausing to pay in the late afternoon drizzle, turning and looking at the facade of Fain's office, then ducking his head and coming across the broad sidewalk to the front door.

"I'm sorry to be in so much of a hurry," Drenner said, sitting down with a wheeze in a banker's chair in Purchas's office, "but my client—"

"Who is?"

"Gerhard Stoltz. A German citizen of Berlin."

Purchas nodded.

"Generally does not buy art from anonymous sellers," Drenner continued. "He understands the drawings in question are excellent, though they have to be authenticated, so he is quite interested. But . . ."

"He does not buy from anonymous sellers."

"That's right."

"What do you want?"

"The identity of the seller."

"Just not possible," Purchas said, leaning his long frame back in his chair. "Sorry."

"Why?"

"The seller has rules as well. Perhaps these two were simply not meant to do business. I understand there is no dearth of potential buyers, and to eliminate one so early is not a discouragement to my client."

Drenner looked at him. The pressure he was under was evident. His face was remarkable for its extraordinarily stout jaw structure and for its unpleasant complexion, which was very nearly jaundiced, with putty gray shadows under the cheeks and around the eyes.

"Why does your client insist upon anonymity?"

"Why does your client insist upon knowing?"

"Security reasons."

"The same."

"Do you have authority to decide this without consulting with your client?"

"Of course."

Drenner's prodigious jaw structure rippled with tested patience. "My client," he said, "is willing to offer, through Mr. Knight, an agreement to buy the drawings at a price of twenty percent above their appraisal value, if they are proven to be genuine Schieles . . . and if the seller will forgo anonymity."

Purchas held his tongue, regarding Drenner from under the bushy outcroppings of his eyebrows. The pause was meant to convey an immediate weakening of resolve.

"That would be done in writing?" Purchas asked.

"Yes. I have the authority to do that."

Purchas looked out at the park across the road, dreary in the rain. He thought long and with gravity. "Would your client," he said, turning back to Drenner, "be willing to keep the transaction totally confidential, between the two parties? Save Mr. Knight, of course. That would be the next best thing to anonymity for both of them, would it not?"

"Yes."

"What kind of identification do you require?"

"I'd like to meet the seller, talk with him about how he came in possession of the drawings."

Purchas was shocked. "Good God, sir. That is *impossible.*"

"Why?"

Purchas shook his head busily and looked away as if in distaste. "No, no, no. A twenty percent increase in sale price doesn't buy *that* sort of thing. My client is not a common 'celebrity' who haggles away familiarity with himself to the highest bidder. I am sorry, sir, but that is out of the question."

Again Drenner, who thought he had been making some headway, showed such frustration at this setback that his jaundiced face flushed, ruddy patches appearing on his cheeks and at the corners of his mouth. It was unpleasant to see.

Purchas thought he had better release some of the pressure before Drenner exploded.

"Mr. Drenner, please, you have to appreciate my position," he said. "The fact is, the 'gentleman' in question here, the seller, is actually a woman."

Drenner's eyes bulged slightly, then relaxed. "Really."

"Yes, really," Purchas said. "So you see why she is cautious. I've represented her family in legal matters for over twenty-two years, and I can assure you your client has nothing to fear from her regarding security. She inherited these drawings from her aunt, an eccentric, a Bohemian, who recently died. She is a widow, in her mid-sixties, a taciturn woman."

Purchas frowned heavily, his eyebrows lowering like dark clouds over his eyes. "I can assure you," he concluded, "if your client insists on your 'interviewing' her, he should count himself out of the running. A woman of her nature would rather forgo a twenty percent profit than to be dragged into that sort of . . . merchandising."

Purchas paused, sighed, and grew grimly sympathetic. "I know that may be difficult for your client, Mr. Stoltz, to understand. But really, sir, this is quite another matter to a woman like that. She simply doesn't see it the same way as Mr. Stoltz."

CHAPTER 51

Mara started talking as soon as they pulled away from Carlos Place. She told Strand everything, speaking hurriedly as he drove through the pelting rain to a nearby hotel on Park Lane. He entered the parking garage and wound upward through the lanes until he found a parking place and pulled in.

He took off his chauffeur's jacket and removed the bow tie and left them both in the car. Together they left the garage and entered the hotel, going up to the room that Strand had taken under the name of one of his passports. There he changed into a suit as Mara continued telling him about the particulars of her conversation with Knight. When he was finished dressing, they left the hotel and took a cab to an Indian restaurant in Knightsbridge, just off Cromwell Road.

After they were seated Mara picked up where she had left off and finished her account of her meeting with Carrington Knight.

"So essentially, you accomplished everything."

"Almost."

"Well, the time. But I don't know how you could have

done anything about that. Carrington's got to talk to Schrade. There's no way he could know otherwise."

"But I've got to call him tomorrow, make arrangements to take him the documentation. I could start then. Did he reach Mr. Schrade? What was his reaction? Is he coming? And so on like that."

"Sure, whatever feels right. The timing of Schrade's arrival is crucial; we'll have to nail it down. That's the whole point of it."

After their drinks came and they ordered dinner, Mara studied him.

"How are you going to do this, Harry?"

"I'll take care of it," he said.

"No." She shook her head firmly. "I want to *know* how you're going to do this."

He swallowed a sip of his Scotch. "It really would be best if you didn't know," he said.

Her eyes flashed. "I'm not impressed by someone wanting to 'protect' me, Harry," she went on. "You know me better than that. This has more to do with you. You're not doing me any favors. I thought we had this settled."

She was glaring at him, her anger controlled, but just barely.

He nodded. "Okay," he said, "you're right." He took another drink of his Scotch and deliberately tried to taste every possible element of its savor before he swallowed. Then he went on. "When Schrade comes to London, he stays at one of three places. They're obvious places for a man like him: Brown's, Claridge's, the Ritz. But there will be few opportunities to approach him at any of them."

"Approach him?"

Strand took a mental deep breath and told her how he planned to kill Schrade. He watched her face as he explained about the saxitoxin, explained the gun, explained the necessity of having to get close to him. She did very well, no shock, no stunned expression, no exclamations. She swallowed once, that was all.

"How . . . did you decide to do it this way?" she asked. "Why not use something that would give you some distance?"

"A high-powered rifle, a bomb?"

She nodded.

"There's less risk for me with those devices, but both of them require detailed long-term planning. I knew I wouldn't have that kind of time."

"But this way the risk is greater that you'll . . ."

"Be killed or caught."

She had to swallow again and covered it by taking a sip of her Scotch.

He smiled at her. "But I plan to avoid that."

She couldn't manage a response.

"Schrade also has favorite restaurants," Strand went on. He named half a dozen. "I think it's a good possibility that I can catch him coming in or out of one of these."

"You said it would make a sound."

"About like a slap."

"That's loud."

"In a quiet place, yes. But outside in the street it could be done without attracting attention."

"What about his bodyguard?"

"Schrade uses them in different ways, and I'm lucky there. When he goes to business meetings, legitimate business meetings, there's only one guard, who accompanies him like a

secretary. He's very understated, in the background. Everybody knows what he is, but it's no big deal. Important men,
at least important men in Schrade's orbit, are accustomed to
seeing their peers with 'assistants.' If you didn't know who
Schrade was, you'd think two businessmen.

"When he meets with his illegitimate associates, always in
environments quite different from those I've just mentioned,
he travels with two bodyguards who look like bodyguards, and
no one would mistake them for anything else. They're there to
intimidate as well as protect."

Strand removed his hands from the sweaty Scotch glass
and touched his face with his cool fingers. He sighed.

"But when he's on art business, the bodyguard is little
more than a chauffeur. He doesn't follow Schrade into restaurants, doesn't follow him around in the hotels, doesn't go into
the galleries. Schrade is in a different world when he's looking
at art. He almost—almost—becomes a different man. He
doesn't want the trappings of his other life to interfere."

Mara nodded. "So, you think you'd . . ."

"Catch him in a noisy restaurant. Catch him coming or
going to the restaurant, in the street. Catch him in the men's
room. In the bar."

Strand went straight into the specifics. He was going to
give her everything.

"My feeling is that in any of these situations I can do a
'brush-by.' To muffle the sound of the 'slap,' and to make sure
the pellet penetrates his clothes, I'll jam the pistol into his
side, just under his rib cage, and fire. He'll flinch, slump. I'll
grab him and hold him up. This will do two things: give me a
chance to hide the pistol somewhere in my clothes, and prevent him from reflexively recoiling from me or gesturing at me

and attracting attention to me. I'll act surprised, confused, then shocked: 'What's the matter! Are you all right?' I'll appear to come to his assistance, call for help, bring people to us. Since I'll be catching him away from his bodyguard, no one will suspect a menacing situation. I think most people will immediately conclude that I just happened to be standing next to the guy when he had a stroke or heart attack."

He stopped, his forearms leaning on the table.

"That's my thinking right now. That's what I'd like. In the confusion I'll manage to slip away. I'll want to be gone before the bodyguard gets there. But even if I'm not, Schrade will be past any ability to communicate. The saxitoxin takes only moments."

"God, Harry . . . you can do that?"

"I have to do it."

She had gone right to the heart of it. He was by no means as confident as he wanted to sound. The risk was the least of it. It was killing the man that he tried not to think about. He had rehearsed over and over everything right up to the instant of squeezing the trigger, then his mind derailed. He couldn't imagine what he would feel like as he walked away, leaving behind him the confused crowd and the dead, or dying, Schrade. How in God's name would that feel?

"How are you going to get that close to him without him recognizing you?"

Strand nodded. "There's a shop in Soho where West End actors buy their makeup and wigs and things. I'll need you to go there and get something for a disguise. A mustache. Maybe a wig. The most expensive ones they have. Very good ones. Subtle. Then we're going to have to change the way I look."

Mara had been listening to him with an expressionless

concentration, hearing things, he knew, that she could hardly believe. Everything he said was being absorbed, being made over in her mind to fit into reality as she had always understood it. He guessed it was as difficult a task as she had ever encountered. A leap beyond, way beyond, what she had been taught in the FIS training course in Virginia.

Her eyes glittered with the impact of the accumulative brutality of the details. All the concern, all the fear, the nearly panicked imagination, gathered in a single crease between her eyebrows. As Strand watched, she gradually composed herself. She took a long, deep breath and slowly straightened her back and set her shoulders.

Strand felt sick doing this to her. Then he thought about Romy and Meret and Ariana. It was too late to get weak in the stomach.

CHAPTER 52

Just after nightfall Claude Corsier hung up the telephone from talking to Carrington Knight, who had at just that moment received a message from Wolfram Schrade. He would arrive at Knight's at ten o'clock the next morning. Corsier looked at the two drawings sitting on the floor of his hotel room in South Kensington. Good God. These Schieles, more Schieles than Schieles themselves now that Carrington Knight believed in them as if they were two Holy Grails, would soon attract yet another knight to his death in his quest for them. Corsier shook his head pensively. It was unbelievable, really, that Wolfram Schrade was coming like this, to two worthless drawings, like a rat to carrion. Corsier had planned it and imagined it, but now that it was really about to happen, well, it was rather a triumph. So, the mighty and powerful could be deceived, too. It was no special thing to be made a fool. And no one was so special that he couldn't be. But it did feel rather special having done it twice to a man like Schrade. To be rid of the murderous freak in the process . . . it *was* a triumph.

Corsier wished he had tried to get in touch with Harry Strand. He would like Strand to know what he had done and how he had done it. After his close call in Schrade's private launch in Venice, Corsier had been convinced that his only hope for salvation lay in cutting himself off from everyone he knew, making it impossible for Schrade to use anyone to find him. With the exception of Edie Vernon, and Carrington Knight just two days ago, Corsier had not spoken to a single soul he knew since the Venetian nightmare. He had diminished into a shadow and floated unnoticed from country to country. Strand had done something like that four years ago, and as far as Corsier knew, the transformation had served him very well.

Corsier's niece, who ran his gallery in Geneva, had eventually reported him missing to the police. He had seen it in the papers and once on the television news. He was sorry he'd had to put her through that, but if he had sent her any note of reassurance, she would never have been convincing to the police or, more important, to Schrade's intelligence creatures.

He had not found it especially difficult to disappear. Of course, he was highly motivated. As had been often observed, nothing was so galvanizing as brushing against the cold shoulder of one's own mortality. Even now just the mere thought of Venice accelerated his heartbeat.

The incident had wrenched a new crease in the folds of Corsier's brain and was now a permanent feature of his psyche. His escape had been born of blind chance, which haunted him. As Schrade's launch pounded the waves and Corsier swore to himself over and over and over in prayerful chant that if he ever got away from this situation he would become as invisible as a breath, the driver of the launch changed course abruptly, leaving the lane to Marco Polo Airport and angling in a traverse course. Corsier was horrified. This was it.

In the quick maneuver of changing course, their launch cut across the wake of one of the public *vaporettos* filled with tourists heading for the airport. The hull of the launch slapped roughly against the large wake at the precise instant that the second of the two men in the launch was turning to reach for something on the dash. Thrown off balance by the sudden slam of the hull, he flailed out reflexively for something to save himself from falling. It was the steering wheel. The launch pitched violently as it turned against the second part of the *va-poretto*'s V-shaped wake, flinging the off-balance man against the side of the launch.

Corsier grabbed a heavy black flashlight from a bin in the hull beside him, leaped at the man, and in a frenzy of panic bashed his head repeatedly. An automatic pistol skittered across the fiberglass floor from the man's jacket. Corsier grabbed it without thinking and fired repeatedly at the driver, who was fighting to regain the steering wheel as he pushed down the throttle to cut the power. The pistol was equipped with a silencer, and the lethal hush of each shot gave an even more surreal character to the frantic sequence. The launch spun around, dead in the water, as the driver was hammered to the floor with each quiet burst from the pistol. Then Corsier shot the second man as well.

He had never fired a gun in his life.

He dragged both men into the cabin, then managed to muddle about with the launch engine until he got the boat started again and followed the distant and diminishing wake of the *vaporetto* to the docks surrounding the airport. There he maneuvered the launch to an isolated branch of the public dock, pulled into a slip, cut the motor, and climbed out of the launch onto the dock, not even thinking to tie it.

He walked away in a daze.

For nearly three weeks he had a nightmare about it every night. More than a few times it drove sleep away altogether, and he lay awake in the dark, hearing imminent death in the creaking walls of old hotels or in the opening or closing of a distant door.

Then one night in a cramped monk's cell at the Great Lavra monastery on Mount Athos, where he had fled to hide and gather his thoughts and nerves among ornate religious art and quiet men, he stared at the blue moonlight on the stone of the deep windowsill and realized Schrade's demonic audacity: usurping God's role, he took it upon himself to grant life or death. If he turned his eyes this way, a man was made to die; with a subtle nod of his head, another was allowed to live. Allowed to live! The magisterial insolence of it hit Corsier like a thunderbolt.

At that moment a sudden and powerful resentment was ignited in Corsier's heart, and even before he could swing his feet off the cot to sit up and look out of his window to the Aegean Sea, a fierce conviction to liberate himself from Schrade began to wrestle with his paralyzing fear and would soon overcome it.

The next day he began growing his mustache and goatee, and the day after that he departed the monastery.

He never wavered. For him there was no moral struggle. Wolfram Schrade wanted to kill him and sought to kill him. And Schrade's life was a brutal witness to the man's appalling turpitude. As far as Corsier was concerned, the sum of that simple equation was quite evident. He never looked back.

❋   ❋   ❋

He checked into his rooms on the third floor of the Connaught Hotel late in the afternoon. The suite had three rooms:
a reception area and two bedrooms, one on either side, each
with its own bath. The reception had the largest windows and
the best view of Knight's second-floor library. Corsier chose
the bedroom on the right.

He had bought a piece of ordinary luggage in which to
transport the paintings so that he did not attract attention to
himself. In another piece of luggage he brought in two pairs of
powerful binoculars and two tripods, which he set up in the reception in front of the windows. He attached the binoculars to
the tripods and looked across Carlos Place into the second
floor of Knight's library. No one was in the room, in which only
a few lamps were lighted against the gray day. Good enough,
though. He hoped he wouldn't have to rely on Skerlic's microphones alone to identify Schrade's positioning. It was good,
too, that the day would be overcast and rainy—he monitored
the television weather forecasts religiously to make sure. The
gloomy day would enable them to sit in their rooms with the
lights out and the curtains open and not be observed from
Knight's library.

Putting the binoculars into the suitcase, he made a mental note always to lock them up before he left the suite. The
maids would take note of binoculars on a tripod.

He sat on the smaller of the two sofas and stared out the
windows. He would spend the night here. Tomarrow would be
difficult because the only thing left to do was wait. He would
install Skerlic here tomorrow night, in plenty of time for them
to be ready for Schrade's arrival the next morning.

After a final conversation with Skerlic about the order of
things to come, he would deliver the drawings around eight

o'clock. Knight had wanted them sooner, of course, but Corsier had presented him with creative excuses, abundant reasons. Now, at least, from his post across the street, he could see and hear whether Knight was tempted to cheat in the two hours he had between the time Corsier dropped off the drawings and Schrade's arrival.

With only the swishing sound of the polite Mayfair traffic on the wet streets to interrupt the silence of his room, Corsier stroked his mustache and goatee and sighed heavily. It was a bittersweet time for him. Though he was about to rid himself of Meister Death, he was going to have to go into exile to do it. The ensuing investigation, by the British and German governments, would quickly identify him as the major suspect. Flight was his only alternative.

Much of the past month had been taken up with arranging his second disappearance, the passports, the shuffled bank accounts, the well-thought-out routes of escape, the detailed study of certain neighborhoods in places like Buenos Aires, Singapore, Bogotá. He thought of his exile as a temporary placement. Perhaps after three years, or five, or seven, he could quietly return. Both governments would make a great flourish of looking for the assassin for a year or two, but in reality, once the media lost interest in the case, so would Scotland Yard and the Bundeskriminalamt. After all, these agencies were not ignorant. As long as the media was not urging them on, why would they go out of their way to pursue the killer of a man like Wolfram Schrade? After a time other urgent criminal matters would demand their attention, and the "Schrade task force" would be reduced to a perfunctory little office with one or two officers assigned to plod through the mounds of paper that would have been generated by the initial inquiry.

That was the way he saw it, anyway. It was not the best of situations in which to find oneself, but he would rather flee the searches of two governments, whose budgetary patience for wild goose chases was limited, than try to hide from an obsessed Schrade's well-financed assassins.

God, but he would miss London and Geneva and Paris and Rome. He loved all these wonderful cities in all the wonderful seasons of their years. To have to say good-bye to their galleries and museums and symphony halls and operas grieved him far more than he ever would have imagined. How long might it be before he would again be able to dine at the quiet little Vecchia Roma in Piazza Campitelli or at the sublime Tour d'Argent on Quai de la Tournelle or have a late morning coffee mélange with his newspaper at the Café Central in Vienna?

The answer was, eventually. As opposed to never, if Schrade was left unchecked. Corsier was French enough to be capable of sentimentality, but he was also a native Genevan and had a strong sense of practicality. It would be Wolf Schrade's great misfortune that Claude Corsier had been a lucky man that day in Venice.

CHAPTER 53

The next morning they walked to Shepherd Market huddled together under an umbrella and ate breakfast at da Corradi, where the bacon and eggs were done to Strand's liking. Afterward they both ordered cappuccinos before going back out into the rain.

"About Carrington," he said, leaning toward Mara slightly on his forearms. "There's a timing concern."

She didn't look at him. She concentrated on her coffee.

"You'll need to retrieve the drawings. We don't want them left there. It doesn't take much imagination to know that there's going to be a hell of an investigation. We need a smoke-screen, something to create confusion, obscure the inquiry. I'm going to use my Geneva files."

Mara looked up. "Harry . . ."

"I can do it without making the source an obvious intelligence leak. It can be done. When that stuff gets out, the potential suspects for the killing will be so enormous it'll swamp the investigation. It'll get murky with spies and criminal organizations. There'll be a frenzy of denials and finger-pointing. They'll never sort it out. It'll go unsolved."

Mara allowed a small smile. She had to; she saw the genius of it, too. It offered a glimmer of hope that this might work after all.

"There's a problem," Strand went on. "When that stuff hits the media it'll be sensational. Schrade's going to be yanked out of obscurity and thrust into the headlines." He paused. "The problem is, it'll heat up the investigation." He paused again. "You know how it works. Where was he going? Why was he going there? Was he being lured? How was it set up? You're going to be caught in the net, Mara. Carrington and his security man are going to bring you right into the middle of it."

The look on Mara's face was not fear. It was calculation.

"The FIS isn't going to acknowledge me," she said. "They're not going to identify any photographs."

Strand agreed.

"I'm not in any police files. But they can trace me through the drawings. I own them legitimately, apart from any work for the FIS."

"That's right. So you've got to get them out of there before Schrade's death is understood to be what it actually is."

She hadn't drunk a drop of the cappuccino, and she was no longer interested in it.

"Let me think," she said, her voice dying away as her imagination shuttled in another direction.

"This is Lenor Paille."

"Oh . . . Ms. Paille. Lenor. I don't think you told me your first name." Carrington Knight paused, his voice inquisitive. "Are you on a speakerphone, Ms. Paille? It sounds like it."

"Yes," she said, "I'm sorting papers." She and Strand were sitting on the paint buckets, cups of coffee in front of them on the scaffolding table. "Listen, I need to ask you if you've got any news on a possible time for showing the drawings to the first client."

"Oh, indeed. You're in luck, Ms. Paille. You're in luck."

"Really? What do you mean?"

"Mr. Schrade will be here tomorrow."

Mara flashed her eyes at Strand.

"The fact is, your suggestion that I contact Mr. Schrade was overlapping another item that I had in the works for him."

"You already knew he was coming tomorrow when I spoke with you?"

"No, no, no. Well, I had contacted him about coming to see another set of drawings, but I had not yet heard from him. I had no idea when he was coming. That's why I really couldn't say anything to you yesterday. He called after you left."

"Did you tell him about the Cao drawings?"

"No, I didn't."

"Why?"

"Well, he had called about the other pieces, and since you had just left, I didn't want to be overeager. Besides, I hadn't yet actually examined your drawings. I do have a responsibility, Ms. Paille. I have to be judicious."

"Of course, I understand."

"Nevertheless," Knight said, "I have, since then, examined your collection, and they are stunning. Mr. Cao is either a very knowledgeable man or a very lucky one—not being a collector—to have come upon these beauties."

"Well, it's about their documentation that I'm calling."

A slight hesitation on Knight's end of the line indicated startled suspicion. "Yes?"

"I'm afraid I can't bring them round today. I have other obligations that have come in the way."

"But you have the documentation?"

"Oh, certainly. It's right here. I'll try to get it to you as quickly as possible tomorrow, before Mr. Schrade arrives. What time is your appointment with him?"

"Ten o'clock."

"Then why don't I come around at nine o'clock?"

"Oh, yes, yes, indeed. Nine o'clock would be perfect."

CHAPTER 54

While Mara went to Soho to get the material needed for Strand's disguise, he began calling the three hotels where Schrade was likely to stay. As it was absolutely essential that Schrade not know of any inquiries about his arrival, Strand tried to think of a pretense for calling innocuous enough that an eager desk clerk would not think it worth mentioning to Schrade upon his arrival. The problem was that Schrade's generosity at these hotels, a result of his wanting to be treated with an almost sybaritic attentiveness, meant that everyone from the doorman to the manager strained themselves mightily to accommodate, and even anticipate, his every wish. If Strand were to pretend to be a business acquaintance wanting to confirm Schrade's arrival, the desk clerk, wishing to be of service to Schrade as he was checking in, would very likely mention it. If Strand called anonymously to confirm the arrival, the clerk would likely report that as well. He could think of no reason so trivial that an eager-to-please clerk would not mention it.

So Strand decided to try a completely different direction. He began calling the hotels, introducing himself as Dr. Morris, and asking if Wolfram Schrade had checked in yet. When he finally located a reservation for Schrade, at Claridge's, the closest of the three hotels to Carlos Place, he explained to the registration clerk that he was a cardiac specialist and his secretary, who was out of the office owing to illness, had apparently confused Mr. Schrade's appointment. Therefore Dr. Morris himself was calling to confirm whether Mr. Schrade had arrived from Berlin.

Mr. Schrade was not there yet, the clerk said, but he did have reservations, and there was a note about an afternoon arrival. Did Dr. Morris want to leave a message?

No, thank you, that was really all he needed to know to clear up the discrepancy. Oh, by the way, Mr. Schrade's appointment with him was, of course, a medical matter and, as such, was of the utmost confidentiality. He would not want it known by the hotel staff that he was consulting Dr. Morris.

The clerk understood perfectly.

Dr. Morris thought he would. Might he have the clerk's name?

The clerk gave it, the changing tone in his voice making it obvious that he knew he was being put on notice.

Dr. Morris thanked him politely. He very much appreciated the clerk's understanding.

Locating a restaurant where Schrade might dine posed a different kind of problem. While one tended not to deviate from a long-trusted hotel, a restaurant was another matter. A person at the reservation desk of a restaurant would be unlikely to report an inquiry, but finding the right restaurant was problematic. Schrade might decide to dine at a new restaurant on a whim. He might dine in the hotel. He might dine

with someone else at a restaurant of their choice. The possibilities were endless.

In addition to all that, Strand was working from his
memory of a dining routine Schrade had kept four years earlier. Things changed, restaurants came in and out of vogue.
Happily, middle-aged men had a great fondness for routine,
and Schrade had a penchant for allowing himself the very
best of everything. It was not unreasonable that Strand might
indeed be able to track down Schrade's dinner reservations.

He was not quickly rewarded. His question to the reservations desk at each of the six restaurants he remembered as
Schrade's favorites—"Just calling to see if Mr. Schrade has
made his reservations yet"—was answered in the negative.

He checked with the concierge at the three hotels he had
just called and asked them the names of the three restaurants
currently considered the finest in the city. All three of them
named the same two, and each named one that the other two
didn't. That gave Strand only three more restaurants to call,
since of the five named two were on Strand's original list. He
hit on the second call.

Wolfram Schrade had reservations for two at eight-thirty
that evening at Ma Micheline, a trendy and expensive French
restaurant near Park Lane. He would surely be driven. Strand
called back and made reservations for one at the same hour.
Schrade's reservation for two was interesting.

Strand looked at his watch. He had one other thing to do
before Mara returned. He went down to the entry hall closet
and retrieved the paper sack with the pistol he had gotten
from Hodge. He took the pistol and went up to the bathroom
in one of the empty bedrooms and turned on the faucet in the
bathtub. The lever that closed the drain in the tub was above

the faucet, so he wouldn't have to reach into the water to drain it.

When the tub was full, Strand turned off the water and stepped back. He removed the clip from the pistol, looked at it, and then slowly pushed it back into the handle. He raised his hand, extended his arm, and then, taking special note of the tension in the trigger, slowly squeezed it and fired into the water.

The slap was not as loud as he had expected, the recoil nonexistent. It took a moment before he located the small plastic pellet at the bottom, ruptured. The clear saxitoxin was dispersed into the clear water. He reached down and flipped the drain toggle.

After removing the clip from the handle, he smelled the end of the barrel. Very little odor from the firing mechanism. If people gathered around the slumping Schrade, there would be no suspicious whiff of cordite in the air.

When the water had drained out of the tub, the ruptured pellet was stuck in the drain. Using a tissue, he picked it up and examined it closely. Then he put the tissue and pellet into the toilet and flushed it.

He left the pistol and clip in his coat pocket and hung the coat in the closet with his other clothes. He walked to the windows and looked out at the rain. This time the next day it would be done. He was tempted to imagine what it would be like for him and Mara after it was all over, but he knew better than to indulge himself in bright hopes. It was too easy to slip into an unjustified optimism, deceiving oneself into believing that the nearest evil was the only evil between oneself and happiness. There was even more of an inclination to do that with an evil like Schrade's, because it so thoroughly dominated the present moment to the exclusion of all others that it was tempting to discount the more subtle demons waiting their turn behind him.

The rain was falling steadily again, running down Chesterfield Hill toward the gutters of Mayfair, on its way to the storm sewers and the Thames.

Strand's thoughts drifted away, distracted by the random pace of the rain as it alternately surged and slacked. He lost track of time until he saw a black cab pull up and stop in front of the town house. The driver got out with an umbrella and opened the back door for Mara, holding the umbrella for her as she gathered up her things.

While they ate the sandwiches that Mara had brought back with her, she laid out on the scaffolding table the items she had purchased for his disguise. She explained why she had bought each item: the three styles of mustaches were of a certain kind of bristle; the wigs were actual human hair, specially woven to more accurately approximate the real thing. This wig could be custom colored, grayed at the temples, or streaked—she had a kit of colors—all colorfast. This adhesive would withstand rain; that adhesive did not require a special solvent to remove. This face latex would remain pliable and would withstand the rain. That face latex was less comfortable, but it had a more accurate color scale and could be shaded. A prosthesis for the mouth changed the shape of his jaw. This sheet of padding could be cut to fit and worn under his clothes to change the shape of his shoulders or to thicken his chest.

"I thought maybe comfort was a big factor," she said after explaining the pros and cons of each item and the possibilities in which each might be used to best effect. As always, she was thorough, never doing anything by halves. "You don't want to have to think about it, about something going wrong. You put it on, it stays on. The better stuff takes longer to apply."

She was trying to cover up her anxiety by being well informed and businesslike. Again, thorough, she turned a natural tendency to her advantage.

"I found him," Strand said.

Mara stopped talking, her eyes remaining on the plastic packet of latex she was holding in her lap. "Where?"

"Claridge's."

She nodded but didn't say anything, still looking at the packet, her fingers kneading it.

"How long will it take to do this?" he asked, gesturing at the items scattered on the table.

"I don't know. A couple of hours."

"Schrade has reservations at a restaurant at eight-thirty. It's a place near his hotel. I'd like to be ready by six o'clock at the very latest."

Mara nodded again.

"If I don't get a chance at him tonight, I won't be coming back here. I'll have to get ready for another chance in the morning, on his way to Carrington's."

"You'll call me tonight."

"Yeah, I will."

"If I don't hear from you, what about tomorrow morning?"

"You're going to have to go to Carrington's tomorrow morning no matter what happens, whether I get Schrade tonight or in the morning. Be there at nine o'clock as you agreed, with the documentation you promised. The timing won't be crucial because Schrade will never make his appointment. Still, it's important that you show up."

"Why? I don't understand."

"Two reasons. When this is all over, after the investigation into Schrade's death begins, they're going to question Carrington, because that's where Schrade was going when he was killed. They'll be looking for a setup, something out of the ordinary, something unusual. It won't be so much of a red flag if you simply show up for your appointment as arranged, an everyday occurrence for Carrington. But if you make an appointment and don't show up for it, it's going to stand out. He's going to make note of it."

He wadded up a napkin and tossed it into a paper bag. "And, just as important, you've got to get those drawings out of there."

"Okay." Mara was still kneading the face latex.

"I won't leave you hanging," Strand said. "I'll keep you informed. But don't panic if you don't hear from me. I'm not going to be in any danger. I'll probably just be in a position that won't allow me to communicate."

"What do I do in the meantime?"

"Clean up this place."

"Anything that can identify us."

"That's right. Don't worry about the mess. Just put anything that might point to us into plastic bags. We'll get rid of them later. After I leave here this afternoon just get ready to go, and stay ready. I might call you from somewhere and tell you to meet me in another country. Be flexible. Don't be surprised at any message from me. Whatever I ask of you will have to do with maintaining our anonymity, not with any dire circumstances. Don't worry about that."

"Fine."

"Don't use the Jaguar again. Take a cab to Carrington's in the morning."

"Right."

"If you don't hear from me at all, leave London. Go back to Bellagio, get a room at the same hotel, and wait for me. Watch your e-mail. That's how I'll get in touch with you."

"Fine."

He looked at her. "Everything okay?"

"Yeah. I've got it."

"I'm comfortable with this. How about you?"

"Yes, it's good. It's clear. I'm okay with it."

They were lying to each other. They both knew it. Neither of them knew how to deal with it any other way.

CHAPTER 55

It took Mara nearly three hours to make Strand into someone else. Monitoring the process in a hand mirror, he watched as his features disappeared one by one until, slowly, a stranger's face emerged and he no longer recognized himself. It was oddly like being invisible. He watched the man in the mirror as though he were seeing him on a small movie screen. The sensations he felt in his own body did not belong to the man he saw. His thoughts did not belong to the man he saw. There was nothing in that man's eyes that Strand recognized, and there was nothing in that man's eyes that he could read.

Mara had had the unfailing good sense to make Strand's new self unremarkable; he was neither handsome nor striking in any sense. He had no identifying mole or coloring or manner of grooming. He was not interesting to look at, and it was highly unlikely that anyone would remember him or be able to describe him after having shared an elevator with him. He had become every man and no man. Harry Strand had disappeared.

"Okay," she said, sitting back, looking at him as though he were a drawing she had just finished. She smiled softly, leaned toward him, and whispered, "I liked the other guy a lot better, mister. A hell of a lot better." She kissed him lightly on the lips. "No offense."

"I'm relieved to hear it," Strand said. He looked at his watch: it was nearly four-thirty. "I'm going to forget the padding. I don't want to fool with it, don't want to have to worry about it."

He checked the mirror one more time. She had done a remarkable job. Not too much latex. It wasn't like a mask, but his nose was broader, brow heavier, jaws rounder, neck thicker. The stuff was sticking to him like a second skin. He did not have to be apprehensive about it coming off accidentally. In fact, he was just a little concerned that it might not come off at all.

"How does it feel? Any problems?"

"No, not at all," he said. "It's good. It looks great." He stood and removed the paper from around his collar.

Mara didn't say anything. She busied herself with cleaning up and putting away the cosmetics and little bottles and tubes and aerosol cans that were scattered out on the scaffolding table.

Strand walked over to the windows and looked out. A misty fog had rolled in, and the evening was growing dim and gloomy. He stretched his neck, twisted his head. Again he took a deep breath, couldn't seem to get enough air in his lungs. Turning, he looked at Mara. She had stopped what she was doing and was sitting there, a tube of something in her hands, watching him. The expression on her face told him volumes about the complex of emotions that churned within her.

Strand came over to her, and she put down the tube of makeup and stood. He raised her hands to his lips and kissed them. He kissed her palms and folded her fingers and kissed them. Her eyes were wide, unblinking, brimming with tears.

"I love you," he said. "Thank you for everything. For everything from the first moment."

He kissed her eyes softly, first one, then the other. He felt the moist salt of her fear and affection against his lips, tasted it on his tongue. This one tender moment was all he would allow. It was all he dared allow.

Turning away from her, he went to the closet and put on his coat. He took out his raincoat and pulled it on, too, and then reached in and got his umbrella and closed the door. When he turned to look at her she had wiped her eyes and was standing with her arms crossed, one hip cocked. She managed a smile.

"Take care of yourself, Harry," she said.

He nodded at her and walked out the room.

At the front door he stepped outside and paused to put up the umbrella. Then he pulled the door closed behind him. It was quiet outside except for the light rain. He went down the steps, through the wrought-iron grille, and across the street. At the corner of Charles Street he turned and looked back. She had turned out the lights. He knew she was standing at the window in the darkness, watching him. He turned again and started down the street toward Berkeley Square.

The light rain had slackened to a mizzle by the time Strand got to Berkeley Square, where he had intended to hail a cab. Now he changed his mind. The weather was not so bad that he couldn't walk, and the walking helped him think. The street lamps came on as he turned north on the west side of the square. The plane trees in the park sagged under the

moisture of the last several days, and the pathways that tra-
versed the lawn were empty and dreary. The wet summer
evening had settled over the city like a soughing breath that
was at one moment too warm and then almost chill.

He tried to stop thinking about Mara. He knew his lack
of concentration was dangerous, but he could hardly get the
image of the darkened windows of their rooms out of his mind.
Gradually over the last month, everything he was and did had
become wrapped up in that woman. She had become his ra-
tionale for everything. When he planned and when he
dreamed, he had *their* future in mind. He did not think of
himself; he thought of *them*.

He peered ahead, through the mist, up the hill toward
Davies Street. He listened to his footsteps on the wet cement
and to the footsteps of the people he passed: the long strides
and plodding steps of men; the quick, rapid-fire steps of young
women in smart clothes hurrying to their futures. All of them,
shrouded beneath their umbrellas, moved along in the late day
gloaming, microcosms of human hopes and disappointments.

Never, throughout the years of this deception, had it
seemed more like an outrageous adventure than it did now.
What had changed? Quite a lot, actually, not the least of which
was the objective. Up until the last few days he'd had nothing
more in mind than stealing stolen money, taking something
that didn't belong to the person who had it and returning it,
not to those from whom it had been taken originally—which
would be an impossibility, like trying to return a cup of water
dipped out of the sea to the exact same place from which it was
taken—but to others in need, to the *kind* of people from
whom it had been stolen in the first place. The method had
been complex, the scheme convoluted, the technology sophis-

ticated, but at bottom he was only running away with a gang-ster's ill-gotten profits. Stealing stolen money.

Now he was only hours away from killing a man. Did he really believe that Schrade would kill Mara—and himself—if he didn't kill Schrade first? Yes . . . he *knew* Schrade would do that. Did he call it self-defense? Yes. Had he argued it ad naus-eam in his own mind? Yes. Then why did he still agonize over it?

He didn't know. But he did know that if he didn't gain control of his thoughts right now, he might as well turn around this very moment, go back and get Mara . . . and start running.

He had stopped at the upper end of Berkeley Square. There was a spattering of cars careening off Mount Street and tilting into the turn that would take them down on the other side of the park, while traffic from behind him came up the near side of the square and headed into Davies Street. When the light changed he followed the dribbling traffic upward in the direction of Grosvenor.

In another ten minutes he was passing the lighted win-dows of Claridge's dining room, which looked out onto Davies Street toward the Italian embassy. A few more steps and he turned into Brook Street and walked under the inviting awning of Claridge's.

Accepting the doorman's assistance, he folded his um-brella and entered the vestibule, removed his raincoat, and proceeded to the front hall, where he approached the recep-tion desk.

"Good evening." The reception clerk was quick and smil-ing.

"Good evening," Strand said. "I just came in from Paris early this morning for a business meeting, thinking I would be returning to Paris this evening. Unfortunately my business is carrying over to tomorrow. Might you possibly have something available for me on such short notice?"

"Let me see, sir." The clerk tipped his head and immediately consulted his computer, typing quietly in quick bursts, studying the screen. While he waited Strand allowed his eyes to follow the extension of the front hall toward three tall arches through which one passed to the more formal foyer famous for Claridge's afternoon teas. A good number of people still lingered around the small tables, chatting quietly, the epitome of decorum in the most decorous of places.

"Nothing available, sir," the clerk said, and Strand turned around.

"Not anything?"

"No singles or doubles, sir. We have only suites."

"One of those will be fine."

The clerk accepted this quiet extravagance with smooth alacrity.

Strand quickly produced one of his forged passports and credit cards, and the clerk got busy putting together the necessary paperwork for the accommodation.

CHAPTER 56

Claude Corsier had an extended argument with the murderous Skerlic that was immensely frustrating and even, at times, comical in its absurdity, over Corsier's insistence that he buy a proper suit and go to a barber. There were surveillance cameras, for God's sake, Corsier had argued—he had no idea if there were—and if the Serb did not want to be conspicuous, he would bloody well dress like everyone else whether he liked it or not. He could not go into the Connaught Hotel in Mayfair looking like a refugee and expect not to be noticed. Skerlic was insulted, and as Corsier argued with him, he actually turned his head away like a child refusing another spoon of green peas.

In the end he relented, and when he arrived at the Connaught carrying an oxblood leather satchel that Corsier had bought for him at Asprey, he did not turn a head. Corsier knew because he was watching from an armchair in the lobby.

He waited nearly ten minutes before folding his copy of *The Times* and following Skerlic up to his rooms. When he got there the Serb had peeled off his suit coat and had thrown it, turned inside out, onto one of the sofas in the reception area.

He was standing at the windows, looking at the tripods and the binoculars.

"What's this?" he asked.

"I don't want to depend on the audio alone. I want to see who's there, and I want to know what they're doing."

Skerlic looked across Carlos Place. "He leaves the curtains open?"

"In the second-floor room, yes. It's a library, a space for viewing paintings and drawings. There's good natural light."

"You can see everything over there?"

"Very nearly."

"No privacy."

"It's a place of business, and it's far enough away that, without something like these"—he gestured to the binoculars—"you really can't see much of anything."

Skerlic looked across as if to double-check that assertion, but the lights were out.

"We still have to rely on the mike," he said. "The mike is how I will know if his face is in the right place."

"I can see if that's the case."

"You cannot rely on what you see. The perspective might be confusing. You could be wrong."

"Of course. I intend to watch nevertheless."

Skerlic regarded him as if he were a simpleton and shrugged. "Where are the pictures?"

"In my bedroom." Corsier nodded to the doorway on the right. "Your bedroom is over there," he added, tilting his head the other way.

"Get them."

Corsier went to his bedroom and returned with one picture, then went back for the other. Skerlic lifted each onto one of the sofas and began examining it, going over the elaborate moldings with his face close to the gilding. Then he turned them over and examined the backs.

"Okay," he said. He carried each of them across the room and leaned them against the wall, facing out. He looked around the room. "Okay. We pull that over there to over here."

Corsier helped him move a writing desk over to the windows so that it sat at an angle to the street. Skerlic removed all the hotel information from the desk, removed the lamp, then carried over the satchel and set it beside the desk. He opened the satchel and began taking out his electronic equipment, putting the pieces on the writing desk like a surgeon laying out his instruments.

Corsier stood by uneasily. The equipment made him uncomfortable. Naturally he was entirely ignorant about it, but he had always had the impression that electronically activated explosives were highly unstable, even precarious. Not reliable. Touchy. He was aware that he was beginning to perspire as he watched Skerlic deal with the wires and the little plastic boxes with toggle switches and readout dials, both analogue and digital. Why was so much electronic equipment always black? He could smell the electrical wiring and the plastic. He noted with surprise that Skerlic was precise in the way he handled the equipment. He didn't remember seeing any of that kind of deftness a few nights ago in the Harley Mews garage.

Half an hour later Skerlic pulled two sets of headphones out of the leather satchel and plugged them into the side of one of the boxes. One set had very long wires attached to it.

"These are yours," Skerlic said, extending them to Corsier. "Put them on and sit over there." He motioned to another chair.

Corsier moved the chair over, sat down, and held the
headphones in his hands as Skerlic looked around the reception area and spotted a radio on a lamp table. He unplugged it
and put it on the floor about five feet away from the paintings.
He turned it on and reduced the volume to a near whisper.
Corsier could barely hear it. Skerlic put on his set of headphones, gesturing for Corsier to do the same, and turned on
the dials of the two black boxes. Needles moved on the analogue dials. Red numbers flew by rapidly on the digital one. In
moments Corsier heard the radio, classical music, at first low,
then louder and quite clear. For the first time since Corsier
had known him, Skerlic managed a tight-lipped smile.

Suddenly he flipped off the switches, removed his headphones, and turned to Corsier.

"Now, the schedule tomorrow . . ."

"I take the pictures to Knight between eight and eight-
thirty. We'll chat awhile in his library so that you will have time
to modulate the reception or frequency or whatever you do.
Then I come back over here. Schrade is supposed to be there
around ten o'clock."

"What if something happens and he comes earlier?"

"Even so, I don't think he would come earlier than eight-
thirty." He paused. "What about the second frame?"

"The second frame?"

"If you get Schrade with one, what about the second
one?"

"Nothing."

"Nothing? You just leave it? You will be giving investigators a guidebook of evidence, wiring signatures, explosive
source . . ."

Skerlic snorted. "You have been watching too much spy

418

programs on television. Bomb makers know all about signatures. Besides, they have never seen this woman's work before." He scratched his head, uninterested. "Now, after the detonation I will pack everything and leave. Within forty-eight hours I will message your e-mail address with instructions for the final deposit."

"Fine." The maneuvering was just about at an end. It had taken him a long time to get to this point.

"There is nothing else to do until tomorrow, then," Skerlic said, standing. "Don't touch any of this shit."

He turned and walked out of the reception and into his bedroom. He left the door open. Corsier heard the television come on, and that was that for the evening.

Corsier turned off the lights. He stood at the windows and looked down into the intersection that circled the small island of plane trees. The bronze statue of the nude woman glistened in the rain. No one sat on the benches beneath the trees. A few black cabs were parked at the curb across the street, and occasionally a car came and went along Carlos Place, going into or coming out of Mount Street.

It was a very strange evening for Claude Corsier. For the past several months, during his methodical planning of Schrade's assassination, it was an abstract, an academic exercise. It had become a little more real with each passing week, and then with each passing day. Now it was down to hours. An imaginary act was about to become a reality, an irreversible one with critical consequences. He felt at once oddly powerful, almost euphoric, and at the same time trepidant. Despite all his planning, a great deal still could go wrong. He would spend the night worrying.

CHAPTER 57

Left alone in his suite, Strand turned off the lights and threw back the curtains. The suite looked out to the Italian embassy on Davies Street, along which he had just walked. He could see the trees in Grosvenor Square. On the other side of that, a few streets away, was Ma Micheline.

Looking into the hazy London night, he double-checked his perspective. Other than Mara, not a soul on earth knew what he was doing. Even professional assassins had to share their secrets with one other person—the one who hired them. It couldn't get any tighter than that.

Yet it really wasn't tight at all. Mara's contact with Carrington was a gaping hole. However, only the intelligence services were likely to see it, and even that would be obscured once Strand unleashed his files on the media. It was highly unlikely that any of the agencies would pursue what they knew. After all, they were among the few entities on earth that feared light more than darkness. There was no turning back on this.

If Schrade's reservation was for eight-thirty, Strand would do well to be in the foyer by seven, an hour and a half from now. Schrade might go to the restaurant from the hotel, or he might fly in from Berlin, go to the restaurant, and then to the hotel. Strand couldn't do anything about that. But if Schrade left from Claridge's, Strand wanted to see if he was accompanied by a chauffeur, if he was accompanied by the second person, if he took a cab. It would even help to know how he was dressed. He had test fired the pistol into the bathtub, but he was still apprehensive about the pellet's ability to penetrate the amount of clothing Hodge had assured him it would.

He had a sharp pain in his stomach, just below his sternum. Disappointed, he pressed his fingers into it. He had thought he was handling the tension better than this. It scared him. How the hell could he be sure of his judgment?

Turning away from the windows, he removed his coat and maneuvered around the furniture to the bed. He tossed his coat on the foot of the bed, untied his shoes, and lay down. He tried to relieve the tension in his stomach by breathing deeply. The shadows in the suite were murky, no sharp distinctions, no clear margins or boundaries. From the window across the room a blue gray light washed over the furniture, the color of night. Christ, he wanted this to be over.

For the next hour—he kept looking over at the face of a clock on the table at the side of the bed—he concentrated on rehearsing several variations of the same scenario. He approached Schrade coming out of the restaurant, jammed the pistol into his side, and fired, catching the slumping figure. He approached Schrade in the lobby of Claridge's, jammed the pistol into his side, and fired, catching the slumping figure. He approached Schrade on the street, jammed the pistol into his side, and fired, catching the slumping figure. He approached Schrade . . .

He began to worry about how many opportunities he

would have before ten o'clock the next morning. Obviously it would be best to finish it tonight. Even if it didn't work out as he imagined it, if the pellet didn't penetrate, if he fumbled the pistol, if Schrade screamed, if . . . if . . . it would be a hell of a lot easier to flee into the darkness. Another reason why a street-side approach was best. If something went wrong inside, getting away would be much more difficult.

He began to worry about Schrade's dinner guest. Was it a woman, and would she accompany him back to Claridge's? That would make it more difficult. If she was with him, she would be close enough to see that Strand's brush-by was more than that. The milliseconds between the contact, the muffled slap, Schrade's reaction, and Strand's own response could say volumes to her. Her impressions would be instantaneous and would be largely formed by Strand's own behavior in those seconds after Schrade's reaction to being shot. If the saxitoxin didn't work fast enough . . .

The next time he glanced at the clock he was startled to see that it was eight o'clock. He swung his feet off the bed and flipped on the light. Eight o'clock. God. What had gone on in his mind to make an hour pass so quickly? Immediately his stomach clenched. He swore, put on his shoes, and stood. He undid his trousers and smoothed down the tail of his shirt, then fastened his belt again.

Walking into the bathroom, he turned on the light and then looked in the mirror. He had the sensation of being a voyeur, as though he were behind a two-way mirror. The latex was holding up well. Nothing had changed. He smiled. The man smiled. There was no hint of resistant tissue. Everything moved naturally, as it was supposed to. He firmed up the knot in his tie. He wanted to wash his face. He turned out the light.

422

THE COLOUR OF NIGHT

In the dimly lighted suite he put on his suit coat, grabbed his raincoat and umbrella, and left.

Strand was relieved to find that the foyer and the front hall were fairly busy, more generally active than he ever remembered them being, with people milling about the marble floors, moving in and out through the arches that led to the foyer. There was no bustle, no sense of collegial acquaintance among any of the guests.

He took a seat as out of the way as he could manage and still see the vestibule. He put his hands on the curved handle of his umbrella and sat back to wait and watch. Senior employees of the hotel stood about usefully but unobtrusively in dark suits while liveried staff glided to and fro across the polished marble floors in their scarlet tailcoats and white stockings.

Strand had no luck. At eight-twenty Schrade had not appeared. He was nothing if not punctual, so Strand could only assume that he was going to the restaurant from somewhere else. He walked out of the vestibule and got a cab in front of the hotel.

Ma Micheline was something new for sedate Mayfair, a result, perhaps, of Tony Blair's insistence that Great Britain should begin thinking positively, reminding itself and the world that it was a modern, progressive, twenty-first-century commonwealth, a place of possibilities and bright futures.

In that vein, Ma Micheline was a wonderful mixture of sophistication and understated adventure. It was located on a quiet street of Edwardian architecture near Park Place, and as Strand approached he saw its softly lighted interior through large plate-glass windows, the pale ice blue linen tablecloths

shimmering as though floating freely in the receding, tene-
brous expanse of the large dining room. Once inside, Strand
entered the warm, polished world of belle epoque decor, subdued lighting, smartly dressed diners, huge paintings along the
walls above the wainscoting reminiscent of Picasso's blue
period.

There was an abundance of serving persons of two kinds.
The first were waiters in tuxedos and glittering white shirts
with wing-tip collars who did most of the work; and the second
were a generous number of young women dressed identically
in black, water-thin cocktail dresses, a single strand of pearls,
their hair identically bobbed, with straight bangs. They all had
blue eyes. They were the only introduction of eccentricity, but
they were striking, and they waited on the tables with a
somber, detached efficiency.

While the maître d' located his reservation, Strand quickly
scanned the dining room. Schrade was not there, but something caught his eye; he came back to a table and looked at a
man sitting alone, in three-quarter profile. Strand tensed. Bill
Howard was buttering a piece of bread.

Strand almost wheeled around, then caught himself. It
took every bit of his self-control to allow the maître d' to lead
him through the aisles of tables to one five or six tables away.
It was in a good location. Howard would have had to turn his
head to see Strand's table.

With his heart working hard to maintain some semblance
of a rhythm, Strand ordered a bottle of wine, which arrived instantly. As one of the young women began opening it for him,
Wolfram Schrade made his entrance.

Strand had not seen him in nearly five years, but Schrade
had not changed. He was neither older nor heavier nor thin-

ner. Even from where he sat, Strand could see Schrade's strange clear eyes, and as he approached, following the maître d', Strand reacquainted himself with the straight, narrow nose, the wide mouth with its thin upper lip and full lower lip, the thick, coarse hair the color of the vellum pages of old books. Schrade carried himself with an erect, straight-backed posture that was saved from being military by his abundant self-assurance, evident in the way he moved with a loose elegance that Strand had never seen matched anywhere.

Strand was not prepared for the rush of emotions that flooded over him as he heard Schrade's deep voice, his heavily accented English. Strand bent his head to his menu and shifted his eyes to one side to watch them. He was suddenly seized by a loathing for Schrade that surpassed any animus he had felt in the past. He watched as one of the black-draped young women poured Schrade's wine; he picked up the glass and drank without even looking at her. He portrayed no expression whatsoever as he talked to Howard. Strand remembered the arrogance he had always thought Schrade's lack of expression conveyed. Schrade picked up his menu, glanced over it once, and then tossed it down, knowing what he wanted from the complicated entries without giving it a second thought, a dismissive gesture that demonstrated his world-weary hauteur in a way that Strand detested.

Watching Schrade, Strand slowly, deliberately dredged up the painful images he had carried with him like secret reliquaries: the harsh light on Romy's wild face as she looked back over her shoulder, horrified, desperate, the rear of her Land Rover sinking slowly into the cold tidewater; Ariana's naked, bloody body stuffed under the bed in the Métropole Hotel in Geneva; Dennis Clymer's headless, limbless corpse being fished out of the Canal de Charleroi in Brussels; Meret's charred skull amid the smoldering rubble of his home in Houston; Claude Corsier.

"Monsieur?"

Strand ordered the first thing that caught his eye.

Goddamn Bill Howard. Had Schrade been dining with a woman, or any person other than Howard, Strand would have had a chance on the sidewalk after dinner. But Howard would see right through Strand's clumsy procedure. It would work only among the unsuspecting, the uninitiated. Howard's world of betrayals and dirty business was far too cynical for him to witness such an act and be fooled by it.

Strand sat back with his glass of wine and looked once again at Schrade. He stared at him, his eyes exploring every minute aspect of his face and dress and demeanor in the same way a sightless man's fingers lightly probed a person's body to gain a sense of understanding. In Strand's case he knew the man all too well. What he was doing as he watched Schrade was more akin to picking at a scab. Everything about the man inspired a disgust that Strand did not want to let go. He worried it and studied it, using it to justify a moment that he felt in his viscera was not long away.

CHAPTER 58

Strand watched them, tantalized by their facial expressions, their gestures, the angle of their bodies, the cant of their shoulders. Bill Howard seemed quite comfortable with Schrade, as much as anyone could be. Their conversation was constant and apparently to the point, since neither of them ever took the time to look around the restaurant, either out of idle curiosity or out of concern for surveillance. Strand took that as a good sign, an indication that he had successfully convinced Howard that he had departed London the previous night.

He watched carefully as they progressed through their meal. He guessed that both men would have dessert. When the time came, they did, accompanied by coffee for Howard and espresso for Schrade. Strand asked for his bill. He wanted to leave just in front of them. They lingered over their drinks. Strand's bill came promptly, too promptly. He perused it. They called for their bill also. Strand caught the eye of the young woman in the black dress, who took his credit card. Schrade did the same. Strand felt as though he were engaged in an intricate dance in which the partners never touched.

His young woman returned. Schrade's returned. Bill

Howard now looked around idly for the first time. He looked straight at Strand, who had glanced up from signing his credit card slip. Their eyes met, and Howard's eyes moved on. That was bad luck. Howard did not recognize him, but ideally Strand should never have allowed himself to be noticed at all, not even in passing. Strand tore off his copy of the credit slip and got up from his table. Neither Schrade nor Howard noticed he was leaving.

He had to wait in the reception foyer for his raincoat and umbrella. If they separated here, at the restaurant, Strand had a chance at Claridge's as Schrade went inside. Or in the lobby, if it was still busy. Or in the elevator, if he could get him alone.

Just as his coat and umbrella arrived, Schrade and Howard appeared at the desk, asking for theirs. One of the blue-eyed women helped Strand on with his raincoat while Schrade and Howard chatted a moment, waiting for their coats to be retrieved from the cloakroom. Strand could hear their voices clearly, but he understood nothing. The blood was driving through his head so violently, his ears heard only the rushing.

As Strand was buttoning his coat he realized the foyer was full of people. Two couples had arrived. There was the noise of conversation. Three young women in black were now among them. The one who had helped Strand turned to the arriving couples to ask their names. A second one was approaching with Schrade's and Howard's raincoats, and a third was talking to the maître d' about something happening in the dining room. Howard turned away, momentarily distracted. Schrade was being helped with his coat.

This was it. Strand thrust his hand into his pocket and

gripped the pistol. He put his finger into the trigger guard and took one step toward Schrade as Howard turned around and looked at him, their faces an arm's length away.

What in the hell was he doing? Hadn't he just told himself at the table that it wouldn't work as long as Howard was with him? The pistol felt like a brick in his hand.

"How are you?" Howard said reflexively in his American drawl, with his American familiarity, like saying "Excuse me" when one found oneself face-to-face with someone in a sudden crowded situation, shoulders touching, hips brushing. Did Howard's eyes linger a moment? Did something catch his notice?

Strand grunted, nodded, turned, the small crowd shifting naturally, never maintaining the same configuration, the new arrivals moving up.

Strand made it to the door and was suddenly outside. He was perspiring profusely and was suddenly worried about the latex. He took the first cab available, got inside, and leaned forward.

"Just pull up a little way and wait, please."

Schrade and Howard emerged and talked on the sidewalk. They were not interested in a cab, and Howard showed no signs of leaving. A dark Mercedes turned on its lights down the street and moved toward them slowly. As it approached the restaurant's awning, the doorman stepped out and opened the door. Schrade and Howard got inside.

"Christ," Strand said. He leaned forward and told the cabdriver, "I need you to follow this Mercedes coming around us here. I think it's going to Claridge's, but if it's not, I just need to know where it's going." He took two fifty-pound notes out of his wallet and handed one through the window. "The Mercedes driver is trained to spot a tail."

"Right, sir. I understand."

He may have understood, but he didn't know what he was doing. He glommed on to the Mercedes, which luckily went straight up the street and around Grosvenor Square to Claridge's. If he had been going anywhere else, the Mercedes driver would have spotted him in five minutes.

"Keep going," Strand said quickly. They passed the Mercedes, which had pulled up to the Claridge's awning, and turned into Avery Row, which turned quickly into Brook's Mews, which brought them around to Davies Street.

"Okay," Strand said, unable to hide his frustration and anger. "Back to Claridge's."

When the cab approached the awning, he gave the second fifty-pound note to the driver and hurried through the vestibule to the front hall. He was just in time to see Schrade's back rounding the corner to the elevators. Where was Howard? Was he ahead of him? Was he now behind Strand, watching Schrade's back? Strand had no time to speculate further. He hurried to follow and got to the elevators just in time to wait a moment with Schrade. Howard was not there, nor was anyone else other than Schrade. Perfect. Strand's heart was slamming against his chest. One hand was holding the umbrella, the other was in his raincoat pocket, gripping the pistol.

The elevator opened, three men got off, and he and Schrade stepped inside. Schrade punched the button for the fifth floor. Strand reached across and punched the button for the sixth. He stepped back. He rehearsed the coming moments. When the doors closed he would shoot Schrade immediately. When they stopped on the fifth floor and the doors opened, he would grab Schrade and pretend to be ministering to him. If someone was waiting there, he would call for help. If no one was waiting, he would shove Schrade out into the hall and go on up to the next floor, then down and out of the hotel.

All of this burst into his mind as an instant template for the next three minutes. He felt for the safety on the pistol. The doors were closing. He flicked off the safety.

Then a bell chimed and the doors jerked back. A man and a woman were waiting apologetically.

"Sorry," the man said. The two of them stepped in, between Schrade and Strand, and the man punched the seventh floor. The woman was wearing a gardenia fragrance that instantly permeated the elevator, a saccharine epitaph for the demise of another opportunity.

Strand was trembling inside when Schrade stepped off the elevator on the fifth floor. That was the end of it for the evening. He got off the elevator on the sixth and then waited in the hall until he could descend again to his own room on the fourth floor.

Once inside, he stood still a moment, panting as if he had run the whole distance from Ma Micheline. Jesus Christ, how could he have been that close without . . . He stopped. He reminded himself again of the reality of what he was doing. It was no different from surveillance work, until the last moment. Up to then it required the same patience, was subject to the same frustrations, required the same instantaneous adjustments in plan to accommodate unforeseen intrusions. One always expected the inevitable unexpected event.

Changing course was routine. Adapting to sudden reversals was the norm.

Back in his suite, he pulled off his raincoat and hung it in the closet, then his suit coat. He laid the pistol on the coffee table. He kicked off his shoes and slumped down on the sofa, looking out toward the Italian embassy. He stared out to the London night for a moment and then picked up the telephone.

"It's me," he said when Mara answered.

"Are you all right?"

"I'm fine. Drained. No luck." He told her about the events of the evening. She listened without comment.

"So that leaves the morning," he said.

She waited a second. "Listen, Harry. Don't . . . don't . . ."

"Don't get desperate. Don't do anything rash," he said.

"Yeah, that's what I meant."

They both seemed to realize how bizarre that sounded, in light of what he was trying to do.

"I was, uh, surprised at how I felt, seeing him after all this time," Strand said. He was speaking softly, as though the telephone were the walls of a confessional. "I was very surprised."

"What do you mean?"

He hesitated. "I *wanted* to kill him. It wasn't dispassionate."

"Did you think it would be?"

"I'd imagined it would be."

They did not speak for a moment, and then she said, "Harry . . ." The tone of her voice hinted at a conversation he did not want to have. "Maybe . . . maybe . . ."

"Don't say it."

"Harry, neither of us is sure we're doing the right thing here."

"I am."

"No, you're not. Where's the wisdom in being blind about this?"

"I'm not looking for wisdom, Mara."

She said nothing else. They stayed on the telephone together, but neither of them spoke for a long time. Then Mara said:

"It's raining again here. And it's lonely."

Strand struggled a moment with the lump in his throat. He thought she must know what was happening.

"I love you," he said.

"And I love you, Harry Strand."

CHAPTER 59

The morning was so overcast and dark that the street lamps were still on as Strand sat in Claridge's plush robe and ate the light breakfast he had ordered. The night had been a grim phantasmagoric passage from one day to the next, during which he had tried to stay flat on his back to avoid inadvertently damaging the face of the stranger who slept with him. He tried to think of anything other than Wolfram Schrade: he succeeded in thinking of nothing else.

He had ordered an extra pot of coffee and already had begun drinking from the second one when he looked at his watch. It was seven-thirty.

He had known two professional hit men during his years in the intelligence business. They were, seemingly, unremarkable men, a little remote, perhaps, but one of them in particular he quite liked. The man was forty-three years old, Strand remembered, and he had grown up in the midwestern United States. He had been trained to kill when he had served in Vietnam, and when he'd finished his second tour in Southeast Asia, his superior officer had recommended his services to the Metsada. It was as though he had simply accepted another assignment. There was a military angle to it, being an Israeli operation, so it had seemed like an extension of his last Saigon assignment. After that the Israelis referred him to someone else, and very gradually the military aspect of it faded away. One day he woke up and realized he was making a very good living being paid to kill people; he was a professional assassin.

At the time Strand had known him, they were staying in a very shabby hotel in Algiers. They spent a lot of time talking, sometimes in their rooms, sometimes wandering in the narrow, alleylike streets of the city. He confided to Strand one hot night as they sat in the dark beside a window in Strand's room, smoking and looking down into the crowded street, that he vomited every time he killed someone. Sometimes before, sometimes after. It was odd, he said, because he was not repulsed by the killing, so he didn't know why it happened. But when it was time, he didn't fight it. He just accepted it as part of the business. It used to bother him, he said, but now he didn't worry about it anymore.

But Strand had always wondered why the man had told the story.

He picked up his cup and saucer and walked to the window with it. He had not turned on the lights in the room, so the suite was washed in a gray luminescence in which the burnished surfaces glistened with a pearlish haze. The light died away kindly into the corners, and colors were reduced to pallid values. It was an effect that he especially liked, though he felt odd about being able to enjoy it at this particular moment.

He had thought of Schrade until he was sick of him. He doubted that he had had a single heartbeat during the night that Schrade had not shared with him. He was saturated with the man. Killing him would be a sweet liberation. He knew it would be a scarifying act, too, like that of a fox that chewed off its own paw and left it behind in the jaws of the trap as it limped away on a bloody stump to freedom.

Mara was sitting on the edge of their bed, fastening the buckle on her shoes, when she decided to go on to Knight's immediately even though she would be a little early. The decision was a result partly of a nagging sixth sense and partly of anxiety. She was worried sick about Strand, her mind generating an endless chain of scenarios about what he was doing and what was happening to him, none of them good. She couldn't help it. That none of these scenarios was hopeful was depressing, which she feared would adversely affect the way she had to handle herself within the next hour.

The sixth sense was, naturally, more difficult to deal with. It was, simply, a discomfiting tug at the back of her mind that was so persistent, it seemed foolish to ignore it.

She stood up and smoothed her dress, a dove gray wool knit that fell to her ankles. She stepped to the windows and regarded her faint reflection. There was no full-length mirror in the bare town house. She entertained the idea of wearing a belt and finally decided against it, preferring a sleeker look. Her stockings were bone, her shoes matched the dove gray of the dress. She had taken the single braid of her hair and coiled it in a complicated chignon. A single black pearl drop dangled from each ear.

After calling for the cab and slipping on her long black raincoat, she stood at the windows and looked down at the street. Whatever was going to happen to them was already in motion and couldn't be stopped or turned back or undone.

THE COLOUR OF NIGHT

She did not feel good about it, and the fact that she was not optimistic filled her with an enormous sadness.

The black cab came down Chesterfield Hill, emerging slowly from the fog and the drizzle. Suddenly she was angry, furious at herself and at the weakness of her feelings. She wheeled around from the windows and started down the stairs.

When the doorbell rang, Carrington Knight was surprised. He glanced at his watch and stepped to the windows to look down.

"A cab?" He turned with a puzzled frown to Claude Corsier, who was sitting in one of the armchairs, balancing a cup of tea on a saucer. "I don't have any idea who that is. Excuse me a moment."

At the landing he pushed a button to unlock the front door and started down the curving staircase.

Upon reaching the ground floor, he crossed the foyer and opened the front door.

"Oh, good Lord, Ms. Paille."

"I'm sorry I'm early," she said, stepping inside. "I hope this isn't inconveniencing you."

"Oh, my goodness, no, no, no, not at all," he said, ushering her inside. "Let me take your coat." He relished looking at her as she turned her back to him and let the raincoat slip off her shoulders. What an exquisite neck, Knight thought, the little wisp of dark hair there at the nape. The supple wool knit fit the woman like a kiss.

"Listen," Knight said, his mind jittering with a way to handle this awkward circumstance as he hung her coat in the closet, "there's a gentleman upstairs, another collector and dealer. He's actually just on his way out, but if you don't mind, I'd like him to meet you, and to quickly look at your collection." He could not, on the spur of the moment, think of any other way to get them around each other now that Corsier had stayed a little too long and she had come a little too early.

"Certainly," she said, "I'd love to meet him."

Corsier was waiting for them when they topped the last step on the landing. Knight introduced her to Corsier, whom he presented as Mr. Blanchard, an impromptu fabrication that Corsier accepted as smoothly as if they had rehearsed it.

Corsier, regal as always, bowed slightly from the waist and took her hand. He did not kiss it, although he looked as if he wanted to. Like Knight, Corsier was a connoisseur of beauty in its endless variations. Everything, even beauty, existed within a continuum, and a beautiful woman was certainly at the highest end of the scale. Ms. Paille was no less stunning today than she had been two days before.

Well aware of their tight schedule, Knight quickly retrieved Cao's drawings from the vault and, while keeping up a rapid-fire, though oblique, explanation of Ms. Paille's situation, placed the portfolio on the library table and opened it with a precious manner.

He stepped back. Claude Corsier silently studied the Balthus encased in the first leaf. Then he methodically went through the portfolio without hurrying, much to Knight's increasing agitation. Occasionally Corsier leaned forward to examine a drawing more closely, his nose nearly touching it. At last he straightened and turned around.

"Ms. Paille, you are in possession of a very handsome collection here. I'm sure you know that."

"Mr. Knight has made me aware," she said.

Corsier elaborated on his thoughts about each of the drawings, turning to look at one of them now and again. Knight could see that the old bear found Ms. Paille to be a bright brush stroke of beauty, eliciting his most charming manner.

After consulting his watch, Corsier excused himself, pleading obligations elsewhere. He took Ms. Paille's hand once again with a shallow bow.

Knight walked him down the stairs to the door.

"Are you going to offer those drawings to Schrade, too, Carrington?" Corsier asked softly, pausing in the foyer.

"I think I am, yes."

"You should. What a remarkable collection."

He walked to the cloak closet and took out his raincoat. "You know, Carrington, you should keep them in the vault until the very last moment, until the Schiele deal is completed. Bring them out just before he's about to leave."

"Don't worry." Knight smiled. "I'm going to squeeze the most out of the Schieles. I won't let the drawings compete. They are a completely separate situation and negotiation—altogether." He handed Corsier his umbrella.

Corsier smiled also. "Thank you, Carrington." He turned to the door. "Oh, the woman, Ms. Paille. Is she going to stay for the meeting?"

"No, I think not. Definitely not."

"Good," Corsier said. He turned and walked out the door, putting up his umbrella. He descended the front steps and disappeared around the corner on Carlos Place.

CHAPTER 60

9:15

He looked at his watch. He had been sitting in the foyer, with yet another cup of coffee, for more than half an hour. Mara would be getting ready to leave for Carrington's in a cab. He guessed that Schrade would wait to come down at the last minute and go straight to his Mercedes. Still, he had come early in case Schrade had an earlier agenda.

Schrade rounded the corner from the elevators, his pace deliberate, his back straight, and headed into the front hall. He was alone, no Howard. Was Howard waiting in the restaurant for him? In the front hall out of Strand's view? Strand quickly left some money beside his coffee cup and followed Schrade, glancing around for Howard.

Just as he got to the sidewalk, Schrade was getting into the backseat of the Mercedes. Alone. Moving without hurrying, Strand stepped across and got into one of the waiting cabs along the street.

As he had done the previous night, he leaned forward and gave the driver a large note.

"I need to follow the Mercedes *discreetly*," he emphasized.

"Yes . . . yes, sir." The driver's eyes boggled at the size of the note as he digested the instructions. "Oh, right, sir." He was suddenly alert, responsible, ready. He flipped on his windshield wipers and pulled out into the traffic of Brook Street.

"The driver's going to be watching for this sort of thing."

"Yes, sir. I understand."

He seemed to. He allowed traffic to get between them, then quickly crowded up close as they approached Bond Street, where all the traffic had to turn right in the direction of Piccadilly. He let the Mercedes move up again several car lengths. The traffic muddled along. These few blocks were something of a bottleneck. Bond Street was not a through street at this point, being interrupted by a pedestrian court a few blocks ahead, after which it began again and went on to Piccadilly. Traffic slowed here since it was forced to turn into side streets or continue on a contorted series of turns to get back to Bond. The Mercedes remained in the left lane, then it pulled to the curb and stopped.

"Hold up, hold up," Strand cautioned. The traffic slowed to a creep. They were still three cars behind the Mercedes. Schrade got out and hurried across the puddle-strewn sidewalk to a shop three doors back from his car: Stefan Kappe: Silver and Goldsmith. He was now directly across from Strand.

"Okay, this is good enough," Strand said. He got out of the cab in the middle of the street and popped up his umbrella as the surprised driver thanked him profusely. At that moment the traffic began moving again, and the cab pulled forward as Strand stepped away and onto the sidewalk.

He stood in the drizzling rain and hesitated. He didn't dare go into the shop. It was too small. The slap of the pistol firing would be obvious. The sidewalks of Bond Street were perfect. Because of the rain everyone was hurrying, umbrellas up. The abundance of smart shops along the way assured that the pedestrian traffic was ample, in spite of the rain, and the streets themselves were full of cars, cabs, and delivery vans. The slap would easily be swallowed by the sounds of the city.

Strand moved closer to the shops to get out of the line of sight of the Mercedes' rearview mirror. He made a quick calculation. Schrade was about twenty to thirty steps from the Mercedes. He was not carrying an umbrella, so he would be in a hurry when he started back to the car. If Strand were close enough, he could easily engineer a collision. If other pedestrians were around them at that moment, all the better.

He walked to a shop window one door over from Kappe's. He peered inside, oblivious of what he was seeing. The rain was steady, splashing his trousers legs. He was so aware of the blood hammering in his ears that the noise of the traffic was distant. How long could he wait? How long dared he wait before he risked having the chauffeur—who, of course, was more than a chauffeur—notice him? He couldn't walk any farther because Schrade might come out any moment, and Strand would be too far away to make it to him before he reached the Mercedes. He looked at his watch. Schrade was due at Carrington's in twenty minutes. He was now ten minutes away from Carlos Place. Could Strand remain inconspicuous for ten minutes, standing still in the rain, pacing in the rain, dawdling in the rain?

He had to admit the situation was perfect. Schrade would come out. Strand would bump into him and fire into his stomach. Schrade would slump. Strand would act confused, then yell for help. He would yell loudly enough for the chauffeur to hear him, and then he would stay with Schrade, holding him in the rain, holding the umbrella over him . . .

The door to Kappe's opened and Schrade paused in the open doorway. He looked up at the rain, turned inside, and spoke to someone.

Strand looked both ways. Pedestrians were converging, God sent as if he had prayed for them: a young woman who looked as though she were an art student—Cork Street and the Royal Academy of Arts were nearby—carrying a large portfolio and coming from the direction of Clifford Street, followed closely by a preoccupied businessman; from the other direction a second businessman, head down, plowed through the rain; while a painter who was involved in remodeling a nearby shop slammed closed the rear door of his parked van and, clutching an armload of wadded tarpaulin, started running diagonally toward Strand.

At the same instant, the door to an expensive luggage shop behind Strand opened and a woman emerged with a plastic-covered bag nearly too large for her to carry.

Schrade said one last thing over his shoulder and bounded out into the rain.

Strand moved toward him.

The art student twisted to miss Schrade, who had burst out in front of her.

The businessman behind the student swerved to miss her and stepped right into Schrade's path.

The woman with the luggage never saw any of them as she dashed to the curb where her car was parked behind Schrade's Mercedes.

The painter and the preoccupied businessman from the

other direction both twisted in midstride to miss the woman
with the luggage.

Strand intercepted Schrade, who had lunged ahead at the
last instant to try to avoid the businessman.

The three men collided.

Strand grasped Schrade's arm as if to catch his balance,
jammed the pistol into Schrade's stomach, and pulled the trigger. Once. Twice. Three times. He heard nothing, felt nothing.
The painter and the woman with the luggage both dropped
what they were carrying as the art student flailed at her oversize portfolio, trying to keep from dropping it. The businessman blurted an apology as Schrade swore in German and
wrenched away from Strand's grip.

The second businessman went around all of it and never
stopped.

As Schrade pulled away, Strand staggered into the first
businessman, who reflexively caught him, steadied him, and
apologized again.

Strand was dumbfounded. After twisting away from the
businessman, he wheeled around to orient himself. Everyone
was recovering: the woman quickly had picked up her luggage;
the painter had snatched up his tarpaulin; the art student was
well down the sidewalk. The businessmen were gone.

Strand wheeled around again, just in time to see Schrade
slam the door of the Mercedes, casting an angry scowl at
Strand through the window. The Mercedes pulled away from
the curb and turned smoothly into Conduit Street.

Strand stood with his mouth open in astonishment, his
umbrella open and upside-down on the sidewalk. He looked
down at the gun in his trembling hand. Desperately he
snatched up the umbrella and ran to the curb. Stepping be-

tween two cars to hide what he was doing, he pointed the pistol into the gutter and jerked the trigger. Once: slap! Twice: slap! Three times: slap!

He was stunned. What in God's name . . . ?

Fumbling with the umbrella and the pistol, he removed the clip from the handle. Two shots were left. He hadn't fired a single pellet at Schrade.

Corsier sat on the edge of his chair, headphones in place, his eyes glued to the binoculars on the tripod. He had said nothing to Skerlic about the gorgeous woman at Carrington's. He was exceptionally uneasy about her. Despite Knight's assurances, Corsier was afraid she would remain for the meeting with Schrade. Ever the opportunist, Knight was probably going to take full advantage of Corsier's carefully planned scheme. Corsier only hoped that this already baroque enterprise did not collapse under the stress of Knight's ratcheting up the complexity to a full rococo encounter.

How extraordinary that this Ms. Paille had brought her client's drawings at this time. It was a bothersome interference. Might it even be suspicious? Corsier could not for the life of him imagine any possible connection here between Ms. Paille and his own endeavor. He had planned this in as near a vacuum as he had been able to manage. He was afraid that what he was seeing here was the appearance of that dreaded poltergeist of every covert operation: the unforeseen intrusion.

The microphones in the frames were working fabulously, and although Corsier was nearly weak from an unsettled nervous stomach, he was mesmerized by his ability to overhear Knight and Ms. Paille.

445

✦   ✦   ✦

When Strand finally came to his senses, standing in the gutter between the two cars in Bond Street, all the confusion and uncertainty that had clouded the previous fifteen minutes turned to an instant understanding and clarity of what had to happen in the next fifteen minutes. He had to get to Carlos Place before Schrade.

The one-way streets pretty much dictated Schrade's route once he had turned left on Conduit Street. Strand had just about the same distance if he ran into Bruton Street and caught a cab that would take him by a different route around Berkeley Square. Neither course had much of an advantage over the other. He broke into a dead run for the Bruton Street entrance directly across from Conduit Street.

CHAPTER 61

Mara stood before the two Schiele drawings, waiting for Carrington Knight to make his way back up the curving stairway. She was struggling with a peculiar sense of disorientation that had hit her the moment she'd seen Claude Corsier. Though his mustache and goatee had prevented instant recognition, within moments his face had reassembled itself in her memory from the Camp Peary files of six months earlier. She was caught completely off guard.

What was happening here? Newly discovered Schieles? Corsier's Schieles? Brought to Knight only a few days ago? Was she supposed to believe all of this was coincidence? She would not believe it. She could not. Why was Corsier being introduced as Blanchard? Her mind fumbled for explanations, but nothing even remotely satisfactory came into focus.

"Can I get you anything to drink?" Knight asked. She was still standing with her back to him, facing the two Schieles.

"No, thank you," she said without turning around.

"Do you know this artist?" he asked, approaching her.

"I recognize the style, but I can't really say I 'know' his work."

Knight smiled with affectionate indulgence. "Egon Schiele. A contemporary and friend of Mr. Klimt in your collection. He is a much coveted artist these days. Very popular." He paused. "Mr. Schrade is an ardent collector of this man's work, just as he is of Klimt's."

She turned and squared herself to Knight. "This was planned, then, having my drawings here with the Schieles?"

"Yes and no. It's the damnedest coincidence I've ever experienced in all my years in the business." Knight's eyes widened theatrically. He told her briefly of how he had come by the Schieles, skimming over the facts.

"So, this Mr. Schrade was coming to London anyway, then, to see Mr. Blanchard's drawings?"

"Indeed. Only . . ." Knight shrugged his shoulders in a way to indicate a delicate matter. "Only Mr. Blanchard is offering these drawings anonymously, as you are. I can't say that happens too often, either—back to back, that is."

Mara nodded. Claude Corsier was selling drawings to Schrade? Incredible. Actually, it seemed too incredible. She couldn't understand what was going on here, nor could she possibly imagine why *something* was going on here. She couldn't gather together enough logical pieces of the puzzle to propose any scenarios at all.

Knight stepped back, pleased with himself. A lock of his white hair sagged over his forehead, and his eyes twinkled from behind his round black eyeglasses.

"So then, we should hurry. You've brought the documentation?"

"Actually, no," Mara said.

Knight frowned. Worry, concern, horrible imaginings, and a little fear instantly embedded themselves in the pale flesh gathering across his broad forehead. "I beg your pardon?"

"I don't have the documentation," Mara said. "I received a communication from Mr. Cao early this morning. There's been a change in plans in Hong Kong. Mr. Cao does not want to sell."

"What? Does *not* want to sell?"

"That's correct."

Knight almost staggered. He looked at the portfolio on the table with disbelief.

"Does he want some other arrangement with me? Would he like to talk about it? I can assure you, Mr. Schrade *will* buy these. And he *will* pay the very highest price. You were absolutely correct in that, Ms. Paille."

"It has nothing to do with anything here, Mr. Knight. Mr. Cao lives in his own world. What he does and how he does it often have nothing at all to do with anything, except what is in his head. I've worked for him for so long, I've become—almost—acclimated to these sudden reversals."

"Why, this is appalling," Knight said. "He, you, could hardly have asked for a more convenient, a more serendipitous circumstance than what you have here. Everything has come together absolutely without plan . . . so extraordinary."

The telephone rang. Knight flinched and looked around at it, and Mara quickly checked her watch. God.

Knight looked at Ms. Paille, held his hand up tentatively as if to freeze the moment, started to speak but didn't, and picked up the telephone.

"Hello, this is Carrington." He listened, his dark brow

lightening in polite ingratiation. "Oh, yes, absolutely. . . . Of course not. . . . No, no, no, not at all. . . . Absolutely. Very good, very good. . . . Yes, good-bye."

He put down the receiver and looked at Ms. Paille, concern returning to his expression. "That was Mr. Schrade. He's in a traffic jam. He'll be a little late, probably another fifteen minutes."

"Good," she said. "Good. That just gives me time to be out of your way." She moved to the portfolio and began closing it up.

Knight blanched. "Ms. Paille, do you suppose it would be possible for me to talk to Mr. Cao? Perhaps he doesn't understand the *extraordinary*—"

"I'm afraid that would be entirely impossible," Mara said, clasping the portfolio as she rallied every nerve in her body to remain in control. She was horrified that Schrade was still alive. What had happened to Harry? She was nearly faint with anxiety. Carrington Knight was talking urgently, but she heard nothing he was saying. She was fighting nausea. God, Schrade was so close.

Knight was coming around the opposite end of the table to meet her. He had put both hands together prayerfully, holding them in front of his chest, gesturing with them, rocking them back and forth. "These sorts of opportunities are rare, really, because Schrade is *the* premier individual collector of these artists. . . ."

Somehow she moved unhurriedly, gracefully, even spoke calmly, though she had no idea what she was saying, and eventually she found herself being accompanied by a loquacious Knight down the long turn in the staircase. She had entered headlong into that surreal and common dream in which quick

flight in the face of peril was impossible, in which her own
legs plowed with slumberous torpor through the thick surf of
her panic.

How much time had elapsed? She had no idea. How
long had Knight tried to persuade her before they headed for
the staircase? How long had it taken them to descend to
where they were now? The foyer that occupied the space between the bottom of the stairs and the front door was generous but not grand, yet in her illusory flight it seemed an
encompassing sea of indigo silk.

Knight opened the cloakroom door, and she turned her
back to him and felt her raincoat on her shoulders. She
slipped her arms into the sleeves as Knight, she only vaguely
realized, was flattering her, his oily, clever manner grasping at
her, trying desperately to hold her with his words.

Where was her driver?

He was ill. She had come in a cab.

Oh, then he should call one.

No, no need to call a cab, she said. There were always
those parked across the street in front of the Connaught. Oh,
but he could call, he would call. She wouldn't have to cross
the street in the rain. Not at all. It was nothing. She said
things, appropriate things.

There were parting words.

She took the umbrella from him and started to open it
when the doorbell rang.

She did not flinch but looked up calmly.

Knight tittered. Don't worry, don't worry, he would pretend she was simply a client leaving, it happened all the time,
there was nothing to worry about, it wasn't necessary to in-
troduce her, it was just business.

She was suddenly composed. The surreal passed, and the present came into focus. She faced the opening of the door with a singular clarity of mind.

She wondered how Schrade would react. He knew her face as readily as he knew his own. He knew all about her. But he wouldn't be expecting to see her. That, at least, would be a surprise.

Knight was as oblivious as a butterfly.

He stepped in front of her and opened the door.

A man burst in, sending Knight sprawling flat on his back on the parquet floor and sliding six feet before he stopped at the foot of the Persian stairs.

CHAPTER 62

Strand was dripping wet, his arm stretched out, pointing the pistol at a dumbfounded Carrington Knight.

"Wolf Schrade," he demanded, short of breath, his lungs burning.

"Wha . . . ?" Knight scrambled up against the last tread on the stairs and gaped, trying to collect his ability to think, to speak.

"Where's Schrade?"

"He's not here," Mara blurted.

Strand looked around at her. "Who the hell are you?" he snapped.

They stared at each other. Silence.

Mara said, "Schrade's not here . . . He called . . . he's late, traffic . . ."

"Jeffrey?" Strand looked up the stairs.

"I haven't seen him."

Strand turned to Knight, who choked, "Not here . . ."

"Who *is* here?" Strand's raincoat was shedding streams of water that puddled around his feet.

"Only us," Mara said. She was standing with her arms

pressed to her chest, a gesture of holding on, of controlling at least herself in this volatile moment.

Strand turned on her. "This is no concern of yours, lady. Get out of here."

She slowly tilted her head to one side. "No . . ." It was a plea, not a refusal.

"Get out!" Strand yelled.

"Oh, no, please don't do this. I can't . . . I won't."

"Get *out!*" Strand screamed this time, furious with her, frantic to get her out of there, to get it under control before Schrade arrived. He glanced at Knight, whose eyes were darting back and forth between them. Even in his confusion he was beginning to calculate the meaning behind Mara's surprising refusal to flee a shocking, dangerous situation.

"You go with me," she said emphatically, "or I don't go at all."

Strand looked at her. She knew very well what she had just done. With that one sentence she had taken them past the turning point. When it was all over, Knight would remember those words. Knight was a witness. It was one thing to kill Schrade . . . It was over.

"Christ," Strand said, looking at her. His shoulders sagged. God, what had he done in that fatal moment on Bond Street, when, even against his will, something in his unconscious had frozen his fingers on the trigger of the pistol? He turned to Knight.

"Get up, Carrington."

This time Knight recognized something familiar in the voice. His eyes narrowed, then he rolled over like a large, awkward child and got to his feet, standing defensively against the newel post.

Strand turned back to Mara. "Okay," he said, "okay, that's it, then. It's over."

In that instant he could see in her face that she was relieved, that although she had committed herself to him, it had been a commitment she had made in spite of her own deepest feelings, not because of them. God, he didn't care anymore, he just wanted to be away from it all. He wanted it to be over, and he wanted them to be together and gone and away from it all, even if only for a little while. He would worry about Schrade later. He would treat him the same way most people treated their inevitable last hour of life, by ignoring it entirely until they were unavoidably face to face with it. Why the hell did he think he should be any different?

"Let's get out of here," he said. He dropped his arm and turned to Knight. "It's a long story, Carrington."

"Harry *Strand*?!"

"Yeah, it's me."

"*Bloody* hell, Harry . . . what's . . . A *mask*?"

"I'm sorry."

"Harry." Mara interrupted him. "There's something else. Claude Corsier is alive, and he was just here."

Strand turned. "He was here?"

"He left just a little while ago. He was already here when I came in. He'd brought two Schiele drawings, new ones that he'd unearthed somewhere. That's why Schrade's coming here, not because of my drawings. It was a coincidence, the drawings. Claude left half an hour ago."

"Coincidence." He knew there was no coincidence. He turned back to Knight. "What's going on here, Carrington?"

Knight, stammering, speaking in bursts, quickly spilled out the story of Corsier and his drawings. In his agitation he

455

confused the sequence of the story and went back to explain and then doubled back again to pick up loose ends. He could hardly speak at all. Though he could not even come close to imagining what was happening here, he knew that he had got caught up in an intrigue that was far beyond his world and his experience. And he knew that it was sinister.

"This is not a coincidence," Strand said to Mara.

"But how could Claude know . . ."

"The timing, maybe. Probably. No one could have known about us and the drawings, our schedule. But the Schieles . . ." He looked at Knight. "The anonymity . . ." He was talking to himself, thinking out loud. "We've all sold to Schrade. We all know what he wanted. What he coveted. I could have chosen Schiele. Claude could have chosen the others. Either way . . ."

"God, Harry." Mara was following him. She saw it all taking shape, too.

"Carrington," Strand said, "Claude knew Schrade was coming this morning? He knew the time?"

"Of course. Yes, yes."

The doorbell rang.

Everything in Strand's mind turned inside out.

"Carrington!" he snapped, again pointing the gun at the art dealer. "Get over here."

Knight looked as though he were going to faint, as though if he let go of the newel post, he would fall down.

"Get over here!"

Knight came over, his face pasty.

Strand looked at Mara. "Get around the corner, out of sight."

"Harry, there's got to be another door, a back door . . ."

"Yes, yes, there's a back door." Knight had stopped in the

456

middle of the entry, suddenly hopeful that this could all be made to go away, literally, through a back door. "Oh, please, yes, the back door."

"Get around the corner," Strand commanded Mara, his mind suddenly jumping track, changing agendas. He waved at Knight, who cowered over to him like a threatened lapdog. Strand grabbed him, speaking hoarsely.

"Just answer the door and get him inside. If you do anything, if you try to run, I'll step outside and blow off the back of your head. Open the door, but step back, don't leave my sight." He looked at the petrified Knight. "Do you understand?"

Knight nodded.

"Hold yourself together just long enough to play the part. Okay?"

The doorbell rang again.

Knight nodded vigorously.

"Just get him inside," Strand repeated, stepping back behind the door.

Knight was massaging his hands and whispering to himself, "Shit shit shit shit." He ran his fingers through his silver locks, shifting his weight repeatedly from one foot to the other in a little mambo. He looked at Strand nervously and punched the button for the electric lock on the door. When it clacked, he opened the door.

"Wolf! Wolf! Good of you . . . good of you . . . Come in, come in. . . ." He backed away from the door, stretching out his right arm in a magnanimous gesture of welcome.

Wolfram Schrade was inside.

Strand closed the door and in the same movement put

457

the pistol to the back of Schrade's neck before he had a chance to react.

"Be very careful," Strand said.

Schrade froze.

"I'll explain the gun," Strand said, remaining out of sight behind Schrade, his left hand on top of Schrade's left shoulder. "It contains a neurotoxin. If it breaks the skin, you're dead. In less than a minute. There's no 'wounding' with this."

Silence.

Knight was standing between Schrade and the stairs, his mouth hanging open stupidly.

"Harry Strand," Schrade said in his heavily accented English, recognizing the voice.

"Is your driver parked in front?" Strand asked.

"Yes."

Strand took his left hand off Schrade's shoulder, reached back without turning around, and punched the electric lock.

"We're going to get away from the door," Strand said. "Upstairs."

They stepped forward, and Schrade caught Mara's figure in his peripheral vision as she waited inside the gallery doorway. He turned to look at her. He stopped.

"Mara Song." He said it as if he were ticking off the names on a list.

"Mara Song?" Knight was completely adrift.

Strand pressed the gun into Schrade's neck again, and they all started up the winding staircase.

As they filed into the library, Strand motioned for Schrade to go into the vault, the door of which always stood open. When he did, Strand closed the door and turned the handle once. Schrade never even saw his disguise.

458

He told Knight to sit in one of the chairs behind the library table. And Knight sat near the two Schiele drawings, as far away from the pistol as he could get.

Strand gave the pistol to Mara and nodded at Knight. "I've got to get this shit off my face," he said.

"What are you going to do, Harry?" She kept her eyes on the mortified Knight as Strand began peeling off the latex features of the man he had been hiding behind.

"I don't know," he mumbled as he worked at the elastic bits of mask.

"The choices—"

"I *know*," Strand cut her off. With trembling fingers he peeled away the layers of the stranger's broad nose. He knew his agitation was noticeable and disturbing to her, but he could do nothing about it. His fingers scrabbled at the bulk of latex over his brow. The adrenaline that had shot through him when he'd heard the doorbell had hit him like a jolt of electricity. He clawed at the ridge along his jaw that had added weight and heft to his head. What had astonished him even more was what he had experienced the moment he'd put the gun to the back of Schrade's neck. Suddenly he had been suffused with a feral hatred that was the most intense emotion he had ever experienced, and he had almost shot Schrade then, at that instant.

"*Good God . . .*" Knight was watching Strand emerge from the rubbery peelings that were gathering in front of him on the table like limp shreds of actual flesh. "*Good God*, man, what in bloody hell is going on here!" Knight's voice rose wildly.

"Shut up, Carrington." Strand's hands were still trembling as he raked and rolled away the last bits of latex from his face.

Then he took off the wig and removed the eyebrows. He took out his handkerchief and wiped his face. He was panting. He felt odd, which scared him.

He stood a moment at the far end of the table from Knight, Mara halfway between them. Across the table in front of her was the closed vault. He put his hands on the table to steady himself. The mandarin red walls shimmered, affecting his eyes.

Without saying anything, he turned and walked over to the ebony liquor cabinet near the settee and searched among the bottles for the Scotch. He found it, opened the doors and took out a glass, and poured it half-full. He stood there with his back to them and sipped it, held it in his mouth, and swallowed. He took another sip, did the same.

He returned to the table and looked at Knight.

"Get him out of the vault."

When Claude Corsier recognized Harry Strand's voice, he froze. He leaned into the binoculars and pressed against them until the tripod rocked and he had to steady it. He couldn't believe his eyes. Strand was nowhere to be seen. But he did believe his ears. He knew Harry Strand's voice. Then the unknown man, incredibly, locked Schrade into the vault, and Corsier watched, spellbound, as the stranger stood at the end of the library table and removed his face.

"Don't touch anything," Corsier whispered.

"He's not even there," Skerlic said. Despite his aloof attitude about the binoculars, he too was using them, hunched over his own tripod like a beetle.

"It doesn't matter," Corsier said. "Everything has changed."

"What?" Skerlic took his eyes away from the binoculars. "What do you mean, 'everything has changed'?"

"Everything has changed," Corsier repeated. "That man who removed the disguise." He finally pulled his face away from the tripod and looked at Skerlic. "You do *not* touch a button until I tell you," he said, and his tone carried a clear note of threat, something totally foreign to Skerlic's understanding of Claude Corsier.

CHAPTER 63

Schrade sat across from Carrington Knight at the far end of the library table, facing the windows that looked out onto Carlos Place and the dark, rainy morning. To his left, a little over an arm's reach away, were the Schiele drawings that had brought them all together. Mara and Strand stood at the opposite end of the table, Mara on Knight's side, Strand on Schrade's.

Strand held the pistol again, but he wasn't pointing it at anyone. He sat on the edge of the table, turned toward Schrade, one leg on the floor. Mara stood next to the windows, leaning against the wall, her arms crossed, hugging herself. Since Schrade had sat down, no one had spoken. Schrade was arrogantly unimpressed by his plight. Knight was miserable with anxiety.

The silence in the room was prolonged, but not deliberately calculated by Strand to ratchet up the tension. He was trying to make decisions that he simply did not know how to make. Knowing Claude Corsier so well, he was sure Corsier had lured Schrade to Knight's for the same reason he had.

Strand ran the fingers of one hand through his damp hair and looked at Schrade, then at the wide-eyed Knight, and back to Schrade. Strand was beyond exhaustion. The struggles in his own mind, committing himself to a course of action and then at the last minute veering off, his efforts to will himself to do what his will would not allow, his fear of what his actions would do to his relationship with Mara when, if, he finally did kill Schrade—all of it had worn him down to a weariness that he had rarely experienced. And he was finding himself unsure of just about everything, ashamed of himself for having planned an assassination and, even worse, for having dragged Mara into it and ashamed of himself for not having the fortitude to do what he had planned.

"Are we waiting for something, Harry?" Schrade asked finally, turning and looking at Strand. "Or are you simply incapable of making up your mind?" He was wearing an elegant double-breasted suit of charcoal gray with chalk stripes. He was very correct, his tie knotted tightly against his starched collar.

Strand took another drink of Scotch. He had to be very careful with that. If he was going to do something foolish, he wanted to do it because he had planned to do it, not because of the Scotch. He put down the glass.

"Well, the end has to begin somewhere, doesn't it?" he said.

The challenge in Schrade's eyes did not retreat.

"I think you should know a few things, Wolf," Strand said, looking down the long table at Schrade, "before anything else happens here."

Schrade waited.

463

"You were very carefully baited," Strand began. "The two Schieles were meant to bring you here—today."

Knight's mouth dropped open.

"There are other drawings here that you haven't seen that were also offered to Carrington for the same purpose. But the plot got complicated, and the other drawings were unnecessary." He stopped, fixed his eyes squarely on Schrade.

"Then I was never supposed to have got here."

"That's right."

"And the meeting in Zurich . . ."

"Fabrication."

Schrade grew still. His clear eyes lost all sense of his personality and became as dead as the glass eyes of a mannequin.

"Then you really . . . *cannot* . . . get the money."

"That's right. Your money's gone. I lied to Bill Howard. The money's exactly where your accountants have been telling you it is. Scattered to the stars. It's been completely out of my hands for years now, almost from the beginning. You could have killed me a long time ago. I was never any good to you."

Schrade's thoughts were buried deeply behind his clear eyes. His face was far more of a mask than the latex shreds of Harry Strand's disguise.

"You are not giving me enough credit, Harry," Schrade said calmly. "The truth is, I have already killed you. And I must say, it was easy." He shook his head slowly, pulling down the corners of his mouth in a disdainful shrug. "You were never really capable of objectivity. You had 'friends,' Harry, the dumbest mistake in the world."

Schrade's hands rested calmly on the library table. He looked down at them. He betrayed no tension, no sign of stress, no anxiety. He looked at Strand again.

"I have killed you, Harry, piecemeal. Dennis Clymer. Ariana Kiriasis. That pretty young woman who worked for you in Houston." Pause. "Marie." He shifted his eyes to Mara. "And this one, sooner or later."

Knight gasped. He was looking at Schrade with an expression of shock that altered the appearance of his face.

"You blame yourself for every one of those deaths," Schrade went on, "and for the ones to come. And you should. You are right about that, at least. You used them to try to damage me, knowing very well what would happen to them, eventually, knowing they would die for it someday. And you used them anyway."

He paused, regarding Strand with glacial disapproval.

"You should have been a philosopher or a theologian, Harry, because real life has always confused you. You would have been better off in a profession where the answer to every real-world problem is just another question. The hard answers in life, the reality of brutal solutions, always made you queasy. You had this . . . exasperating weakness for empathy."

He paused, and again he almost smiled.

"But you were very good at deception, I'll give you that. It isn't much, manipulating shadows, orchestrating subtleties, subterfuge, but you did have a natural ability for it. In fact, you have proved to be altogether too good at it in the end, haven't you, Harry? Predictably, you have finally succumbed to the single greatest risk of your profession: self-deception. Even at this very moment you are befuddled.

The moral gray stretches out from you in every direction, and you have lost your way in the barrens of your own confusion.

"That business about the hospitals . . . about the schools . . . that thin, sanctimonious soup for the weak conscience. I think you actually convinced yourself that those things would absolve you from the guilt of all these deaths that you so willfully pretended would not happen."

Outside, the summer storm intensified and leaden clouds descended over the city, pulling a shroud of gray over Carlos Place, the little island of plane trees, and the tarnished statue of the inward shrugging nude. The rain quickened and began to fall in drifting sheets. The windows now let in not light, but darkness, and the mandarin red walls of the library deepened and turned a grim, hematic hue.

Strand said nothing. Schrade was right, of course. Strand did feel guilty for all the lives lost. There were ways to rationalize their deaths, ways of escape that sounded reasonable, and he had tried them all. But the guilt remained, a stain with just enough of the truth mixed into it to make it indelible.

Strand walked halfway down the length of the table and stopped a few steps from Schrade, who, having satisfied himself momentarily with his bitter soliloquy, had turned away from Strand again and stared straight out the windows.

Strand had to acknowledge Schrade's despicable form of bravery. He was still holding the gun, and in the face of the kind of loathing and threatened menace that Schrade

466

had just unleashed, any man might be expected to be provoked to a sudden rash impulse.

Schrade showed no fear that such a thing might happen. Yet he remained seated. He made no effort to leave, a tacit acknowledgment of Strand's control of the situation. Schrade was not feeling comfortable enough to offer a physical challenge. He recognized the instability of the moment and stared straight ahead, toward the muted light of the storm.

Strand sat on the table again, as before, one leg on the floor, the other one dangling from the knee. He continued to study Schrade. Then he lifted his chin, indicating the two pictures leaning on the bookcase counter behind Schrade.

"The two Schieles," he said, "the ones you came to see. Do you know who's offering them?"

Schrade didn't bother to answer.

Strand looked at Knight. "Tell him, Carrington."

Knight actually hesitated. Avarice was a strong rival to the survival instinct. Finally he said, "Claude Corsier."

This time Schrade reacted sharply, glaring at Strand.

"I'm curious about him," Strand said. "I noticed you didn't list him among those I'm responsible for killing. How did you miss him, Wolf?"

Schrade was suddenly distracted, not listening closely. Conspiracy was his heart's milieu. He was good at it, and he fell to it naturally. He understood its intimacies. Only a hint of it in other men leavened his imagination.

"Yeah," Strand said, "I suspect the Schieles are forgeries. I wasn't the only one who wanted you to be here."

Schrade's eyes turned thoughtfully to the library windows, to the gloom that had swallowed Carlos Place and obscured the buildings on either side, and to the windows of the Connaught, some of which were lighted, some of which were dark.

Corsier held his breath as he peered into the lenses of the binoculars, his back tight and aching, his headphones in place. He strained to hear more clearly, to see more clearly through the ashen dusk that had descended during the last few minutes of the storm.

"Damn! What do the dials say?"

"He is too far away to be killed outright," Skerlic answered. "It would tear him up, he might linger . . . but he would eventually die, I think."

"So would Harry."

Skerlic said nothing. For a moment he studied Corsier's sooty silhouette a short distance away, then slowly put his eyes back to his own pair of lenses.

Suddenly Corsier grabbed the telephone off a little table nearby and dialed. He cocked up the earphones on one side of his head, put the receiver to one ear, and bent again to his binoculars.

The telephone rang once, and Corsier saw everyone in the room turn to look at it. It rang a second time, a third. No one in Knight's library moved.

"Come on, Harry," Corsier coaxed under his breath. "Answer it . . . answer it."

Suddenly Schrade leaped up, grabbed the telephone, and threw it, jerking its cord out of the wall.

"Oh! God . . ."

Corsier slammed down the receiver.

"I need to do it," Skerlic said, his voice steady. "While he is standing."

"No!"

"If he moves any farther away . . ."

"*No!*" Corsier had practically crawled into the room on the other side of the rain. "No one is *talking.*"

Schrade's outburst brought everyone to their feet. Tension filled the room. Schrade's attention was still focused on the windows. No one said a word.

Strand knew exactly what he was thinking.

What happened next covered a span of twelve seconds.

Schrade suddenly turned and lunged for Strand. But Strand had been expecting it, and with a full swing of his arm he hit Schrade on the side of the head with his fist, staggering him. Having missed his opportunity and dazed by the blow, Schrade thought only of getting away from the windows. He fell back away from the table to take refuge behind the column of bookcases that separated the two broad windows. Knight, seeing that Schrade perceived a threat from the windows, fell back with him, and the two of them stopped against the bookcase cabinets, their backs to Schiele's naked women.

The two explosions were horrific.

A surprising amount of detail can be absorbed by the brain and retained with remarkable clarity in the infinitesimal duration between the blast of an explosion and its effects. Strand was too close—twice as close as Mara—to retain more than a flash, but the detail of what his brain perceived was as precise as if the instant had been

469

photographed for him to study: Schrade was lifted, disem-
boweled, and hurled in halves across the distance that separated him from Strand. His rib cage preceded his lower
torso and legs, which followed like a whorling, unraveling
ball of twine thrown whipping and twirling into the air. His
head hurtled past Strand's face, whistling like a banshee, far
in front of the rest of him.

EPILOGUE

QUAI DES GRANDS AUGUSTINS, PARIS

Mara Song sat at a table by the window and watched the early autumn light soften to a pale peach on the spires of Sainte-Chapelle across the Seine. The lunch-hour crowds had long since cleared out of the restaurant and the few customers who remained were outnumbered by the waiters, who generally ignored them as they went about their business of changing tablecloths, sweeping the floors, preparing for the evening clientele.

Eugene Payton came into the restaurant and spotted her immediately, waving off a waiter who had started toward him. Mara turned her face away and listened to his footsteps on the floor, slowing as he drew near. When he stopped, she looked up.

"Well, it's good to see you again, finally," Payton said.

Mara nodded dismissively.

"No, honestly." Payton grinned. "It is." He unbuttoned his suit coat, pulled out the chair opposite her, and sat down. "We've talked so much by telephone and fax and e-mail during the last couple of months that it doesn't seem as though it's been that long since Camp Peary."

"It seems that long to me," she said. "And more."

Gene Payton was second in command of the Foreign Intelligence Service. Strand had said that Payton was among the best of them. He had always been on the fast track to the top, and he understood the intelligence business in a way that very few did. He believed that the FIS was important, that it was even essential. He did not believe that it had a holy mission, which made a big difference in the way he saw the role and responsibilities of his officers.

"You're looking good, Mara," Payton said, clasping his hands on the table after ordering a cup of coffee from the waiter. He rigorously avoided letting his eyes go near her scars. She imagined he had rehearsed it, repeated to himself over and over not to look at them. He must have decided that he would candidly refer to her wounds right at the beginning. That would seem open and honest, without being gratuitous or unnaturally oblivious. "We were worried when we saw the photographs after your first operation." He smiled. "But I can see those concerns were unwarranted. You look great."

"I don't have any complaints," she said. Fine. She didn't want him to say any more about it. He had something to tell her and she wanted him to get on with it. There was no need for small talk, as if their meeting was social, as if they could actually relax with each other. Cordiality seemed ill-suited to the circumstances.

Payton paused a moment as the waiter left his coffee. He poured in some cream and stirred.

"Okay," he said, putting down his spoon. "I'll get right to the point." Payton was no fool. Whatever else, he was not that. "I can't say that the final decision on all of this was unanimous, but it was a solid decision. Everyone understands that it's *the* decision. Anybody who doesn't like it can take a hike. It's that solid."

Mara lifted her glass and sipped the Bordeaux she had been nursing for the past twenty minutes.

"FIS is walking away from it, Mara," he said. "Officially, unofficially, on the record, off the record, casually, formally, on the books, off the books, any way you can describe it. We're out."

Mara couldn't help herself. She dropped her head and closed her eyes. She was suddenly weak, as if she had received an injection of morphine. Jesus Christ.

"I've got to tell you," Payton went on, "letting the money get away from them, that killed them. Some of them couldn't believe it. The scheme has their grudging admiration, but if it hadn't been for the offsetting circumstances, the grudging part would have far outweighed the admiration part. For some of them, it always will."

"What about the investigation? Where do they all stand on it?"

Payton cautiously took a sip of coffee. "Scotland Yard and the Bundeskriminalamt," he said, "are inundated with possibilities, hundreds of leads, thousands of names, scores of new relationships and connections. They'll be investigating Schrade's assassination for a decade. They'll never solve it. The German intelligence community is shut tight on this. So are the British. So are we."

He looked out the window to the Seine, and Mara thought he was trying to decide whether or not to bring up something else.

"The wild card was that the international media got hold of the information about Schrade's double life first. That pissed off the law enforcement agencies *and* the intelligence community. Rumor got way ahead of reality. The gaudy headlines made everyone cringe: 'RECLUSIVE BILLIONAIRE TIED TO INTERNATIONAL CRIME SYNDICATES. GERMAN BILLIONAIRE LINKED TO GLOBAL CRIME LORDS.' That kind of thing was alarming all of us. It could've gotten out of hand and pulled us all into a full-blown international scandal."

Mara remained silent.

"A lot of questions had to be answered. People are still scrambling. Once the cat was out of the bag, the media wanted to know what else was in the bag and what it was doing in there." He paused, looked down at his cup. "Whoever did that created a firestorm."

She said nothing. He wasn't going to get any reaction from her.

Payton took another sip of coffee. "But the mitigating factor was that the media received no information connecting Schrade to the FIS, or to any intelligence service. Just information about his crime world connections. That gave the whole intelligence community deniability when the inevitable spy rumors started flying around. No one ever definitively tied Schrade to any agency."

"That was good."

"Yeah"—Payton gazed at the quayside again—"that was good."

Another couple left the café. The place was practically closed.

Payton turned back to Mara. "As far as your situation was concerned, the clincher was the information about Bill Howard." He paused. "You know, Mara, we didn't have a clue about him. The son of a bitch, he might've retired and we'd never have known."

"Have you found him yet?" Mara asked.

Payton shook his head in disgust. "No, and with the kind of money he's got he'll be able to buy a hell of a lot of ghost help. This could take a long time. Plus, it's got to be done in silence. Rules of the game."

She nodded.

"Anyway, everyone knew you didn't have to do that. I mean, it worked to your advantage, it was a score on your side of the ledger."

"That's not why—"

"I know, I know," Payton held up his hand to stop her, "that's what I mean. Everybody knew that, and that's why it gave you the edge."

He was silent a moment, looking at the buildings on the Ile de la Cité. Mara looked out to the Seine also. Her face ached, but it didn't matter anymore. Time would pass, the scars would heal. The ones on her body, anyway. Right now was not the time to think about the others.

"One question," Payton said, turning back to Mara. "This is for me—just me, believe it or not."

Mara did believe it. "What's that?"

"How did you get away from there? I know Mayfair was immobile with shock after the explosion. It's not exactly on Scotland Yard's hot patrol list. The weather was bad. The response time was bad. But still . . . shit, you were both blown up."

A simple question. It seemed ingenuous enough. But within the last year her life had undergone irreversible changes. Ingenuous. The word had almost lost its meaning.

"I can't talk about that," she said, dropping her eyes to the last deep mulberry sips of wine left in her glass. "If it's over, it's over." She hesitated, then looked up at him. "I don't know how you people do this, how you make a life out of it. There are always more questions than answers, more tragedies than triumphs . . . and more secrets than all of it put together."

Even for a man as circumspect as Gene Payton, even for a guy who knew the ropes and the rules as well as he did, the frustration was written all over his face. Still, he was destined to disappointment. That was the nature of his business. Almost all of the men and women in the intelligence profession died taking an entire nightful of secrets with them.

They visited a little longer, but they really had nothing to say to each other beyond the business of business. Though Mara's connection to Payton and the FIS had been intense and indelible, it had been brief. And it had been stormy. She had breached trusts; she had abandoned loyalties. Regardless of the extenuating circumstances, the bridges lay smoldering and in ruins. There just wasn't anything else to say.

Payton left. They would never see each other again. There would never be any need to.

Mara reached up and absently touched the side of her face, the tips of her fingers tracing the silky surfaces of the tender, helical scars. Touching them, checking them, had become a habit. She was trying to break it. She was the only patron remaining in the café nearly half an hour later when the door from the Quai des Grands-Augustins opened again and Claude Corsier walked in. He was dressed like the most correct member of the Académie Française. He walked over and stood looking down at her. She was never self-conscious about the scars with Corsier. She always had the feeling that when he looked at her they disappeared. It was a way he had.

"Sit down, Claude."

Corsier shook his head at a questioning waiter and sat down.

"I followed him for a while," he said. "There was no one else." He had kept his mustache and goatee. The look suited him.

"They're walking away from it," Mara said. "They're not going to come after us. Your name never came up. It's over."

"My God." Corsier gasped and sat back. He had been fatalistic about the outcome. In the three months since the explosion Corsier had been glum. He had gained little peace from his deliverance from Schrade. Too much—and too many —had been lost in the process.

The Swiss turned his face away to the street, and Mara studied his profile. Corsier had been horrified that he had allowed the Serb to deceive him about the precision of the explosives. He should have known better. And he was horrified that Skerlic had detonated both bombs, slaughtering Carrington Knight for no reason at all. What he had found most difficult to live with was that he himself had benefited enormously from Knight's death. Knight was the only person who could have tied Corsier to the assassination. He had been the only unresolved flaw in Corsier's plan, the one reason Corsier had resigned himself to being a fugitive for the rest of his life.

He had been lucky, but the price had been steep, and he would not pay it off in a lifetime.

Though Mara had been badly hurt, none of her wounds had been life threatening. Because the Schiele forgeries had been sitting on the bookcase countertop, above the level of the library table, and because Mara had been twice the distance from the explosion as Strand, the extra millisecond had given her time to react. The top of the heavy table had shielded her from the greater force of the blast. By the time an appalled Corsier had run across Carlos Place, Mara had already dragged Strand, bleeding badly, down to the first floor, away from the fire and smoke. Corsier had gotten them out the back door, into Mount Row, and away from the building as the crowds had begun to gather in the rain in Carlos Place.

"This is quite incredible," he said, turning back to her.

"I think so, too. There were so many other possibilities."

Corsier thought about it for a while, absorbing it. Then he sighed heavily. "I went to Rome," he said. "Ariana had given quite a lot of money to Santa Maria del Priorato, near her home on the Aventine. The priory allowed an urn with her ashes to be placed in those lovely gardens there. It seems it was her request."

He drummed his fingers on the table.

"She had drawn up legal papers to have her house converted to a residence for young Greek women who come to Rome to study art. She had set aside a large endowment for it, to be administered by a private university in Athens."

He drummed his fingers on the table.

"I went to Santa Maria. The urn, of course, is beautiful."

For the second time he turned to look out at the Seine and the Palais de Justice. The afternoon was quickly slipping away.

"My God, Mara, look at that light."

They watched as the softening light stained the stone architecture and the slate roofs with tea rose and pale coralline.

The shadows were turning dusty blue, poised for the deeper hues of dusk.

He turned to her.

"I am back in Geneva," he said. "Back with my niece in the gallery." He smiled. "It's heaven."

"Good, Claude. That's good."

"Come to see us, Mara. Let us hear from you. We must never lose touch. It would be a sad mistake."

"I promise."

"What will you be doing?"

"Staying on here for a while."

"In Paris?"

She nodded, but offered no clarification. Corsier studied her a few moments.

"You know," he said, choosing his words carefully, thoughtfully, "they say that a wise man will befriend the shadows that move into his life. They say that if he will embrace them and make them his companions, they will teach him how to live with his regrets."

Mara said nothing. Then, suddenly, inexplicably, she felt her eyes moisten. She concentrated; she didn't blink; she managed to stop it.

Corsier reached across the table and gently put his heavy, bearish hand on hers.

"Come to see us in Geneva."

Mara was now alone in the empty café. It was finally over, and it had ended the way such things end, with a quiet conversation, a mundane and almost feckless dismissal of the extraordinary.

She stood and made her way out of the café just as the

first few dinner-hour clientele began to trickle in and evening was settling over the Seine. She crossed the Quai des Grands-Augustins and walked slowly along the quayside toward the Pont St.-Michel. The lights of Paris were aglitter in the lilac air, and in the Seine the large *bateaux mouches* plied the approaching darkness, their swags of tiny lights sparkling doubly bright against the water.

She walked past the Pont St.-Michel and went on to the Petit Pont where she turned and started across the Seine. She was nearly to the other side when she saw him. He was waiting at the edge of the trees, leaning on his cane against the stone ramparts. He was watching her.

REQUIEM FOR A GLASS HEART

David Lindsey

Irina Ismaylov kills men and women and she kills at the behest of Sergei
Krupatin, the Russian crime lord who exerts a monstrous hold over her.

FBI special agent Cate Cuevas, still in mourning, has just learned of a
devastating betrayal by her slain husband. Wounded and shaken, she is
plunged into the most dangerous assignment of her career. The leaders of
three great international crime organisations are to meet in Houston. The
implications are stunning, and horrendous. But the FBI has a chance to
stop this unholy alliance, if Cate Cuevas can infiltrate the Russian
contingent – and if she can get out alive.

When Cate and Irina meet, they are drawn to each other strangely and
powerfully. And as Cate and Irina fight to survive amidst the intricate and
deadly stratagems of men of violence, their relationship becomes an
evermore-intimate dance of sexual attraction and murderous intent.

'Lindsey takes us to the very depths of human evil'
New York Daily News

FICTION/THRILLER
0 7515 1852 2

AN ABSENCE OF LIGHT

David Lindsey

Marcus Graver, an officer in the Criminal Intelligence Division of
Houston Police Department, is understandably concerned and upset
when a colleague commits violent suicide.

But when the inevitable investigation begins to unearth worrying details
about the dead man's apparently unremarkable life, Graver realises his
concern should be more professional than personal. The evidence points
to a betrayal of terrifying import, forcing Graver to face the murkier
realities of modern information technology, where everyone's privacy is
for sale – at a price.

And as the trial leads him nearer and nearer to the dark core of a vast
criminal intelligence network, Graver has no choice but to acknowledge
an uncomfortable truth: that when men's desires are shaped in an
absence of light, only the corrupt survive . . .

As gripping as the clutch of a drowning man, *An Absence of Light* is a
dazzlingly superior thriller from the acclaimed author of *Mercy* and *Body
of Truth*.

FICTION/THRILLER
0 7515 1279 6

IN THE LAKE
OF THE MOON

David Lindsey

The first five photographs were perplexing; but the sixth seemed to be
the chronicle of a death foretold.

Houston homicide detective Stuart Haydon opens the anonymous
envelopes to find two photographs of his late father, and three
photographs of a beautiful woman he doesn't recognise, all dating from
around fifty years ago. Photo number six is of Haydon himself, taken a
few days earlier, and is marked with a felt-tip pen to show the trajectory
of a bullet into his right eye and the resultant explosion of blood from the
back of his head.

It's not the first time Haydon has had a death threat, but as if becomes
clear that this one could well be his last, Haydon is flung into a desperate
search for the murderous maniac who's tracking him down – a search that
leads to the sprawling mass of Mexico City and the unknown world of his
father's past.

Gripping, utterly compelling, *In the Lake of the Moon* is a superbly
constructed thriller from the bestselling author of *Mercy* and *Body of
Truth*.

'Chilling'
New York Times Book Review

'One of the most unusual and fascinating thrillers I have read'
Hammond Innes

FICTION/THRILLER
0 7515 1428 4

BODY OF TRUTH

David Lindsey

In a remote country with no rules, people –
and the truth – just disappear.

Lena Muller, daughter of a wealthy Houston businessman, went missing
in Guatemala. Now, six weeks later, homicide detective Stuart Haydon
receives a phone call from Guatemala City. Lema is alive – and in
trouble.

But Guatemala is synonymous with trouble. Thirty years of guerrilla
warfare have turned it into a surreal and violent netherworld where fear
rules; where no one can be trusted; where a small coterie of American
expatriates is deeply involved with the corrupt military and an elusive
guerrilla faction, and where everything is tainted by greed and cynical
political motives.

When Haydon arrives he finds himself embroiled in the menace, the
complex mystery and the tension of life in Guatemala. He also finds that
Lena Muller is not the young woman either he or her parents thought
her to be – and that he is searching for a harsher truth than he dared
imagine . . .

'It is, as a thriller should be, precise and immediate'
Independent

'Entertains, educates and breaks the heart'
Chicago Tribune

FICTION/THRILLER
0 7515 0109 3

<u>MERCY</u>

David Lindsey

The chilling malice that lurks in the mind of a serial killer . . .

Carmen Palma is a homicide detective in Houston, Texas; a strong female
in a world still almost exclusively male. When two women are found
murdered in an identical, grotesque fashion, Palma suspects the worst: a
sexually motivated serial killer.

But, when yet another woman is murdered, Palma discovers an
underground network of wealthy Houston women living secret
double lives.

Inexorably she is drawn into two strange worlds: the underground world
of bisexuality and sadomasochism, and the twisted, perverted world of
the killer – unlike anything she could ever imagine. Or could she?

'A sexually charged thriller . . . written with masterly skill'
Publishers Weekly

'Outstanding . . . a convincing, intense, and scary trip into the soul of a
sexual maniac'
Kirkus Reviews

FICTION/THRILLER
0 7515 0239 1

Warner titles available by post:

❑ An Absence of Light	David Lindsey	£6.99
❑ Body of Truth	David Lindsey	£6.99
❑ Mercy	David Lindsey	£6.99
❑ In the Lake of the Moon	David Lindsey	£5.99
❑ Black Gold, Red Death	David Lindsey	£5.99
❑ Requiem for a Glass Heart	David Lindsey	£5.99

The prices shown above are correct at time of going to press. However the publishers reserve the right to increase prices on covers from those previously advertised without further notice.

WARNER BOOKS

WARNER BOOKS
Cash Sales Department, P.O. Box 11, Falmouth, Cornwall, TR10 9EN
Tel: +44 (0) 1326 569777, Fax: +44 (0) 1326 569555
Email: books@barni.avel.co.uk

POST AND PACKING:

Payments can be made as follows: cheque, postal order (payable to Warner Books) or by credit cards. Do not send cash or currency.

U.K. Orders under £10	**£1.50**
U.K. Orders over £10	**FREE OF CHARGE**
E.E.C. & Overseas	25% of order value

Name (Block Letters) _____

Address _____

_____

Post/zip code: _____

❑ Please keep me in touch with future Warner publications

❑ I enclose my remittance £_____

❑ I wish to pay by Visa/Access/Mastercard/Eurocard

Card Expiry Date